Adriana Rizak-Healing, this one's for you. Had your love for Nathan never existed, his story might never have been finished in words. I have so much love for you. ❤

we are Forever

a.e. murphy

Chapter One

"**D**illan!"

Something crashes; it sounds like Dillan's toy train against the door. At least I hope it's his toy train. The destructive little sod that he is has broken more dishes than we own.

"He's possessed." I hear Nathan yell and smile when tiny feet hammer across the wooden floor, followed by the sound of larger ones. Dillan's little giggle echoes through the large house. Snort. "He's possessed!"

"I heard you!" I shout down the stairs, stifling my laughter. I gently ease Emily, our gorgeous one-year-old baby girl, out of her cot bed and carry her down the stairs.

"Mama," she coos softly and rests her head on my shoulder. Her fingers go to her mouth and she sucks on them as we watch Dillan race through the hallway, his little bare butt wriggling as he passes. His laughter is evil. He knows exactly how much trouble he's causing. He just loves to wind up his daddy.

"I swear on all that is holy…" Nathan stops beside me and we both watch Dillan slam the kitchen door. He sighs and turns me into his arms, squishing Emily between us. She squawks uncomfortably so I place her on the ground and tilt my head back to receive his kiss. "You need to go."

"I know." I press my lips to his and smile when I feel his fingers drift over my cheek and into my hair. "Will you be okay?"

"Uh-oh." Emily sounds and Nathan stiffens.

"You little…!"

I turn and pinch my lips together when I see Dillan holding his top up with his hands, releasing a stream of pee aimed at the wall by the kitchen door.

He takes off running, giggling like the crazy little bugger that he is.

"Dillan." I chastise. "Now daddy is going to have to bleach everything!"

I grab Emily before she can crawl to the puddle and splash in it. Yes, this has happened before.

"He'll be potty trained soon. Keep persevering." I assure Nathan, who has Dillan in his outstretched arms.

Nathan glares at me so I take this as my cue to leave.

"I love you!" I yell at them all before depositing Emily on the floor and rushing from the house.

Today is my First day training to be a chef after leaving Valentine's only three weeks ago. I've only been working part time since Emily became eight months old so I know how challenging this new venture is going to be.

Kerim Dal, the leading chef in the UK is training me. ME! He's a culinary genius. I've tried and tested ninety percent of his recipes and I issue my stamp of approval for everything but one weird minty aubergine creation. I wasn't a fan of that one but I'm sure if I had the taste buds for it I would have *loved* it.

If I could happy squeal and clap my hands while driving, I would so do that right now.

It's not until I've pulled up outside the restaurant 'Little Ambrosia' that my nerves really begin to kick in. The building is fancy, huge and... did I say fancy? For an untrained chef to start here is unreal. I am extremely fortunate.

My phone vibrates in my pocket and I pull it out, using the moment of distraction to collect myself.

Sasha: You got this.

Mum: Bring me the leftovers.

Nathan: We love you. I love you and I am so proud of you.

Nathan's is the only one I respond to.

CHAPTER ONE

<u>Gwen</u>: Thank you Spongebob. <3

Tucking my phone into my bag, I climb out of my car and make my way to the entrance. According to the instructions I received, an outfit will be waiting for me in the staffroom by the kitchen.

Where's the kitchen?

The lobby is huge; the walls are little more than glass panel doors with net curtains drawn to the sides. I move to the first set that leads into the large room. It stinks of money. The theme seems very royal and flowery. Heavy-looking chairs surround large round tables that are surrounded by smaller round tables. There are no booths here but there are tables in the corner, partially hidden beyond six-foot-tall dividers that offer a little more privacy.

"No!" I hear bellowed and a pan clatters loudly from the back of the room. I spot the kitchen through a large gap in the wall. Of course the kitchen staff will be open to view. That doesn't make me more nervous at all. "You don't put sweet potatoes and parsnips in with lamb. It's too sweet!"

My teeth find my lower lip and bite down hard. My feet suddenly feel leaden. I'm not sure I can move.

<u>Gwen</u>: This place is legit cool. It's like... billion-dollar cool.

<u>Sasha</u>: And Nathan hasn't taken you yet?

I watch as two men in chef's whites wave frantically at each other and shout in another language as a female in a matching white double breasted coat stirs something in a pan over one of the many stoves. My mouth drops open when the man on the left, who I recognise as Kerim Dal, grabs the guy on the right, who I think is his Executive chef and cousin – thank you Wikipedia – and throws him three feet backwards before throwing another dish at the wall. A dish full of food. Is this how they behave when the restaurant is full?

Now I'm scared.

As if sensing my thoughts, Kerim's eyes cut into the dark restaurant seating area and find me, standing, my bag over one shoulder, no doubt trembling. His eyes narrow and he says something else to the Executive

Chef before coming out to greet me through a set of large, grey double doors that say exit on them. A smaller door on the other side of the wall gap has the word, 'entrance' printed on it.

"You." Kerim barks striding towards me. He has at least five inches of towering height over me. "What are you doing here?"

"I..." I take a step back as he continues coming for me. "I'm Guinevere."

"Guinevere?" His lips, shadowed by a narrow, well-trimmed goatee, curl with confusion.

"I start training today."

"And you came in through the front door?"

My mouth falls open. I'm unsure why I'm suddenly a target. "Was I not supposed to?"

"What the..." His almost black eyes widen with surprise, the contrast making his dark caramel coloured skin seem darker. "Seriously? What chef takes the front door?"

I want to go home now.

"You come through the kitchen, through the back or you don't come at all." He shouts, his Turkish accent light though noticeable. My eyes follow his arm which waves towards the kitchen area. "I'm assuming you've parked using the customer car park too?"

At this point I feel as though silence is best.

"And Nathan assured me you were smart...next joke. Move your fucking car and come in the appropriate entrance or fuck off. And bring your brain with you." With that, he turns on his heel and storms back to the kitchen.

I think I might cry.

"Fucking arsehole," I mutter under my breath instead of sobbing like I want to. I stalk from the restaurant, back the way I came. I've dealt with worse than him. I refuse to crumble, especially on my first day. "I've got this."

It takes me a while but when I finally find the secret entrance for employee vehicles, I park in a spot I hope isn't reserved and head to the large, metal double doors. One of them is propped open with a fire extinguisher. It leads to a small, white tiled area and another set of double doors.

The door on the right opens and the executive chef, whose name escapes me, storms past, throwing his hat on the floor as he goes. He stops at the stone steps leading down towards the parking area and screams to the heavens.

"Don't worry about him; they are always like this," the female states and motions for me to enter the kitchen.

"You're seven minutes late," Kerim bellows, dipping his finger into a white coloured sauce in a pan on the stove before sucking it into his mouth. "Better, Umut."

"Fuck you!" The Executive chef yells and Kerim rolls his eyes.

"You're Gwen?" He asks, knowing full well that I am Gwen.

I nod.

"Good. Patience!" He barks and at first I think he's telling me to have patience, but then the woman who greeted me moments ago appears by my side. "Take her to change. Show her around the kitchen." He steps into my space and narrows his slanted black eyes. "If you need telling twice, you're not right for this kitchen."

"No pressure then," I mutter and his nostrils flare.

"This, my *dear girl*," his tone is heavy with disdain, "is the kitchen of the damned. It is one of the *busiest* restaurants and most *expensive* restaurants in the whole of the United Kingdom. The pressure is unbelievable, but your boyfriend…"

"Fiancé," I correct unnecessarily.

"Assured me you could handle it," he spits, clearly annoyed at the fact I've opened my mouth to speak without his permission. I can't help it; it's an illness.

Before I can answer, Patience, the thirty something female with gorgeous sandy blonde hair peeking from beneath her white hat, pulls me towards a door on the far left.

"This is the staff quarters where we get to just take a moment if we have time to take a moment." The room is cosy; it has a couch, a day bed and two doors leading to female and male toilets. I notice a secondary fire exit too and the windows allow a lot of light, even though the blinds are drawn. "We rarely get time to take a moment though, so don't be surprised if the only time you see this room is to hang your things up on arrival."

I place my things in the designated area and wave goodbye to my phone.

"You'll start with Delphine," Patience tells me. "She handles the pantry. Today you'll be learning how we work together as a team and where things go. I suggest you study the pantry now because if you screw up, there will be no second chances."

"Exactly," Umut puts in, giving me an apologetic smile. "It's nothing personal. We all suffered this way in the beginning."

"How many have come before me?" I ask, attempting not to gulp with fear.

"Too many, most of them already trained in the finest kitchens." Patience whispers, her light green eyes glittering. "Most of them quit before the end of the day." She leads me to the pantry. "Study until I call you. I won't over complicate today for you."

"Thank you." She leaves me by the heavy metal door that looks better built than a bank safe. "Holy fuck," I mutter under my breath. What the hell have I gotten myself into?

The living room light is on when I pull into the residential carpark just across from our three-bedroom townhouse. For the price we paid for this tiny building in London we could have afforded a mansion in the countryside or smaller towns of Britain. Unfortunately needs must. After the country house burned down, we have yet to decide what to do with the land and Nathan needed to be close to his newly opened store. It has prospered so well with his gorgeous jewellery line, he has been able to open another in Newcastle.

London is where we need to be and luckily it has all worked out okay, with my new job being here too. If we'd stayed in Skegness where my mum lives, I'd not have this opportunity and Nathan would need to be away five of seven nights.

I see the curtains twitch in the living room window and make a move. I sure hope Nathan has coped better than I have today.

My fingers find the zipper to my jacket and pull it down as I cross the one-way street and ready my key to unlock the door quietly.

It opens before I get the chance and I'm yanked inside by the man I love within the space of a second.

He kicks the door closed and presses me to it.

"Careful," I moan, my voice a whisper. The fact there's no noise means the kids are sleeping. "I ache everywhere."

His light brown eyes find mine in the dim lighting and the back of his knuckles trace my cheek. "I know how to make you feel better."

"You do?" I raise a sceptical brow. If he's thinking what I think he's thinking, that definitely isn't going to make me feel better.

I squeal when he lifts me into his arms and carries me into the living room, where the scent of vanilla and cherries settles gently in the air.

"What are you doing?" I giggle when his hand finds the light and flicks it down, leaving nothing but candlelight to illuminate the space.

"Looking after you," he states and finally places me on the ground. He motions to where the couch cushions are spread in a line on the floor, a thin blanket and towel draped over them.

"I'm confused."

His answering smile is so handsome it still, to this day, takes my breath away. "Step out of your shoes."

"Umm..."

"Just do it," he orders, his tone exasperated, so I quickly kick off my black leather shoes and flex my ankles. His hands peel my jacket down my arms before tossing it onto the naked couch. "I love this." Fingers tickle the space between my shoulder blades. "You have a trail of the finest hair." His lips touch the space where his hand just wandered. A shiver slowly weaves down my spine, twisting and pulsing along the nerves. "It makes you look shiny."

"No, I think that's just the sweat." I turn in his arms. "You shouldn't touch me; I'm gross."

"Be quiet," he chuckles and pulls my thin vest up and over my head. "How was your first day?"

"Hard," I admit, closing my eyes when his hands smooth down my arms and tickle to the inside of my wrists. "I'm so tired."

"I bet." His lips find my jaw as his hands unfasten my black trousers. They drop to my ankles. "Step out of them."

I take a step backwards, putting a small space between us. His eyes gaze upon my body, a hungry glint in their almost chocolate brown depths.

"Your beauty mesmerises me," he states, holding out his hand. I take it and allow him to lead me to the pillows. "On your front."

When I'm comfortably situated on the pillows, he immediately rids me of my bra and drips warm oil onto my back.

I laugh gently and wriggle, though he soon stops that by parting my thighs and kneeling between them after ridding himself of his T-shirt and jeans. "Stop laughing."

"'Kay," I murmur, resting my head on folded arms. "You spoil me."

"I seem to remember all of those days I'd come home from work exhausted and you'd have this exact layout prepared for me."

"What can I say? I'm such a caring fiancée." His hands begin to smooth the oil into my skin. I smile when I feel the leather of his gloves. It isn't often that he wears them but he still has his triggers, sticky substances and grainy substances being amongst them. The road to recovery is a long one but I'm extremely proud of how far he has come. "That feels so good."

His thumbs dig deep into my neck, pushing the oil around the surface of my skin, nudging the aches away. I groan loudly, unable to contain it, and I feel his boxer clad cock harden. It taps against my thigh and I smile into my arm. I love that I can still turn him on just by being me.

It makes me feel powerful and beautiful. It makes me feel sexy.

"So, was it as terrifying as you expected?" His voice is soft, lulling me as I drift on a wave of relaxation.

I hum a yes.

"Was he nice to you?"

"There was no time to be nice to each other. From the second the restaurant opened it was mayhem." I mumble. "I just passed ingredients to everyone and familiarised myself with the kitchen."

"Good." His hands dig deep trails down to my hips and then circle around to my navel before coming back again. "We missed you."

"Did Tommy use his potty yet?"

"Not yet."

We both sigh. He's proving extremely difficult to potty train. "He'll get there when he's ready," Nathan adds and I really hope he's right. "At least they went to bed easily enough."

"That's because you stuck to the routine."

"Exactly." He grins and circles his strong fingers around my arse cheeks. "You have the smoothest skin."

"Stop tracing my tiger stripes," I snap, as his fingers follow the stretchmarks on my hips.

"They're beautiful."

"I'm getting a spray tan to cover them first thing."

His slick hand connects with my right arse cheek. I squeal and buck as the sting tingles across my skin. "You'll do no such thing. Besides, that orange spray women insist on getting transfers onto their poor husbands."

"I love how you just assume they're all married."

"I'm an old fashioned kind of guy. Now hush and let me rub you."

"Rub away," I insist and close my eyes. "I love you."

"I know," he mutters playfully and tickles gentle patterns on my ribs.

"Are you going to make me shower before bed?"

I hear the smile in his voice. "Naturally."

Sighing heavily, I close my eyes again. "Well then, don't stop rubbing until there's not a single spasm of pain in my body."

"Yes, ma'am."

"You spoil me."

"Are you hungry? I didn't even think about that."

"No, I got to taste more food than I can cope with during work." I wet my lips at the memory. "It is so good. You just don't find the quality ingredients they use in the local supermarket, you know?"

He shifts down my body and works on my legs. "I want to kiss every inch of you but you're all oiled up."

Grinning, I wriggle my butt at him. "Just keep rubbing then. If I'm still oily then you're not done."

"Yes, ma'am."

"Is it twisted that I love it when you call me that?"

"Yes." His slippery, leather clad fingers slide around to my navel. A gasp escapes me when I'm hoisted up at the hips a few inches and another pillow is placed under my groin.

"Mind if we do this old style?" He asks, his voice playful and deep. Before I get the chance to respond, I feel him pushing against me, parting my folds with his thumbs. I release a moan of pure pleasure as he sinks into my depths. Every inch of him brings me a tingling ache that I doubt I will ever get used to. "So good." His hands move back to my hips and rub deep patterns.

I feel torn between sleeping from the slow massage or bucking against him so as to get him to move faster. My body is a mess of contradictions.

"I have been waiting all night for this," he admits. "All week, even."

"Has it really been seven days?" I ask. We normally don't go more than two but both of us have had so much to do this week. "You've stopped moving."

"It's been a week," he tells me as way of explanation.

"And?"

"And..." His hips join my arse, burying his full length into me. He groans; I groan and I feel his length contract inside of me. "I'm so close to finishing."

I shouldn't laugh but this hasn't happened before. "I feel that good, huh?"

"You do." He misses the joke entirely, or maybe he didn't and he's joking too. "Now stop talking; you're distracting me."

"How can I distract you? You're literally balls deep."

His laughter vibrates through his body and directly into mine. I think I'm as close to coming as he is right now. What an odd pair we make. He begins thrusting slowly and his hand continues massaging. Then suddenly he sobers and snaps, "Also, stop calling me SpongeBob."

"Well that was random." I try to look at him over my shoulder but his hand pushes my head into the pillow. Ouch. "Smothering me here."

"You like it."

He's not wrong. Fingers tangle in my hair and pull sharply until my head comes back. I push myself up with my hands.

"Now shut up while I fuck you," he orders and picks up his speed. I push backwards to meet him and every time I do, the deep burning spreads through my limbs and navel until it dances along my spine and pulses through my veins. "You need to get there."

"I'm there."

"Now," he begs. I imagine him gritting his teeth in a strain to gain some semblance of control.

As if my body is rigged to his command, I shudder and my womb ripples with pleasure. My chest tightens and I find it hard to breathe.

"Ugh..." Nathan grunts, hammering his hips into mine so hard there will probably be bruising but I don't care. It's intense. "Christ, I love you. I love this. I love doing this."

"Me too," I grin, flopping into the pillow as my orgasm dissipates, leaving me breathless and sated. He stands almost immediately, leaving his boxers on the ground. "Shower?"

"It's the oil; I'm sorry. It's everywhere."

"It's a good thing I love you." I drag myself to my feet, yawning unattractively, and follow him into the darkened hall and up the narrow, steep staircase which creaks on the fourth and tenth steps.

Chapter Two

I BALANCE DILLAN ON my hip as we both watch Nathan attempting to feed Emily. She's too fussy. It's not that she doesn't like food; it's just that she likes to feed herself. I don't think Nathan is quite ready to accept the fact that she's now at the age where we're supposed to teach her to use a spoon.

"Open," he coos in a happy, baby talk voice. "Open wide. Ahhh."

I hear the spoon clatter onto the highchair and wince.

"You're naughty," he laughs, still using his happy voice. He turns to me, his smile gone. "She's impossible."

I nod my agreement. "She's your daughter."

"Hair," Dillan says softly and nuzzles his face into my locks.

"I love it when he does that." He's so warm and soft and he looks exactly like Caleb. As he grows, looking at him is hard and, even though I have Nathan, I still struggle with the fact that Caleb is missing out on so much life. He's missing out on his son and his son is missing out on him. Though Nathan is an excellent father, Caleb will never have that level of happiness in his life.

"He's obsessed," Nathan points out. "He loves hair."

"Yep," I agree. "Our kids are weird."

He stands, giving up and handing the bowl and spoon to Emily, who makes a mess within the first five seconds. Her light, wispy hair is already covered in the orange gloop we've chosen for her lunch. "Are you looking forward to your second day?"

I crinkle my nose as a way to show him that I'm honestly dreading it. "I don't think I'm cut out for kitchen life."

"All jobs are hard in the beginning." He leans in to kiss my lips and Dillan protests by slapping his cheek with a chubby hand. "You're just training. This time next year you'll be better than Kerim. You'll see."

I find that so hard to believe but I appreciate the support all the same. "Your faith in me is astounding."

"Well, we still have three hours before you have to go." He takes Dillan from my arms and places him on the ground. Emily remains strapped in her highchair to the left of me, happily squishing the lumpy orange bits in her bowl with her hands. "What do you want to do?"

"Well, there are lots of things I'd love to do, or, more importantly," I step into him, wrap my arms around him and tuck my fingers into the back pockets of his jeans, "someone I'd love to do…"

"You are insatiable," he whispers and my eyes drift closed in anticipation of his kiss that I know will come. He sucks my lower lip into his mouth. "I wish I could bend you over this counter…"

Smiling, I pull back and raise a pointed brow. "You're really into that at the moment, aren't you?"

"It has its perks."

"You just like pulling my hair." My mouth falls open. "You don't think Dillan has seen…"

"No!" Nathan practically yells, looking horrified. "Of course he hasn't seen us!"

"I was kidding," I soothe, realising my error. To say that Nathan still has issues with regard to his horrifying upbringing would be an understatement. We're working on it. "I'm sorry; that wasn't a good joke."

He pulls away and I know that the moment has gone. He just needs time.

"Come on, sweetie," I say softly to Emily and unclip her confines. "Let's clean you up."

Nathan pretends to be searching for something in the fridge but I can tell he just needs some time alone.

"I love you," I call over my shoulder as I move into the hall. Dillan follows, clutching his toy train tight to his chest.

"I wuv oooh," Dillan copies and I smile down at him.

Nathan doesn't respond; he just continues staring into the fridge. Sighing heavily, I take Emily up the stairs, closing the stairgate behind me to keep Dillan from following and quickly wash her down in the bathroom sink.

It's not until I'm back downstairs, clean and clothed baby in my arms, that Nathan has finally gotten over his fun. He kisses me the second he can grab me and all is right in the world.

So we're not perfect. We're dealing with it the best we can.

"I love you too," he responds. It's late, but he responds.

"You don't have to tell me. I already know." I assure him and place Emily on the floor. She immediately seeks out her brother. Their love-hate bond is beautiful until one of them is screaming.

"I like telling you."

"I like you telling me, but you show me enough every day."

"You're so not needy, and you wonder why I want to marry you?" His lips find my jaw. "Let's go and permit the kids to use us a climbing frame as we watch endless amounts of colourful TV shows with dancing parrots and puppets."

"Oooh, our lives are so exciting," I snort and we move to the living room.

"Have you put any more thought into the wedding?" Nathan asks after tangling his body with mine on the couch. Emily climbs up his legs and demands to be played with. As always, he acquiesces. Her little giggle as he draws her to him and nibbles on her neck melts my heart.

"I umm…" I snap myself back to focused. "I've got a few venues for us to look at but…"

"What?"

"Well, we don't really know anybody to invite," I admit solemnly. "And I don't want to hire a huge venue for a tiny wedding."

"We could always elope."

"Hmm…" It's romantic but I love the idea of planning a wedding.

"Intimate weddings are nicer, aren't they?"

I roll my eyes. "At this point it'll be me, you, the kids and my mum."

"And Tommy and Sasha." He grins and I let out a grunt when Emily crawls over to me. Dillan, seeing his sister get close, immediately becomes jealous and demands that I lift him. "Don't worry." Nathan strokes the side of my cheek with his nose. "It'll all work out. Just hurry up and let me give you my last name."

"I will."

"When?" His thumb tugs on the ring on my left hand.

"Let me focus on training, okay?"

He smiles, leans in and kisses the tip of my nose. "Okay, you're right. Too much pressure."

"Do you want me to make you something for dinner before I go to work? You can warm it up later."

"Another reason I want to make you my wife." I'm practically shoved off the couch. "I don't know if you noticed but I got you all of the ingredients to make that chilli pasta that I love."

I laugh, roll my eyes heavenward and move to the kitchen. I hope that I'll never lose my passion and love for cooking, despite the stresses my new job may put on me.

"You'll get faster," I'm reassured as I botch slice a potato.

"If you say so," I mumble.

I feel my arm snap backwards as I'm spun and my boss... head chef guy... is directly in my face. "What kind of talk is this? If you don't have faith in yourself then why should I have faith in you?" He drops a knife beside the potato and his brown eyes narrow with annoyance. "Fucking cut the thing and cheer up about it or get the fuck out of my kitchen."

I hate him. He swears too much. Now I understand why Nathan hates me swearing. It's such an unattractive language add on. At least he has pretty eyes and his breath always smells minty. If he was yelling in my face with horrible breath, I'd have quit already.

"He has a point," Patience says, shrugging one shoulder. "You're slowing us down as it is."

"Such a joy isn't she?" A young guy who introduced himself as Sean smirks from the other side of the table. He's peeling the potatoes that I'm chopping, though he's actually the designated cleaner.

I don't comment. I don't want to slag off the people I work with on my second day, or at all for that matter. I simply smile and concentrate on the potatoes.

Potatoes.

Just potatoes.

Talk about starting at the beginning. I'm just so nervous; I don't want to mess up.

I don't want to let anyone down. I know I can do better than this.

CHAPTER TWO

I mean, I know how to peel and chop a bloody potato. If I was alone, I'd slap myself.

"We need onions diced," Kerim yells when I finish my last potato. "Quickly."

"Yes, Chef!" I call over the noise of the kitchen and pop a piece of chewing gum into my mouth. A little trick to stop your eyes from watering is to chew on gum as you chop onions. Although when I grab the bucket full of onions, I realise I might need more than chewing gum in my arsenal to stop my eyes from watering. I want to cry just from seeing the mountain. Fortunately, I'm an excellent dicer. I know I can do this quickly.

I get a fifteen-minute break when the restaurant settles at eleven PM. Normally I'd call Nathan but I have a feeling he'll be sleeping, so instead I call Sasha to check in. It's been a few days since we talked properly. I know she's definitely awake due to the fact she just updated her Facebook status two minutes ago.

"Hey, stranger," she greets me immediately, her tone happy.

"I don't have long; I'm on a break." I sip my drink and check the time on my phone. "I have exactly six minutes left."

"I'm honoured to be chosen." She laughs a little. "How's work?"

"I'm exhausted."

"It's only day two; you'll get over it."

"Gee," I grin. "Thank you for the support."

"You're welcome. How is Nathan coping?"

"Better than I would be," I admit, thinking of the handsome man with whom I'm spending my life. "I love him. He's so good to me."

"Yeah," she agrees. "Speaking of partners, I think Tommy is going to ask me to marry him."

My jaw hits the floor. "You're kidding?"

"No, he's been all jittery recently and he keeps fiddling with something in his pocket."

At that, I snort. "You're sure he's not just playing with himself?"

"Hardy, har."

"We need you back inside," Patience yells through the double doors. "Now!"

Sighing heavily, I stand. "I have to go."

"I heard."

"We'll talk more about Tommy and his pocket fiddling tomorrow."

"Love you, bitch."

"Love you more, asshat."

I hang up and rush inside from the cold. I was enjoying sitting. I'm so tired.

"Eat," Kerim demands, sliding a peculiar-looking red dish in front of me. "It won't poison you."

"Thank you," I murmur, not meeting his eyes as I spear a piece of aubergine with my fork and place it on my tongue. Oh my god. I can't fight the groan. That's so good.

"You like it?"

"It's amazing."

I spear a piece of lamb and onion and chew them slowly to savour every second. I didn't realise how hungry I was.

Kerim cocks his head to the side as he watches me eat and I find it a little unnerving. "Finish it all. Have a coffee. I need you to stay until four."

Blink. "But we close at midnight."

"Yes," is all he says before going back to his work. I stare after him, wondering why on earth I'm being forced to stay so late. I shan't argue though, as tired as I am. I want to be here. I *need* to be here. Maybe this is a test to see if I have what it takes to make it in his kitchen. I sure hope I do. All I can do is try.

"Okay, Chef," I mutter under my breath and finish my delicious food.

Midnight comes around and clean up begins. Mostly we have somebody designated to clean as we go along through the evening, but we all pitch in at the end of the day. It's not until all the lights are off, apart from the dim white light above the central unit, and everybody has left that Kerim finally reappears from the staffroom.

"Come." He beckons me to the large metal surface under the light. "Tonight I will teach you two things."

"Okay."

"One, how to chop with your eyes closed."

My eyes widen involuntarily when he brings a long, flat blade to the table followed by a bucket of carrots, potatoes and leeks.

When he rounds the table and holds up a long, silver scarf, I immediately take a step back. My face is no doubt as panic stricken as my heart. Endless thoughts of him tying me up and mutilating me flit through my mind. I mean, how well do we really know this guy? For all we know, it could be humans he's using instead of lamb. Do we even taste of lamb?

Why am I wondering what humans taste like?

The world goes black as the soft silver fabric tickles the bridge of my nose.

"You want me to wield a sharp knife without my eyesight?"

"Not immediately; I'll aid you."

I feel his chest against my back and my entire body tenses. I've never been in such close proximity with another human in the past two years, except for Nathan. I don't like it. It makes me uncomfortable.

"Relax." His hands cover mine and guide them to the knife and the potato. "I want you to learn the sizes our recipes require."

"Without my eyesight?"

His laugh carries his breath through my ear. "This is how I learned and I learned quickly."

"I'll lose a finger."

"No, you'll be more careful because..."

"I have no sight," I finish and blow out a breath. His hands shake mine loose and make quick work of sliding through the potato. "Carrots and such are easier as we have the slicer, but you still need to work the slicer and you still need to know the sizes."

"Got it."

"Chef," he snaps.

"Sorry," I mumble and he clears his throat, a persistent nudge to get me to finish the way he wants me to. "Chef. Sorry, Chef."

"Inside this kitchen I'm not your friend. I am not your husband's friend. I don't know you beyond this kitchen while I'm in this kitchen. So when I yell at you," his hands continue to move mine, carefully chopping the potato, "nothing is personal; everything is professional. I tell this to all of my staff and I stand by it. Do you understand?"

"Yes, Chef."

"There will be no personal arguments that don't involve this kitchen within a mile radius of this kitchen."

"Y...yes Chef."

"There will be no flirting or chatting with other members of this kitchen, unless on break, and even then no personal attachments will be formed."

He barks, slicing the final slice of the potato. I feel its moist smooth texture under my fingers. "There will be no meeting outside of work. I want no drama brought into this kitchen. Human nature forces us to act like fools when angry at another. Do you understand?"

"I think so." I clear my throat and wet my lips that have dried from the nerves.

"You think so?" His tone is high, disbelieving. "You only think you understand?"

"No," I quickly correct. "I understand, Chef."

"Good, then fucking say that next time." He releases me. "Keep cutting those very same sizes. You were paying attention, weren't you?"

"Hard not to when you're trying to step into my body, *Chef*." I remark and his answering chuckle surprises me.

"Good. There may be hope for you yet. Now chop."

Chapter Three

The sun is lightening the sky when I finally make it home. It's almost five in the morning and even at such an hour, the traffic in London can be a battle.

"I know." He smiles arrogantly before smacking my arse and exiting the kitchen. The kids follow closely behind him.

Quietly and slowly I unlock the front door and head inside. It's dark save for the small lights on the wall, dimly lighting my path.

I can't recall a time I've ever come home to a sleeping Nathan. It's surreal.

He looks so peaceful. I almost daren't undress in case I wake him, but somehow I manage it. Once I'm stripped to skin, I sit on the bed and kiss his temple. He rests on his stomach, his arm hugging the underside of his pillow. His lips are smushed to the shape of a wonky heart. I kiss the corner and run my fingertips down his arm.

Not a single ounce of me recalls falling asleep. When I finally awake at noon the next day, it's to find a note on the side that reads:

'Taken the kids to the store. I didn't want to wake you. Sleep well; call me when you're up. I miss you.'
x N x

Smiling, I quickly tie my hair back and seek out my bag and phone. My body aches badly from the day before. I try to focus on the silver lining - all of the weight I'll be losing and muscle I'll be toning.

Unfortunately, due to being so bloody tired when I arrived home, I didn't put my phone on charge, so in order to use it I have to stand by the plug. This means I can't cook and talk at the same time and I am famished, but my partner means more to me than my stomach so calling him wins.

Sigh.

The second my phone turns on it rings. My mum's face and number light up the screen. I contemplate disconnecting but I owe her a call.

"How is it going? Is it marvellous? Are you learning a lot?" She jabbers, hardly pausing in between each question. "I've been trying to call you all morning…"

"I was sleeping," I explain, smiling at the franticness with which she's speaking. "Late night last night; yes it's marvellous; it's hard, but I'm learning."

"Do you need me to come and stay for a while? Help you with the kids?"

"No, we're good. We'll save that token for when we're desperate." My mum would come to us at the drop of a hat, but she only gets so much time off work. I'd never force her to use her holiday time if I weren't desperate. We're lucky to have her.

"You should consider hiring a nanny."

"Nathan is certain he can cope and he's doing amazing so far."

"So far." She emphasises the words. "It's only day two."

"Ye of little faith." My smile becomes a frown. "Don't be so negative."

"Sorry, I don't mean to be. I miss you guys."

My smile returns and so does the softness in my voice. "We miss you too. Emily can say 'Nana' now. She sees your pictures and videos and her face lights up."

"Good. Kiss those chubby cheeks for me."

"I will but I have to go. I need to call Nathan."

"Where is he?"

"At the store most probably. He loves taking the kids there. The customers love it." I check my phone as it vibrates with each incoming message I've received during the time it has been switched off. "I'll call you later. I love you."

"Bye, Sweetie. Love you too."

The line disconnects and I waste not a single second to call my one and only.

"Hey, you're alive." He sounds happy and also breathless. I love the deep, husky sound of his voice. It awakens my very soul.

"Barely, I ache." He chuckles at my moaning. "I miss you; where are you guys?"

"We are having lunch after a pleasant stroll through Hyde Park."

I hear Dillan yelling, "Pigeon!"

Nathan sighs and I laugh.

"Or it was a pleasant stroll." He mumbles so quietly I only just hear him.

"You know how much he loves birds."

"No, it's not that... can I call you back?"

"What? Why?" My heart begins pattering a quick beat. "What's wrong?"

"My umm... my mother."

Holy crap. My face flushes with fire. I'm so angry knowing she's even within five miles of my children. "She'd better not be trying to talk to you."

"Of course she won't, but I'd rather she didn't see our children. I'll call you." He hangs up before I can protest, not that I would. Clearly he needs both hands free to steer the children away from that wicked witch.

Speaking of his parents, his dad's trial is soon. He had a heart attack two months after he almost killed us both and they postponed the event, though he hasn't been let off in the meantime. I'm not entirely sure how he has been dealt with; Nathan hates speaking about it. What I do know is he's looking at a life sentence. I just hope his pull in the business world, his money and his lack of a criminal record don't influence that.

That man is a monster and he deserves every single ounce of pain and punishment that he gets. If I could personally shoot him in the face, I would.

His mother is no better. Vile monsters, the pair of them.

Though thinking such dark thoughts hardly makes me much better. I shouldn't be thinking of them at all.

Deep breaths.

Nathan doesn't call me back and I don't want to bother him if he's ushering the kids around, so I take the time alone to do the chores and have a shower. I have to be at work at four, thankfully not too early, so I have time to recover, though I'd really like to see my babies before I vanish for twelve hours again.

<u>Gwen</u>: Are you coming home at all? I have to leave again soon.

Nathan: We're on our way. Traffic is terrible. X

It always is, but I'm too scared to use the underground alone. I grew up in small towns and big cities scare me. The moment I get the chance, I'll be out of London and back in the countryside. As awful as the memories are that that house held, it was the first place I ever truly felt at home. I miss the quiet. I miss the scents. I miss how I felt being there with Nathan. I smile when my mind calls upon the memory of the time Nathan proposed to me in a letter and I avoided it for days. This then triggers the memory of the conversation I had with Sasha last night.

Gwen: Has he proposed yet?

Sasha: He's not home from work yet.

Gwen: Oh...

Sasha: Should I check his pocket?

Gwen: Absolutely not! Let him do this his own way.

I'm surprised that Tommy hasn't mentioned anything though. I only spoke to him last Friday. We don't text much these days; we call and chat. He hates texting; he feels as though it's too impersonal. That and he doesn't want to waste time typing when he can get what he needs to say out in less than five minutes.

Sasha: You wouldn't snoop?

Gwen: Nope.

Sasha: Boring. Where's the excitement in that?

Rolling my eyes but smiling broadly, I place my phone down and limp into the kitchen. I need lunch before work. Because I slept until late, my body clock is all wrong. I didn't get breakfast until lunchtime and even though I'm not yet hungry, I don't know what time I'll get a break at work and be able to eat, so I'm going to stock up on energy foods now. A fruit salad and some Greek yoghurt should do the trick. I hope.

I also pop a couple of painkillers with my lunch to help with the aching.

"I'm sorry I'm so late," Nathan calls as he enters but I don't care about that. I'm just happy to see him and my little cuties.

Dillan takes a running leap at me and immediately buries his face in my hair. Nathan balances Emily on his hip and nuzzles her nose with his. The way she smiles up at him with sleepy eyes to match his, I almost melt.

"What happened with your birth lady?" I ask, not wanting to ruin this precious moment but I need to know.

He shrugs and his eyes evade mine. "Nothing."

Somehow I don't believe him. "Nothing?"

"Yes, nothing." Now he meets my eyes, his brows raised with indignation. "I'm serious. I took the kids and left."

"She didn't see you?"

He shrugs again and nuzzles Emily's nose. She laughs and hits his cheeks with both hands. "We missed Mummy, didn't we?"

"Yeah," Dillan grins, making me grin just as wide.

"I love you all." I kiss Nathan firmly on the lips and then my little girl, as Dillan clings tightly to my neck, and then I kiss him too. "Have you had a good day?"

"The best! We've sold out of Forever Connected charms; there are only a few left."

"They're becoming so popular," I grin, proud of him for all of his accomplishments.

"I'm going to have to design and make new ones. I've had quite a few requests."

"Maybe you can do a competition or something? See if people can design their own and the one you like the most will win an entire bracelet or something?"

"Hmm," he hums thoughtfully. "Not a bad idea; I'll have a talk about it with the others."

"How bad is traffic?"

"Gridlock."

Kissing him once more, I step back and thread my fingers through Emily's wispy hair. "I should go then or I'm going to be late. Can we talk more about this later?" Taking our daughter from his arms and manoeuvring Dillan into his, we share a group hug and numerous kisses, and then I'm on my way.

I'm grateful that I have the night off tomorrow or I think I might die.

As expected, the traffic is manic but I'm ten minutes ahead of time when I finally make it to work. The relief I feel is substantial. I might have to start taking the underground though; it'd save me a lot of time and money. It's just so scary!

"Good, you are here. Taste this." A spoon is forcefully pushed into my mouth by Kerim. Patience stands beside him, looking hopeful.

The tangy soup hits my tongue and I'm not sure if I'm a fan.

"How is it?" Patience asks.

"Too much salt," I state and Harold, the Station Chef claps his hands and calls, "I told you so."

"Fuck," Patience hisses, scowling at me as though it's my fault she fucked up the dish.

"Next time don't fucking argue or you're fired," Kerim bellows at her, throwing the spoon onto the same counter we chopped potatoes at in the early hours. "If I say it's shit then it's shit."

"But..."

"No, you are the sous chef. You follow ME!" Kerim shouts, his nose an inch from hers. "Do you understand?"

"Yes, Chef." She mutters, her cheeks flushing with humiliation.

"Come." Kerim grips my arm and leads me out of the door. "You will follow me. We need to order meat."

"Will the kitchen be okay without you?"

"Probably not, but we need to order meat." He half drags me around the restaurant. "You need to learn the best cuts versus the worst cuts as this job will be yours as of next week."

"Why?"

"Because you need to learn meat quality, fish quality, you must know it all."

My legs can hardly keep up with his long strides.

We stop at the corner and two large, unlabelled chiller vans come into view.

CHAPTER THREE

The men inside climb from the driver's seats as though performing a synchronised move. I almost laugh when they both scratch their heads at the same time, though the performance ends when only the first man at the first van opens the sliding door on the side.

Kerim steps in first and then tugs me up alongside him.

There are pallets full of red meats on the left, all carefully sealed and contained, and the same for white meats on the right.

"We need goose meat, lamb, beef, chicken and duck." Kerim barks at me. "See this?" He holds a full, small duck up. "This is no good. Why?"

"Because... umm..." I don't see any imperfections.

"Because it is not balanced. There is too much fat."

"So, no fat?" I enquire.

He rolls his eyes. "Meat must always have fat. Fat holds a lot of flavour and makes the sauces taste good. It needs to be balanced. Seven percent fat to ninety three percent meat for the ducks. They are too small to allow more." He throws the duck into the bin behind him. "Are you following?"

"It makes sense." I watch as he skilfully fondles each individual bag of meat, looking for the best cuts, until he has four plastic pallets full of the meats he needs. He pays the van man from a packet of money stuffed into the breast pocket of his white coat.

"Okay, now the fish."

"I genuinely don't know much about fish."

He turns to stare at me, his face an expressionless mask. Then he turns back to the second van as the van man from the first van takes the pallets towards the restaurant.

"Then we will teach you this too." He waves his hand and, like before, we step into the second van and he immediately peruses the many fish within. I can't tell a haddock from a bass. This is going to require some serious research.

"You stink," Nathan insists the second I step into the house. He pinches his nose with his fingers. "I kind of wish I hadn't waited up for you now."

"I know; I'm sorry. I've been at the fish market for the past hour studying fish."

"Studying fish?" He sounds bunged up from being unable to breathe through his nose. I start stripping off my clothes the second he holds a bin bag open for them. "That sounds... odd."

"I can't tell the difference between cod and every other fish," I admit, dropping my knickers to the floor with my leggings. "Well I can now, but I couldn't before."

"Nice."

"I'm immune to the smell. Am I horrific?"

"I'd still do you." He leans in to press his lips to mine but makes a hasty retreat. "After you've showered."

"Coward," I cry jokingly and make my way up the stairs. Nathan follows closely behind with a bottle of disinfectant in one hand and a sponge in the other. If he plans on cleaning *me* with that, we'll be having issues.

I'm forced to shower three times before he's satisfied and by the end of the third time, the house stinks of disinfectant and Nathan is fast asleep in bed, the empty bottle of cleaning fluid resting on its side on the bedside table.

Also my skin is red raw but I smell of raspberries so I'm not totally unhappy about it.

It's a good thing I love him.

I'm awoken when a child lands heavily on my stomach. I "oof" as the wind is knocked out of me. A mess of brown curls tickles my nose and Dillan's giggle as he climbs up my body makes this sudden wake up the best kind of wake up.

"Mummy," he yells and pulls up my eyelid.

"Hey!" Batting his hand away, I roll us over and bite his chubby little shoulder.

"Noooo," he giggles hysterically and thrashes to get me away.

Obviously I stop when it gets too much for him. "Love you."

"Wuv ooo," he responds and accepts my kiss. "Daddy uh-oh."

"Daddy what?"

"Uh-oooooh," he frowns and scrambles to move out from under me. I sit up and scan the empty room.

"Where is your daddy, I wonder," I murmur, climbing from the bed. I close the bedroom door so the little terror can't escape and quickly dress. "NATHAN?"

He doesn't answer so I lift Dillan into my arms and step into the dark hallway that still stinks of disinfectant.

"Nathan?"

CHAPTER THREE

I can hear him speaking and it sounds as though it's coming from the kitchen. I can't quite make out what he's saying.

When I enter the well-lit room, I immediately spot Emily in her highchair eating slices of banana. Nathan must have dropped Dillan in my room and left. He's standing in the doorway leading to our small back garden and seems to be captured in a deep conversation. His tone is so low, I can hardly hear him.

When he senses my presence, he quickly barks, "I have to go. *Now.*" And then hangs up the phone.

"What the hell was that all about?" I snap, feeling out of the loop and a bit nervous.

"Nothing," he responds. His brows draw in, making the lines on his forehead deep and concerning. "Just shop stuff. I hate it when they bother me at home."

I blink, disbelieving his lie. "Since when?"

"Since now," he snaps back but quickly softens when he sees that he has upset me. "I'm sorry. It's just they've been calling non-stop all morning and it's for stupid things. I've been up since six. Dillan has been driving me crazy, pulling everything from the cupboards."

"Are the child locks broken?"

"The clever little git figured out how to open them." I'm pulled into his arms and kissed slowly and wonderfully. So wonderfully I forget everything else for a moment. "We'll either have to upgrade them or tie him to a chair." A plate clatters on the ground, but fortunately it doesn't break.

"Dillan," I chastise and pull him away from the immediate danger. "Come on, let's go and play in the room while Daddy cleans up your sister." Before we fully exit, I turn back to my future husband. "Are you sure you don't want to hire a nanny? It's not like we can't afford it right now."

"No, we can handle this," he barks, offended at my suggestion.

"Okay, I'm sorry. I don't doubt you; I just don't want you overworking yourself."

"I know, I just… I don't want them being raised by other people." His lips twist with a grimace.

"It'd only have to be for a day or two a week. Just to give you a break."

"No, okay? We're fine. Now, are you hungry?"

I nod my head. "Starving. You?"

"Same. Shall I cook?"

"I'll whip up some porridge and then we can go to the store to sort out the thousands of calls you've apparently been getting."

"That's fine." He waves me off. "It's sorted. Let's take the kids to play instead."

I nod my agreement. "That certainly sounds like a better plan."

"I'm glad you agree. I'll sort out the changing bag; you make porridge and we'll both argue over who gets Dillan and who gets Emily."

"As is our normal routine," I grin, laughing a little. "I love our life." He hums and pulls me tight to his chest. I tuck my head under his chin and ask, "Don't you?"

"Of course."

"Are you happy?"

"One hundred thousand percent."

"Me too." I move away and reach for the cupboard that holds the porridge.

Chapter Four

"He still hasn't asked me!" Sasha screeches before I even get the chance to say hi.

"Did you ever think that maybe you're wrong and he isn't going to just yet?"

There's a long pause, where even her breathing has stopped. "FUCK!"

"Chill out." I have to hold the phone away from my ear to prevent any long term damage.

"You're probably right, oh my god... what if he's cheating on me?"

Eye roll. "He isn't cheating on you."

"But..."

"Sasha..."

"Okay, okay but what if he is?"

"I'm hanging up on you."

"No! Okay, I'm sorry, I'll quit obsessing. Tell me about you. How are the kids?"

I sink back into my seat and prop my feet up on the coffee table. "They're fabulous. Dillan used the toilet twice yesterday."

"Toilet?"

"Yeah, he didn't like the potty so we got him a little toilet training seat and a step. It's so adorable."

"Yuck." She laughs. "Only a mushy parent such as yourself could find toilet training cute."

"Whatever, it was a good day yesterday."

"And what about today?"

"Well we've been at the store all morning so he had to wear a pull up."

"I don't know what that is." She takes a noisy gulp of something. "I fucking love coffee."

"Me too."

"So, how do you think he'll propose when he does propose?"

And we're back to that. "Ask him; maybe he'll tell you."

"You suck at this."

"Goodbye, Sasha," I laugh.

"Wait maybe you could ask…" I hang up before she can finish. No way am I being pulled into her madness. Not this time.

<u>Kerim</u>: Need you at work ASAP. Patience is ill.

Fuck.

"Nathan!" I call and moments later he appears in the doorway.

"Yes?"

"I have to go into work."

The shutters come down in his eyes. "But we just got the kids to sleep."

"I know, but I need to make a good impression."

He sticks his lower lip out in a pout. "I get it. Don't worry." Walking over to me, he holds out his hand and pulls me up from my comfortable position. "At least we had all day yesterday and today together."

"Exactly." I flop like a dead weight, knowing he'll catch me.

He grunts, holding me under the arms as I hang from him like an extremely heavy noodle.

"You might have to drag me there."

"Get up," he laughs. I love making him laugh. I don't love it enough to actually get up though. "Come on, Gwen. Either go and get them or stay and let me use your body in delicious ways that please me."

"Ugh, now you've made being an adult even harder."

"Just ignore it. You have kids…"

"Don't be an enabler." I stand upright and slap his arm.

"I'm not sure that word works in this scenario."

Blowing out a breath, I stretch my body and give him a frown. "Don't correct me when I'm being cute."

"When were you being cute?"

"Bugger off," I smile and pick my phone up off the sofa.

CHAPTER FOUR

<u>Gwen</u>: I'm leaving now. X

Nathan, who watched me type over my shoulder, immediately snaps, "What's with the kiss?" His tone reeks of jealousy and annoyance.

Immediately I regret my error and not just because my partner has pointed it out and it has caused him to feel uneasy, but because I just sent my boss a kiss.

"Total habit. I genuinely didn't mean to send that." My teeth sink into my lower lip and it's painful. I deserve it. "Think he'll be weirded out?"

"I think he'll be thinking with his dick."

Nathan, unused to having feelings, can sometimes overreact to situations such as this. He's not overbearing by any means and never stops me from enjoying myself, but when it comes to men, he gets nervous. I can't blame him for that and I'm helping him with it.

"Don't be silly. Kerim is extremely... *extremely* strict on the no fraternisation in the workplace rule. He won't even let us take breaks at the same time."

"I trust you. I just don't want him thinking he has an in."

I can't help but laugh. "Because of one accidental X in a text message?"

"Go to work," he pouts, nudging me towards the doorway. "Before I change my mind."

"I'm going, I'm going."

<u>Kerim</u>: Hurry. You have twenty minutes.

What an arsehole. How does he expect me to get there in twenty minutes?

"Oh, I'm not even kidding," I growl to Tommy on the phone. "He was all, 'you're late'. Like... I'm not even supposed to be there."

"What an arsehole. But you're so fucking lucky to be there."

"And don't I know it? Hence the fact I just say, 'sorry, Chef. Yes, Chef.' Like a submissive little fool."

"You've been reading those whip and chain novels again, haven't you?"

"Yes, during my work breaks." My eyes roll heavenward. "So... anything new to report other than the usual?"

"New as in what?"

"I dunno," I lie because I'm fishing for information about the proposal. "Just asking."

"Nothing that I haven't told you already. Why? What's wrong?" He suddenly sounds panicked. "Although Sasha has been acting odd lately."

Oh no. "She has?"

"Yeah, I caught her searching through my pockets. Though I didn't tell her I saw her. Any idea what that's all about?"

Oh dear.

Sasha, what are you doing you crazy bitch?

"Nope, why don't you ask her?" Their level of communication is below par.

"I asked her what's wrong. She said nothing and then the next day I caught her searching my pockets." He clears his throat. "Does she think I'm having an affair? Because I literally spend no time away from her, excluding work hours."

"I umm... I have to go. I think Dillan is crying."

"Don't use the brat as an excuse to escape an awkward conversation," he laughs.

"Why else did I have him?" I look at my beautiful babies who are napping happily on the sofa, a thin blanket thrown over both of them. "And don't call him a brat. He's an angel."

"If you say so," he jests. I know he's kidding. He loves how cheeky Dillan is. He taught him most of it. "I'll come and visit soon with the psycho woman I love."

"Make sure you do; we miss you."

"As you should." I hear a door close on his end. "She's home. I should go or she'll be checking my phone next. Speak later."

"Later."

I rest my head back against the wall, enjoying this moment's peace. My body aches. My brain aches. I don't know how people work this hard and enjoy it. I haven't had the chance to enjoy the things I'm learning because I'm so tired.

Have I jumped into this too soon?

No. It's just the start; I'll get used to it. Soon Kerim will allow me to actually cook something. So far all I've done is cut, chop, slice, clean and watch him order things for the pantry. We all have to start from the

CHAPTER FOUR

beginning and, considering I'm going into this blind, without a University degree up my sleeve, it's a huge accomplishment just to be there and holding my own. I'm more surprised that I haven't yet been fired. Kerim hates me. He's told me so on two occasions when I botched the length of an asparagus tip. I was supposed to cut them all to the same length and I was sure I did, but I was out by a millimetre.

No word of a lie.

A fucking millimetre.

But when one works in a twenty-million-star restaurant, everything must be perfect and I'm not moaning about that fact. I just wish he wasn't so aggressive. It makes me panic and when I panic, I make more mistakes.

Like now, just thinking about how he makes me panic is making me panic.

Dillan sits bolt upright, like a meerkat peeking over grass. I laugh at the suddenness of it and open my arms ready to welcome him when he scrambles towards me.

"Mumma." He nuzzles my hair that rests over my shoulder. I had to cut a lot of it off after the fire so it's not as long as I'd like, but it's getting there. Hair takes so long to grow.

The living room door clicks open and Nathan pokes his head around it. He's so handsome, especially now he's had a shave and doesn't have a ton of scruff circling his mouth. "When's your next day off?"

I shrug. "I'll have to let you know."

"I thought we could ask Jeanine to babysit. I want to take you out for the night."

Yay. "Date night?"

"If that's what you'd like to call it."

"Woohoo!" I whisper cheer. "Date night."

"You're adorkable."

"Thanks." I give him my cheesiest grin and Dillan does the same, simply to copy me. "Where are you taking me?"

"I haven't gotten that far yet. I'll let you know."

"Oooh, exciting!" I blow him a kiss and he blows me one back. I can't deny the fact that we are a sickly sweet couple. Even I find it nauseating how happy we are sometimes. It worries me too because happiness like this doesn't last forever according to everyone else in the world. We need to be unhappy more often so that when a blowout does come, it's not so huge.

I'm being moronic.

This gorgeous man walked through fire for me and chose to die beside me. How could we ever be unhappy?

"You're staring." He frowns; he really doesn't like it when I do that.

"I can't help it."

Quirking a brow, he vanishes back into the hall and moments later I hear him whistling to himself. He's happy. I'd know it if he weren't.

"Mama," Emily coos and I see her chubby little arms straighten as her legs stretch so high the toes of her right foot hit her lips.

"Emmy!" Dillan yells and scrambles from me to help his baby sister off the sofa.

I love them both, so much.

"Yes, Chef!" I yell for the thousandth time in ten minutes.

"You've got this, Gwen," Ahmet whispers in my ear as he passes. Ahmet is the name of the Executive Chef. We finally got an introduction in between all of his arguing with Kerim. Though considering they fight so much, there seems to be no love lost between them. Apparently they're cousins but they have such a brotherly bond. It's nice. I can understand why Kerim wants to keep everyone separate. This place, though they yell a lot at each other, is such a well-oiled machine. One kink in the cogs and it'll fall apart. Anyone can see how much effort Kerim has put in to create the perfect team.

I can't be the one person who screws that up.

"Good," Patience tells me when I slide the tray of sliced vegetables towards her. "Another week and you'll be laughing."

I sure hope she's right.

"Prepare the duck," Kerim yells and at first I ignore him because he can't possibly be speaking to me.

"Sorry?" A duck in a small metal dish is practically thrown my way.

"How would you prepare it?"

Holy fuck. This is happening.

The problem is, I've never cooked duck before. As if sensing this, Kerim steps beside me. The bustle of the kitchen is louder than his voice. "You have only half an hour. Prepare it how you like it. Go crazy. I want to see what you're made of."

"No pressure then."

"Don't panic; just have fun. The whole point of doing this is because it's what you love and supposedly you're good at it. Rely on your instinct, your talent. If it exists, we'll soon see."

With that he wanders away, leaving me and the bald duck in the middle of the kitchen.

Crap.

I cheat and keep it simple. If I was to have duck, I'd want the skin to be crispy and salty and the rest to pull apart like string cheese.

Or should I follow the recipe Kerim has taught the others? I'm not totally sure what the formula is.

When it has finished cooking and it comes time to taste it, Kerim does so but gives me no feedback other than the fact he doesn't spit it out. It isn't terrible in my own personal opinion. Could use some potatoes and gravy.

"Back to chopping and rid the fat from this beef. There's too much. My error." Kerim yells from across the kitchen. "Jamal, wash your fucking hands before you touch the equipment, you idiot."

"Yes, Chef." The man darts past with red oil covering him to near elbow.

I've never handled so much raw meat in my life. There's a dirty joke in there somewhere.

Chapter Five

NATHAN CLIMBS INTO THE driver's seat, a happy smile on his face. Flexing his glove covered hands, he looks at me and then beats a rhythm on the steering wheel. "Are you ready?"

"After the week I've had, is that a serious question?"

He pulls me to him and places his lips against my forehead. "You've worked so hard."

"As have you." He so tirelessly puts my needs before his own.

"I'm used to it and the stores are doing so well, I'm thinking of opening another."

Grinning, I throw my arms around his neck, leaning over the console so as to hold tighter to him. "That's amazing! I'm so happy for you."

"Thank you." He seems uncomfortable, not with the way I'm holding him but with the subject. I feel as though he has something to tell me. When I get this feeling, it's usually correct.

"Where were you thinking of opening another?"

His phone startles us both at the same time as a car, wanting to pull into the space we're about to vacate, blares its horn at us.

I reach for his phone, as is normal while he's driving. Normally I'll answer and ask them to call back. Just as my fingers touch the edges, he snatches it away and drops it into the hollow pocket on the door, beneath the handle.

What just happened?

"Umm... what was that all about?"

"Just some company calling. Probably wanting to help me claim back my PPI," he laughs and I immediately know he's lying. "Nothing to worry about."

He backs out of the parking space, glancing at Jeanine's car as we pass. We're so lucky to have her only an hour away; she's always eager to help out when we need it.

"Nothing to worry about?" I repeat, tasting his words on my tongue and willing them to actually banish my worry.

I don't want to be paranoid but there is only one reason I can think of that he'd hide his phone from me for the first time in our entire relationship and I doubt it's because of a surprise party. If it was a text message, I'd understand his hesitancy to let me see it, not that I'd try. I've never tried. But because it's a phone call, surely if it was my mother calling to discuss a secret that I'm unaware of, she'd act natural so as to not make me suspicious.

Unless it's a venue calling and not somebody we know. In which case I can understand his hesitancy to allow me to answer the call.

My head hurts. Nothing about this is right.

"So, I thought we could go and grab a quick bite to eat before going to see that movie you've been going on about for months."

This perks my mood up a little bit, though not enough for me to fully get excited as my mind is a torment of questions. I don't want to be the type of woman that searches his phone, destroying his privacy because of my own paranoia. I should trust him. If I can't trust him then I shouldn't be with him.

"That's great. I'm starving." I force a smile, not that he sees it as his eyes are on the road.

"Good." His hand leaves the wheel and finds his phone in the hollow pocket. I hear it beep as he turns it off and the panic in my heart sets a deep scar. "Let's go."

"I want popcorn."

He frowns; he has such an aversion to it. "Fine."

"And nachos with melted cheese."

"Really?" His disgust amuses me.

"Yep."

"Your funeral."

I blow out a breath and stare out of the window for a long moment. "Who was on the phone?"

"Nobody, as I said."

I give him a sideways glance, hoping my disbelief projects onto him. "So why'd you turn your phone off?"

"Because I don't want our evening to be disturbed. I turned yours off too."

He did? I pull it from my handbag and stare at the black, unresponsive screen. "When?"

"Back at the house."

"What about the kids? Jeanine?"

"They'll be fine. I have my secondary phone on vibrate." He pats the breast of his jacket. "Against my heart."

My panic dissipates as I recognise my ridiculousness. He wasn't doing it to be sneaky. He was doing it purely because he didn't see anything wrong with it. It's me making an issue.

He walked through fire for me. I remind myself and allow the worry to lift from me like a wet blanket from my skin.

"I'm sorry for creating. I'm such a drama queen. I have no reason not to trust you." I place my hand on his thigh and trail my fingers up to his crotch. He shudders and shifts in his seat. "I'll make it up to you later."

For a few seconds he says nothing. I put it down to the fact I'm teasing him whilst he drives, definitely not the safest move, so I stop groping him through his trousers. His groan of disappointment makes me laugh. The slow speed with which his cock grows along his thigh makes me laugh harder.

"You're dealing with this before we eat. You know I'll be hard for hours otherwise."

"I might give you a sneaky hand job in the cinema if you're lucky."

"So romantic." He takes my hand and places it back on his solid groin. "Ugh, that feels great."

"I'm hardly touching you."

"Well, it still feels really good." I slap his thigh and cross my arms, smiling with mischief when he hisses through his teeth and rubs his thigh with his fingertips. "I forget sometimes what a bitch you can be."

"Don't insult me. I have the vagina, remember?"

"Please, you couldn't deny me sex even if you wanted to. I'm too good at persuading you."

He's not wrong. "I'm so happy we're getting to do this."

"Me too."

We share a smile.

"So, where are we eating?"

"There's a deli place open around the corner; we'll just grab something quick. The movie starts in half an hour. Unless you want to eat afterwards?"

"Hell no!" I cry, his suggestion abhorrent. "Then I can't have popcorn."

"Oh dear," he remarks sarcastically. "How tragic."

"What is it with you and popcorn?"

"What is it with you and broccoli?"

"Broccoli is vile."

"You're a chef. You shouldn't hate broccoli. I'm certain that disliking such a basic vegetable is against the rules."

"Good point. I won't tell Kerim." I shudder at the thought that he'd find something else to yell at me about.

"How are things going at work? We've not had chance to speak much this week."

"Great." I know I moan about it a lot but my answer is honest. "I love it, all of it, even the stressful parts."

"Are you learning a lot?"

"I'm trying, though it's hard to learn when you're constantly stuck in one area of the kitchen."

He frowns thoughtfully. "Maybe he's waiting for you to take initiative?"

His point is an excellent one. "I'll try to be bold."

"You can do this. You're the best cook I know, which is fortunate for me because I love food and I get to keep you."

He's too sweet.

We step into the little deli shop and a sweet, peppery scent lingers in the air. As we peruse the many fresh items of food, I hear a high pitched, feminine voice squawk, "Nathan?"

Nathan tenses beside me. "Hey, Millie."

"Millie?" I ask, one brow raised as the woman behind the counter comes around and envelopes him in a hug that is far too familiar.

Her pretty, silvery blonde hair is tied back into a bun and hidden beneath a hair net. She's wearing far too much makeup.

"I didn't know you worked here," he states, still making no effort to introduce me after finally releasing her from an awkward one-armed embrace, the other arm remaining tense by his side.

"Yeah, I just started last month. It's been," she blows out a breath through her lips, "four years?"

"Hmm," he agrees and clears his throat.

"What are you doing here? Are you busy? I finish soon; it'd be great to catch up." Her eyes finally come to me standing close to his side. "Oh I'm sorry, are you waiting to be served?"

"We were just grabbing something quick to eat before hitting the cinema." Nathan interjects and steps back so as to put some distance between them.

"Oh, I apologise. I didn't realise you were together. Perhaps we can catch up another time?" She moves back around the counter and I'm grateful for the space between them. I'm not liking the chemistry flowing here; it's too familiar. "I was so sorry to hear about Caleb."

"A tragedy," Nathan responds as my heart flutters with mourning.

"Do you see much of his kid? He left one behind didn't he?"

"Actually…" I start but Nathan cuts me off as if I hadn't even started to speak. "Yes." He looks at me. "Do you know what you want?"

"Just a chicken salad wrap," I bite out, feeling frustrated at his ignorance. I doubt I'll eat it all as I'm not particularly hungry.

"So how long have you two been together?"

"Just over two years," I respond. "We're engaged."

"How lovely." Her words seem flippant and disinterested. "How's your mother?"

"Fine." Nathan takes my hand in his. "I'll have the same as Gwen."

"Sure." The other girl behind the counter sets about making it as Millie handles the payments.

"It's so great to see you again," Millie sighs, looking lovingly at Nathan. Yes… fucking *lovingly*. Her eyes are big, blue and round. She looks like Bambi. I feel almost threatened. I've never been in a position with Nathan where I've felt threatened.

"Yes." Nathan gives my hand a squeeze as his lips touch my temple. "We're on a schedule though…"

"You always were punctual," she giggles and places one wrapped wrap into a plastic carrier bag. "Oh!" She quickly scribbles something onto a piece of torn receipt. When she hands it to *my* fiancé and I see that it's her number, I turn a mixture of red with anger and green with envy. Especially when he folds the stupid thing and pockets it. "Call me and we'll get together. It'd be nice to catch up."

"Sure," Nathan responds and takes the bag that she holds out. "See you later."

See you later?

Maybe I'm being irrational but can I kill her?

Nathan's hand leaves mine and presses against the small of my back as he leads me from the store.

"Well, how nice of you to introduce me," I snarl the second we cross the street.

He seems surprised. "To who?"

He's kidding? "To Millie."

"Oh, sorry, I was just... in shock." He frowns and his hand goes to the breast pocket of his jacket where her phone number is. "It's been a long time since I saw her. She looks different."

She looks different? "Okay, you're going to need to start explaining or I'm going to grow increasingly paranoid. Who was she?"

"An old friend." He presses the button on his keys and the car unlocks. I climb into the passenger seat before pressing him by asking, "An old friend?"

"Yes, she used to hang around on the park near my parents' house when we were kids." He smiles wistfully. "Back when Caleb was having good days and I wasn't forced to stay with..." His sentence trails off but I know what he's referring to. "She's the first girl I... umm."

"Fancied?" My heart tingles with envy even more powerfully than before.

"Had sex with." He finishes honestly as though speaking to me about the weather.

My entire body stills with panic and alarm bells blare in my head. "Are you going to call her?"

"No." He brings my hand to his lips and kisses the knuckles.

The envy in my heart dies a little. "Why not?"

When his eyes come to mine and then his lips, the envy in me dies completely. "Because it'd be entirely inappropriate. I just didn't want to reject her for fear of insulting or upsetting her. That would have been unnecessarily mean." He's right. As much as I'd have loved him to toss her to the ground and laugh in her face, that would have been evil. He handled it quite well, now that I think about it. "Here. Dispose of it yourself if you don't believe me." I wait for him to place the number in my lap and my love for him rises tenfold. How I ever doubted this man for a second is beyond me.

I climb across the console and smother his mouth and face with kisses until he laughs and pushes me off him. "I love you."

He grins and winks at me. "I love you more."

"Why didn't you introduce me though? Or tell her who I was to Caleb and what Dillan is to you?"

"And prolong the conversation further? To satisfy the curious mind of someone who means nothing to us?"

"Okay, stop being clever." I fold my arms across my chest, annoyed with myself for being so petulant. Nathan is so logical; he never acts on emotion. Everything he does is so well thought out.

"You're upset?"

"No." I shake my head and rest my head on his shoulder, ignoring the way the arm rest between us digs awkwardly into my ribs. "I'm just playing."

"Good." He squeezes my thigh. "Shall we go and see this movie or not?"

"Why are you still talking? Drive already."

"Yes, boss," he chuckles and finally switches the engine on. "To the cinema!"

"Aye aye, SpongeBob."

His eyes roll. I love it when he rolls his eyes at me.

The movie was a lot funnier than anticipated. So funny even Nathan laughed out loud at some parts. He was too distracted by the movie to care about my popcorn binge too, always a bonus.

I know that we have to head back now but I don't want this night to end. I've needed this break. Together we have needed this break.

As we step out of the cinema into the cold air, Nathan winds his arm around my shoulders and nods at a passing man. He's always so polite.

"I hope the kids slept okay," I say softly.

"They'll be fine."

"You sound so sure."

"Because Jeanine knows what she's doing." He shakes his head and stops us by the carpark. "I might have to go away for a few days on the thirteenth."

I feel as though he's been building up to this moment. "Where to?"

"Essex."

I blink a long blink. "Essex?"

"Yeah, to open a new store."

"That'll only take a few days?" This is more of a probing question. I know how long it takes to find and open a new store. I just want more information on this sudden venture.

"No but I can come and go. For now I just want to find a decent location for a new store."

I frown. "You sound like you've put a lot of thought into this."

"I have. I know you've been busy so I didn't want to bother you."

My hand rests against his chest. "You never bother me."

"Did I say bother?" He turns and wraps me in strong arms. "I meant burden."

My eyes roll much like his did earlier. "You're an idiot if you think anything in your life could possibly burden me."

"Still…" He rests his forehead against mine. "So you're okay with it?"

"I'll miss you but I'm okay with it. Though I won't be able to get time off work any time soon."

"I know. I'm going to take Emily and Jeanine said she'll watch Dillan."

"You can handle that?"

He scowls. "Can I handle my daughter?"

I see that I've insulted him and now I feel bad. "I didn't mean that. I just meant with you being busy and all…"

"I knew what you meant." He pulls away from me and rubs his eyes. "Let's go. I'm exhausted."

I want to argue to stay a little longer. I know we have to be back but I've missed this alone time with him. I love my kids, I wouldn't trade them for the world, but I love my partner too and sometimes it's okay to want alone time. I hope. Right?

"So how long have you been thinking about opening another store?" I knew it was a possibility but I'm worried he's biting off more than he can chew. It's only the second year. His jewellery is doing so well, but don't all new things in the beginning? I don't know. I shouldn't be judging; I should be cheering him on. "Can we afford it?"

"We can now that you're working and the insurance money for the house is just sitting there." He shrugs and my temper spikes.

"We're building a new house with that house money, remember?"

"We will." His frown deepens and after he climbs into the car, he slams the door a little harder than usual. "Have faith in me."

"I do!"

"Sounds like it."

"I just…"

"What?" He turns to face me, the darkness and dim artificial light making his eyes glow dangerously.

I shrug. "I don't know. I'm just scared."

"You don't think my jewellery will sell?"

My mouth drops open. "Now you're just looking for an argument."

He turns to face the front, giving me his profile. "Well it's what you're implying."

"No it's not." Is it? "That's not what I meant." He doesn't speak and I fear my hesitation in supporting him has ruined the evening so I bite the bullet, close my eyes and take a deep breath. "I'm sorry, truly. You're amazing and I believe in everything you do. This is… well you haven't said anything until now and I guess I don't like being out of the loop on something so huge."

"I understand that, but you're not out of the loop."

"We should have decided this together."

"Why?" He looks incredulous. "We would have come to the same conclusion, regardless."

Gah. He is so frustrating. "Just forget it." Now I'm the mardy one.

"You're being ridiculous."

Scoff.

"Guinevere…"

"Just stop. Everything you say is making this worse."

We both bite our tongues and stare ahead. I really hope we can reach some kind of neutral ground before we get home. Besides, I already apologised; it's his turn now.

He doesn't.

"Hey, Jeanine." I grin when the silvery haired woman greets us in the hall. She hugs me tight. "Were they good?"

"They were wonderful, as always. Straight off they went." We step into the living room and I take immediate note of how clean it is. She's so good to us. "Dillan used his potty before bed too."

"He's getting so good at it," Nathan grins, looking every part the proud father. "Would you care to stay for a drink?"

"No, I regretfully have to shoot off. Jen is coming with Tyler." She hasn't seen her daughter or grandson for a while due to her hectic schedule. Now I feel bad for asking her to come all of this way.

"Thank you for watching them. You're too good to us." I hug the lady I have such a loving bond with. She helped to safely bring my son into the world so it's only right that I'm close to her. "Drive safely."

"I always do," she grins, hugging me back. "Give those beautiful angels a morning kiss for me. I'll call you tomorrow night; we'll plan a lunch."

"Sounds good to me." I step back and walk her to the door. Nathan follows close behind, his smile hiding the fact our date night ended in disaster. Though the night isn't over yet, is it?

The second she drives away, we shut the door and turn to face each other in the narrow hallway. It's almost dark, only the dim light from the living room illuminating our bodies and surroundings.

"I daren't speak," he admits as we both lean against opposite walls. His eyes come to mine. The shade of brown looks black, making him seem angry though his voice is level. "I don't want to further upset you."

"You always twist what I say."

"I don't mean to," he admits softly, looking towards the door. "It's the way you say things; they come across that way."

"You should know me well enough by now to know what I…"

"Don't," he snaps, his black eyes coming to mine. Even now, at this point in time, regardless of my feelings, he looks so completely handsome. "Don't force me to believe that I need to read your mind. I'm human and we have only been together a short amount of time. I don't know everything you think and feel and I don't want to." He doesn't want to? "I like discovering new things about you."

Maybe I've been unfair. "You weren't completely wrong. I don't doubt you, but I do worry."

"Me too." He admits. "But I need you to have faith. If you lose faith, then so will I."

We both breathe heavy sighs. It takes a few seconds but he extends his hand to me. "Come to bed. Let's erase this displeasure in the best way possible."

Finally smiling, I place my hand in his and step past him to the stairs. "We can't."

"Can't what?"

"Erase this in the best way possible."

"Why's that?" His hand strokes and squeezes my arse as I ascend the stairs.

"You don't do oral."

I feel my thigh sting as his hand connects with the sensitive area below my arse cheek. "Cheeky."

It's a long running joke between the two of us. He knows I don't mean harm or even care that he can't give me oral sex. I'm more than satisfied with what he gives me.

Stepping onto the landing, I feel Nathan's hands glide around my hips and hold tight. His footsteps match my own quiet, careful ones as we enter our bedroom and switch on the light.

I flop forward onto the bed, exhausted despite the fact it has been a night of rest. Nathan flops beside me but props his head up on one arm. I hum happily when his fingers trace a gentle pattern on my lower back, where my top has lifted slightly, showing pink flesh above my jeans.

"My dad's trial is in a few days," he says and every fibre of me becomes rigid. Why is he bringing this up now of all days?

"That's good. It's been a long winded process."

I roll onto my back so that I can see into his eyes. They seem detached, distant, as they always do when conversing about his family, which is very rare and only when necessary. The brown irises don't hold the shine that they normally do. Even when they aren't around, these people seem to suck the life from him.

Has seeing his mum had any pull on why he's suddenly talking about the one thing I've been trying to get him to open up about since we almost died that day? My hand reaches up and my fingertips lightly press against the scar on his neck. He winces, not because it hurts but because of the painful memory.

"Thank you for saving me," I whisper when his hand grips my wrist and he presses the inside to his lips.

"Thank you for loving me." His voice is a breath. His eyes are closed but the depth of emotion behind his words almost brings tears to my eyes. I feel my bottom lip tremble so I grab his hair and yank his lips to mine.

We claim each other in a deep kiss, heated and sweet, soft and so bloody beautiful I never want to experience another for fear of losing the memory of this one.

Then it's over and Nathan is rolling onto his back beside me. It's my turn to prop myself up on one arm and trace his forearm with my fingertips. He loves it when I do this so when he pulls away, his eyes alight with nerves, I feel uneasy.

"I think I might go."

"Go where?"

"To my dad's trial."

Holy fuck. "You're not joking, are you?"

He shakes his head, brown, lifeless eyes scanning me for my reaction.

"We paid the barrister a fortune to make it so we didn't have to go."

"No." He sits up and I follow suit. "We paid him a fortune so *you* didn't have to go. It was you he almost killed."

"And you."

"But I raced into the house after the event. You were already in there and there's an extremely good chance that he knew that."

I don't know what to say so I allow the silence to stretch.

He releases a heavy breath so I place my hand on his shoulder. "Do you want me to come with you?"

"No." He bites as if the thought of it is abhorrent. "God no." I'm suddenly on his lap, tight to his chest as he holds me as though we're back in that awful moment. "I guess I just need to hear the sentence for myself."

I nod in understanding and try to pull free. When he doesn't let me, I know that he just needs a moment to compose himself, so I let him have it.

"He'll get ten years minimum." His tone is so certain, so demanding. "He almost killed you."

Chapter Six

Unfortunately, in real life, things don't always take the path we most want them to. Despite the fact that Nathan and I are genuinely good people, despite the fact we lost a house, despite the fact we almost died, Nathan's father has walked free.

"A good man." Nathan throws a glass and I watch it shatter against the wall. "His first offence, they said." I've never seen him so angry. He rips at his hair. "An accident. Our experience and the near fatal *accident* is clouding *our* judgement on a good man. The fire was unintentional." He yells out a play by play of the court hearing, his tone mocking and disgusted. His eyes are wild with anger and in between each sentence, he bares his teeth and breathes as though ready to hyperventilate. "A fucking ACCIDENT." I jolt back when he slams the cupboard door shut after reaching for a fresh glass.

"Nathan!" I yell to stop him from destroying another glass. My hand goes to my mouth, catching hot tears I didn't realise were cascading down my cheeks.

"They said there was no motive and if there was a motive, they were never made aware."

Oh god. I watch him pour two fingers of whiskey into the tumbler.

"Please," I cry, holding my hand out to him. "Come to me, Nathan. Let me take care of you."

"I..." He looks at me with bloodshot eyes. "I can't do this right now."

"What?"

He looks around the room, his eyes taking in the destruction that he inflicted.

"There must be something we can do." I hold out my hand to him, relieved when he takes it and allows me to bury my face in his chest. I know his eyes are staring at the mess he's made so I stroke his back to try and take his mind off it, as a way to soothe him. I've never seen him so angry. I've never felt him tremble so badly.

"They need a motive…"

"They won't get one out of what we gave them," I reason, pulling back and looking at him through my thick lashes. "Regardless of his motive, the fire wasn't meant to kill me."

He yanks away from me. "That's not the point."

"I don't even think it was supposed to burn the house down."

"Are you saying he doesn't deserve to go to prison?" His tone has deepened dangerously; his eyes glitter with anger. I need to watch what I say next.

"No, I'm saying that… you might have to report him for what happened to you as a boy." My teeth sink hard into my lower lip.

The horror on his face when he realises what I'm trying to say breaks my heart. "No."

"But…"

"I said, *no*."

He's gone in an instant, leaving me cold and wanting his heat. I hear the front door slam, shaking the house with the force of it. My leg itches to take the first step after him but the rational part of me knows that going after him now won't make anything better.

Tears fill my eyes and spill down my cheeks as I get to work on cleaning the kitchen. It has been a long time since he has walked out on me, not since long before Emily was born. Not since before we were almost killed in that horrific fire.

I don't like it.

It scares me. I like our relationship how it is now; I don't want things to change. Nathan dotes on us. He loves us. We love him just as much and I can't do this without him. He's starting to really become himself. Something this major could set him back.

CHAPTER SIX

After cleaning up the glass and disposing of it properly, I lean against the side and inhale a heavy breath. My body is still shaking, confused and sad. I don't know what to do.

Once I've swept up the glass and vacuumed the tiled floor, I slide down the wall and bury my face in my knees. It's not until I hear Emily begin to witter through the baby monitor that I remember that I actually have responsibilities and, regardless of Nathan's feelings, so does he.

Gwen: Come home. I won't talk about it anymore. Not today anyway.

I get no response. I wasn't expecting one. He needs time and I have faith that he'll return tomorrow. He has to; I have work at one and he knows how badly I'll worry if he doesn't.

Besides, he isn't the only one who is angry and upset at this revelation.

We did have some warning - the barrister said this was a possibility. Nathan's father has friends in high places and investments in companies that will bail him out if necessary. Nathan just refused to believe that these professionals would not see through his father and his lies.

It almost makes me want to laugh.

Instead, I head upstairs to check on my babies and when I'm satisfied that they have been untainted by the drama, I crawl into bed and wrap my arms and legs around Nathan's pillow.

Sleep is as evasive as smoke between my fingertips. I know it's there but I just can't get a grasp on it.

What am I going to do? I want to be there for Nathan and I want to respect his wishes but while his father roams free, we and our children won't ever be safe. This has to be settled. His father has to pay for everything he has done.

I climb out of bed and have a long, hot shower, praying that the heat relaxes my tense muscles. It doesn't and I climb back into bed, still slightly damp and teary eyed.

Nothing will bring on sleep, nothing but my fiancé. Or the powerful bite of exhaustion.

Gwen: Please come home.

Yet again, no response. I cry my final tear just as exhaustion takes a hold of my wilting body.

"I'm so sorry." The bed shifts and my hair is pushed to the side by cold fingers, making my heavy eyes lift just enough to see his face coming towards my own. "Forgive me," he murmurs against my lips before tucking me into his clothed front and wrapping his leg around mine to keep me in place. His arms hold me tight, almost too tight. I don't know how much time has passed since I finally began to drift. It feels as though I only shut my eyes for a moment before he appeared. I can't say I'm not relieved.

"Always." I find his throat and place a gentle kiss below his jaw. "I'm sorry this is happening."

His chest deflates. "Me too. I should never have lost my temper like that. I never…" He leans back and places a gentle hand on my cheek as his eyes search my own. "*Never*, want to make you feel scared of me. I would never hurt you. You know that right?"

"I know." My hand rests over his. "You don't have to reassure me. I know. I wish you hadn't gone."

"I won't walk out again, I…"

"No." My eyes search for his in the dark. "To the trial."

"Me too. It was too much to bear. I don't know how to handle this."

"We'll get through it together." My hand presses against his shoulder firmly enough to force him onto his back. "We always get through things together."

Strong fingers curl around my neck and a thumb presses against my pulse. I feel him pulling me closer right before his soft lips trap my lower lip between them.

I grin, followed by a squeal when I'm quickly flipped onto my back so that he can deepen the kiss.

"That tickles," I laugh wildly when he nips at my neck and buries his face below my ear. I try to press my shoulder to my temple to keep him out but he's too strong. "Stop," I beg, now laughing so hysterically I can hardly catch my breath. "Nathan, the kids!"

He finally lifts his head, a cheeky smile shining in the dark. I watch his pupils dilate and know that he's swiftly changing from playful to aroused. He'll do anything to change the conversation or make me forget it entirely. I'll do anything to help him heal from it, even if only for tonight.

Groaning, he pushes his tongue past my tingling lips. I accept willingly, loving the way his hands roam up and down my sides, grasping at my flesh desperately.

"You smell like peaches," he mumbles against my breast before drawing a nipple into his mouth. My back arches as the beautiful, stinging burn spreads through my breast with each lash of his tongue and pull of his lips.

The heat it creates twists and writhes in my womb and groin, so when he releases himself from the confines of his trousers and sinks into me with little to no warning, the relief I feel is brutal; the moan I release is untameable. His answering groan only furthers to ignite my pleasure in a way only he can.

"I love you," I cry out on a whisper, tugging on his hips with my hands. His pelvis hits the apex of my thighs, pushing softness against my aching clit with each thrust.

"Gwen," he pleads, lifting my thigh over his arm so he can force himself deeper. "Lift your hips for me."

He raises himself onto his forearm as his hand pulls my lower back up. This is new. It feels amazing. I can see stars. My heels dig into the mattress after he releases my leg. Warm lips seek mine. I feel his panting breaths on my face and then his tongue against my lips. As he pushes all of him into me straight to the hilt with every thrust, I can hardly cry out from the ache it causes deep within.

"I'm there," I warn him, hoping that he's there with me.

His grunt is loud and I feel him swell, filling me so perfectly. It's when his swollen cock throbs with the first spasm of orgasm that I follow him and allow myself to release the pent up pleasure in my stomach.

"Yes," he pushes harder. "Gwen, god... don't stop."

"I'm not doing anything."

I'm too lost and limp. My insides keep twitching with delicious tingles.

A shudder flutters through my body as Nathan collapses on top of me, bringing both of our bodies against the mattress. He rolls instantly, still panting from the exertion but thankfully not crushing me beneath his weight. His sculpted and toned body certainly doesn't weigh nothing.

"That was incredible," he whispers into the darkened room and holds me tight to his side.

I count down from six in my head and, when I reach one, he pulls away to have his after sex shower. Rolling my face into the pillow, I smile at the routine of it. It used to offend me but now I don't care. Soon I'll follow and I wouldn't have it any other way. The thought of not showering after sex is almost repulsive to me now that I'm in the habit of it.

A heavy breath leaves me when I drag myself to sitting and finally hobble into the bathroom where Nathan is already under the hot spray. He holds the door open for me and smiles when I step inside. It's then that we hold each other under the heated water, our rapidly beating hearts synchronising.

"I love you," he tells me as his slick hands admire every inch of my back from shoulder to arse. "I'm sorry."

"Me too." I tip back and kiss his jaw. "Don't get my hair wet or you will be sorry."

His brow raises defiantly as his hand grabs the shower head and twists it so the spray is hitting me face on.

Arsehole.

Chapter Seven

<u>Sasha</u>: August nineteenth, my birthday, we're going to Alton Castle in Windsor and there's nothing you can do to get out of it.

I sigh heavily and move to the right when Emily throws her breakfast spoon at me. It hits the wall, spraying porridge everywhere.

"Maybe if you weren't staring at your phone you'd have been able to prevent that." Nathan wipes down the wall as I pick up the spoon with my free hand, my other hand responding to Sasha's message.

<u>Gwen</u>: That actually doesn't sound so bad.

<u>Sasha</u>: Good! I'm so excited!

I smile at my friend's enthusiasm but it quickly vanishes when I notice Nathan scowling at me. Wincing, I point to my phone. "It's Sasha. It couldn't wait." He looks unconvinced. "She wants us to go to Alton Castle for her birthday." He looks repulsed. "It'll be fun! I haven't been to a theme park since before Dillan."

After a moment's deliberation he finally bites out, "Fine, but only because you seem so happy about it."

"Yes!" I fist pump and snatch Dillan from the ground. "We're going on some big rides!"

"Beeeg wide," he mimics, staring intently at the toy train in his pudgy little hands. "Chooo choo. Beeg wides!"

Nathan kisses my temple and removes his nappy clad daughter from the highchair. "No hotdogs though."

My eyes roll so quickly I almost lose them in my head. "You're so predictable. I mouthed those very words as you said them."

"Hotdogs aren't food."

I pat his cheek lovingly and condescendingly. "Be quiet."

"Beee carrot," Dillan mimics, making us both laugh. Emily laughs with us simply because we're laughing.

I love my family.

"I have to go," I softly say, feeling the weight of having to leave them rest on my heart. "Make sure you finish packing your bags today. They're basically done, just toothbrushes and more nappies."

Nathan nods and follows me to the door, both kids following closely behind. "It'll be sorted before you get back."

"I don't want you to go." I lean against the door frame after opening the door and Nathan presses his body against mine. "I'm only going to have an hour with you in the morning before you leave."

"I'll miss you more, trust me." His hands rest on my hips and his mouth touches my own.

"Morning," our neighbour calls from across the fence as he enters his garden.

"Morning." Nathan and I smile back as I slide free of Nathan's heat. I lean into him and touch my cheek to his. "See you later."

"Bye." He waves before battling both kids back inside. As I climb into the car, the front door to my house closes.

I know I was resigned to Nathan leaving for this trip but it'll do both of us good. Time apart will only make us stronger and the opportunities this trip could bring are too big to miss out on.

"Kerim," I call over the noise of the kitchen. He swiftly moves around his station, throwing salt over fish in a pan before moving on. His arm raises and he crooks a finger for me to follow him. "Can I have a word?" I shuffle around two co-workers in my attempt to keep up with his speed.

"Outside," he says and nods to the back doors before yelling, "HAROLD, COVER."

"Yes, Chef." Harold responds and I follow Kerim outside.

He snatches a dish from the side on the way and the second I step outside he presents it to me. I recognise the creamy scent immediately. "This is beautiful," he compliments. "On Tuesday I want you to make me more just like this."

"Sure." I watch as he dips a piece of bread into it before presenting it to my lips.

"Eat."

I open my mouth. I don't have another choice and my stomach doesn't protest either; it lets out a demanding growl.

"You're hungry?" His accent is heavy and his brows furrowed. "I'll make you something."

"That's not…" I run a hand over my hair to make sure it's still in a neat bun. "I actually want to ask you if I can take the day off on August the nineteenth."

He blinks slowly and stares at me for the longest moment. "Day off?"

"Yeah, it's my friend's birthday and we're going to Alton Castle." I can't contain my excitement.

He smiles and I can't recall ever seeing him smile. It's nice. I'm steadily feeling more comfortable. "I'm sure we'll manage without you for one day." The tip of his finger taps my nose. "Come, let's feed you before you waste away. My mother would be sorry at what little meat is sitting on your bones."

I giggle because that only just makes sense. "Thank you, Kerim, for feeding me and for this opportunity."

His answering grin is full of warmth. "I made the right decision. You deserve to be here."

My responding smile is blinding; I can't hold it in. This is becoming an awesome day, despite the fact Nathan is leaving tomorrow. And on that thought my smile is gone.

"So, Alton Castle, I've never been." Kerim stretches his arms above his head and flexes his thighs as though preparing to race.

"Me neither but I've always wanted to go."

"I hope you have a good time." He holds open the door to the kitchen and motions for me to enter first. Patience stares at me from across the way with narrowed eyes. What's her problem? "Mark it on the calendar in my office or I'll forget."

"Yes, Chef." I grin and practically skip in that direction. Who would have guessed that Kerim is actually a nice guy beneath all of the insulting, shouting and swearing he does?

Surprisingly, since starting work in this fabulous restaurant, I've never once ventured into Kerim's office. It's nothing spectacular and it would no doubt give Nathan hives with how disorganised and messy it is.

I have the urge to organise the papers strewn over the desk and the floor but I have a feeling that Kerim knows exactly where things are in here. If I touch his stuff, I'll be in deep shit. It's not worth it.

The calendar hangs by the side of the door at eye level, a pen hanging loosely on a piece of ribbon from the wire binding at the top. Skipping forward a month, I circle the correct date with the red pen and write my name and reason for absence in the small box.

When I'm done, I find Kerim working over my station and I spot a lamb cutlet sitting in the centre of a plate. It's rarer than I like but I'll eat anything he gives me. He adds potatoes and a drizzle of gravy before sliding it in my direction. "Eat."

I do as I'm told, trying not to mouthgasm with every bite. He's just too good at food.

"Good?"

I nod. "The gravy is different."

"Too many customers complaining about the mint so I made an alternative."

"Good plan." I'm surprised when he cuts into the lamb on my plate and takes a bite.

"Your husband," he speaks around the food in his mouth, covering his lips with the back of his hand, "invited me to dinner, but as I'm still training you, I politely declined. I wanted to tell you, so you would know not to take offence."

Nathan didn't mention anything.

"He's my friend, yes, but you know my rules on socialising. Once you're trained and have the qualifications you need, I'll gladly accept." He dips his head and asks, "You understand?"

"Of course."

Harold knocks an empty pan away and it clatters on the ground, splashing dirty water across the tiles.

"I'll get it." I brush past and reach for a mop. Kerim returns to work mode faster than he left it.

"You fucked the fish!" Harold bellows at Patience who, true to her name, has enough to just roll her eyes and start again.

She scowls at me in response to my reassuring look. I was trying to show her a united front but she can go fuck some more fish if that's how she wants to be.

If I could drop to the ground and cling to Nathan's leg I would, but people are watching and he'd hate the spectacle. So instead I cling onto his arm and smother his cheek and neck in kisses as he tries to move to his car. His smile lets me know that this is the kind of attention he enjoys.

"Gwen, I'll be home in a few days."

"That's a few days longer than now though," I grumble petulantly.

"My Angel is going to get upset if I leave her alone for a moment longer." He's referring to Emily, who he has just fitted safely into her car seat. I look around him at the bright eyed baby girl who seems far too happy to play with her father's phone. She likes bashing it against the arm of the car seat.

"You're so full of poop," I state haughtily and straighten myself.

He grins, tugs me into his body and slams his lips onto mine, "I shall miss you every second that I'm gone."

"Good."

"Daddy." Dillan tugs on Nathan's jacket and Nathan gathers him into his arms for a long hug and a deep inhale. "Daddy be long. No."

"No, Daddy won't be long." Nathan kisses his son's chubby cheek and hands him to me. I balance him on one hip as I tap Nathan's nose with my own. "I'll call you when we arrive."

"Good."

"Have fun at work." He squeezes my fingers and reaches through the rear passenger side window to snatch his phone back from the naughty baby. Now she screams. I lean through the window and annoy her with more smooches, despite the fact I already said my goodbyes before we strapped her in. "We'll be fine."

He climbs into the car and turns to face me. We look at each other over Emily and through the gap in the front seats.

"Promise?"

"Of course." He winks and turns to face forward.

"I love you." I move away and tell Dillan to wave. Seconds later Nathan is driving away, leaving me feeling empty and uncertain.

"Daddy gone. Bye bye." Dillan continues to wave to nobody.

I swallow, shake myself off mentally and carry my son inside. Jeanine will be here soon to care for Dillan while I work and I need to make the most of the short time I have left alone with my son.

The house is pitch black when I arrive home past midnight, much later than expected. Jeanine must already be sleeping. To take my mind off the reality of life, I buried myself in my work, working myself to the brink of death. I've never felt so exhausted nor have I ever pushed my limits so entirely. I have impressed Kerim and the others though and for that I'm happy. I didn't realise just how able my body is to handle so much. I'll be pushing myself more often.

I creep into my little boy's room on shaky legs and kiss his forehead. The guest bed is set up in the corner. Nathan did that for me before he left; he's such a sweetheart.

Jeanine stays in our bed when she comes due to her bad back. I don't mind, though it's hard getting ready in the dark and I daren't turn the light on for fear of waking Dillan. If only Emily's room was big enough to fit a spare bed; it's only just big enough for her cot and furniture.

<u>Nathan</u>: We miss you.

The phone lights up the room like a sun in a can, so I pull the blanket over my head and stare at the text and three missed calls until my eyes adjust to the almost painful brightness. I should respond but I don't want to wake him or Emily. He sent me this at nine so I know he'll be sleeping now. He has a busy day tomorrow and Nathan is always responsible. He likes to be well rested before a busy day.

Instead, I tuck my phone under my pillow and wince when the quilt sounds loudly against the bed sheet. I'm going to be so stiff when I wake up in the morning from being too scared to move all night.

Never mind.

Chapter Eight

THE PAST FEW DAYS have been the longest. Dillan has suffered without his father, Daddy's boy that he is, and I've suffered right there with him. Why do I seem to become afflicted with the need to fornicate whenever Nathan isn't here to satisfy me? Maybe that's why, because on a normal day, he'd be here to fornicate. I never go wanting when he's around.

Unfortunately, I'm working when he returns in around an hour if my calculations were correct based on our phone call this morning. He will relieve Jeanine of her babysitting duties; she has been amazing.

"Pay attention," Kerim bellows so loudly my right ear rings and tingles almost painfully.

"Sorry, Chef!" I rush, panicking, and unfortunately, in my panic, I drop the plate in my hands and it clatters to the ground with a loud smash. Pieces of ceramic fly in all directions.

"CLEAN UP!" Patience yells and one of the crew gets to work with a brush.

"Are you fucking stupid?" Kerim slides another plate in front of me before turning to Harold. "We need another duck over here."

"I'm sorry," I say meekly. I need to get my head in the game.

He flips me off and stalks away, grumbling in Turkish. I can't imagine the translation would be very pleasant.

"Oh great, just what we need," Kerim growls as I finish dressing the final plate and slide it towards the collection point. His fingers are suddenly gripping my bicep and I'm being dragged to the back entrance. "You have thirty seconds to say your hellos and goodbyes."

I'm left in the exit area, feeling flustered and annoyed at being suddenly dragged without my permission.

"Did he just put his hands on you?" Nathan's voice utters dangerously. I feel the tension radiating from him and slowly turn his way.

Before giving him the chance to further question about Kerim and his temperaments, I throw myself at the love of my life and bury my face in his neck. "I missed you."

He returns the embrace and cups the back of my head with a large hand. "You smell like herbs and vinegar."

"Sorry?" Pulling back, I glare up at him. "That's the greeting I get?"

"It's nice. I'm not complaining."

Kissing him firmly on the lips, I push up to my tiptoes and hold him as tightly to me as I can. "You're never going away again."

He smiles against my mouth and then tastes me with his tongue.

"Gwen," Kerim barks loudly, making me wince.

"I have to go," I whisper and step away from the man I love. He entwines our fingers. "Don't wait up for me; you need your sleep."

Nodding, he kisses me again and watches me go back inside before heading to his car.

The smile on my face is so wide my cheeks are in different countries.

"You focus now?" Kerim asks harshly, though I'm too happy to allow his mood to sour my day. "Good. Get working."

"Yes, Chef."

"And no more visits."

My smile still doesn't shift. He rolls his eyes at me but before he walks away I see his lips twitch. I'm off the hook.

Yay.

"Remind me to take my car in for its MOT next month. I think my radiators are broken. They take a lot longer to heat up than they used to and sometimes they don't work at all."

Nathan blinks, his eyes holding no small amount of irritation. "You're talking about that now?"

"We're finished so it doesn't count."

CHAPTER EIGHT

"How is it even on your mind?" He grinds his hips against mine and kisses the corner of my mouth.

"Ask yourself," I remark, shoving him off me.

He laughs as he rolls to the side and slaps the side of my thigh. When I spin around, tempted to punch him in the face for making my skin sting, I melt when I see his cheeky smile. There's no way I'm going to be able to mark that handsome face.

"I love you," I tell him as I grab my dressing gown and tie it tightly beneath my breasts. "Shower?"

"Are you seriously asking me that question?" He's up and out of the room before I make it around the bed.

As I reach for the handle, the sound of Nathan's phone vibrating on the bedside table forces me back a step. I put it to my ear after noticing the number has been withheld. "Hello?"

"Gwen?" A man asks, sounding taken aback.

"Speaking."

"I thought... is Nathan available?"

"He's just stepped into the shower." I hear the spray hitting the shower curtain from across the hall. "Can I ask who is calling?"

The line goes dead before he answers; he either hung up or we were disconnected. Either way I can't call him back due to him withholding his number.

How strange.

What kind of person calls and doesn't introduce themselves?

Then a thought hits me, regardless of the fact I doubt Mr Weston, aka Nathan's father, would be stupid enough to call at such a delicate time.

Would he?

Something tells me that he most definitely would and something deep down tells me that I know his voice. I really hope that he doesn't call again.

"Are you coming?" I hear Nathan ask and I really wish he wouldn't be so noisy while the kids are sleeping.

To stop his racket and also because I need to feel clean, I finally enter the shower. My mind is a war of, 'should I, shouldn't I?'. If I tell him his dad called and I'm wrong, I'll be causing him unnecessary panic. If I don't tell him and he finds out, he'll be really upset with me.

I'll tell him tomorrow. There's no need to upset such a peaceful night when I haven't seen him for so long.

"So, now we have a second..." I turn the shower head so it's pointing more towards me. Nathan's soapy hands move around my back. He always knows just what to do to make me shiver. "How was your trip?"

"Successful. I've found a store and I'm looking to buy it as soon as I can."

Annoyed that he hasn't discussed this with me *at all*, though I don't show it, I simply hug him instead and tell him how wonderful that is. It really is wonderful; I just wish I'd been a bit more included. I suppose I will be once we've gotten more of a routine established and I can get time off work to actually enjoy it over there with him.

"I'm not sure when I'll be going back as we both know how much we've got going on here and I need to oversee the manufacturing of the newest line of Forever Connected charms."

"Well as long as we don't miss Sasha's birthday gathering. I think Tommy might propose."

"That's nice." He coughs a little and I worry that he might have caught something during his time away. "It'll be nice getting together again; it has been a while."

"Yeah." I turn off the shower and step out, the chill instantly tightening my skin. Nathan wraps me in a towel and kisses the tip of my nose. He coughs again into his shoulder quickly after and my hand, despite the moistness of my palm and his skin, goes to his forehead to feel for any sign of a temperature. He rolls his eyes but lets me check him over. He knows how paranoid I get when somebody gets ill. I can thank Caleb for that one - his sudden death has tormented me forever. I know it was his fault; he should have told me and I don't want to hate him for it, but I think a small part of me will always blame him.

"I'm fine," he whispers and backs me into the bathroom door. "I can see your head spinning a thousand tales, but I'm fine. It's probably just a cold."

"In summer?"

"This is England," he points out. "Is there such a thing?"

Fair point.

"Did you take your vitamins?"

"Of course."

"You better not be contagious," I mutter then pull away from him and tuck the towel tightly beneath my armpits.

"Stop worrying." He grins and nuzzles my cheek with his nose.

CHAPTER EIGHT

"He's such a baby," I whisper down the phone to my mum.

"He's male; of course he is."

"All he wants to do is lie in bed."

"Again, revert back to my previous statement." She laughs and I smile along with her. "How are my grandbabies?"

"They're great. I missed Emily so much." I watch my baby girl play happily beside her brother.

"Why didn't he take Dillan instead?" She enquires.

"Dillan wouldn't have sat still while Nathan worked. Emily is less of a handful."

"Makes sense. I need to come and see you all."

"You do!" I really wish she could. It feels like a lifetime has passed since we saw each other last. "You're always welcome here."

"You too, we'll have to make a plan. What about in August?"

"Well I'm away for Sasha's birthday and then there's work... apart from those two things I'm free."

"I'll speak to my boss about the rota and let you know. Now go and look after your fiancé. I can hear him whining in the background."

Nathan has been whinging like a baby for the past twenty minutes. He likes me to cuddle him when he's poorly; he says it soothes him. To be fair, I enjoy him cuddling me when I'm poorly and I do like holding him. Feeling his heart beating in his chest settles my own nervous heart.

Unfortunately, he's fallen ill at the worst time because I have the kids and in an hour I have work. I can't leave them to cuddle him.

"Will you get up and stop being such a wuss?" I yell up the stairs.

"I just need a cuddle before you go." He blows his nose and then sniffs heavily. "Please?"

"Come downstairs then," I order and usher my kids back into the room. They're like little chubby shadows of mine.

"Ugh," he grunts but I hear the bed creak as he moves. "I feel awful."

"I know, Baby," I say softly as he descends the stairs, wrapped in a blanket. "But you've got to start being active or the kids will kill you."

He nods and opens the blanket for me to embrace him. The heat his body is emitting is crazy. I feel sweaty before I even get my arms around his toned waist.

"You're so soft," he coos in my ear and nips the lobe with his teeth.

"I need to make something for the kids for dinner." He doesn't let me pull away so I add, "Unless you feel like cooking for them?" His arms, blanket and heat leave me faster than water from a tap. Giggling silently, I pad into the kitchen and pull a few things from the fridge.

"With you working so much I hardly get to eat your food anymore," Nathan pouts from the doorway. I love it when he pouts; he looks so adorable. His cheeks are glowing pink through his light stubble; no doubt his fever is a leading contributor to the colour. It's not often that I get to see him with a bit of scruff on his face and I really like it. "Stop staring at me like that."

"Like what?"

"Like you want to eat me."

I wag my eyebrows. "I do want to eat you."

"I'm too poorly today, you insatiable creature."

My head falls back with a laugh. "You're insane."

"I'm also too poorly for your sexual deviance. Away with you. He backs out of the room, his eyes dragging down my body so slowly it feels like a caress. He's not wrong. I am insatiable at the moment and that look that he just gave me has not helped at all to soothe my latest case of horniness. If anything it has only poured fuel onto that fire.

To distract myself I make them an easy to heat pasta bake and leave it in the oven for later. I just hope Emily likes it; she's so awkward with food at the moment. She survives solely on biscuits, raspberries and milk.

When I enter the room, almost ready for work, I sigh happily when I see my entire life snuggled together under a duvet on the couch. Some kind of kid's TV show is on the TV and Nathan and Emily are lightly napping. I had wondered why they'd quietened. Dillan is sat by Nathan's hip, enthralled in his TV show, so I back slowly and quietly from the room and close the door behind me.

<u>Gwen</u>: I didn't want to wake you or disturb the mini demon so I've left you with air kisses and dinner in the oven. I love you, good luck and take it easy. Xx

I have a feeling he's going to need all the luck he can get.

Chapter Nine

WHEN I LEFT FOR work I had this daunting, sinking flutter within, a peculiar nagging that something wasn't quite right. At first I thought it was because Nathan is ill. Now I've discovered it was a sixth sense, my instincts warning me of something coming my way.

A woman I haven't seen in years, whom I never want to see again, is sitting only four tables away from the kitchen with a man who I don't recognise.

Nathan's mother.

She's so pretty. It doesn't suit her ugly soul.

I'm surprised when she leans around her companion and peers into the kitchen.

"The nerve of her!" I gasp and my hands tighten around the carrot and the knife that I'm slicing it with.

"The nerve of who?" Harold asks, flipping a fish in a sizzling pan.

"Nothing," I mutter, still seething over the fact that vile woman just waved and smiled at me. As though she knows me! How *fucking* dare, she?

"Calm. You're going to cut your fingers off." Kerim's hands cover mine. "I notice you have seen her?"

I nod.

"Do not let her bother you. She's not worth it." Kerim doesn't know about what happened to Nathan but I have no doubt that he's aware of Nathan's sour relationship with the bitch. "We don't have time for drama. Come." He pulls me towards the desserts. "You can finish these."

I nod, willing myself to keep my mouth shut for fear of losing control and running it where I shouldn't. The urge to go out there and slap her across the face, job be damned, is just unbearable. So I distract myself with the desserts.

From my position in the kitchen I can no longer see her, but that doesn't stop me from tensing every single time I think I hear her laugh. How dare she find any joy when her poor son suffered for so long?

"These look great," Kerim compliments as he passes. "Keep up the good work."

That small gesture has helped me smile a little bit. Though only a little.

I need my break so I can call my fiancé and vent to him about this.

What are his parents playing at? First his dad calls and now his mum is where I work. Why can't they just leave us alone? Haven't they done enough? Does she know that I work here? If this is intentional, what does she want?

Patience, adding to my discomfort, decides to sneer at me from over the metal table on which she is now preparing plates for table delivery. Which was my job. Her beady eyes narrow to almost slits and I now know that Kerim's kindness towards me has earned me an enemy in this kitchen, which is disappointing because I don't want any conflict. I just want to work in a hassle free environment, where I enjoy coming to every day.

"Don't mind her." Harold winks at me as he passes. At least now I know I'm not going crazy because I'm not the only one to notice her animosity towards me.

There is one thing I'm grateful to her for - her dramatic glaring has distracted me for long enough to almost forget about the infamous Mrs Patricia Weston.

Hopefully she's gone already.

I daren't look to see. I just want her out of my mind. Her and that poisonous husband of hers.

How on earth he got away with what he did just sickens me. Nathan needs to come forward. I know it'll be hard but that man is roaming free. And what will happen if something happens to Nathan and I? They have money. They'll gain custody of our children if they wanted! What if his father is as vile as his father before him?

My heart stops and tears fill my eyes at the thought of my babies, my beautiful babies, being subjected to such a torturous life.

With trembling hands and a roiling stomach, I plough through my work, willing it to end so I can go home and speak to Nathan. We need to safeguard the future of our children. If this is the only way to do so, it needs to be done. His feelings be damned. He has me. I'll help him through this. I'll be there every step of the way.

Unfortunately, when I get home and I see my beloved Nathan snuggled into our blanket, his arm around my pillow, I just can't bring myself to disturb his peaceful rest to bring up such awful times. My revelations and worries can wait until he's better.

"Mm." Nathan's arms come around my middle and his chest presses against my back. "Something smells amazing."

"That'd be me," I joke, tilting my head so that he can kiss the tender space beneath my ear.

"Bacon scented perfume? You spoil me." He licks the space he just kissed, leaving a cool trail of tingles and unfortunately no small amount of saliva.

"Gross," I laugh and wipe at the spot with my sleeve.

"NEEOOOR!" Dillan yells and flies his toy plane around the kitchen and then back into the hall. Emily sits in the doorway and watches him, a teddy in her hand.

"How are you feeling today?"

"Better." He slides his hands down to my groin and cups it over my jeans before grinding his own into my arse cheeks.

A shudder pulses through me but I shake it off and concentrate on the sizzling pan in front of me. "Let me cook lunch."

"I can be your lunch," he whispers and nips at the lobe of my ear. My thighs press together and my teeth sink sharply into my lip. I feel him swell against me and the ache it causes makes me want to collapse onto the ground and beg to be taken. I may or may not have done this before.

"Food," I mutter, my energy all in one place, not leaving enough for me to speak at a normal volume.

Soft lips move across the back of my neck as one of his hands gathers up my hair.

I moan; I can't help it. My hands leave the pan and my arse pushes back against his swollen length.

"Fuck," Nathan hisses when the sound of the doorbell has us both instantly alert. "Such crappy timing."

"You're telling me," I breathe and focus again on the bacon which is now crispier than I'd planned to cook it. "Can you get that?"

"Certainly my lady," he bows playfully and backs out of the kitchen, almost tripping on Emily's abandoned teddy as he goes. I can hear Dillan babbling to her from the living room so I know they're okay. There's nothing dangerous for them to get their hands on thanks to Nathan and his paranoia when it comes to the safety of his children.

"Who was it?" I call when I hear the door close.

A low whisper comes from the hall and then I hear her sweet voice cry, "SURPRISE!"

My best friend, Sasha, appears in the kitchen doorway.

I scream, she screams and then we embrace.

"HEY!" Dillan yells, unhappy with our noise.

Nathan shakes his head, his smile emitting happiness as he scoops up his son and leaves Sasha and I to reunite.

"What are you doing here?"

"I wanted to surprise you. I'm only here for a few hours. Tommy has a meeting at a sports place somewhere over that way." She points at the far wall. "I figured I'd come and spend it with you."

I hug her again. "I'm so glad you did."

"I come bearing gifts." She points to the bags she dropped upon entering and gives one a little kick. It rattles. "For the kids, not for you."

"Oh," I feign disappointment, she punches my arm. "Aggressive." When I see her look over my shoulder at the abandoned food I smile. "Hungry?"

"Possibly."

"Sit, I'll finish this."

"I'm going to properly greet Nathan and my beautiful God babies. You make us all some delicious food."

I kind of wish I'd planned for something better than just bacon sandwiches, though the bread is homemade so it's not a complete shame and I just know Sasha will enjoy it regardless. She's a greedy bitch.

When I've served the food, Sasha and Nathan take their seats at the small, drop leaf table as I usher the kids to play. They've eaten theirs already.

"Nobody makes bacon like you," Sasha groans and Nathan quickly quips, "She cooks it, she doesn't make it. Pigs do that."

The blank look she gives him has me stifling laughter with the back of my hand. I almost choke on the bread in my mouth.

"I'm guessing by the lack of ring, he has yet to propose," I comment, bringing her face back to life as her eyes come to me.

"He will." She sounds so sure that I really hope he does. I hope they're both in the same place emotionally and mentally otherwise she's going to be in for a world of hurt.

I'm being a pessimist.

It's all of this drama and stress.

"How is everything going with you two anyway? Have you set a date yet?"

"No," I say as Nathan says, "I'm trying."

We fall into an awkward silence. I take Nathan's hand over the table and give it a reassuring squeeze. It'll happen; we just need to take our time with everything else first, especially now he's opening a new store.

"How excited are you for Alton in August?" I've mastered the art of subject change.

Sasha's frown is quickly flipped. "Literally I am dying. We've never done anything like this before because you're always pregnant."

"I am not."

"Are too."

"Well, no more for me. I'm done now. Time to focus on our futures and careers."

Nathan nods. "For now anyway."

Maybe one day we'll have more, but it's unlikely. We got lucky having one of each sex. Besides, until I'm certain that I can put both of them through college, I'm not even going to consider having any more. I know that Nathan feels the same... or am I being as blind as Sasha could be in regards to her marriage wishes?

Wow, I really am a pessimist.

"I love what you've done with your hair." Sasha tugs on my trimmed, brown locks. "It's grown nicely since..."

"That it has." Nathan threads his fingers through the back of my hair. It sends a pleasant feeling down my spine.

My hair was a mess, it took over a year to get it all level and for a long time I had a bob that just didn't seem to grow. Now it skims my shoulders and rests in layers around my face. I might actually prefer it to how it was before, long and wild. I feel more grown up and womanly with it this style.

"I feel pretty," I say around a broad grin, no doubt making myself look anything but pretty.

"Ey wah wah la la," Emily sings as she waddles into the kitchen with a headless doll.

"That's not creepy," Sasha sniggers and holds out her arms to my chubby little princess. "Are you coming?" Emily's face lights up and she quickly forgets the headless baby doll and rushes past Sasha and straight to her father.

"Good girl," Nathan grins and nuzzles his daughter's nose with his own.

Sasha looks on, offended. I just laugh, used to my daughter choosing her father over all else. Especially now that they get so much time together alone, their bond is stronger than ever. I love it and hate it all at once.

"Sell out," Sasha grumbles and turns her attention to Dillan who is now in the kitchen with the head of the headless doll. "Come here little boy, come to Auntie Sasha."

"Oh no," Dillan gasps, his little lips form the shape of an O. He rushes to his dad and clings tightly to Nathan's trouser leg.

Nathan snorts, I wince and Sasha glares at Nathan as though it's all his fault. Which in all fairness, it is.

"Don't worry, they treat me this way too," I explain but her death glare doesn't subside at all. Now it's my turn to snort.

Nathan looks unaffected. He's always been unaffected by anyone's ire but mine. Possibly because mine is the only ire he cares about.

"So, where do you want to get married anyway?" Sasha asks, bringing the subject back to one I'd rather avoid.

"Kensington Palace orangery," Nathan states and the look I give him should surely freeze him in place.

"Never heard of it," Sasha admits, her head tilted in thought. "I was thinking of somewhere like the Washingborough Hall hotel for mine." And that was her plan all along, to talk wedding details. I can't help but smile secretly at her cleverness.

"I want a pastel colour theme, which means you'll probably be wearing a mint green dress. I do love mint green."

"It is a nice colour," I agree and sip my drink.

"I already went to look at wedding dresses."

"Sasha," I laugh, rolling my eyes.

She giggles with me and leans closer. "I can't help myself. I'm so excited. I'm considering booking the venue now to guarantee my place."

"You're insane."

"I wish my fiancée shared your enthusiasm," Nathan deadpans and I feel a small amount of guilt.

"She will, when she's got time to become enthused about it."

I mentally cheer my friend on; her defence of me is appreciated. At least somebody understands.

"Maybe my wedding will help elevate her levels of excitement."

Nathan winks at me and then stands. "I'll leave you ladies to do your catching up. I smell something foul brewing in our child's nappy."

"Have fun with that," I tell him and smack his jean clad arse as he steps around my seat.

"Don't touch me," he snaps, though I know he's only joking. His lips touch the top of my head and then he leaves the kitchen.

"The love that man has for you makes me fucking swoon," Sasha sighs, her cheek resting on her hand.

"Tommy loves you just as much."

"Tommy loves me. Nathan worships you. There's a massive difference."

She's not wrong. Nathan certainly is one of a kind.

She continues, "It makes you wonder how two such noble, loving men came from such vile beings."

"Amen, sister." we share a look of disgust at the mere mention of Mr and Mrs Weston.

"Speaking of his parents, what's going on with the trial? Is Nathan's lawyer appealing to reopen the case?"

I shake my head. "There's no point; nothing will happen."

"So he's basically gotten away with it?"

"Yep."

"Fuck him, that absolute wanker."

"Right?" I drain the rest of my drink. Sasha's remains on the table untouched. Then it clicks. This sudden light pings inside of my head and everything becomes clear. "Oh my god."

"What?" She looks at me inquisitively.

"You're pregnant!"

Her mouth drops open. "No!"

"You so are! That's why you've gone all psycho bride!"

"I'm not! Do you think I'd be going to Alton if I were?"

She makes a good point. "Oh... I got excited then."

"Trust me, if I got pregnant you'd be the first to know." She finally sips her drink and grimaces.

"What's wrong with your tea?"

"Did your mum make it?"

My jaw hits the floor. "Are you trying to say it's bad?"

"It's bad, there's no *trying-to-say* about it."

"But... I made it. You love my coffee."

"Not since I discovered Lavazza. No coffee tastes the same." Her eyes grow distant and dreamy. She's so dramatic.

"We have that at work. It is great coffee."

"The *best*," she corrects and pushes her cup away. "I'll never look at Kenco the same again."

"Nescafe is my life."

"Nescafe... blegh." With her fingers in her mouth, she makes a vomiting noise. I throw a tea towel at her and it covers her head, saving me from her vomiting demonstration. When she sobers and drops the towel onto the table, she snaps, "I can't believe you thought I was pregnant."

"Well you had all of the signs."

She punches me on the arm and we share a laugh at my stupidity.

"What time do you start work?"

"Not until four."

"Is it proper fancy like?"

I nod. "It's literally the best. I've never known a place to be so clean and yummy."

"Yummy?"

"Yummy."

"You're so weird."

"It really is though. You need to come sometime. I'll ask Kerim to cook for you! If you think I'm good, you should try his food. It's the best."

She raises an eyebrow. "Kerim, the guy who made you cry?"

"He did not make me cry."

"Almost."

I wave her off. "Whatever. The kitchen is a stressful place."

"Whatever," she repeats my word and waves me off with a mocking look.

"Cow bag."

Her mocking becomes a satisfied smirk and then her eyes light up with an idea. "Do they host weddings there?"

Sigh.

"They do actually."

"I need pictures."

"Google has them."

"You can do a video walkthrough of the place!"

"No... no I can't." I stand and place our cups into the sink. Sasha follows close behind and then leans around me to help herself to a home baked biscuit from the biscuit barrel.

"You're such a let-down," she jests, her voice muffled and her cheek full of biscuit.

"You're so nice to me." I deadpan.

Her response is to throw a biscuit at me.

It bounces off my temple and lands in the sink.

"Why did you come, again?" I ask sardonically and her answering cackle is all I receive as she helps herself to another biscuit.

Dillan, with his super hearing, rushes into the kitchen with his hand outstretched. "Bicket."

Sasha hands him one and then Emily, who follows her brother purely to be nosy.

"Yay, sugar rush," Nathan sighs and rubs his temples.

"You can thank me never." Sasha grins and picks Emily up, despite the fact the kid now has soggy biscuit around her lips and fingers. "Is that nice?"

"Bicket," Dillan yells and runs around our legs.

"EY!" Emily shouts, purely because she likes shouting.

"And so it begins." I laugh and nudge Dillan towards his dad.

"It's always a joy to see you, Sasha." Nathan ushers Dillan back out of the room, leaving us with my pretty little girl.

"I just want to kidnap this kid," Sasha growls and bites at Emily's neck, who giggles and presses her chin to her chest. I smile at the sight of her joy and the sight of her cheek chub squishing outwards.

"I'm not sure I'd stop you, though Nathan might."

"Yeah, I could take him."

Sasha checks her phone and a cute crease forms between her brows. "Let's take them to the park or something and get a coffee."

"That actually sounds pretty good." I point to Emily's pram which sits behind the kitchen door. "Stick the kid in there; I'll go get Dillan and Nathan."

"And matching socks."

I look down at my black and grey feet and flip her off. I don't have time to pair socks these days.

When I step into the room after following Nathan's hushed voice, I catch him scrambling to hang up his phone and stuff it into his pocket. That's odd. That's not like Nathan.

"Everything okay?" I ask, frowning with confusion.

"Yeah, just a company," he states but I notice his hand trembling as he runs it through his hair. "They don't stop."

His eyes avoid mine so I know that he's lying and my heart begins fluttering painfully in my chest.

"Yeah, well, companies are arseholes," I mutter, wanting to push him on what the fuck he's hiding from me but not wanting to cause a scene in front of Sasha.

"Is everything okay?" He asks, still avoiding my eyes.

"Sasha and I are going to take the kids to the park and go for coffee. Do you want to come?"

He smiles softly, his nerves seeming to slowly vanish. Or maybe I imagined them? "You go and have fun. I've got a few things to do today and being kid free will make it a bit easier."

"Of course." I try to smile but it comes out as more of a grimace. My heart is still fluttering. When he steps into me, I try my best to become soft and pliant in his arms but my hug is almost as stiff as his.

What the hell is going on?

"I love you," he tells me intimately and pulls away. The way he says it is almost as though he's reassuring me... or himself. I don't like this vibe at all.

"The baby is in the buggy," Sasha yells, startling me and bringing me back out of my head.

"Coming," I call and hold my hand out to Dillan. "Shall we go get our shoesies on?"

"Oosies," Dillan mimics and pulls me into the hallway.

Nathan helps to put his shoes on as I sort out Emily in her pram and grab the changing bag.

CHAPTER NINE

"I'll see you in a couple of hours," I tell him, looking in his eyes for any sign of deceit, for any sign of a secret he could be keeping.

I had thought we told each other basically everything but I just know, deep down, that something is going on here that he doesn't want me to know about.

Chapter Ten

Because I got home so late that day, I had to quickly change and leave for work. Since then, I've noticed Nathan has been actively avoiding being alone with me. When I finish work he's sleeping and for the past three days, when I've awoken, he's left the kids with me and disappeared into his office. Also, yesterday he went out for two hours with no explanation as to where he was going.

I'm hoping this sudden change is nothing more than store demands but deep down I know it's something more. I have a feeling that his Dad's lack of conviction is weighing heavily on him and is affecting him far more than he's letting on. Though surely he'd tell me? Who else better to listen to his ranting about that awful man than the one person who knows the history?

A little voice in the back of my head pushes other possibilities forward too. Ones far scarier than I can cope with.

I want to trust him but how do you trust a person who is lying to you? Is he having an affair? Is he tiring of me?

This man walked through fire for me. This man constantly pushes for us to set a wedding date. This man is supposed to be the love of my life.

The thought of losing him to somebody else makes me feel sick and I just know that's not the case. It can't be.

So what is it?

If it's not another woman, why is he suddenly being so shady?

All of this stress is going to turn my hairs grey.

My performance at work today has been less than stellar. I need to stop letting my home life interfere with my work presence but I can't help it.

I'm exhausted. Between battling the kids, work and keeping an eye on Nathan, I'm exhausted. I've had no time for myself in weeks, not that I regret anything. It's just that I'm going to lose my mind if I don't find some quiet time to gather my thoughts and reflect on things.

That and speak with Nathan about his inability to meet my eyes.

Is it selfish that I don't want this on my plate on top of everything else? I don't need relationship drama right now. I can't cope with that now.

"Everything okay?" Harold asks.

I nod, smile and continue working. I really need to focus.

"It's your turn to go on break," he adds and nods towards the staffroom. "Go."

I don't need telling twice.

When I make it to my bag and grasp my phone, I'm surprised at the message lighting up my screen. It's as if he's psychic and knows that I'm struggling to come to grips with the mess that is my mind.

Nathan: I'm sorry I haven't been around lately. I miss you. Shall I get a sitter for tomorrow?

Gwen: Yes, definitely, even if it's for a few hours. We need to talk.

I check my pinned hair with my free hand as I wait for him to respond. I know he's going to ask what we need to talk about but I don't want to tell him over the phone for fear of giving him time to create a tale to tell me to my face.

Wow.

My own thoughts have set such a deep chill in my heart. Never, since the day we almost died, have I had to worry about Nathan lying to me about anything. This is awful. I hate this.

Nathan: Yes, we do. <3

Holy shit. That is not what I was expecting. Suddenly I need tomorrow to come right now. The anticipation is going to kill me.

The next day drags. I love my kids but I need them out of the way today so that I can focus on other things for a while without worrying about how my tone of voice will affect them. So when Nathan leaves to drop them off with Jeanine, the first thing I do is strip naked and climb into a bubbling hot bath. It's genuinely the best feeling in the world, apart from Nathan induced orgasms.

I'm so lost in my bubbling paradise that for a moment, I forget all of my woes. This... this is just what I needed. Suddenly all of my problems don't seem so bad and the aches in my body vanish, helping to melt the tension in my muscles.

I remain prone in the bath until the water turns cold. When I exit, I wrap my hair in a towel and pat my body dry before heading into the bedroom and checking the time. Nathan will be home in about an hour. I have time to just lounge naked and read until he gets back, or maybe I should start the jigsaw puzzle he got me for Christmas. I do love doing jigsaw puzzles.

There's nothing worse than having a small portion of time to waste and not being able to know what to waste it on. You spend the majority of it trying to choose because later on, when you look back on this blissful moment, you don't want any regrets.

I chose the jigsaw.

"I'm back," Nathan calls unnecessarily as he ascends the stairs. I'd heard his car when it turned onto the street and heard the door unlock, open and then close. My hearing is just that good.

He steps into the room and blinks at the sight of me, sitting naked on the ground, jigsaw pieces scattered around me and an almost finished jigsaw edge in front. "I'm not sure if I should be aroused or not."

I grin at him over my shoulder and the towel falls from my head, dropping onto the puzzle box beside me. "You should always be aroused at the sight of me."

"Good." He holds out his hand, so I take it and stand and sigh with contentment as he threads his fingers through my hair, pushing it into the right places.

"You wanted to talk," I state softly, my eyes closed as he continues to tease my hair.

"Yes." When he clears his throat, my eyes ping open and my skin feels the chill in the air. My bliss has ended; it's time to be an adult. "So did you."

"Yeah."

We both pause, the silence between us wrought with sexual tension. His breathing is shallow; mine is heavy. I feel as though I've just run a marathon.

"Maybe I should get dressed," I whisper and reach onto the bed where my gown rests.

"It won't erase the mental image of you sitting gloriously naked on our bedroom floor. Or standing, looking and smelling so clean and fresh in the middle of the room." His hand curves around my hip and my lips tremble with a ragged breath that pushes through them. I want so badly to concede and let him take me in a way that I know will plunge me back into the state of bliss I just vacated, but I can't.

"No." I step away and pull the robe around my shoulders. My arms are trembling so badly, I struggle to get them through the arm holes. "We really need to talk."

"We do." He sits on the bed and gnaws on his lip, his eyes casting a mournful glow on the ground as I tie the rope around my middle. "I'm leaving on the twelfth of August."

I can't breathe. I grip hold of the edge of my chest of drawers for support. "Leaving?"

"It's full steam ahead with the store. I have to go." His eyes hit mine, sparkling with guilt and sorrow. "It's the only time Kendrick can fit me in."

Kendrick is the man who helped him hire staff and get all of his other stores up and running.

"Otherwise it'll be another six months."

"And you can't do it yourself?" I choke, wondering why now, of all times. "How long will you be gone for?"

"A few weeks, but it's only Essex. I'll be able to commute back."

My eyes fill with tears and my heart thuds to the bottom of my stomach with a heavy beat. "And the kids?"

"We'll have to figure it out," he admits, wincing. "I won't need to be there every day and the days that I am, I'll take the kids if I can."

"And if you can't?"

He shrugs. "We'll figure it out. We always do."

"We should hire a nanny or put them in nursery."

"No!" He snaps, standing suddenly.

"Nathan."

"I said no. I can't..."

My fingers slide around his wrist and squeeze gently. "I understand your reservations. I know it must be so hard for you to trust after all you've been through, but..."

"I said no."

"Nath..."

"NO!" He shouts, startling me so badly I take a step away. My hand goes to my chest instinctively and his eyes soften almost immediately. "I can't put them in the hands of somebody we don't know or trust."

"Then I should quit now," I snarl petulantly. "Because how the hell am I going to cope if I can't find a sitter?"

"Guinevere..." His tone is chastening. I roll my eyes and turn away, done with this conversation. "You're being unreasonable."

"No, you are."

"If I have to take them with me, I will. I'm not going to leave you stranded."

"And what about you?" I pull open the door and descend the stairs, with him following closely behind. "How are you going to get anything done?"

"I'll figure it out."

"And if you can't?"

"I will," he assures me and though he sounds truthful, I don't have much faith in this right now. Everything is changing, again. I don't like it. "Aren't you happy? Another store is more money."

"I know." I push open the kitchen door and snag the empty kettle from its base. "It's great. I'm happy for you, truly. It's just difficult timing."

"We'll make it work." His arms come around me, resting below my breasts, and his chin touches my shoulder. "We're strong enough."

"Are we?" I mumble and he tenses at my back. His arm holds me so tight it's almost painful.

"What was that?"

Do I dare bring it up now? Maybe this is what he's been hiding? The fact he has to leave? Am I overreacting?

"Nothing." I try to pull free but he holds me even tighter.

"What did you mean, Gwen?"

"Nothing!"

"Guinevere."

"Let go," I yell and he does, immediately.

"What the hell?" He pants, his hands raised and his eyes wide with horror. "Did I hurt you?"

"No, I just... I need to breathe."

His lips thin to a white line. "You need to breathe?"

"Yes."

"Away from me?"

Grunt. "Don't twist this."

"Twist what? The fact you don't think we're strong enough to make this work? The fact you don't have faith in me anymore? Or the fact that you just shouted at me to let you go?" He lets out a humourless laugh. "Or am I reading this all wrong?"

"I'm just..." Gah. "You've been avoiding me lately."

"I've been busy."

"You've been secretive too."

He doesn't deny this. "I've been busy."

"What are you hiding from me?"

Licking his lips, he crosses his arms across his chest and raises his chin. "You think I'm hiding something?"

"I know you are." I prod him in the chest. "Tell me what it is."

"You don't know what you're talking about."

"Fine, swear it, on our lives, swear that you're not keeping something from me."

He laughs again and runs his hands through his hair. It's a nervous tic; he's about to lie. "This is ridiculous. Are we ten?"

"Do it. If it's so silly then what does it matter?"

"After we almost died?"

I narrow my eyes. "Don't bring that into this."

"Then stop being silly. Come here; let's make up and not waste our few hours of freedom on arguing."

"No." It's my turn to fold my arms. "You either tell me or we don't talk at all."

"Fuck," he snaps and turns away from me. "I can't do this right now."

"Do what."

"This." He presses his forehead against the wall and blows out a heavy breath. "I don't want to argue."

"Then tell me what's going on."

"Nothing!" He hisses and opens the door beside him.

"Don't walk away from me, Nathan."

"I'm giving you space to breathe and calm the fuck down," he shouts, stomping towards the door. "Is that okay? Or would you like me to sit down and allow you to call me a liar some more?"

"I can't label what can't be labelled."

"What does that even mean?"

He grips the metal handle of the front door. "Last chance to stop this nonsense."

"Chance not taken." I step into the living room. "Go, run, but I'm not talking to you when you get back."

"Oh my God," he whispers and breathes deep, calming breaths. It won't do him any good. I'm too pissed off now. I'm determined to get this from him. If he chooses not to trust me with the truth then maybe we aren't right for each other. "Gwen, please. I booked us in at a really nice restaurant around the corner. Please, come and eat with me."

"I'm not hungry," I lie. I'm always hungry and he knows it.

"Come on," he prompts, smiling as though I don't hate him right now. "You know you get grumpy when you're hungry."

"You're a patronising shit!"

"Fine." He raises a brow and leans his shoulder against the door jamb. "Suit yourself."

I sit on the couch and pout at the unresponsive TV. Nathan, after a few more seconds, sits beside me and places his hand on my thigh.

"I hate this. I feel as though there's no way out of this." He murmurs and strokes down to my knee and back up again. "I'm worried..."

"Then be honest."

"You wouldn't understand," he whispers solemnly and I wonder if his aversion to telling me is something as simple as the time I caught him sneaking away to watch SpongeBob in his office. Maybe he's embarrassed?

"Try me."

"No," he sighs. "Can't you just trust me? Can't I have a secret of my own? Just for a while until I'm ready to tell you?"

Ready to tell me? "Are you cheating on me?"

His expression is one of horror. "You think I'd cheat on you?"

"I hope not but..."

"This conversation is over." He stands and straightens his shirt. "If you honestly believe I'd do that, after all we've been through, I'll..."

"What? You'll what?" I press when he doesn't finish his sentence.

"I'll never forgive you," he responds and exits the room.

"Where are you going?"

"I need space to breathe," he snaps, repeating my own words from before, rolling his eyes.

"Fine," I snap back and all but shove him out of the house. "So do I."

Arsehole. I slap the door with the palm of my hand and silently scream to help relieve the stress I feel. I am so fucking wound up right now. I want to break something.

"Calm," I tell myself and lean back against the door. "This will pass." It's just a rough patch. We just need to get past it. Things are tense with all that has been happening lately.

Now I feel bad, knowing that Nathan has been dealing with the knowledge that his father is roaming free. He's no doubt suffering and I'm hardly helping.

Shit.

I didn't get the chance to speak to him yet about who gets the kids in the worst case scenario. We really have to put all of this in writing. Life is too fragile.

I've seriously messed this up.

Nathan: Call me when you've calmed down.

Gwen: You're the one who left.

Nathan: Enough. Enough. Enough. I can't take this.

Why am I pushing this?

Gwen: Sorry, I'm just in a really bad mood right now. This entire thing has escalated to silly proportions.

Nathan: Agreed. We need to reboot this entire night.

I sigh heavily and squeeze my phone tight in my fist. My mind constantly chants at me to calm down and be rational but it's so frustrating, especially now that I know he is definitely hiding something.

<u>Nathan</u>: Are you hungry now?

I will the stress to melt away along with my petulance.

<u>Gwen</u>: I could eat.

The door opens less than a minute later and I find myself smiling. It doesn't matter how badly we fight, I love Nathan so much I'll always be happy to see him.

"Let's go and eat then." He grins, winks at me charmingly and holds out his elbow for me to take.
"We're a hot mess; you know that, right?"
"We're passionate," he corrects and kisses my temple. "The day we stop fighting like this is the day I'll be scared, because it means neither of us care."
"What about if we keep fighting all the time? What if we break up because of that?"
He locks the door and leads me to the car, all the while saying, "I'd rather break up because we can't handle the feelings we have towards each other than us break up because we just don't care enough to confront each other."
"I'd rather us not break up at all. We need to work together."
"Isn't that what we're doing?" He opens up the door for me and holds my hand as I lower myself into the seat. I wait until he's beside me in his before I respond. "I hope so. It sure doesn't feel like it."
Bringing my hand to his lips, he kisses just below my engagement ring and closes his eyes. "The sooner we make this official, the better for the both of us."
"Marriage won't change anything."
"I'll feel more secure."
"More secure in what?" I ask as he puts the car in gear and twists in his seat to see behind us.
"Us."
"Us?"
"I can't lose you."

"I'm not going anywhere." I wish he'd see that. What else can I do to convince him that he's it for me? I don't want anyone else.

"It's not just about that," he mumbles conspiratorially.

"Then what is it about?"

"Not tonight." He kisses my hand again and holds it against his thigh. For once I don't push it; I'm just too drained. We'll not reach any conclusions to anything while we're both stuck in such a stubborn mindset. Like with everything Nathan, I have to wait for him to come to me. I chose to respect that when I decided to marry him, to be with him. I'm not going to suddenly stop because it frustrates me.

He'll open up when he's ready and when he does, I'll be ready to listen. I just have to have love and patience.

Which is extremely hard because I just want to know *everything* now.

We're late for the reservations but fortunately not by much. I've never been to this place before and a huge part of me feels as though I'm cheating on my own restaurant, but there's no way we could afford those prices right now. Not with how much we're paying out at the moment and that's just an estimated guess based on how much Nathan spent the last time we opened a store.

Sure it makes the money back; it's just the limbo before the profit that we suffer through. We're still not poor by any means of the word but we do have to watch our pennies until we're sure the store is going to continuously pull in profit.

"You look lost." Nathan taps my fingertips that rest around the bottom of my wine glass.

"I'm always in my head these days."

Tickling gentle patterns over my knuckles, he doesn't speak. I think he's as scared as I am that it'll start another war between us.

"We should order," he tells me and I realise that I've been sitting here completely ignoring the menu that rests open on the table. His laughter is quiet and loving. Giving my fingers another tap, he removes his hand and takes a sip of his drink.

"I'll have the salmon."

"I'm having the steak."

"Ribeye?"

"Always."

I flag down the same waiter who escorted us to the table. He comes our way, smiling and happy, looking smart in a three-piece suit. "Are you ready to order?"

Nathan instructs him on our food and how we like it as I peruse the dessert menu. I have to be prepared for later.

"I hate seeing you this lost," Nathan mutters as the waiter leaves us. My finger circles the rim of my glass, causing a high pitched but quiet ringing noise to sound.

"I hate that there's something between us," I respond before my brain can come up with an excuse to push it back.

"There isn't anything between us."

"You don't trust me with your secrets. You know everything about me."

"Not everything." He winks as though this entire thing is a joke. That's frustrating because it's not a joke; it's the opposite.

What's the opposite of joke?

Serious?

Well this is definitely serious.

"It's good to have a bit of mystery in a relationship."

"Mystery, yes." I snap and lean back in my chair. "Lies, no."

"I'm not lying to you."

"You're not?"

"No, I just... I need time."

"So you've said." I mumble and look away. "This isn't going to change until you talk to me."

He blows out a heavy breath. "I'm starting to see that."

"Put yourself in my shoes."

"It's complicated."

"It always is with you."

"Please," he begs and reaches for my hand. "Please let's just enjoy tonight."

"I'm trying. Honest to God, Nathan, I am trying." My teeth bite on my lip. The urge to stand and pace is unbearable but I remain seated purely so I don't look foolish.

"I love you, Gwen."

"Then tell me the truth."

"It's not that simple."

"So you've said." I hiss. My hand clenches my glass so tightly I worry it will shatter so I loosen my grip and try desperately to relax my body.

"You're not going to let this go, are you?"

When I shake my head, 'no', he sighs and rubs his eyes with the palms of his hands. "You used to be more patient."

"And then I found out my *was-to-be* husband set me up," I point out. "I'm feeling a little bitter about patience, as you can imagine. I don't like not knowing things."

"We're really bringing that up now?"

"It brought itself up," I grumble, no longer feeling hungry or happy. "Don't look at me like I'm being unreasonable when I'm on the receiving end of your inability to communicate."

"Okay, let's stop. This is spiralling again." He closes his hand over mine and dips his head so our eyes meet. "Please, Gwen, I'm begging you. Just give me time to figure out how I feel about everything that's happening right now."

When he asks me so desperately, how can I refuse? "Not forever."

"No." His fingertips squeeze mine. "Not forever. Just a little while."

"Fine, I'll do my best to leave it alone." I use my free hand to bring my glass to my lips.

"I love you; don't ever doubt that," he implores.

"I love you too," I reply and we share a loving smile. "I do have faith, you know?"

"I know."

"Now that things have calmed a bit, I've been thinking." I clear my throat and mentally prepare myself for the conversation about to follow. "We need to decide who gets the kids upon our deaths and get it in writing."

He blanches and I notice him visibly pale. "Why?"

"Because your parents are awful enough to get custody in the events of our deaths."

He pales further and nods slowly in agreement. "You're right."

"I'm just thinking of worst case scenario…"

"No, I understand. I think it's smart. Life is short and can easily be made shorter." He sneers with disgust as his next words spill from his mouth. "And the thought of Dillan and Emily in my father's care."

I place my hand over his clenched fist and tickle the knuckles of his fingers with my thumb. "Then we need to get this all in writing as soon as possible."

"Yes, now we just need to choose who gets them. I don't particularly trust our parents."

"My mum has changed. I'd much rather them go to her than them go to your parents."

"Definitely, but I still don't feel as though she'd be a good choice for the rest of their lives."

I wish we had more people in our lives. Good people.

"Sasha and Tommy would be our only other option and I doubt they'll want to be stuck with our kids," I murmur and take a large gulp of my wine. It makes my throat tingle.

"We'll figure it out."

"Can't they contest it, though? I mean, if we don't leave them to family, maybe they'll contest it and there's a good chance they'll win."

Nathan looks like he wants to punch something... or somebody, hopefully his dad and not the waiter who is heading our way with plates of our food.

"Is this your way of coercing me into going to the Police?" Nathan asks, his brow raised.

"No, of course not, but it would make sense for you to."

"I just..." His lips thin to a white line and I sense him struggling to meet my eyes.

"I know it's hard." I pause when the waiter places our plates in front of us and asks us if we'd like anything else. As soon as he's gone, I lean forward. "I can only imagine how you feel, but if we take that video footage to the Police, it probably won't even go to trial. We'll have his motive for burning the house down too. Not only will he be put away on aiding and abetting a paedophile, he'll also be on trial for attempted murder and arson."

He pokes at the food on his plate with a fork, his mind working no doubt a mile a minute. I don't expect him to speak. I know how difficult it is for him to talk about this. Not only is it traumatising, but to him it's also embarrassing. He doesn't like me thinking of him in such a vulnerable position and I don't blame him. I'd feel the same in his shoes.

My poor Nathan.

"I need time to think," he whispers after too long of a pause. "Okay?"

I mentally cheer because I know I've gotten through to him. "Of course."

"Shall we eat?"

I nod, feeling lighter from the weight lifting off my chest. "Sounds good. This looks delicious." Another startling thought hits me, one that sets a childish panic through my heart. "You are still coming for Sasha's birthday right? Since you'll be in Essex, which isn't that far."

"Of course," he grins, a stark contrast to how he looked minutes ago. "I wouldn't miss it. I know how excited you are."

"Yay."

When he rolls his eyes lovingly, I know things are good again. At least for tonight anyway.

Chapter Eleven

The morning comes and passes all too soon and work begins even sooner. I miss the days where I just lounged on the couch with new-born Emily, watching TV and trying to nap as Dillan ran riot with his toys.

"Not at all."

Working is hard. I thought I could handle it but some days I'm not so sure.

Fortunately, I work with a pleasant group of people, minus the odd one or two grumps that keep to themselves, so it does go quickly. When I'm not constantly preparing plates, I'm laughing with my co-workers. Kerim, though he's the most intimidating of them all, has to be my favourite person at work. When he's not being a total twat he's actually quite fun to be around. He likes to play pranks on the others, like the other day he left a novelty mouse trap in Harold's pocket and yesterday he hacked into Rex's phone and changed his ring tone to porn. It was hilarious.

Today it was my turn. After taking off my hat on my break I discover noticeable blue lines across my forehead. He'd painted the inside of the seam blue and I hadn't even noticed when putting it on. Now I have a jagged stripe across my peachy skin.

"It's on," I warn, pointing at him with my blue finger, blue because I used it to try and find what everyone was sniggering about. That saying, 'Do I have something on my face?' It came true for me. "It is so on."

"I'm shaking my shoes," Kerim laughs, his accent heavy and his sentence lacking proper English, but it only seems to make him funnier.

"*In* my *boots*," I correct, only to receive a napkin to my face. "Ass."

He grins wickedly as I stomp towards the bathroom to wash the blue off. I'm just praying that he didn't use permanent marker.

As I'm about to bring water to my forehead, my phone rings on the edge of the basin so using my dry pinkie I accept the call and put it on loud speaker.

"Did you get my text?" Nathan asks.

"No, I've only just got on break." I bring some wet tissue to my forehead and scrub at the blue. It only seems to smudge so I frown at my reflection and resist growling angrily. "What's wrong?"

"What's that noise?"

"I'm washing my face," I respond. "Don't ask."

"Okay," he laughs, dragging the word out and I hear Dillan cheering gleefully in the background as though part of the conversation. "I've booked your car in for its MOT on the seventeenth. It was the only day they could fit you in. I'm going to get your wheels changed and whatever else needs doing."

"But Sasha's birthda..."

"I'll be home that weekend so we'll go in my car; it's no big deal. I figured you won't need it for work so the timing is pretty good."

"Yeah." He makes a valid point. "That makes sense. You promise you'll be there though?"

"Of course!" He sounds slightly offended that I'd even ask but I daren't be too hopeful.

"Sorry, I'm just so excited for a day of fun."

"I know. I understand."

"Well, thank you, sweetie. For taking me to Sasha's birthday and for fixing my car."

"You're welcome." He clears his throat. "If you're working that day, you'll have to take it in before you go because I don't think I'm going to be back on time."

"Got it." I finally make progress with the blue. "I have to go."

"Enjoy the rest of your day." His voice is soft, like velvet, and sweet like melted chocolate. "I miss you."

"I miss you too," I smile, wishing I was there with them all.

My smile soon vanishes when I hear an unfamiliar female voice call, "Dillan, look wha..." The line goes dead before she finishes her sentence.

My heart hammers against my ribcage as I try to figure out who it could belong to but nobody comes to mind. I'd know the voice if it was my mum or Sasha. We don't know anybody else apart from Jeanine and it definitely wasn't her.

Unless he's at one of his stores...it could be one of the staff there; they all fawn over our kids when we go in. Though I could hear the wind and cars in the background so he can't be inside his store.

Fuck.

Who was it?

I want to trust him... I need to trust him. He wouldn't be stupid enough to call me if he was with another woman. Not unless he told her to be quiet and then she decided not to be just to let herself be known to me.

How dare he let some female be around my children without my approval? I can't just let this one go. Ignoring the message Nathan already sent to me about the car, I quickly type and send:

Gwen: Who the fuck was that?

Nathan: Who was who?

Gwen: The woman who yelled Dillan's name at the end of our conversation.

Nathan: Just a lady who works at the ice cream stall on the park.

Oh. Well... don't I feel like an idiot? He's just out being a good dad to our kids and I'm stuck here being an irrational bitch as per usual. What is wrong with me?

Gwen: I'm sorry. I'm an idiot.

Nathan: You have nothing to apologise for. Stay calm. We'll see you later.

I'm losing it. I need to stop losing it so much but it's hard. My hormones are all over the place and it's so hard to trust after what Caleb did. I'm trying so hard to get over it but it's not always that simple. His deception left a seed that took root and now I'm forever taking it out on Nathan.

Gwen: I need a girl's night.

Sasha: Me too! When?

Gwen: I don't know; we're both always so busy. I need a new friend.

Sasha: Normally I'd be offended by such a suggestion but you really do. You just don't get out enough at all.

Gwen: Gee... thanks. :-p

Sasha: You used to hang out with tons of people all the time. It's only since Nathan that you've become a hermit. The world doesn't revolve around him. He can live without you for an hour or two.

Gwen: I know he can. He's not the reason I'm so secluded.

Sasha: I know he's not, but still... put yourself out there a bit more. Go to a local mummy and baby group or something. Find the kids some play mates; they need friends too.

She's completely right.

Gwen: That's actually not a bad idea.

So after some research on Google, I find my local children's centres and book us in for some tea and toast sessions. I really hope this goes well. My anxiety is already skyrocketing.
"You can do this," I whisper to myself. "You got this."
"Are you talking to yourself?" Harold asks.
"Shut it."
"First sign of madness."
Raising my hand to his face, I move to the outside. This kitchen gets too warm. I need to breathe.

Sasha: Remember that I love you, bitch.

Gwen: Like a rash.

Sasha: Duh.

Gwen: Did he propose yet?

Sasha: Do I seem happy?

Gwen: Do you ever?

Sasha: Fuck off, I'm a ray of sunshine!

Gwen: I seriously can't wait for your birthday. No joke. I am so excited!

Sasha: Me too, you better go on the big rides with me.

Gwen: Of course!

"Why are you so happy?" Kerim asks as I come back in from my break and put away my things. "You're working and your face is blue; you shouldn't be happy."

I slap his arm. "My face is not blue." Is it? "And I'm happy because I'm going to Alton in just over two weeks!"

"Ah, yes, your day off to ride the rollercoasters and spend ridiculous amounts of money on watered down drinks." He raises a brow. "What's not to get excited about?"

"Right?"

He rolls his eyes at my glee and returns to his work. "Your break is over. Stop disturbing my employees."

"Didn't realise you employed yourself," I mumble, still grinning.

"Nobody else will," Harold adds and we all laugh. All of us but Kerim, who hisses at the man in Turkish and as aggressive as it sounds, we can tell that it's in jest.

This makes Harold laugh harder.

I wish I could speak Turkish; it seems like such an interesting language. I wonder if all Turkish people use salt as eagerly as Harold and Kerim do.

"Again?" Kerim suddenly sobers and throws a rag onto the side.

My eyes follow his and I immediately tense when I see the thing that has caused his ire. Mrs Weston.

When her eyes meet mine and her lips tilt up at the edges in what should most likely be a friendly smile, my hands clench into fists by my sides.

"Before you started working here she never came as far as I'm aware. This is the fourth time she has been." Kerim tells me, his hand gently touching my wrist just above my hand. "Ignore her."

"Fourth?"

"You weren't here the previous times."

"I hate her."

"I know," he states and pulls me to where Patience is preparing the herbs for the evening. Her back is to the restaurant thankfully. "Here, just ignore her."

I take a pizza cutter and begin chopping through the fresh basil leaves before dropping them into a bowl beside the cutting board.

"That's a neat trick." Patience seems impressed and my heart swells with pride.

"I find it easier." I roll the pizza cutter blade through the green and swipe the fragments of leaves to the side.

I can't help but glance over my shoulder, though I wish I hadn't because she looks my way the second I do and just the feel of her eyes on me makes me want to scrub my skin until I feel clean.

When I turn back, my bad mood evaporates when I see Patience and Johnny using pizza cutters on their piles of herbs.

"You're right," Patience states. "This is easier. By far."

"I'm glad you approve."

"It doesn't matter how long you cook for, how long you do *anything*, for that matter. There are always new things to learn."

"Such a wise woman." Johnny pats Patience's shoulder and tosses more herbs into a separate container from the one I'm using. "I'm done. Get to it before Kerim shouts at all of us."

"He thinks he's boss since Kerim allowed him to be head chef for two hours." Patience whispers and I can hear the envy in her voice, though she'll deny it if I point it out.

"He did really well though," I admit, because it's true. "Kerim just couldn't handle it."

"Yeah," Patience giggles a little and it's such a foreign sound. I've not heard her laugh before. "No one can even try to better him. He's too competitive."

I shrug and nudge my shoulder against hers. "I like that about him though. He doesn't kneel before anybody."

"Only beautiful women," Kerim comments loudly, pulling all eyes to him.

I'm caught off guard when he winks at me. I'm not certain what kind of wink it was and I decide not to dwell on it. My mind produces little to no good thoughts these days. I don't trust myself to not twist this most likely innocent exchange into something more sordid.

There I go… I just inadvertently turned it into something sordid and now my cheeks are heating in a way that confuses me. Why am I blushing?

Patience sighs quietly, affected by our Head Chef's charm and appearance. Wait until she meets my Nathan. I have yet to meet a man more beautiful than he.

Although his charm leaves much to be desired.

I giggle at the thought of how unapproachable my partner is. The only person he has ever been remotely friendly towards is me. I love that and hate that all at the same time. I love it because it was me that cracked him. Out of every woman in the world, it was me he fell in love with and I just know that no other woman could ever penetrate his barriers as I have. Yet I hate it because I'm the only person he has ever been able to open up to and that breaks my heart.

Now I feel even guiltier. Have I been putting too much pressure on him to be somebody he isn't? I want him to tell me everything but that isn't the kind of person he is and it's not the kind of person he has ever been. I'm being extremely unfair to him. Of course he should tell me his issues, but it should be on his terms, not mine.

Fuck.

I have been a raging bitch.

I feel like sobbing. Yes, I know it's not all entirely my fault and I have every right to give him a few prods, except I haven't been prodding; I've been shoving and that's not fair on him. It isn't fair on us.

So when I roll in from work, later than anticipated, and find him sleeping on his back in bed. I slide the blanket down to his knees as gently as possible and trail gentle kisses from his sternum to his boxers.

I feel him shudder and tense in his sleep as my tongue sweeps across the skin above the elasticated waistband. Tiny little bumps break out over his arms and he groans in his sleep. The sound is extremely erotic. When I finally suck as much of his delicious, swollen length into my mouth as I can, he jolts awake and lets out the most feral, lusting moan I've ever heard.

"Gwen," he pants after a moment and his hands go to my hair. Fingers clench and I can tell he's torn between ripping me away and forcing his hips up to my nose. I smile; I can't help myself. I love how receptive he is to my teasing. I love how easily I can please him because I'm the only one who knows how.

His breath leaves him. It sounds ragged and heavy as I swallow him to near gagging.

"I love you," he groans, still holding onto my hair. His hips buck as I continue to slowly glide my lips and tongue up and down his cock as my hands explore his body and remaining inches of him. He feels so hot. "You need to stop soon." Fingers tap me on top of the head. "Babe... Gwen..." Hands try to gently pry me from him but I shrug him off. "Please... I... God... Gwen."

"I want to taste you," I whisper after releasing him from my mouth and caressing the delicate apex of his thighs with my tongue.

"Isn't that what you're doing?"

He knows what I mean and I know he's going to try and stop me, so I quickly suck him back into my mouth in a way that I know will render him speechless for a moment. As expected, he falls back onto his pillow and groans loudly. His hands grip the headboard and I hear the wood squeak under his tight grip.

"Enough," he whispers through another moan. I know he doesn't mean it. He just doesn't want to finish before giving me the chance. He has always been a generous lover. It has always been about my pleasure before his own. "Gwen..."

I bat away his hand, working his cock eagerly with my warm mouth and swollen lips. I've yet to taste him, yet to swallow his essence, because the thought of it doesn't appeal to him like it does most men. His extremely tough upbringing made sure to ruin such desires for him.

I just want him to experience it, just once. Mostly for my sake, but also for his.

The thought of it is so erotic. I bet he tastes as good as he looks.

"Gwen," his tone is pleading, though for what, I doubt even he knows.

"Let me make you feel good," I beg when he manages to pull my head up. Our eyes meet and his dilated pupils stare through the darkness and into mine. My fingers trace the trimmed hair around his solid length as we silently communicate. When his eyes close and his grip on my hair loosens, I get back to it, smiling around him when he whispers my name with such intensity my womb clenches. The need to bring myself to my own release using his body is unbearable. Every time he tenses, every time he groans, every time he whispers my name, tingles burn through my veins like lava through the grooves of a rock.

"I'm nearly there," he warns as he always does and usually I'd allow him the reprieve. On any other evening, he'd flip me over and take me from behind, his favourite position and one of mine. Not tonight. "Gwen."

I slap his hands away.

"*Gwen*," his voice is more urgent this time. His hands grip my hair almost painfully and his legs tense. "Come here."

"Nuh-uh."

He hisses through his teeth and thrusts upwards. "Christ."

This is it, I can feel it. His balls tighten as I roll them between my fingers. His hands tighten to the point my scalp aches. It only seems to make me feel more alive.

My body burns. How I wish I could feel this alongside him.

"GWEN!" He yells, no longer in control of himself, when I suck him farther into my mouth than I've ever managed before. His tone is saying one thing but his body is asking for something entirely different. "FUCK! Move!"

I've never heard him swear before. Is it so wrong that it excites me? My womb clenches in response and my body shudders with a tingle so powerful, I almost bite down with a groan.

He doesn't get the chance to pull me away and I know that he didn't want to.

When I feel him spilling himself onto my tongue, I grip the base of him and hold steady. He tastes just as I imagined and I'd do this again, just to hear him cry out the way he is and just to watch him fist the bedsheets in his hands just as he's doing now.

After swallowing and kissing a trail up to his neck, I rest on his chest, smiling with pride at myself, though he can't see because his trembling fists are pressed to his eyes. Sharp breaths escape through slightly parted lips that I want to kiss so badly but I don't want to weird him out.

"I don't think I can move." He murmurs, making me giggle and drop my face into his neck. When his arms come around me and his lips touch my forehead, I feel so tightly embraced by such a powerful love. There's no stronger bond than ours. "You blow my mind."

"I definitely blew something."

His answering laugh vibrates through his throat and chest. My body shakes involuntarily with his and then I'm being rolled onto my back and soft fingers are brushing my hair from my face while chocolate eyes scan around my head to make sure not a single strand is trapped under his weight.

"It suits you this length." He tells me and twists a lock around his finger. I wriggle beneath him, ensuring a comfier position. "Though it suits you at all lengths. You're one of those fortunate beauties that can pull off almost every look and style."

"Fortunate beauty?" My brow quirks as I stifle my smile. "You have such a way with words, Mr Weston."

"I try, almost Mrs Weston. Have you looked at any more venues yet?"

"I haven't really had the time."

"Make time." His frown hurts. I don't want to be the one to put such a look of frustration on his face. "Why are you stalling?"

"I'm not stalling." My hand reaches up to caress his face and I feel the stubble along his jaw prickle the palm of my hand. "I just haven't had time."

"Hmm." He doesn't look convinced and I don't blame him. I'm not stalling; I just don't see the need to rush. I'm looking forward to marrying him, but first I want to focus on us.

"What's gotten into you lately?" I ask carefully, not wanting to cause another argument after such an amazing breakthrough. "You seem so..."

"I'm fine."

"Don't interrupt."

"I know what you're going to say."

"You can read minds now?"

He places his warm hand over my mouth and kisses the tip of my nose. "I'm going for a shower. You coming?"

I huff but I let him pull me from our bed anyway. As we creep through the room and step into the hall, I change the subject to not only distract him, but also to distract me. "So... are you going to comment on the fact that I totally just swallowed you?"

"I feel guilty," he responds, confusing me.

I close the bathroom door behind us and wait for him to switch on the shower before prompting him to continue.

"I'm never going to be able to do that for you."

My eyes roll before I can stop them. "I didn't do that to receive. I did it because I wanted to. No hidden agenda."

"I know but..."

"Nothing. But nothing." This time I place my hand over his mouth. "We got this, Nathan. We're happy. I'm happy."

"Promise?" He whispers and pulls my naked body flush to his. One hand threads into my hair as the other pushes against the small of my back.

"I promise."

A vulnerability shines from his eyes; it's slight but I see it. Not only can I see it but I heard it in his voice.

"Should I be worried about whatever this is?" I ask softly, not wanting to close away his soul from my view.

Chapter Twelve

My mum arrived early this morning. It's so nice to see her and the kids are ecstatic. They love their nana, as they should. She's great with them.

"Your tea is always the best," she comments as she sips a healthy amount into her mouth.

"And yours is always the worst."

She rolls her eyes but doesn't deny it. At least she's finally out of her denial.

"How's your better half?"

"He's good." She smiles warmly at the thought of him. "How's yours?"

"He's also good." I mirror her smile.

"I'm the better half though." Her words are mumbled against the rim of her cup.

I snicker and hum my own agreement. "As am I."

"PENGINN!" Dillan shouts and I hear his heavy little footsteps come from the living room, right before a penguin doll sails into the room and skids across the floor.

"He's so weird," I comment and my mum bursts into a fit of laughter.

"He's definitely something." She clears her throat. "He looks just like..."

"I know." My hands clench on my mug so tightly my skin squeaks against the ceramic. "It's unnerving how much he looks like him."

"You don't have any pictures of Caleb anywhere."

I look around and wince. She's right. "I know. It's not really something I've thought about."

"It's okay to have a picture up somewhere. Dillan is going to learn about his father eventually. You should make his face familiar so it's not a total shock."

Placing my cup on the side, I look around the room before settling on a spot on the microwave. "I just got this really nice silver photo frame from that home store around the corner. It'll look lovely here."

"It's up to you; don't feel pressured by me."

"No, God no, I swear I don't." I rush to grab the frame from the cupboard under the stairs. "You're right. It'd be nice to look at his face again. I avoid it usually but it's been enough time. I want to see him again."

"Will Nathan be okay with that?"

"I don't see why he'd have an issue with it."

A look of scepticism comes across her face, only briefly, but I caught it. I let it go. She doesn't know the ins and outs of my relationship so she can't foretell how he'll react. Besides, if he does somehow react in any way other than nonchalant about it, I'd be concerned about his mental health.

"In other news," I announce loudly to the room, my face set in a beaming smile, "on Wednesday, I am going to be the line chef!"

"That's like floor manager, right? But in a kitchen?"

"Kind of." I bounce on the spot. "I overheard Kerim and Patience talking about it. Patience is ill and somebody has to cover."

"But you've not been there long."

"He needs to see if I'm capable."

"Are you?" She's asking out of concern but it still stings with the feeling that she doesn't have any faith in me.

"I hope so."

"You can do anything you want. You're so clever. We're all proud of you."

"That's what Nathan always says." I motion for her to follow me to the room where the kids have pulled out all of their toys and have no doubt misplaced all of the remote controls.

Yep, not a single remote in sight.

"I guess we aren't watching TV then," I sigh as Emily comes to me with her arms outstretched. I lift her and snuggle her close before she pushes me away and goes to her Nana. After pulling my phone from my back pocket, I check it for the thousandth time and frown.

"How's he doing in Essex?"

"He's been there since yesterday morning and we only spoke when he arrived."

"That's unlike him." She seems as concerned as I feel. "How many times has he been over there now?"

"This is his fourth visit in two weeks, but we spoke as much as possible."

"He'll be in touch."

I can't hide the concern from my eyes. "I'm supposed to be taking the car in for its MOT and a couple of fixes tomorrow."

"Is it desperately needed?"

"It can't wait any longer." I go to rub my tired eyes but then recall the fact I'm wearing makeup so I stop that error immediately.

As if an angel from heaven sent the message herself, my phone rings.

I snatch it, grinning like a happy bunny once more, and exclaim, "You literally have no idea how much I've missed you. It's not nice to keep a girl waiting."

"In that case, you'll be saying yes to what I'm about to ask then?" Kerim's voice shatters my good mood and adds a thick layer of embarrassment to my now sad mood.

"Sorry, I thought…"

"I know." He coughs away from the phone. "I have to go to a friend's opening night tonight. Only for an hour. Normally I'd take Patience but this time I'll take you; it'll be a good experience for you."

"What?"

"Bring clothes to change into. We'll be working until it begins. Nothing difficult."

"Nothing difficult?"

"You'll have less than a minute to dress and makeup yourself before we leave."

"I'm so confused," I admit and Mum looks at me as if to ask what she's missing. "Formal?"

"Yes, a dress or something."

"Okay."

"So… you'll come?"

"I'll still be getting paid, right?"

His answering laugh is loud and melodic. I find myself joining in and my sad mood melts away to a happier one. "We shall see how well behaved you are."

He hangs up before I can say anything else.

"Not Nathan then?"

I shake my head. "Apparently, I'm going to a restaurant opening night tonight."

"When? You're working until almost midnight."

"I think it's a during work time thing?" I'm still so confused.

Gwen: I miss you. :(

"Well, have fun." Mum throws a small ball back to Dillan and he laughs when it bounces off his face.

"I shall, hopefully. I just need to find something to wear."

"Wear that black dress that you wore to the store's opening day. That was lovely."

"It's a bit windy for the skirt." I look outside and try to get a reading on the crappy weather.

"You'll be fine; you'll be inside."

"I hope." I nod. "It still fits and it's the only formal thing I own so... the dress wins."

"See? I'm so clever." Mum smiles and scrunches up her nose playfully. I roll my eyes lovingly and check my phone *again*. Still nothing. "Maybe his phone broke."

"Maybe." I know that's not the case though as he knows my number off by heart. He's just busy. Really busy. It has nothing to do with how distant he has been recently. Absolutely nothing.

I think back to before he left yesterday morning. It might be my increasing paranoia but I swear I walked in on him whispering down the phone to somebody. He was too quick to shut his phone away so I can't be certain and I didn't want to suddenly start accusing him. I know all too well how frustrating that can be.

It's me. I need to reassess my mental health.

My phone rings again and this time I check it before jumping the gun.

Relief fills me like warm water in a ceramic mug when I see his handsome face light up the screen.

"Is your mum definitely coming today?" Are the first words he speaks upon my answering.

I want to snap at him for such a business-like approach to our first conversation in two days, but I think better of it. "She came early."

"Good, I was worried."

"No need."

He falls silent but I can hear his steady breathing. "Are they okay?"

"They're fine."

"I can hear Emily singing to herself."

"She does that."

He chuckles. "I'll be home tomorrow evening."

Thank heavens. "Text me the garage details; I need to know where to take the car."

"Will do."

Will do?

"What are your plans for today?" I'm scraping at subjects now to gain his attention.

"You already know. Just store stuff."

Store stuff? I knew he'd be doing '*store stuff*' but I didn't anticipate his tone or description to be so... unlike him.

"Right." There's a loud crash in the background. I don't have to be looking at him to know he's biting his lip.

"Honey, I have to go. I'll call you later."

Honey? "Honey?" I ask and the line goes dead.

Since when did Nathan start to use the endearment 'honey'? When did he ever say 'stuff'?

"You look troubled." Mum shifts in her seat, her face awash with concern.

"I'm fine. I just heard a bang and he didn't tell me what it was before hanging up."

"Think he's okay?"

"I don't think he's hurt but still..."

"He'll call you back."

"Yeah, he said he would." My lies are so effortless I'm impressing myself.

His voice lingers in my mind, repeating the name "Honey" over and over again.

Who has been saying that enough for him to start repeating it so naturally?

"Okay, what is it? You look as though you're about to cry."

"I..." The lump in my throat swells. I try to swallow it down. "I just realised I don't have any tights to go with my dress."

My mother cackles so loudly Emily comes running to me, fear in her eyes. The lump in my throat vanishes as my baby girl whimpers into my neck.

Dillan, the little jokester that he is, thinks we're laughing at something he did so he stands facing us, giggling his evil little boy giggle.

"Let's go shopping then. Also... everyone knows you wear stockings, not tights. You're not fourteen anymore."

"Won't they fall down though?"

Her smile turns into a look of shame. "You're kidding?"

"Umm..."

"Oh dear Lord, I didn't raise you right."

"I've been trying to tell you that for a while."

"Cheeky," she laughs and motions for Dillan to come to her. It takes a few goads but he finally does as he's told and soon enough we're on our way to our local shops to get me some stockings.

I've never felt so womanly or so sexy. I wish Nathan could be here to witness me in such a divine set of underwear.

I take a picture to show him later because I don't think he'd believe me if I tried to describe it over the phone. I should send them to him but I want to see his face when he sees me like this.

Mum really knows what she's talking about. I didn't think she was that kind of lady.

I twist and turn in the mirror, admiring the way the lace knickers hang perfectly onto my curves without cutting into the flesh. The tan stockings tie to a lace belt that rests on my hips. I run my fingers across the top, tickling my own flesh gently. I wish Nathan's hands could replace my own.

"You're going to be late for work!"

"Fuck," I whisper, annoyed that I can't admire myself for a minute longer. I pull on my work uniform and grab my dress, which is protected in a plastic bag and dangling from a hanger in the wardrobe.

"Have fun, beautiful," Mum adds as I race to kiss the kids and tie my hair atop my head. "Did you spray your face to make it stick?"

"Yep, I have backup makeup in my bag too."

"You're nailing this vanity thing like a pro."

CHAPTER TWELVE

I give her a finger wave and skip out of the house and to my car, my beautiful little silver baby as I call her.

Gwen: Starting work now. I have SO MUCH to tell you and show you. ;) Call me tonight if you can. I miss you.

Nathan: I miss you too.

His response is almost immediate; it seems I'm not too far from his thoughts thankfully.
I wonder what he's doing right now.

"Are you going to explain to me what exactly it is we're doing tonight?" I ask loudly over the sound of pots clattering and concoctions on the stove bubbling. The chatter from the restaurant is louder than usual tonight too, though I believe it has a lot to do with the celebrity guest over on table sixteen. I can't see them; they're in a private area and I'm not entirely certain who they are. Long since gone are the days that I followed any kind of pop culture.
"Later," he calls back, his forehead shining in the bright light. It's too warm in here.
Always later. I hate that word.
My hands make quick work of the plates before me. I admire how good I'm getting at preparing the food. I remember the days when doing this made me nervous. Now I get creative and just flip Kerim off when he tells me he doesn't approve. I try not to deviate too much from the set plans but sometimes I can't help it. I get a vision and I act on it.
"What's going on tonight?" Patience asks, her tone cheery, but I can tell it's forced to cover up her annoyance. It's been obvious since the beginning that she has a thing for Kerim. It's a shame he doesn't reciprocate; they'd make such a pretty couple.
"Kerim wants to take me to an opening night restaurant thing. That's about as much as I know." I don't look at her as I say this; I simply slide the dishes onto the opening so a waitress can take them.
"But... he always takes me."
I shrug, still avoiding her with my eyes. "I think it's just because we've never been to one before."

"Oh."

"We'll be an hour tops... I think." This time I do look at her. "You should just ask him out, Patience."

Her eyes widen, startled.

"The longer you leave it, the less likely he'll be to reciprocate."

"You think?" I've never heard her sound so timid.

"Just go for it."

"I'll lose my job."

"Then go for it in a subtle way. I don't know. I'm not good at this stuff. I'm marrying my fiancé's brother, so don't ask me." I giggle and then realise what I just said. I've never laughed at the situation before. Has enough time passed for me to be permitted a laugh about it?

"You're what?"

I wave her off. "It's complicated and we're busy. I'll tell you another time."

"I'll hold you to that."

We share a smile and I notice the softened stretches by her eyes. I think I may have finally bonded with Patience. This is good. This makes me happy.

"Right, GWEN!" Kerim yells and I watch him throw his hat into a box in the corner. "You have sixty seconds!"

"Kay," I call back and drop what I'm doing before racing into the staff area, locking the door behind me.

I rip my leggings down, careful of the stockings which still seem to be in place and carefully hang my white coat up on my designated hanger.

As I'm reaching up on my tiptoes to grab my heels from the shelf, I hear the door open.

What the fuck? I locked it. I know I did.

My entire body freezes, my eyes closing as I pray for sudden death or anything to help me escape this situation.

He clears his throat and I release the breath I'm holding. "The lock is broken."

I look at Kerim over my shoulder, expecting to find his back facing me or at least his closed eyes. No such luck. Instead I'm greeted by his eyes, looking me up and down like only a man can look at a woman. His pupils are dark, huge spheres set behind heavy lids. Parted lips release a slow breath.

"Kerim!" I chastise and try to snatch my coat to cover my lower half, but it gets stuck on the hook it dangles from. "Fuck."

He seems to ignore my ire as he strolls across the room and to his own space. "Quickly, we have little time. Pray there's no traffic."

"So we aren't addressing this?"

"No." He tugs his chef's coat off, revealing a thin grey vest. I look away and unzip my dress from the bag while trying to keep my rear covered with my bunched up leggings. This is humiliating.

"Can I have some privacy?" I ask quietly as I go to pull my own vest over my head.

"I am done," he states and I look at him over my shoulder. He exits the room wearing grey jeans and a black turtle neck, long armed jumper top that clings tightly to his body, accenting muscles I didn't know he had. I'm happy to see that he keeps his eyes off me.

After pulling on the dress and straightening it into position, I pin my medium length hair into a messy style twist, leaving a few tendrils dangling around my face and neck. My makeup still looks decent so I leave that, slip my feet into my heels and carefully race through the kitchen where my co-workers whistle like children, calling the eyes of the restaurant to us. My cheeks flame.

"Hurry," Kerim says and I feel his hand on my elbow. He guides me to our cosy little carpark and leads me around his flashy, dark Bentley. After opening the door and waiting for me to take a seat, he races to his side and starts the car.

I'd call him a gentleman but after his display in the staff room, he's the farthest from that.

He mumbles under his breath in Turkish.

"What was that?"

"I'm just begging for there to be no traffic." He glances at me and smiles. "I have a reputation for being late, but not this late."

"How late are we?"

"Just under an hour."

"Kerim!" I whine, his name a long note. "We're going to look like idiots."

"It's fine; our table is on hold. Besides, the food will be tastier now the pans have been used for a while."

"So, what restaurant is it?"

"Silver Kitchen."

"You're kidding?"

"You've heard of it?" He asks, glancing at me again.

"I went to university with the owner's son a few years back."

He nods. "Darrick Silver?"

"The one and only. Massive nobhead."

His bark of laughter confirms his agreement. "The entire family is one ball of nobhead."

This makes me giggle quietly, purely because of his accent and the fact it didn't make sense. His smile of pride at his ability to make me laugh only makes me giggle harder.

"We shall go, eat, have a drink or two as we socialise with idiots and then return to the restaurant. Good?"

I nod. "Sounds good."

My phone starts to vibrate in my clutch. It startles me and for some reason I panic as I try to pull it from my bag and drop it between the seat and the console.

"Oops."

"You have little fingers; you can reach it," Kerim laughs as I twist to try and pull my glowing phone from its dark grave.

When I finally grasp it and slowly pull it up, I look at Nathan's handsome face on the screen and notice I answered the call about twenty four seconds ago.

The second I utter a breathless, "Hey," he yells, "Who the fuck is that?"

"It... it's Kerim." I respond, startled at the anger in his tone. I've never heard such an angry tone come from him. Well, not for a long time.

"Why are you with Kerim on your own?" He still sounds angry. His tone is menacing, fuelled by jealousy.

"We're going to a restaurant opening."

"A what?" He snarls.

"Stop speaking to me like that. It's for work."

"You're being wined and dined... for work?" His sceptical tone is completely unwarranted.

"I tried to tell you."

"Did you? Where in your messages does it say that you're going on a date with your boss for work?"

Kerim curses in Turkish and I only know it's a curse because he uses it on Harold frequently. "Shall I talk?" He whispers but I wave him off. I feel so embarrassed.

"I'll call you later," I whisper to my future husband, wishing I knew what had gotten into him.

"Don't you dare hang…"

The line goes dead when my thumb shakily hits the red button on the screen to end the call. I'm unsurprised when he calls back immediately but I am worried. This is unlike him. He has never reacted so untrustingly and so unstably towards me or anything I've ever done. The shock of his reaction is sending painful tingles over the surface of my skin.

"Are you okay?" Asks Kerim softly as I take a few calming breaths.

"Yeah, he's just tired. He's not usually so hostile." I make out like it isn't bothering me and I can't tell if he believes me or not. "I'm hungry; do you think the food will be good?"

"I hope not or we'll lose even more business."

"Such bad sportsmanship."

"I never claimed to be a good loser."

"Have you ever lost?"

He thinks on it for a moment as he navigates the car through the dark, complicated streets of the city. "No."

"Unsurprising."

"You like my food?" He grins as though this is a huge success.

"I love your food."

"So does everyone."

"So why'd you ask if you were so sure I'd like it?"

His grin widens. "I like to have my ego stroked, especially before entering the presence of an adversary."

"You're such a guy."

"Sexism," he cries loudly. I slap his arm, laughing so hard I can hardly breathe. "Assault!"

"Stop," I plead, forgetting about my phone and the conversation with my fiancé. That is, until it vibrates again.

We both sober and just as I reach for it, Kerim picks it up and holds the power button. It switches off and I just blink with shock when he drops it into the pocket on the inside of his door.

"Do not worry; there is no use battling him tonight. When a man is that fuelled by jealousy, there's no reasoning with him. There's no facing it over the phone. It will only escalate if you answer that call."

He's right, I know he is, but I feel as though Nathan deserves my attention. It won't do any good, I know it, yet I yearn to explain myself.

"We'll have a good night. Try not to think about it."

I need a drink. A large one.

Maybe then my mind can be at ease. Until then, all I'll hear in there is Nathan's angry tone. It shakes me deeply.

The restaurant is stunning, though not as stunning as ours.

I feel like a celebrity as we walk along the sidewalk on a glittery red path leading to the main doors of the restaurant, set in thick grey stone. People loiter around, sharing smiles and cigarettes which fog the air. I'm thankful to be inside and away from the stench, though I doubt it bothers Kerim as he's a smoker himself.

A firm hand rests on the small of my back as I'm guided into the restaurant.

"Glitter," Kerim scoffs after we've been led to a table and we're away from the ears of the servers and hosts. "Tacky."

"I like it," I smirk, knowing it'll annoy him. He only rolls his eyes and clucks with displeasure. "They're very formal."

"Too formal, it'll scare people away."

"They can probably afford to."

"Hmm." He looks around and then orders us drinks after clicking his fingers at a passing waiter. I just know that he's disapproving of the fact that they didn't ask us immediately after seating us, but this place is packed to the brim. I see the servers, dressed head to toe in tailor cut uniforms, glancing over at us with panic every so often. They have obviously been told who Kerim is.

"Relax." His warm hand suddenly closes over mine. It isn't until he does this that I realise I have been tapping my fingers against the wooden table top. "Your vodka will arrive shortly."

"Vodka?" I choke. "I haven't drunk spirits in years. I'll topple."

"You are eating soon; you'll be fine." He looks over the menu, his eyes set again with disapproval which often switches to amusement and then back again. "That's if I can find something I desire."

CHAPTER TWELVE

"Just pick already." My stomach growls its agreement. "I fancy chicken."

"Chicken what?"

"I don't know... chicken something."

"Attitude," he says but his smile tells me he's not upset by it. "You're sassy when you're hungry."

"The term is hangry and yes, yes I am." Finally our drinks arrive.

The female waitress bows slightly as she speaks. "Mr Silver says he'll be with you as soon as you've finished your meal."

"Tell him not to worry. I have to leave to attend to my own restaurant. I will call him later."

"Erm... sure," she stammers, looking flustered. "Enjoy your meals."

"They haven't arrived yet because we haven't ordered them," he points out and I kick him under the table. The poor girl looks as though she wants to cry. He grins at me and I know that he knows exactly what he's doing to her.

When she's gone, as much as I want to tell him off I can't. It's too funny.

"So what are we eating?"

"Silver will send us something."

"How do you know?"

"Because I'd do the same."

Oh.

"I'm very impressed with your orders."

His change of subject catches me off guard. "Sorry?"

"The meat and fish you have been choosing. I will be honest." He steeples his fingers beneath his chin and scans my face, for what I don't know. "I make the orders. I go out after you've put the order in and I check every single ounce of meat that you have chosen. To date I've only changed a handful of things. These last few times I haven't manipulated an order at all."

"Oh." I'm speechless and also thrilled.

"You have talent. I'm glad you're working in my kitchen."

My face burns from the strain of holding back my smile.

"Which brings me to my next question..." When he leans back, a server I didn't see places our drinks before us. I have a sparkling water in one glass and a small sip of vodka in the other. Both glasses are made of such beautiful, patterned crystal. "Eyes."

"Sorry?"

"I want your eyes."

What the fuck?

He laughs at my bemusement. "I mean I want to see your eyes."

"Oh." I make contact and hold it.

"Better. Now. What are your plans after I've trained you?"

"I…" I sip my vodka. "I haven't really thought about it. I didn't think I'd get this far, if I'm totally honest."

He dips his head, his eyes still on mine. "Do you want to stay and work in my kitchen?"

My jaw hits the floor. Is he serious? I think I might be on the verge of having an excitement attack, which I assume is much like a panic attack except I'll be smiling while I'm dying of suffocation. "I haven't really thought about it."

"Or are you planning on opening your own restaurant?"

"And compete with you? I'd fail."

Breaking eye contact, he laughs and looks at his phone before stuffing it back in his pocket. "You don't know your talent or worth." He brings his glass to his lips. The amber fluid is gone in a second and he's chasing it down with a sip of my water. "That's excellent whiskey."

"It's Jack Daniel's," I point out. "Hardly fancy."

"No, but still excellent." He takes another sip of my water before sliding it back to me. "Where is our food? I need a cigarette."

"You should quit."

"So you've said." My cheeky grin shines at him, though it vanishes when he pushes, "So, your plans?"

"Honestly, I haven't thought about it."

"Well, I'm offering you full time employment in my kitchen. Eventually I'd like you standing by my side."

I'm not sure how to take this. "Standing by your side?"

"Perhaps one day we can enter a partnership."

"I don't understand."

"We'll be head chef, side by side, tackling the culinary world."

My lips form an O. He's serious. I feel like crying with excitement. "What about Patience? Harold?"

"They're excellent but they're not you."

"Not me?"

CHAPTER TWELVE 121

We're interrupted by a delightful, warm scent as our food is placed before us.

"The first course," Kerim states. I look down at a simple pate with redcurrant jam and what looks to be freshly made, thinly sliced bread. "I'm impressed with the presentation."

"Me too," I say, distracted from our prior conversation by the delicious looking food. "Can I eat?"

"Go ahead."

The food, I'm horrified to admit because Kerim is really annoyed by it, was beautiful. Never have I ever tasted such beautiful chicken. It's as if Silver read my mind.

Kerim thinks so too because he's done nothing but mutter in Turkish since we left.

The dessert was glorious too.

"That was fun." I break the almost silence.

He doesn't look pleased with my words.

"It was more fun when you were being fun."

I feel his anger begin to dissipate.

"I'm still fun," he whines, his voice high.

"You're grumpy is what you are. You shouldn't be grumpy, not after that cake."

"That was good cake," he mumbles so quietly I can barely hear him.

"Didn't it feel good to admit that?"

He rolls his eyes and rolls the car to a stop at a red traffic light. "Quiet."

"But I'm so much fun."

"It was good, wasn't it?"

I nod, yes.

"Better than mine?"

"Not a chance." I smile and place my hand on top of his on the gear stick. I don't know why I'm touching him but now that I am I wish I hadn't made the decision to. "His is good; yours is life-changing."

When he turns his hand beneath mine, grips my fingers and brings my hand to his lips, I find myself struggling to breathe. This just became so inappropriate so fast and I think I may have instigated it.

"Sweet Gwen," he murmurs and places my hand onto my lap.

I release the breath I was holding as he moves the car. Now I simply feel embarrassment, an emotion I've been feeling a lot as of late.

The way he placed my hand on my lap and patted it as though to make it stay...does he think I'm trying to push things with him? If so, that wasn't a very subtle rejection. At least now I can safely say the kiss he placed was purely one of a gentlemanly kind and not one of lust.

My heart feels a little less heavy.

My mind feels a little less heavy too now that the vodka is swimming around up there.

Chapter Thirteen

I don't turn on my phone at all for the rest of the work evening. My hands are shaking as I carry it into the house. In fact, I'm so focused on the phone in my hand finally turning on that I don't notice the light come on as I enter.

A jolt strikes through me when I feel Nathan at my back the second I close the door. His hands turn me and press me against the door and his forehead presses against mine.

"Don't you ever... EVER," he shouts the word, forcing me back against the door. "Turn your phone off again."

"I..."

"You've no idea what's been going through my head."

"Like what?" I snap, angry that he thinks he can even begin to tell me what to do. I shove him back, not hard but just enough for him to release me.

His eyes become wide with shock. Then he spits a ridiculous, "He wants you."

"What?" I laugh incredulously.

"Kerim."

"Oh... Nathan. Don't."

"Don't what?" He frowns, looking at me as though I'm the crazy one.

"Don't become this guy." I step around him and move towards the kitchen. My body is weary. I should be happy to see him but instead I'm just tired.

"What guy?"

"This paranoid, untrusting being that I can't live with."

His silence seems to cool the air. I turn to face him, leaning on the bar that's now between us.

"I'm exhausted," I admit.

"What?"

"I said I'm exhausted. I've been at work all day."

"Not all day," he mumbles petulantly and leans his back against the wall.

"Why did you come back? You have an early start today, don't you?" I glance at the clock and wince when I see that it's nearly one in the morning. Why must we serve food so late?

"Aren't you happy to see me?" He seems less angry and more concerned now.

I shrug. "I would have been, had you not pushed me up against the door the second I walked through it and started telling me off like a fucking child."

"Then answer your phone!"

"Why? Because you'll think I'm fucking my boss if I don't?"

His eyes become narrow slits, shooting dangerous vibes directly at me. "I didn't say that."

"You didn't have to. You said it earlier when I was in the car with him."

"I'm not allowed to get jealous?"

"You are, but not at the expense of my bloody job. Or your own bloody sanity."

His teeth sink into his lip and then release it as we stare at each other. "Will you come here?"

"No."

"No?"

"No. I'm not in the mood."

"You…" He stammers as though trying to find the right words. "You aren't in the mood?" Taking a step forward, he places his hands on the bar between us. I lean back, needing distance. "I'm worried."

"I hate that you're worried," I state honestly, "but I'm not just hugging and hoping this will go away."

"What happened between you both?"

Oh my god. "NOTHING!" I bellow, ripping the grips from my hair and dropping them on the bar.

"Gwen, that's disgusting."

"Clean it up then," I hiss and stomp around him.

He grips the back of my top, stopping me from leaving, and gently wraps his arms around me, just under my breasts. I feel his chin on my shoulder and his warm, slow breath fans across my cheek.

"I'm worried."

I sag a little. His words, though repeated, cut through me worse this time than the last. "Don't you trust me?"

"I do but it's the images..." His lashes tickle my neck when he buries his eyes between my ear and shoulder and gently rocks us. "I just can't get them from my mind. The picture of you and him doing things, in his car or..."

"Stop." I pull free and turn to face him. His words bring back memories of when he thought Caleb and I had had sex in the car. His eyes seem so worn and sorrowful, it breaks my heart. "You humiliated me today. He heard everything."

"I know." He doesn't seem fazed by this at all, which is extremely irritating.

"How?"

"Because he didn't answer his phone either."

Now I'm really angry. "You called him?"

"I'm sorry, I..."

"No. I am mortified. Absolutely mortified."

"Me too, but I got scared. I didn't know you'd be with him."

"Because you didn't call!" I whisper shout. "I've texted you and you didn't respond."

"Why not tell me in the text?" He folds his arms over his chest and raises a brow. Unfortunately my silence prolongs his look. "If it was all so innocent..."

"Don't flip this around onto me! I didn't text you because I wanted to talk to you. You know I'm not a fan of texting."

"Convenient."

I don't think I've ever wanted to punch him in the nose more than I do right now. I've never been a huge fan of texting and he knows it. "You are infuriating."

"Did anything happen between you both?"

"Nathan!" I cry, annoyed and upset by his question. I feel winded.

He glares at me through narrowed eyes, as thin as slits. "You're not answering. A simple yes or no would suffice."

I stare at him, my eyes filling with tears. "I would never do that to you."

His gaze is observing, as if waiting for a lie to reveal itself. When he's satisfied that I'm truthful, he nods his head and holds out his hand. When I don't go to him, his lips thin to a white line.

"I'm going to bed," I announce quietly.

"Okay, I'll just tidy up down here and then I'll be up."

"Don't bother." I drop my things onto the arm of the couch, promising myself that I'll deal with them tomorrow. "Go back to ignoring me in Essex."

"Gwen," he whispers, his tone laced with hurt.

"Shut up saying my name like I'm the one who is hurting you!"

"What did I do?"

My jaw drops. Is he joking? "You're tearing us apart!"

"How? I'm simply asking you a question about your actions."

"Exactly!"

He quirks an arrogant brow. "So you never get jealous?"

"Not to that extent!" I need to stop shouting; my mum is going to hear. "I've never accused you of anything."

He doesn't deny it because he can't.

"You're always with other women at work, but I never say anything."

"I've never been to dinner with them," he points out, sounding almost petulant.

"It was for work!"

"Can you promise me his intentions are honest?"

With my fingertips rubbing circles on my temples, I respond, "I can't promise anything from him because I'm not in his head, but I can promise you that he has been professional and kind ever since I started in his restaurant."

A muscle twitches in his jaw. "Really?"

"The fact you're questioning my honesty is really starting to piss me off, Nathan."

We're at a standstill, both of us staring at each other. My shoulders sag before his. "I'm tired. I had a busy night. I've had vodka and I have to be up early."

"Right."

CHAPTER THIRTEEN

"Don't come to bed. I won't welcome you," I snarl and shoulder past him. He remains standing, his back to me as I ascend the stairs. My heart is hammering. I feel nauseous and stressed.

Why is he being such an idiot? What has gotten into him?

Suddenly he's insecure and I don't like it at all. I can't live my life like this.

When I ascend the stairs with heavy, stinging eyes, Mum peeks her head out of Dillan's room, a quizzical look on her face.

"Nathan's home," I whisper, though I know she's gathered that already. Unless she thinks I've completely lost it and I've been shouting at myself. It wouldn't be the first time, in all honesty.

Her brow furrows. "He's early."

I shrug. "He's also grumpy. I'll tell you tomorrow. I'm so tired."

I hear Nathan's footsteps on the stairs behind me so I hastily retreat to my bedroom, leaving the door open for him behind me.

"I'm sorry," he says the instant he enters. Then he closes the door behind him and leans against it. "I'm sorry, Gwen. I don't want to anger you. I'm just... I miss you."

"I miss you too," I say to the wall as I pull my vest from over my head and push my leggings down to my ankles.

"What the...?"

I remember the seductive underwear that I dressed myself in before work and every inch of me tenses. In our anger, I completely forgot about it. How this must look to Nathan in his tense, insecure state, I'm most definitely about to find out.

"I took pictures for you!" I spin to face him, finding his eyes hungrily eating up my scantily clad form.

"Did he see you like this?" Are the worst words he could have spoken.

"Not like how you're thinking." My hands are raised defensively and assertively, but I can tell he's not going to listen to anything I have to say.

"He saw you like this?"

"It was an accident!"

"Was it?" His dangerous tone sends a shiver through me, a cold one. It also makes me pulse between my thighs with excitement.

"The lock on the door was broken."

"He saw you like this?" His pupils are dilated fully and every inch of me he scans with his piercing gaze feels like a caress. A long, gentle, electric caress.

I want to moan, I feel so aroused. I know that's wrong given the circumstances but I can't help it.

"You don't know what you do to me," I tell him as I reach for him with a hand. "Come here."

He doesn't move. I can tell he's conflicted.

"You know me," I whisper and grasp his collar. I pull him to me and run my nose along his jaw. He smells delightful, spicy and sweet. I want to taste the bitter tang of the aftershave resting on his tightening, pebbling skin. "I want you." My lips touch the underside of his chin. "Only you."

"Does he know that?"

I spread my hands across his chest and move them under the shoulders of his jacket.

"Does he?"

"I've not had the opportunity to tell him. We've never been in any position where I've had to reject him."

Finally, after what seems like a lifetime, he bends into me and grabs my arse with leather clad hands. I gasp a short inhale and nuzzle his neck.

"You look amazing."

"Thank you."

He kisses my neck and walks me backwards until my legs hit the bed. "You always look amazing."

"Thank you," I grin and press my chest to his tightly so I can reach his lips. "As do you. You smell good too."

"New cologne," he murmurs as his lips travel down my neck.

"Nice, where from?"

"It was a gift." He lowers me onto the bed into sitting position and pushes my thighs open with his hands.

"From who?"

As he drops to his knees he begins to stammer, "From... Trevor at work."

Trevor? "Who and why is he buying you cologne?"

"It was just a shop warming gift."

Now I know he's lying as he's trying to distract me from the conversation by pulling his shirt over his head.

"A shop warming gift from a guy called Trevor?"

His eyes hit mine. "You don't believe me?"

"I will when you're truthful." Why is he lying? Who bought him the cologne? Why not just say he bought it himself? I'm thoroughly confused and suddenly no longer in the mood for sex.

"I am being truthful."

"Fine." I push at his chest and move backwards on the bed so he can't get me back in the mood. He frowns at the distance now between us. "Call Trevor."

"Sorry?" I see the panic in his eyes despite the fact his tone is neutral.

"You heard me. Call Trevor and ask him to join us for dinner as a thank you for the cologne."

His lips part and his throat bobs with a gulp. "Well he'll be sleeping."

"Okay, then we'll call him in the morning." I snap, feeling my eyes burn from the pain of his deception.

"Gwen, honey."

"Honey?"

What the *fuck*?

"I..." He runs his hands through his hair.

"What's going on with you, Nathan?" A tear falls from my eye.

"Nothing!"

"Nothing?"

"As I said," he stands and looks away from me, "you're paranoid."

"*I'm* paranoid?" Now I'm not only heartbroken, I'm really fucking angry. "Get out."

"Excuse me?"

"I said out!" I point at the door. "And don't come back until you actually want to give me the respect I deserve!"

"You can't be serious!" He looks incredulous. "Honey..."

"Stop fucking calling me that!"

"It's just an endearment."

I bring a pillow to my chest to shield me from everything. "One you've never used. One I dislike greatly from you."

He bites on his lip and reaches for his shirt. "I don't know what you want from me, Gwen."

"The truth, Nathan. Or leave."

"Or leave?"

"Yes."

"As in... over?" His voice cracks on the final word.

"I can't be with a liar." My heart shatters when he pulls his shirt on and looks around for his jacket. Panic sets in and my resolve weakens immediately. "You're actually going?"

"I don't know what you want from me." His voice is quiet and pitiful, his body language oozing defeat, and despite my anger, I find myself softening, wanting to take away his pain. Pain that he's bringing on himself, mind you.

"You're breaking me, Nathan."

"Tell me what to do."

"Tell me the truth."

"You'd never understand," he states to my eyes and no longer is he breaking me because now I'm officially broken.

"Get out," I sniff, holding the pillow to me so tightly my arms ache.

"Nothing is that simple, Gwen. I need time."

"So do I," I whisper and my meaning isn't lost on him. "Especially with regard to the fact that your accusations are too many and too often and you're the one with the secrets." My trembling hand moves to my mouth to hide my quivering lips.

He takes a step towards me and raises a trembling hand. "Please, Gwen... please. Don't do this."

"Don't *you* do this."

"I need you."

My following laugh is harsh and cold. "If you needed me, you'd talk to me."

"I will, just... not yet."

"I can't wait that long. I won't survive it."

He lowers his hand and stares at me as I stare at the curtained window. This is how we remain for the longest time. It feels like a lifetime passes before he speaks. "I won't survive leaving you."

Leaving?

I meant for him to sleep on the couch, not to actually leave. I assumed I'd just blank him for a while but it seems his mind has other options.

"Is that the only option?" I croak, looking at him through swollen eyes. Please don't let it be the only option.

"You don't understand."

"Then help me understand!"

CHAPTER THIRTEEN

"I... I can't," he sighs and turns to the door.

All of me, every single ounce of me and my soul, ache to race after him as he leaves. Every step I hear as he walks further and further away from me forces a tear from my eyes. Then the door closes and I find my body trembling violently with sorrow.

He just left.

He just walked away.

The morning comes, though sleep evades me until the sun greys the morning sky. In zombie mode, I leave Mum with the kids, all the while evading her questions, and then set off to take my car in for its MOT and service. My mind is a warring mess and my fear of my failing relationship makes every move I make feel forced and jittery. Nausea bubbles in my stomach making me unable to eat.

I can't cope with this. Why is he doing this?

Have I been wrong all along? Is it him that's seeing somebody else? Does she call him Honey so much that now he says it too?

Now I feel even worse so I find an excuse to make contact with him.

<u>Gwen</u>: Car is in for repair. What's going on for tomorrow? You promised me you'd be here for Sasha's birthday.

I get no response. I didn't expect to get one. This also makes me cry. I'm so sick of crying.

"He's not going to come," I say to mum when I finally arrive home.

"Who?"

"Nathan." I rub my eyes, hating how tired and upset I must look.

She looks concerned. I would too if I were in her shoes.

"He won't let you down." She rests her hand on my arm and it soothes me, though only a little. "He loves you. That man has never done a thing to hurt you in the entire time I've known him."

"He's..." Wiping my nose on a tissue, I shake my head and try to, again, figure out what my fiancé is going through. "He's changed, Mum. He's not the same as he was."

"Surely it's not that bad? Maybe he's just tired?"

"No, he's keeping something from me."

When she rolls her eyes I want to get angry at her. She doesn't know what I'm going through to judge me like that.

"I'm serious!" I snap, emotional from all that's happened.

"You both need to sit down and talk about it. Kicking each other out in the middle of the night won't help anything."

My jaw hits the floor. "I didn't kick him out of anything but the bedroom!"

"Still..."

"Would you be able to sleep next to a man who suddenly starts calling you new names? All the while lying to your face and telling you that you wouldn't understand."

"Gwen," she says softly. "I don't want to fight with you."

"I don't want to fight with anybody," I cry and my shoulders sag. "What if he doesn't come home?"

"He will."

"What if his new girlfriend is nicer than me?"

"He doesn't have a new girlfriend."

"How would you know?"

She pauses and peeks around the doorway to check on the kids who are both watching the TV. When she's satisfied they're occupied, she leads me into the kitchen and pulls out her phone.

"What are you doing?"

"Asking Dave if he knows any good private investigators."

"You're not serious?" I almost laugh at the ridiculousness of it.

She shrugs. "You want to know if he's cheating?"

"Well..."

"Then what's the issue?"

"It's so invasive." I admit but I can't help that the thought is enticing.

She grins. "It's not invasive to him if he doesn't find out."

Oh my God, she's terrible. I laugh a little. "I'm not spying on him."

"Suit yourself, but he just texted me three numbers. I'll forward them to you in case you change your mind."

"You're insane." I point at her and then move to the kettle. "Coffee?"

"Please. Ooh! This guy's not too pricey." She holds her phone up to my face, showing me the website of one of the contenders.

"Stop!" I giggle, pushing her arm away so that I can reach the sink to pour water into the kettle.

"What's the big deal? You need to put your mind at rest and he's not being forthcoming. Just give it some thought. I won't say anything if you don't."

I pretend to ignore her, not wanting to admit that her words are ringing through my mind like a harmonious symphony of bells. "Two or three sugars today?"

"One, I'm being extra good."

"Two it is."

"You know me well."

If only I knew my fiancé well.

Gwen: We really need to talk about all of this.

Nathan has never let me down. Never. Surely he wouldn't let me down with something so important to me?

Gwen: You can't just leave. You're completely overreacting. It's unfair. So unfair! Why are you hurting me like this?

Nathan: Why are you hurting me? Why am I always the villain in every piece?

Gwen: What are you talking about?! I haven't done anything!

Nathan: He fancies you.

This is infuriating. My palms begin to sweat as I become angrier by the second.

Gwen: He doesn't! You're being silly and that's beside the point!

Mum: Smile.

I look up from my phone and find her staring at me from across the room. I'm neglecting them all. I need to calm down.

"Sorry."

"It'll work out, Chicken. You'll see." She sweetly reassures me, her lips tipping up with a kind smile. "Things just seem dreadful in the moment. In a few weeks you'll look back and laugh. I promise."

"I doubt it," I mutter and slide onto the floor to play with my children. If anyone can make me feel better, it's them.

"He'll come home later; he's just busy and distracted. If he weren't working, he'd have come back by now."

Something tells me she's wrong, though I really wish she was right.

When I arrive at work, a horrid nagging feeling in my gut, I crack on and ignore all distractions. Kerim included. Not including when he asks things of me with regard to the kitchen; he's still my boss after all.

I'm upset and annoyed that with all the Nathan drama I didn't get the chance to celebrate Kerim asking me to join him in business. That should have been such a happy and proud moment for me. I didn't even speak to Mum about it and Nathan certainly never gave me the chance. He'd probably only tell me it's because of the fact Kerim wants me and not because I've put in so much hard work. I can't handle being dismissed in that sense, not while I'm feeling so fragile. It'd push me over the edge with Nathan. Our relationship would plummet.

"Hasn't it already plummeted though?" I ask myself quietly as I sauté potatoes. The hissing sound the butter makes when dropped in the oil is a strangely pleasant sound.

Maybe Mum was right. The last time Nathan held something back from me it was terrible and it wasn't even about him. I can now rationalise why he didn't tell me about Caleb. It would have done me no good to know while I was so weak and deeply grieving. This time... what could it be? If he isn't having an affair then what is it that he's so frightened to tell me?

I'm told to go on break. I consider it a moment of fate and grasp my phone the first chance I get. Then I scroll down to the text from Mum and look at the three numbers she forwarded with names.

I call the first one before I can convince myself not to.

"Jackson's office, who's calling please?" Comes a soothing female voice after a couple of rings.

"Hi there, I'm umm... I'm Gwen and I..." Christ this is stupid. I clear my throat. "I'm sorry."

"You've never done this before?"

"Definitely not."

"That's okay, sweetie," she says, even softer than when she answered. "I'll talk you through it. What is it you need?"

"My partner has... secrets."

"An affair?" I hear the phone rattle and it sounds as though she's placed it between her shoulder and cheek.

"I don't think so but I'd like to rule that out."

"Whatever it is, Jackson will find out. He's not failed yet."

I can't believe I'm doing this. "When can he start?"

"I'll get him to call and talk through his price plans. His phone will ring through as a spam caller. It's safer that way."

"I get tons of those PPI guys and accidental injury claims callers. It drives me crazy."

"Exactly," she giggles. "It's the perfect disguise. He'll call you within the next twenty four hours."

"Try to get him to push it to the next four; I'm at a theme park all day tomorrow with family, friends and the man in question."

I hear the smile in her voice when she responds, "I'll do all I can. Take care, Gwen."

"Thank you." I hang up, swallow the lump in my throat and exhale the breath that got stuck painfully in my chest.

I can't believe I'm doing this.

I escaped from work quickly, still avoiding everyone, and on the way home I popped into my local supermarket to print off a few new photos, one of Caleb included. It took me a long time to decide what picture to choose but I'm happy with the one I have. It's of Caleb on the beach, not long after he asked me to marry him. He's holding his hand out to me as I hide behind the camera. I remember it so well, as if it were yesterday. He was so happy, smiling so handsomely as the wind swept his hair across his eyes. The skies were surprisingly blue, making him look as though he were glowing.

He kissed me immediately after I took the photo and pinned me down on the soft sand. That is until a shallow wave came and wet our legs. The tides in Skegness come in far too quickly. We went home happy, in love and extremely soggy.

This is the picture that will sit on top of my microwave.

Blinking back tears, I head towards the underground and hope that I don't have to wait long to catch the tube home.

Thoughts of where Nathan stayed last night assault me. My paranoid brain paints pictures of him and that girl at the sandwich place. Maybe he sought her out?

No. I'm not turning into Nathan. He wouldn't do that. He wouldn't hurt me that way. This is all something so silly and simple. I just know it.

I weave through a crowd of people as I descend the stairs, the stench of sweat, urine and burning rubber helping to keep my thoughts to myself.

The underground has always made me extremely nervous. I keep my bag tight to my front, so tight my arms ache. Luckily everybody seems as distracted as I did moments ago. You can always tell who the frequent underground people are; they look unfazed by it all. They can stare at their phones as they jump onto the trains without even looking at the maps and information boards. The rest of us, with chattering teeth and fear of thieves and catching the wrong trains, move slowly and carefully like prey about to enter an open field.

Gwen: I'm underground. I might smell like a dirty old man when I get home.

Mum: Ew...

Gwen: Yup. Ew.

Mum: I'm going to have to shoot off as soon as you get home. The better half is ill and whining like a little bitch.

Gwen: Poor Dave. I understand. See you soon <3

My train, or at least I hope it's my train, pulls in and I dash on, still clutching my bag as though it were the only thing holding my body together. A disturbing image of my body separating into two right here across the plastic fold down seating makes me shudder.

My imagination has always been a bit random.

Gwen: What time will you be home? I'm really looking forward to going tomorrow.

It's not until I'm almost home that he responds.

Nathan: I'll be an hour. <3

The love heart symbol quirks my lips though not by much. I'm too hurt by his actions to muster up an actual smile. My energy for my emotions is spent.

Nathan: Shall I bring food?

Well... I am hungry. I didn't eat at work, not much beyond the odd taste test.

Gwen: Sounds good.

Nathan: Excellent. What would you like?

Gwen: Surprise me.

Nathan: Surprise a master chef? I'll do my best, but don't hate me when it's wrong.

I smile but then frown when I see the elderly man two seats down from me staring at my phone screen. When I turn it away from him, he shifts back to a frontal position and taps his fingers against his knee. What an odd one.

Gwen: Don't ever make me use the underground alone again.

Nathan: Never, baby. I promise.

Gwen: I'll hold you to that.

A name I wasn't expecting lights up my phone with an incoming text.

Kerim: Are you okay? You seem very upset today.

I read it but don't respond as the train begins to slow and I'm not sure where we are. My focus was on said phone, not the speaker announcing where the next station was.

I make it off the train safely and to the stairs that lead to the surface, trembling less with fear than I was half an hour ago. As I ascend the stairs, I quickly type a generic response to Kerim with promises to concentrate harder next time. Then I collide with a hard, warm body and a familiar arm closes around me.

Looking up, surprise on my face, I notice my husband-to-be smiling down at me. His hand that isn't around my waist is gripping a beautiful bouquet of mixed flowers. I can smell them from here and they eliminate the stench of the underground.

"For me?" I ask, grinning as he pulls me to the side out of the way of the pedestrians weaving around us and clucking their annoyance.

"Of course." His voice is deep, loving and all him. He kisses me sweetly and briefly before turning and tugging me the rest of the way up to the surface. "I trust your train ride wasn't too unpleasant."

"I can think of worse things." I reluctantly admit. "Like being sawn in half whilst still living."

His chuckle makes me smile and he tucks me tighter to his side. "Snob."

"You'd never take the underground."

"I would and I have," he responds haughtily, but there's a twinkle of amusement in his eyes.

"Oh really?" I raise a brow. "When?"

"When I was fourteen, with my mum."

This is the first time he's spoken about his mum at all. "Really? I'm sceptical."

"It was one of the rare times she was nice to me. We went to the theatre to see Aladdin."

Smiling, I lean into him and remark, "I bet that was a good show."

"It was."

"What was life like after your grandfather stopped hurting you?" I only ask because I know that from age twelve the abuse stopped, though that's really all I know and if he's volunteering information I'm going to pry a little.

"Normal I guess. I didn't really speak to anyone." He shrugs as though this doesn't affect him but I know it does. "I grew up so isolated from everyone that it was hard for me to open up. Eventually I just got used to being alone."

"Until me."

"Until you." His lips touch my temple. "My mum did try. I remember after Caleb got better, she started trying to spend more time with me but I wouldn't really let her. I did as she said but my mind was never present."

"Understandable, after all she put you through."

He nods and focuses on the cars as if trying to recall where he parked. "I've missed you."

"Me too." I shiver from the chill I receive when he releases me to open the car door for me. "Don't leave like that again."

"I won't. It was very childish of me."

I'm happy with his answer and I show it by reaching across and squeezing his thigh.

"Before we move on from this topic, I'd like to add that not only have I never walked away from you by my own choice, but I also never would."

"I know." He seems remorseful, not only in his tone but in the dimming light of his eyes. "I promise I'll erase all anguish from your heart tomorrow. I can smell the candyfloss on you already."

"I love candyfloss."

"I know."

"I'm so excited!"

"I know," he grins, showing his wonderful teeth.

"I really did pick the perfect breeding partner, if I do say so myself."

His bark of startled laughter makes me grin with glee and when he pulls me to him and kisses my forehead, still laughing, my grin becomes a smile. I love having the ability to make him laugh.

Chapter Fourteen

Mum looked as relieved to see Nathan as I felt when we walked into the house together. She didn't mention the night before but she did give me a look that said we'd be discussing it later. I must have her worried. Nathan and I have been stable since the fire. I guess we're exiting our honeymoon period. Is that why he's so desperate to marry me? Is he worried that now the constant happiness is wearing off, I'll leave him when the going gets tough? He's a fool if so.

Packing the kids up for a day at the theme park is easier than expected. We manage to bag their things into one changing bag, thanks to Nathan. If it weren't for him I'd have had two full bags on the double buggy.

Sasha texts me endlessly as we drive to Alton Castle. I'm giddy with excitement and so is she. I wish I'd done more things like this growing up. My shyness and inability to connect to anyone properly has always held me back. Well, not anymore.

"We should start doing more things like this," I tell my fiancé as I stare at the large gates and the multiple booths where we're collecting our tickets from.

"Let's get through today first," he chuckles, his hands holding the handles of the double buggy. Emily sleeps soundly in the left of it; Dillan squirms in the right, eager to run away from us and get himself into all kinds of trouble.

"I'm serious though. When we get more time, let's go on a proper family holiday." Then I gasp as a thought comes to mind. "Let's go glamping!"

"You hate fields."

Good point. "I'll tackle my fear."

The look he gives me is heavy with scepticism.

"I'm serious." I nudge his shoulder with my own. "It's not like we can go on a beach holiday."

"What about Italy?"

"Italy?" I repeat, thinking of the romantic cities that I've only ever seen on TV. "That's a good idea; it's warm, it isn't sandy and it has lots of historical places to see."

"Exactly."

"Can we afford it?"

"We can definitely afford it," he insists and nudges me back. "Just see what two weeks you can get off work and we'll take it from there."

"Promise?" I'm extremely excited for this. A holiday with my family is sorely needed.

"Promise."

I squeal and clap my hands, before throwing my arms around his neck and peppering his face with kisses. "I love you."

"So a trip to Italy is what it takes, huh?"

"And candy floss," I wink, still practically hanging from his neck.

"Oi, love birds!" I hear Sasha's voice over the steady crowd around us. "Stop sucking face and give me my birthday present."

I immediately release Nathan and race to my friend to hug her tight. She returns the hug, tense with happiness, as am I.

"Seriously, this better not be my gift."

"Of course it isn't; you'll get that later." I step away, still beaming from ear to ear. "Where's my third favourite man?"

"Here." Tommy and Nathan step apart after greeting one another and Tommy envelops me in a bear hug. He's gotten even more buff since the last time I saw him. How is that possible?

"You're a mountain," I comment, squeezing his massive arm with my hand. I can't even nearly get my finger and thumb to meet. Not for lack of trying either.

Tommy, other than Caleb and Nathan, must be the most handsome man I've ever seen. Sasha is absolutely gorgeous too though. They make such a stunning couple and I can't wait to see what their spawn looks like, though hopefully they can wait. Parenting at our age is not something I'd choose to do a second time if I had to live another life, although I wouldn't change my life for the world, given the chance.

"Yeah, he's working out a lot these days," Sasha responds, grinning at her man and squeezing his other arm. Nathan wraps a leather clad finger around the belt loop of my jeans and tugs me away from my close friends.

I wink at him and his lips twitch with amusement, but I see the jealousy in his eyes. He'd always trust me with Tommy, though not to the extent of letting me fondle him. Not that I blame him.

"Let's go, daylight is burning!" Sasha cries, startling the few individuals around us.

"It's not even open yet, you freak." I mutter. "Also, you're forgetting your niece and nephew."

"I'll smother them with affection when we beat these fuckers to the front of the queues." She looks at Dillan and coos, "Right, my little man? You can wait, can't you?"

"Come out!" Dillan squawks, holding his chubby hands up to her.

"Patience, little man." She skips ahead to the wooden rails that organise the queues. Only two people stand ahead, waiting to buy their tickets and progress to the park. We came at the perfect time. It's not dead but it's not so busy that I can't push my pram through without feeling entirely frustrated.

"We pre-booked," Sasha tells the lady behind the glass when it's our turn. She hands over a printed A4 sheet of paper and we're soon waved through. "It was cheaper to get a family ticket." She defends herself, purely because I'm glaring at her for paying for us.

Nathan will be sure they receive the money by the end of the day. I can tell already that he is itching to pull out his wallet.

His independence and inability to accept gifts from elsewhere can be frustrating. The few times I've spent money on his birthdays, he's found some way to pay me back which is ridiculous. I spend way more of his money than I do my own. Though I suppose there is no 'his' and 'my' money. It's all 'our' money now. I let him deal with that side of things. He likes to keep it all organised and I'd only mess it up.

"That looks unsafe," Nathan says as he stares up at a large, twisting rollercoaster that can be seen over the other attractions in the far distance. If only he knew that once we turn the next corner there are three even larger ones that I cannot wait to try.

"That looks bloody AMAZING!" Sasha yells and throws her hands up in the air. "Can we? Can we? Pleeeease!"

"When we get to it," Tommy laughs, pinching her nose and shaking his head lovingly. "Let's go in turn. Okay?"

"Yes, boss." Then she turns to me. "Speaking of bosses, is yours still a grumpy git?"

"Nah." I glance at Nathan, hoping the subject of Kerim doesn't sour his mood. "He's all right. We have our ups and downs but don't hold it against each other."

"Good, more on that later." She points to the closest fast looking ride with a giant gorilla on the front. The cars that run along the tracks are shaped like bananas. Creative. "Let's go."

"We'll have to take it in turns," I say, nodding to the kids. "Somebody has to watch the brats."

"It's fine; you two go. I'll feel sick if I start riding those things so soon after a fry up," Tommy says, looking casual and cool about it all.

"Are you sure?" Sasha asks, worried that he might just be being chivalrous.

"Go," he insists, kissing her nose. "I'll stay behind with Nathan. He looks as keen on the idea of riding that thing as a man about to be stabbed."

He's definitely right about that. Nathan gives me an apologetic shrug and I make a mental note to drag him onto something later. For now I'm just happy that I get to experience this shit sitting beside my best girlfriend.

"Let's do this!" Sasha cries like a woman preparing for battle.

We make it on the first ride, though we're forced to take the second to last seats. I was hoping to get first.

"What do you think they're talking about?" Sasha asks as I wave at the boys below and the sleeping Emily. A metal bar lowers to my middle and we both instinctively give it a push to check it's secure.

"One second while I read their lips."

"You can lip read?"

"No, I was being sarcastic." I'm laughing purely because I'm having to explain sarcasm to the queen of sarcasm herself.

"Oh." She looks at her hand. "My finger feels naked."

"Oh my god," I laugh again, this time at her obsession with marriage. "You're worse than Nathan."

"Is he still pushing for marriage?"

CHAPTER FOURTEEN

I shrug and bite my lip.

"What's the hold up? You said yes two years ago."

"I know, I just..." I pull on the fat under my biceps. "I'm not physically perfect enough to marry him. I'll look awful."

"Seriously? That's your reason?"

"It's not my only reason," I grumble but soon scream, giddy, when the ride begins to move. The sound of the chains below the car makes me nervous and puts thoughts in my head that I don't appreciate at this point in time. I can't deny that they make the ride that much more exhilarating.

"This is it!" Sasha grins and takes my hand. "Hold'em high, bitch!"

We only brave the no hands thing for the first four seconds, then we're gripping onto the metal bar for dear life, screaming at the top of our lungs. I'm pretty sure we're the only ones screaming. That's what happens when small town girls experience new things. We scream.

I've never been tossed around so much. As we hit each bend I'm thrown into Sasha but it's the greatest time ever. I feel sick, I feel high…I've never been high but this has to be it. My veins are pumping a heavy, static buzz around my body that I'm sure if there was no light you'd be able to see in the form of a bright blue glow.

And then it ends. My lungs constrict, my throat is sore, but holy crap. "I want to go again."

We turn towards each other, grin and burst into a fit of giggles. Her messy hair no doubt mirrors my own.

On trembling legs, we exit the ride enclosure down a set of metal steps with small and random ovular holes in them.

"You okay?" Tommy asks us both as he and Nathan check our shaking bodies for any damage.

"Yeah," we both respond breathlessly at the same time and we share another giggle.

"So, who's got the map? Where are we going next?"

Nathan pulls it out of the breast pocket of his jacket and unfolds it. Now that it's open I just know that there's not a single chance in hell any of us are going to be able to fold it the same way again.

Then, after deciding which path around the theme park we're going to take, Nathan makes me eat my words and refolds it back to its original state without issue.

"Show off," I mutter and shove him when he grins smugly at me.

After three constant hours of rides, swapping rounds so everybody gets a turn, kids and Nathan included, we stop for extremely expensive theme park food where Tommy and Nathan battle over the bill. Nathan wins. The burgers aren't actually that bad; even Nathan agrees and he usually hates fast food. That said, the lettuce within is pitiful; it's a quarter piece and the ends of the leaf are wilting.

The rest of it is great though. I've never felt so hungry but now that I'm full, I'm dreading the loopy rides. We settle on taking the kids on a few rides instead; they're slower and safer on our bloated bellies.

Out of everything, I think the sea lion show was the shining point for Nathan and Dillan. It had nothing to do with the fact SpongeBob made an appearance… nothing at all.

I'll never understand their obsession with said cartoon. It's good but is it obsession worthy? Not in my opinion, though I never make them switch the channel. It makes them happy and that makes me happy.

"Are you having fun?" Nathan asks as we sit in a round boat on a magical water ride through colourful tunnels, each telling their own story with peculiar looking miniature people.

I rest my head on his shoulder and hum, hating that with every passing second we come closer and closer to the end of our day out. It feels as though we're in a completely different life. Tomorrow it's back to reality, back to work and back to how things are between us. Let's hope the past few weeks of tension don't come flooding back the second we step into its familiar environment.

"I've never seen you smile so much."

My smile has been a permanent fixture all day. So much so that my jaw is aching and so are my cheeks.

"It's nice." He kisses my temple and then turns to look at the boat behind us where Tommy and Sasha wrestle with the kids. We both laugh at their struggles.

"It really is," I agree and sigh away my troubles. I worry too much. Maybe it's me who has been bringing the tension into the home and that's why Nathan avoids me so much lately, because of my moods. Or am I talking myself into happiness again based on something that doesn't exist?

Who knows anymore?

Tommy didn't propose like Sasha had hoped he would. I'm honestly on the fence now about it. I don't think he's ready yet and Sasha being so insistent about it, even behind his back, is going to drive a wedge between them. She needs to calm down and he needs to be prodded. I have zero doubts that he's completely clueless about Sasha's constant marriage babbling. She's becoming so frustrated with it all that she's going to start taking it out on him. It's going to become one of those all or nothing things, I can just tell, and that makes me sad. I don't want either of them to rush into something they aren't ready for as a couple, but I don't see them often enough to judge this deeply. I'm probably wrong and I can't really push on her a thought on a subject I know little about.

It's easy to have opinions when you're on the outside looking in.

I'm sure that Sasha herself has many comments on my own life that she's withholding for the same reasons.

<u>Sasha</u>: Thank you so much for coming today. You made my birthday the best. I had so much fun.

<u>Gwen</u>: Me too, I miss you all ready. Send me all of your pictures as soon as you can.

<u>Sasha</u>: Open a FB account and I'll tag you. Save me a time uploading them.

<u>Gwen</u>: Ugh... screw that. Just print them off like the olden days. You have a printer. Use it.

<u>Sasha</u>: And demote it from its legendary place on my shelf as head dust collector?

<u>Gwen</u>: Print the photos.

<u>Sasha</u>: Please... rude bitch. ;-)

<u>Gwen</u>: Please, you rude bitch. Better?

I can hear her laughter despite the fact she's hundreds of miles away once more.

"Go to sleep," Nathan grumbles directly into my ear. He nuzzles my neck and holds me tighter as I reach across to place my phone onto the table beside the bed. It crinkles on a sweet wrapper, reminding me that I really need to tidy up and stop eating junk in the bedroom before Nathan has a heart attack. Or I do from the number of snacks I've been consuming lately.

His teeth nip at my ear after I wrestle with him and the blanket to find a comfortable position. I end up sprawled on my back, one leg tossed over both of his. He reluctantly rolled onto his and now his fingertips trail lazy circles on the inside of my thigh. I love this feeling. It's so tingly and relaxing, almost as good as having my back scratched. Almost. Not quite.

"You're not sleeping yet," he mutters sleepily as his arm creeps under my neck. He pins me to his side, both of my legs now over his. I must be heavy but he never complains.

"I want to start going to the gym."

His body tenses. "Why?"

"To be healthy. We can go together. I know you enjoy working out."

"Fine, go to sleep."

"Really?"

"Yes," he mutters sleepily. I can hear the smile in his voice. "Now sleep."

"Is it weird that I'm excited?"

"Gwen." He warns, but I can tell he's still tired.

"I'm kind of horny now though." He stills at my words and I feel his cock thicken against the underside of my thigh. Giggle. "I get horny when I'm excited."

"Well, who am I to deny my excited wife her fill of me?"

With a strength I was unaware of, he throws me from him and rolls on top of me. Normally he'd take his time, kiss my body and massage every inch of me with his hands, only sometimes allowing me the same. This time he's almost feral as he seeks out the source of moisture between my thighs and when he's convinced I'm wet enough to be comfortable, he thrusts inside and swallows my screams with his mouth.

Each thrust is more powerful than the last and the fullness of it causes a sweet, tingling burn so deep I feel it in my throat when I moan. My body shifts up the bed. Sensing this, Nathan places a hand on the top of my head, using me as an anchor and protecting my head from the headboard.

I've never felt it like this before with him. He's never been this hard, this rough, this powerful. Tears spring to my eyes as the sensitivity he's teasing below burns with more fire than ever before. I find myself on the brink of orgasm yet unable to grasp it, so my muscles clench with pleasure so potent it feels almost painful. My hips try to keep up with his but the speed and strength of him keeps me pinned.

"Oh God!" I cry out as that deep sensation finally unfurls its static wings and pumps a light through my veins that carries me in and out of consciousness.

Nathan releases a desperate roar so loud I'm forced to cover his mouth with my hand. When his eyes meet mine, it only triggers a longer climax shared by the both of us. Each frantic, unmeasured plunge takes us closer to the edge of oblivion and then suddenly, leaving us with a lingering wave, he stops and collapses onto me with a groan. His chest heaves heavily with his breathing which seems to have no natural pattern.

When the pleasure hums to a low murmur, I begin to feel the ache his welcome forcefulness has subjected my body to. As he softens, entirely spent and tired, I feel even achier at the loss of fullness.

"Wow," he says softly and buries his entire face in my neck. His breath tickles. "I think I like tired sex with you."

"Hmm," I agree, too sleepy to respond in any language. "Shower?"

When he doesn't move, I blink into the darkness and rub slow circles on his back and shoulders. Then my eyes widen when his breathing finally evens out, my lips parting with a silent gasp. This is the first time he has ever had sex without showering immediately afterwards.

He'll wake soon. He will.

I'm too scared to sleep just in case he does. Nothing worse than being forced to shower when you're dead to the world.

"You look exhausted," Nathan states as I struggle to make breakfast for him and the kids. "Are you ill?"

"No, I just didn't sleep well last night," I confess, smiling at him over my shoulder.

"Why? Did I not fuck you hard enough?"

I choke on laughter, triggered by my shock.

When he winks at me, I turn to face him fully and shake my head to clear it. Who is this man? "You did. I just stayed up waiting for you to wake me and force me into the shower."

He spoons a mouthful of mushed banana into Emily's mouth, seeming unaffected by my admission. "I had one when I woke up."

"I know that, but still... this is new territory. I couldn't sleep."

He grins, shrugs and battles with Emily for the baby spoon she just stole. "I didn't mean to confuse you."

"Don't apologise," I laugh and slide onto his lap. "It's nice that you didn't immediately force me to shower."

"Does it upset you when I do?" His free hand rests on my hip.

"Not at all. It used to, but I understand. To be honest, I'm so used to it now I feel icky when I don't shower."

His lips touch mine. "I'm trying to be a little more lenient with my routine. I don't want you to feel..."

When he falls silent and looks away, I gently tip his face back to me with my finger and thumb grasping his chin, just below his thick lower lip which, before speaking, I suck into my mouth for a brief moment. "Feel what?"

"Trapped." This breathless word is full of so much emotion, primarily anxiety laced with a ton of insecurity.

"With you? Always, in the best way, not the worst. Don't release me."

Forgetting our lives for a moment, he pushes his lips to mine and we kiss for the longest time. It feels like an eternity, though in reality it's only a fraction of that. What a glorious fraction though.

"I love you."

"So you've said." I peck his lips with a final gentle kiss, run my hands through his hair, kiss the underside of his jaw and stand to finish making breakfast.

Now that I know he's in a good mood, I decide to confront the elephant in the room. Staring at the sizzling pan on the stove, I gather my courage and say softly, "Don't give me a hard time about Kerim anymore."

The pause between us lasts another fraction of eternity, this one nowhere near as pleasant as the last.

"I'll do my best." He finally says and I release the breath I was holding. "I trust you. It's unfair that I hold against you the thoughts, feelings and possible actions of another."

This makes me smile. Good progress has been made today. I'll be on cloud nine for a while.

Chapter Fifteen

"YES!" I cry, happy when I see the rota that Kerim has pinned on the board in the staffroom.

"What?" Patience asks and checks her hours over as she gathers her soft blonde hair up with both hands. "What am I missing?"

"I've got Thursday and Friday off."

"And?" She ties her hair up using the hair band that she held between her teeth.

"Those are the two days Sasha and Tommy are having the kids." I feel like dancing. "Now I just have to convince Nathan to get the time off."

"I'll keep my fingers crossed for you," she states, though she is as insincere as the bitter smile on her face. That woman blows so hot and cold all the time. It drives me mad. One day I'm going to punch her in the face.

"Yeah right," I whisper quietly so she doesn't hear me but loudly enough for me to feel as though I've vented a little bit of stress towards her.

"Ladies," Kerim announces as he steps into the room with Harold behind him.

"Hey guys." I grin through the fabric of my white jacket as I pull it over my head. I can't be bothered to undo all the buttons. "I'll be with you in a second."

"Are you sure you're not stuck?" Harold laughs.

I finally tug my head through the neck hole and stick my tongue out at him.

"I need to make a call before I go in, is that okay?" I ask meekly, knowing that I'm already pushed for time.

"Go." Kerim waves his hand at me. "Make it quick. You're on line today."

"Really?" Patience and I say together, though mine is excited and hers is insulted.

"Yep, you did so well last time."

"Yay!" I throw my arms up, wishing somebody other than Patience was close enough for me to high five.

"Yay?" Harold questions.

"People say Yay!" I snap playfully, annoyed that everyone always seems to question my happy word whenever I release it.

"What people?" Kerim adds teasingly.

I glare at him as I take my phone into his office.

"I didn't say you could go in there!"

In answer to his playful grumblings, I lock the door and pull up the number for Jackson, the investigator I hired.

"Jackson's office, how may I help?" I recognise the voice immediately.

"Hey, umm..." Why do I always stammer when I'm on the phone to new people? "It's Gwen. I hired Jackson recently to dig a little."

"Oh, yes, I recall. He's working your case now in fact."

He is?

"So he's not there?"

"No but I can assure you that I'll relay any and all messages with perfect clarity," she tells me and I have no doubt that she will.

"Actually it's not really a message, it's more of a cancellation."

The line goes quiet for a moment. "I see."

"I just feel as though I've made a huge mistake."

"I see."

"You guys can keep the money. I just know there's no point him investigating further because he'll not find anything. It was just me being paranoid." I'm rambling. "I don't want to waste any more time."

"I understand, honey. This is more common than you think."

That brings me relief. "I feel silly."

"Don't feel silly; we all go through rough patches that have us guessing. I'm just so happy that it has all worked out for you."

"Thank you." I hear the clattering of pots and pans coming from the kitchen. "I have to go. I'm sorry."

"No problem, I'll let Jackson know immediately. Take care."

"You too."

Work time. A weight has been lifted. I can't believe I ever even entertained the idea of spying on Nathan. What is wrong with me?

<u>Gwen</u>: Make sure you're home for Thursday and Friday! I'm not working! YAY! <3

<u>Nathan</u>: I'll do my best. <3

"Are you done?" Kerim asks the second I enter the kitchen. I nod. He adds, "Good, wash your hands and get to work. Listen up, Gwen is overseeing your shit so don't fuck up it!"

We all snigger at his language error but we don't let him see. Never mess with Kerim in his kitchen; he gets angry and stays angry.

Everyone is helpful and happy under my ruling, despite the fact I've been there the least time. We all get on great so that helps, but knowing that they respect me is the biggest cherry on top of this cake.

I don't have to yell at them; I'm only forced to raise my voice when it's noisy. Even Patience listens, though I can tell she's not happy about it.

This, apart from the first time I was line manager, is the best work day to date. I am so happy right now. Almost too happy.

<u>Gwen</u>: I'm ready to start looking at venues. <3

I send this message to not just Nathan but Sasha, Mum, Jeanine, and Tommy. They immediately send back excited replies with promises to help me pick. Nathan, however, sends me a list of places he's already considered.

This makes me smile. I only manage to check two before my break ends, but they're both gorgeous and paint such wonderful visions in my mind.

For the first time in a long time, I find myself feeling excited about my future wedding. This is good.

No.

This is great.

Cloud nine seats me comfortably for the rest of my work evening. It holds me tight in the strong embrace of Nathan when I arrive home. It floats in the steam of the shower we share after hours of love making and tickles my arms on the tips of his fingers as we browse the internet late at night, looking over venue after venue across the UK.

The next day, even though we wake up groggy and exhausted from lack of sleep, I call Kerim and pick two weeks I'd like to take off. Nathan and I head to his travel agency friend to book a trip to Rome, Italy.

Cloud nine needs to start charging me rent; I'll be settled here for a while.

"Will you come with me to the store next Thursday? I really want to show you around before the renovation." Nathan asks as we share a cup of coffee in our kitchen. The kids are both napping, a rare occurrence but a welcome one. We're hiding in the kitchen so as to not wake them. The slightest noise sets Dillan off these days. He's almost passed his nap stage, though they occur randomly still, very rarely.

"On our day off from the kids?" The thought of working on our one time away from the kids for so long doesn't appeal to me but how can I deny him such a request when he seems so excited? "Sure, but not for long!"

"Of course, there are a few places I want you to see in Essex."

"Like?"

"You'll see," he grins and takes the mug from my hands to have a sip. "Damn I make a good coffee."

"You do," I agree. "You're a coffee snob."

"Only since you." He taps the top of our little percolator. "You shouldn't have gotten me this for Christmas."

I shrug. "You love it and you make me delicious coffee on demand."

He grins, waits for me to finish the last of the coffee and turns to place it by the sink. When he stills, my hand goes to his arm, concern flooding my brain at his sudden stop.

"What's wrong?" I ask, panicked.

He slams the cup down on the side but his eyes remain on something ahead. I peek around him to find the source of his sudden ire. The only thing in his line of sight that I can determine to be the cause of this drama is the picture of Caleb on the top of the microwave.

"Nathan?"

He stares at the photo emotionlessly and I wonder if seeing his brother again is upsetting him. It has been a long time; surely he's ready to have a piece of him in our home now?

"Why is he on display?"

That wasn't the question I was expecting, nor was I expecting the cold, low tone it was carried forward on.

I reply, "Because we've all missed him and I want Dillan to…"

"Dillan?" He snaps, his tone higher now, angry.

"Yes. What's the issue?"

He doesn't respond; he only looks away and licks his lower lip slowly. When I step into his body and wrap my arms around his waist, I try to smile but it comes out as more of a grimace.

"What's wrong?"

"Do you still think of him often?"

"What kind of a question is that?" I laugh, though nothing is humorous about this situation. "I think of him whenever my brain conjures a memory over something familiar."

"So a lot then?"

"I'm not doing this," I warn him and step away.

"Doing what?"

"Arguing over a dead person!"

"Who's arguing?"

"Stop," I snap, feeling my anger rise. "He's dead, Nathan. Dead. He's your brother; he's somebody I loved once very dearly; he fathered my child; he took my virginity…"

Nathan winces but I don't stop.

"He was my first love. The first guy I brought home to my mum. My first fiancé. I was going to die with him. I was going to grow old with him and I'll not let you force me to abandon all of that because you're bloody jealous."

His jaw tenses and I see the muscle twitch. "Are you finished?"

"Yes. And so are we."

"What?" His eyes widen so I roll mine and hiss, "With this conversation!"

"Fine," he hisses back and runs a hand through his hair.

"Fine."

"You should have spoken to me about it first!" It took him a few moments of silence before he blurted this.

I rub my temples. "Nathan, I don't have to tell you shit…"

"Language!"

"About SHIT!"

"Gwen…"

"You're not my dad; you're not my parent; you are my PARTNER! Start acting like it!"

"Partners discuss things!"

"Yes, things…" I run my own hands through my hair and resist the urge to rip it out. "Such as where we're going on holiday. Who has the kids and when? We should discuss things like the bills, what we need when going shopping, the weather and it's potential to ruin any plans…"

"Gwen…"

"Plans that we make together! Unless one of us already has plans with somebody else. Partners do NOT dictate to their partners about what pictures go where when they've never had an issue with said partner putting up all of the other pictures around the house! If…"

"Gwen, can I just…"

"If we've discussed it before, then we'll discuss it, but I won't be told or made to feel guilty over a fucking photo of somebody no longer with us." And breathe.

"Are you done?" He asks, his arms folded and his brow quirked. I nod. He continues, "Good, then I'm sorry. You're right. Just… things have been tense between us lately."

"No kidding," I whisper but he ignores it.

"I've not been forthcoming with a lot of things and I guess I'm scared that I'll do something to push you away."

I unfold his arms and step between them. "Then be forthcoming. I'm listening."

"I will," he says, nodding. "On our two days off. We'll sit down and talk about it all. Okay?"

This brings me a tremendous amount of joy. "Promise?"

"I promise." He grins. "Is your meltdown over?"

I pinch his side. "Is yours?"

"Yes, my Queen."

I think we handled that a lot better than the last few times we argued. We're making great progress, he and I.

"Maaaaa!" Dillan yells loudly. "Wha doin?"

"I'm coming," I call back, giggling. "He's getting so good at talking."

"Unfortunately, he'll be talking back before we know it," Nathan jokes and follows close behind.

"Maaa!" Dillan screams again as we enter the room. Emily awakens with a screech, unhappy to have been woken prematurely. Nathan goes to her as I tend to Dillan. This is going to be a tough afternoon for Nathan, though not for me. I'm at work soon. I do love my job, though I love being at home more.

Chapter Sixteen

These past two days have gone as slow as could be, but finally Thursday is here. I couldn't be more excited if I tried.

He laughs and off we trot into the horizon. Literally.

Sasha arrives at ten in the morning and I'm too quick to kick her and the children out, which has her laughing. The second she's gone I dive on my fiancé, legs around his waist, lips all over his, and we crash onto the bed, only to wake two hours later feeling groggy, warm and suffocated under his body.

"We're late!" Nathan yells suddenly, jolting me from my near slumber.

"Huh?"

"We fell asleep." He peels his body off mine, allowing me to roll over. I'm fully dressed. Didn't we have rampant animal sex? "Gwen, move."

"Tired," I tell him, blinking the sleep from my eyes.

"Gwen!" He grabs my wrist and pulls.

"Don't make me." I roll back over and bury my face in the blanket. His hand connects with my arse but I'm too tired to do little more than grunt. His laughter follows.

Hands grab my ankles and pull me down the bed. I drip from it like slime, my body boneless.

"Gwen, come on."

"Just five more minutes."

He sighs heavily and sits beside me. "You promised."

He's right, I did.

I roll back over and give him my biggest sleepy smile. "I'm up." Then I raise my arms and allow him to pull my wobbly body from the floor. I stagger into him and inhale deeply when he holds me tight. He doesn't moan or rush me, just holds me for as long as I need.

"Love you," I murmur into his dress shirt before pulling away. "I need coffee."

He slaps my arse again as I leave the room. That one stung.

"Make me coffee."

And again. Ouch.

"Stop," I grin, picking up my pace to avoid his assaults.

"I like it." He tries again but misses when I jump down the last three steps and skid around the bottom of the stairs.

"Be careful," he laughs, still chasing me. "I just cleaned the floors this morning."

He likes cleaning first thing in the morning. He's so strange. I think it's because he enjoys the stench of bleach when it lingers throughout the day. I have to admit, I do enjoy walking in and smelling the fresh citrus scent of cleaning fluids when I walk through the door.

I'm becoming as queer as him.

"Stop running with your socks on," he finally grabs me from behind and pushes me into the wall. Teeth scrape at my neck making me laugh so hard my stomach hurts. He won't let go. Tears are streaming from my eyes.

"You said we're late!" I cry, giddy and now wide awake.

On a sigh, he slides his hand down my arm and spins me under his before pulling me back into his chest. I love it when he gets in this kind of mood.

"Let's go." His lips touch the tip of my nose.

"Where are we going exactly?"

"To Essex, to the store."

"And then? Maybe we could go holiday shopping! I need bikinis."

He clears his throat and shifts in his seat and I sincerely hope that the reason for this and the added flush to his cheeks is because he's thinking of me in a bikini. "And then to eat. If we have time to shop we will."

"You've found a place?"

"Of course." He grins and helps me into my jacket. "Come on, we can sleep in tomorrow."

"Liar."

I watch his relaxed profile as he leads me from the house. He does seem happy now and that makes me joyous beyond compare. Whatever burdens he carried before don't seem to be burdening him anymore.

Maybe this is the reason he's ready to talk to me about it?

Because whatever it is, it's resolved so I won't have to worry about it alongside him?

The sooner we get that conversation out of the way, the better. I'll not push him for it though. I'm just going to enjoy the two days I get with him alone.

"Is it your choice or my choice?" I ask, referring to the radio.

His hand goes to my thigh. "Yours."

"Yay!" I turn the dial and the stations blur in and out. Why is it that whenever it is my turn to choose the music, there's no good music on? Sod's law. In the end, as if fate planned it, we listen to what he wants anyway, not that I mind. I still sulk a little though, just for the hell of it.

"So, what are we doing afterwards?" I ask, excited to see what plans he has in store for me. "You said 'if we have time to shop'. I doubt going for food is going to take up the rest of the day."

"Nothing gets by you, does it?" I shake my head in reply and bite my lip. "I'm not telling you." The twinkle in his eye and smile playing on his lips shows his excitement. Whatever it is, it must be good. I can't wait; my chest is tingling.

"I'm looking forward to seeing your designs for this store. Are you following the same themes as the others? With the glass cabinets in the middle of the store? I love that."

"Yes, but I've gone for a subtle grey with green accents this time. It's far from done but I'm extremely excited for this project."

"I can tell." I place my hand on his thigh and his hand comes to rest on top. With my free hand I pull up the switch for the window and sigh happily when it rolls down, allowing a cool breeze to filter into the warm car. "Summer has been crap this year."

"Agreed." He brings my fingers to his lips and kisses just below the knuckles. "Hopefully today will stay warm."

"Agreed," I mimic, beaming from ear to ear. "We're going to Southend, right?"

"Yeah, the store is facing the beach."

"How wonderful! You should do mermaid charms." I sigh wistfully but scowl when he snorts as if my mermaid charms are silly. "What? Everyone loves mermaids."

"You're so weird."

I poke my tongue out at him and turn the radio up, only amusing him further.

We both get peckish on the way and stop to pick up some chips from a popular chippy on the way to Nathan's store. Long ago seems the time that Nathan wouldn't allow me to eat in the car; it still makes him nervous but he gets over it.

<u>Gwen</u>: Are they being good? Thank you so much for this! <3

Sasha doesn't respond which surprisingly doesn't worry me. I trust her and Tommy. They're so good with the kids and the kids love them to pieces.

I wonder if Nathan has put any more thought into who we're going to leave them with, worst case scenario. We really should get life insurance. As morbid as my thoughts are, I just feel as though I can't sleep soundly until this is sorted.

"We're almost there." Nathan's soft voice carries over the noise of the ocean waves splashing against the shore. It's a gentle day but the sea is powerful.

I run my hands through my hair and try to stretch as best as I can in the confines of the car. My body aches from being sat for so long.

"Here we are," he states, slowing down to find a parking space. "There's a private allotment around the back but it has a trailer and a ton of junk. I want to buy it, clear it and turn it into a little car park."

"Good plan," I say, relieved when he pulls up only two stores down from his. It's rare that we'd find such a great parking space so close to the beach. "Though I'm sure people would use it to go shopping elsewhere."

"That's my concern." He holds up his hand when I place mine on the door handle. His smile is entirely sweet and makes me feel warm inside. "Please, allow me."

I release my hold of the handle and wait for him to exit the vehicle and come around it, purely to open the door for me.

CHAPTER SIXTEEN

"You're so cute," I giggle as I take his hand and slowly allow my cramped body to exit the vehicle.

Growling, and glowing with mirth, he tugs my body to his and presses his lips harshly to my own. It's brief but it's powerful enough to light a fire within my body that can only be doused by his body on mine.

"Let's go." His leather clad fingers entwine with mine and pull me towards his store. I notice immediately what I didn't notice before.

"New windows?"

"Yes, extra security." He knocks his fingers against the glass.

"The outside is nice. I love the bay windows. It'll make for a great display." I inhale sharply as another thought comes to mind. "Can you imagine it all lit up at Christmas? It'll look like something out of a movie!"

My excitement is making him happy, I can tell.

We enter the store through the slightly open door and I immediately hear a jigsaw as the scent of burning wood fills my lungs. I tense. The burning feeling in my throat as my lungs constrict to protect themselves from the intrusion brings back painful memories. Nathan seems affected too as he sighs with relief when the noise stops and we're greeted by a large man in overalls, boots, safety glasses over his eyes and a white mask over his face.

"Sorry, boss." He looks apologetically at us both. "I totally underestimated the speed of time."

"No problem."

I'm assuming Nathan warned him to not do any cutting while we are visiting. For this I'm relieved.

"How's it going?" I ask before Nathan does.

"Great actually. The lads have gone on their break; I'm keeping watch and keeping busy," the tall, stocky man says and I see his eyes crinkle with a smile hidden by the mask. "I'm Carl by the way. I'd shake your hand but..." He shows me his blackened, dusty hand and shrugs a sorry.

"No problem." I'm relieved to avoid the shaking of his hand. I look around the open space; it's narrow but it's long and I can see where they're building the displays.

"Floor looks like it's going to be good." Nathan comments, kicking part of the dust cover to the side to view the wooden floor beneath.

"Boys'll get it all polished up. When we're done, it'll gleam like a new penny."

Nathan nods, his lips smiling subconsciously. I love seeing him in his element. I know he's imagining all his jewellery in displays across the room. Seeing his visions come to life in his other stores really shines a light into his mind. He has such a good eye. I knew that already from his jewellery but his creativity astounds not just me, but the many people who have offered him partnerships.

This reminds me of the partnership offered to me by Kerim. I really need to speak to Nathan about that. There seems to be so much going on in our individual lives at the moment. I've been focusing so much on Nathan's future, I haven't yet processed my own possibilities.

What do I even want to do? I always wanted to own my own restaurant. Could I consider the possibility of joining Kerim? Do I really have the talent he claims I do? Or is he after something else? Was Nathan right?

"What do you think?" Nathan asks suddenly, catching me off guard.

I nod, unsure what to say because I drifted while he was talking.

He grins knowingly and loops his arm around my neck. After touching my temple with his lips he whispers, "Come on, let's check out the back and then we'll go."

"The back?"

"Staff area and product exchange."

"Cool."

I give a little wave to the joiner as Nathan pulls me through an open hole in the wall that I assume will become a door.

"Panic room space?"

He nods when he sees the corner I'm pointing at. "Same as the others."

"Good." I love that he's cautious enough to think of such things. I certainly hope the panic rooms never get used though.

"I'll just check on the staff area and we'll go," he comments quietly and I'm pulled towards an actual door this time, by what looks to be a half built counter. "The plumbing still not done?"

"Not yet, nearly!" The joiner calls back. "Had to replace the majority of the piping to get it to where we needed it."

Nathan remains silent as he inspects the area. Then he finally asks, "So... what do you think?"

"I think I like it even more than the place in London!" I smile with glee and launch myself at him so he feels the full power of my excitement in my hug. "I'm so proud of you, Nathan."

The loving look he gives me as he holds tight to my hips, keeping my body flush to his, makes me tingle with warmth. "This is the start of such a bright future, don't you think?"

"That I do. And with Italy around the corner, what more could I ask for?"

"Exactly."

"I am on cloud nine."

"Me too." His thumbs slide under the edge of my top and tickle the bare skin of my hips. "Come on. Let's go."

"Where?"

His secretive grin only makes me giddier. "I really hope that whatever we're doing today, it involves coffee."

"We could scout out the local cafes before we leave?"

"Let's go."

We wave to the joiner and make our way onto the busy street. That's the one thing I hate about living in the city; it's always too busy. If the locals aren't cluttering the streets, the tourists are and the paths just aren't wide enough to accommodate.

The worst part about pushing through the crowds is the cigarette stench. Instead of stepping off to the side to smoke and then continuing their journey, people deem it okay to smoke as they wade through limbs. It's gross and unfair. Just because they want to smoke doesn't mean I do. I've had many of my clothes marked because people can't keep their cigarettes to themselves. Nathan feels the same; he's voiced this many times and it's always evident on his face.

Fortunately, we don't have to shuffle too far before we come across a cute little Italian style café with garlic braids hanging in the windows. Just for that detail alone I skip inside and order us both drinks and a muffin to go. Fingers crossed it's good.

When we both agree that it is exceptional, I make a note to commute to this store more often, purely for the coffee only a few buildings down the street.

"Okay, so we have our coffee," he grins, tapping his cup to mine over the console of the car. Taking a sip, he puts the paper cup in the cup holder next to mine and buckles his seatbelt. "We have each other." When he taps his forehead to mine in the same manner that he tapped his cup to mine, I burst into a fit of giggles. Playful Nathan is the best kind of Nathan. "We have our instruments."

"Our what?" I ask, still laughing, but then he starts to fumble with his jeans button. Images of him trying to tap said instrument against mine force me to slap his hand, laughing even harder. Turning to me and smiling, he finally places his hands on the steering wheel and asks, "Ready?"

"Yes."

"You have the most beautiful smile."

"Can we just go already?" I giggle, eager to get to my surprise.

"Fine, but you're paying," he jests and somehow manoeuvres the car onto the busy road.

I sigh dramatically. "I kind of maybe left my purse at home."

"Clever." His hand goes to my thigh and squeezes. "You'll just have to pay me in other ways."

"Now? While you're driving?" I reach over and start to pull on the zipper of his jeans. "Well okay then."

"Gwen!" His tone is panicked yet happy as he grips my hand in his to stop my assault. "Behave."

"Boring."

My thigh stings when he slaps it. I try not to react, knowing how much he loves it when I squeal. "Nob."

"Language."

"*Language*," I mimic in a whiny, annoying tone.

"Don't start that again."

"*Don't start that again.*"

"I'm serious."

"*I'm...*" His hand covers my mouth, which only makes me laugh harder. I'd lick his palm to get him off but he's wearing his leather gloves so I'll settle for nipping at it with my teeth instead.

"You're such a child," he smirks, finally releasing my mouth.

"Yet you love me."

"I do. Without you my life would certainly be missing a lot."

I melt over the console and nuzzle his shoulder and neck. "You're the best."

A solemn wave seems to pour from him into the space between us and his eyes cast a sad glow onto the road ahead. What I said has clearly upset him and my heart flutters painfully with the need to know what.

CHAPTER SIXTEEN

For now, I'll continue to live in a state of blissful ignorance because I know that whatever it is, he'll talk to me about it later, as promised. Please, whatever it is, don't let it be so bad that I can't deal. Whatever powers are out there in the universe, give me the strength to handle this alongside my future husband. Don't let me fail.

The drive is fairly long and I'm totally unsure of where we are. I wasn't following road signs; I was too busy annoying the love of my life by poking him repeatedly whilst asking, "Are we nearly there yet?"

Also I was texting Sasha about the kids. She's unresponsive and part of me wonders if they've killed her. It wouldn't surprise me; my kids are vicious.

I miss them.

"Almost there," he grins, breaking the short break of silence between us.

"How close is almost?" I ask, pressing my face up against the glass of the door window. The weather is lovely, the sun shining over vast amounts of countryside. Are we going for a picnic? Or a stroll? This is so frustratingly exciting!

Nathan switches off the air con and rolls down the windows with a flick of a button. The scent of fresh fields in full bloom assaults my nose in the best way. Regardless of the fact I'm sneezing, I'm still enjoying every second.

"That breeze is the best," I sigh wistfully and relax back into my seat. "Right?"

"Most definitely," Nathan grins, looking as relaxed as I feel.

We finally slow on the long road and I see a large white house in the distance. Horses canter and play around a field across from it.

They are beautiful. There's a particular horse with a large white patch across its rear that calls to me the most.

Nathan pulls into the wide driveway by the even larger country house, mindful of the two cars already parked.

My heart begins to quicken, my palms tingling with excitement.

"What's going on?" I ask when the front door of the home opens and an older man steps out, beaming from ear to ear.

Nathan, still grinning, opens his door and climbs out to greet the man. I don't wait for him to assist me in exiting the vehicle; I'm too excited to find out what on earth is going on.

"Mr Weston." The man takes my fiancé's gloved hand for a brief moment before turning to me. I can tell he's a grafter simply by the coarseness of the skin of his hand that envelops my own. "Soon to be Mrs Weston, am I correct?"

"Well if you were wrong you'd have made my mistress very uncomfortable," Nathan deadpans. I roll my eyes and slap his arm before telling the man, "Just Gwen is fine."

"I'm George; this here is my farm and those are my horses…"

I want to scream for him to get to the point but that would be rude.

"The stable help are ready for you both." He leads us around the house to a large area hidden by tall trees.

Stable help? Now I'm even more excited.

"We chose for you; I hope you don't mind."

"You know their temperaments better than anyone else, I'm sure," Nathan says as he folds me under his arm and helps me walk along the cobbled path.

The walkway is narrow, surrounded by beautiful flowers in pots and hedges hiding what lies beyond from view. By now though I have it sussed but I don't want to say it out loud until I'm sure.

Finally the large barn style stables come into view and I can't help hissing out an ecstatic, "YES!"

Nathan winks at me and George finally allows us entry where two well dressed employees suit us up in the proper horse riding attire. I've never seen Nathan in breeches before. I need to see him in them again. I wonder if they'll let us keep them. His legs look so powerful, toned and smooth. I have never been so turned on by the sight of such shapely man legs before. I'm officially weird but I have no regrets.

"These are yours too." We're passed helmets and Nathan helps to tighten the buckle of mine under my chin before allowing me to help him buckle his. I scratch at the scruff of his beard, kiss it and give an excited squeal when they inform us that we're ready to meet our horses.

"I can't believe you've done this," I whisper, feeling all kinds of emotional. "This is…"

"Save it for later." Nathan brings my gloved hand to his lips, his eyes holding mine. "Let's go and meet our horses."

The scent of the stables is exactly how I imagined it to be. It reminds me of rats. Everything in nature reminds me of rats but my happiness at the situation overrides my fear of the mini demonic buck tooth creatures with tails like a dying worm and...

"You look pale," Nathan whispers.

I shake my head to rid myself of the thoughts. It doesn't take much to distract me as I'm too busy inwardly screaming at the sight of a beautiful dark brown horse coming my way. It's a lot bigger than I imagined.

"This gorgeous boy is Retro." George pats his beautiful, long brown nose and tugs on the saddle. "He will be your chauffeur for your ride."

Nathan walks me around the side of him. My nerves are shot. I've never ridden a horse before, although I've always wanted to.

He takes my hand as the others verbally guide me up a set of wooden steps. I'm instructed to put one foot in the stirrup and swing the other over the horse's wide back. This is extremely nerve wracking.

"I'm going to fall," I laugh and Nathan uses this as permission to place a firm hand on my rear. "Stop."

"I'm just helping," he jests and I count down out loud before hopping onto the horse. I'm not very graceful but after sliding around on the saddle a little I finally get my leg over and breathe a sigh of relief.

"Are you okay?" Nathan asks, gripping my thigh as the horse takes a sideways step.

"Oh my god." I feel the power of the beast beneath me and my fear floods a huge amount of adrenaline through my system. I've never felt so tall, high and powerful. "This is amazing."

"Am I okay to leave you so I can situate myself?" Nathan asks, rubbing my thigh with his thumb.

I nod, smiling down at him, and watch as he's guided to his own even larger horse than mine. It's pure black with the most beautiful braided mane.

Nathan slips onto his horse without guidance and with such ease. He aims a smug grin at me and I flip him off and show him my tongue.

"What's your horse called?"

"Moon Vessel," he chuckles and I follow suit. What an odd one. I love it though. It suits him.

"You certainly planned this on the perfect day," George comments as he brings out his own horse. "Zephyr and I love walking in the sun."

"I'm glad," I state because I'm not sure what else to state.

"I'll be taking point, but I won't bother you as promised. I'm a safeguard because you're new to the horses and you," he nods at me, "Are new to horse riding."

I smile sheepishly and scrunch my nose up at Nathan.

"Are you clear on all of the instructions you were given?"

We both confirm we are. I can tell by the quickness of Nathan's tone that he's as eager to actually start as I am.

"Let's go."

It's the moment of truth.

With little nudges from the heel of my boot, Retro takes his first steps. My body sways with it. It's surprisingly comfortable at the moment, but I have no doubt that will change with time.

"Pull to a stop just beyond the doors and I'll take lead," George calls as Nathan spurs Moon Vessel to my side.

"Where are we going?" I ask, staring down at my horse with wide eyes. He's holding such a steady and controlled pace; does he know I'm new? Somebody once told me that horses can read people better than people. Whether that's true or not I don't know, but I sure hope he isn't getting spooked by my fear. I'm trying my hardest to be calm.

"See that footpath just across the street?"

I nod in response and shield my eyes with one hand so I can get a better glimpse of where I'm looking. The sun is so high in the sky it seems. Its heat is beautiful. I feel as though I'm in a foreign country.

"I'm going to take you along there to an opening in the fence. The route is all mud paths. Just follow my lead and keep off the fields and you'll be fine.

Fields. Shudder.

I wonder if Nathan put a lot of thought into that too. Did he ensure that I wouldn't have to be crossing through any kind of grass that is higher than my ankle?

"This is crazy," I whisper when Nathan lags a little to fall into step beside me.

"It is," he agrees, grinning widely.

Seeing him sitting on his horse, his posture relaxed, his hand holding the saddle between his legs as the other lazily holds the reigns, I feel as though I want to climb onto his lap, wrap my legs around his hips and ask him to gallop. The horses aren't the only things that are going to be ridden today.

CHAPTER SIXTEEN

The sun hits his face, lighting up his beautiful features, shining on his easy smile and making him glow with a calming aura that I hope to absorb into myself. He's stunning. Every part of him.

"You're staring," he tells me, but instead of being irritated like he would have been once upon a time, he only seems amused.

"Sorry," I mumble and look ahead. George has kept his word as he keeps his distance. He only glances back every so often to ensure that we aren't up to no good. "I wish I had the time, patience and money to adopt such beautiful creatures."

"Agreed." Nathan leans forward and pats the strong neck of his broad beauty. "Alas, I think I'll stick to just hiring one out every now and then."

"Amen," I giggle.

"I've missed you."

"Huh?"

His eyes hold that same sadness to them that they did earlier and it twists my heart. "Every day that I've been away has been torture."

"For me as well."

"It's wrong that I'm relieved to hear you say that." He shakes his head, smiling, and then stretches high, releasing both hands off the reins and saddle. He's crazy. I daren't even scratch my nose with my pinkie. "I really wish I'd insisted on wearing my own attire. This shirt is itchy."

"You look so sexy though."

To further prove my statement, he wags his brows at me and gives me just a glimpse of his teeth as he smiles a seductive smile.

We've come such a long way he and I. Sometimes I think back to those first few months together and how lost and hostile he was towards me. Underneath it all was such a wonderful person just aching to connect with somebody. I'm fortunate enough to be that somebody.

"What's wrong?" His smile fades to concern. He can read me like a book.

"I'm just happy."

When his smile returns, so does mine, but it soon vanishes when he reaches out a hand to me for comfort.

I shake my head, "Are you crazy? I'll die."

Chapter Seventeen

I was right earlier about aching after a few hours. My thighs are killing me but I don't regret a second of it.

Nathan truly has made this day so special. Immediately after we finished riding, we used a guest room in the house to shower together. That was nice. I was sweating so badly, it really ruins the romantic image. It was especially hard keeping our hands to ourselves but it had to be done or we'd have been late for our dinner reservations at a highly exclusive little cottage restaurant in practically the middle of nowhere.

All it serves are home cooked grandma meals as Nathan refers to them. Stews, hotpots, dumplings, proper mashed potatoes and sausages, etc. Personally, I love mash and gravy so I chose that whereas Nathan chose a lamb hotpot. Then for dessert we received home cooked pie and custard. It was lovely. I'm almost crying at the thought that we have to go home, back to reality where a certain conversation awaits us.

I can tell that Nathan is dreading it too. The closer we get, the quieter he becomes until finally, he's as tense as a rod with the personality to match.

His breathing quickens and I worry that this might be the beginning of a panic attack.

"I'll put the kettle on," I say softly, hoping to give him a minute to gather himself. I hate that whatever he's bearing is weighing so heavily on him. He needs to let it all out. He also needs coffee because once he sees how ridiculous he's being, he'll hopefully be up for that ride I promised myself earlier.

"My mother contacted me," he blurts. Clearly the pressure just burst because I've never heard him speak so quickly before. It's followed by a hefty exhale.

Luckily, my back is to him as I'm filling the kettle so I gather what little I have left of my composure and turn to the kettle base. "Oh."

"After my dad was released of charges."

"Okay... and?" I place the kettle on the base and flip the switch. The side glows blue and I focus on that so I don't explode along with Nathan's pressure switch.

"And... umm..." He scratches his growing beard. He's hiding something. "Nothing really. I just wanted to know how you felt about that I guess."

"You know I hate your family... all of them." And I don't have a single apology for it. "What did she say?"

"Just that she wanted to be in the kids' lives and that she's left my dad."

Is that why she's been coming to my restaurant? To make contact?

"What did you say?" His silence panics me. "Nathan... what did you say?"

"We spoke a little, but nothing." Stepping into me he cups my cheek with his hand. "I can see you're upset."

"I can't stand her."

He nods, not quite agreeing but understanding. "I made the right choice then?"

"No, you should have cursed her arse back to hell." I smile softly and melt into him. He wraps his arms around me. "Is this truly what you were worried about?"

"Yes," he answers quickly, too quickly, so I lean back and narrow my eyes to push him for more. "Promise. I just didn't want to worry you after all of that talk of them gaining custody."

My hand flies to my mouth. "Oh my goodness! We really need to sort that."

"I agree." He pulls me back to him and kisses the tip of my nose. "This week. If it'll make you feel better."

"It would." Then I slap his arm. "Don't frighten me like that. Don't you ever think that you can't come to me. I won't judge you. I understand; she's your mum at the end of the day. It was probably a really tough situation."

His sigh is heavy and long. I tuck my head under his chin and kiss his throat. "I love you, Gwen. More than anyone and anything."

"Not including the babies."

"Well that goes without saying."

I love to hear him say that. "I wish I grew up with a dad like you."

"Me too. Our kids won't know an ounce of what we knew growing up."

"Exactly." I clear my throat and hand him his coffee. He's going to need all the energy he can get for what I have planned. "Are you sure that's it? That's truly what's been eating at you?"

"It was just confusing. My mother was abused for so long, as you know. Part of me can't help but feel some small amount of sympathy for her."

"I get it; just don't get suckered in." I press my lips to his. "She's poison; both of them are." His eyes soften but still seem troubled. Perhaps it's just time he needs now, to accept all of this. Having his mum return a seemingly different person has to be a bit disorienting. "I actually have my own news."

"Oh?" He grins and lifts me onto the breakfast bar so easily I feel as though I don't weigh an ounce. "Do tell."

I part my thighs so he can stand between them and hook my arms around his neck. "Kerim..." The second I say that name, Nathan's mask of happiness twists into a look of hatred. I don't stop though, I need to get this out. "Has offered me a partnership, kind of."

"What?" His deep voice doesn't mirror my own voice of joy. Strong hands that were stroking my thighs now squeeze as though afraid to let me go.

"He said that I'm really good and he doesn't want me as his competition, he wants me as his partner one day so he's giving me a permanent place in his kitchen."

"I bet he does," he mumbles while rolling his eyes.

Slapping his arm, I cut him with a look that tells him to behave. "Nathan, this is brilliant. He's *the* chef. He's my idol. You know I look up to him! The fact he's told me this..."

"Has absolutely nothing with him wanting in here?" He bucks his hips against my groin, startling the absolute hell out of me.

Shoving him away I snap, "Yes because it's all about my pussy and has absolutely nothing to do with how hard I work or how good I am?" I drop to the floor and try to shoulder past him but his firm hand on my bicep stops me.

"I know you work hard and maybe his intentions aren't completely impure. He'd be a fool not to want that; I just don't..." He releases me and runs both of his hands through his hair. "I just don't trust him."

"He's your friend."

"Hardly. We're connected, that's all."

"I'm going to promise him my loyalty in return for a future partnership. We'll get it in writing."

His eyes narrow. "Just like that?"

"I'd be a fool not to. I'll have a better chance of becoming a recognised chef by his side than trying to wing it on my own."

"By his side?"

"Yes, professionally. He's so good at what he does."

His voice deepens dangerously. "Tell me you don't *feel* for him."

My jaw hits the floor. "Because I want to better my career means that I feel for him? Whatever that means."

"It's all a bit much too soon. You've hardly worked there and suddenly he wants you permanently?"

"Maybe I'm just that good." His face tells it all by the way he raises a brow and tears well in my eyes. "You don't think I'm that good?"

"Gwen..." Every part of him softens as he reaches for me, but it's too late. I pull away and he snaps, "Don't be naïve! I'm not saying you're not good enough..."

"That's exactly what you're saying." Tears roll freely down my cheeks.

"Please," he pushes, taking a step towards me and placing his hands on my shoulders. "That's not what I'm saying at all. I just don't trust him."

"No, you just don't have faith in me as your wife or as a chef." I snarl and break free of his hold.

"Gwen," he calls as I move through the hall, grabbing my bag and my keys as I go. "Where are you going?"

"Away from you."

"Don't be ridiculous." His hand on the door stops me from leaving. "Please, let's just calm down. This has all been blown out of proportion."

"Tell that to my broken heart." My chest deflates as I exhale a shuddering breath.

"Gwen," he whispers, sounding as broken as I feel. "I'm sorry. That's not what I meant."

"Then what did you mean?" I don't look at him. I stare at the lines in the wood of the door, trembling almost violently.

"I just meant that it's possible he wants more and you're not seeing it. Maybe he's asking you to stay, not just because you're good but because he wants you."

"Isn't that the same thing?"

"No, it's just... I'm a man."

"Bravo."

"I know he wants you because there isn't a single man in the world who would get as close to you as he has and not want you."

I laugh harshly. "And what of every other man that works there? Do they all want me too?"

"I don't know, but I don't feel threatened by them because they aren't the male equivalent of you. Kerim could offer you so much more than I can."

My body stills. So this is what it all boils down to? "You're feeling insecure."

"Aren't I allowed?"

"Of course, but not at the expense of my mental health or your own," I snap, finally turning to look at him. He presses his lips to my forehead and wipes away my tears with the back of his hand. "Stop talking about Kerim and I like that. It's not true and if it is then you have to trust me and know that I would never hurt you like that! I swear it. I wouldn't touch Kerim."

"You can't help who you fall in love with, Gwen," he snaps, his tone almost mocking. "If you could, do you honestly think you'd be fucking your dead fiancé's brother? Didn't you promise Caleb that you'd stay away from me? Yet here we are. How much are your promises truly worth?"

Oh my God.

"You didn't just say that," I whisper, feeling devastated. Absolutely devastated. "What the fuck is wrong with you?"

"I'm sorry, I went too far."

"Oh, no, you went the perfect distance." I laugh coldly and rip his hand from the door. "I'm leaving."

"Don't, please," he begs, following me out into the cold. "Come back inside."

"Don't touch me," I shout, ripping free from his grip when his hand circles my wrist.

"Please," he begs, sounding desperate and panicked. "I'm sorry, I couldn't help it. I didn't mean it."

"I can't take this anymore," I say quietly, feeling pain in my heart with every stabbing beat.

Pulling open the door to my car, Nathan grabs the top of it to stop me from closing it after I climb in. "I'm sorry."

"Are you?"

"Don't go. Come back inside. Let me make it up to you."

Snort.

"Gwen, I'm begging you." His voice takes a saddening echo to it. He sounds as close to the verge of tears as I do. "Come back inside. Please. *Please.*"

"No," I say, my eyes front and centre. "You're out of order and I literally can't stand to be around you right now."

"Then I'll stay out of your way. Just don't go…"

I try to pull the door closed.

"Please." He goes to grab my arm but the look I hit him with instantly stops his movement in mid-air. "Where will you go?"

"Oh, I don't know. Maybe I'll run to Kerim, just like I ran to you." I snap and finally manage to pull the door closed. Reversing out of there, I try to ignore the look of devastation on his face but it's impossible. It'll be forever burned onto my retinas.

But I can't simply let go of the fact that he holds such circumstantial things against me. Does he regret it? Does he wish he never made a move on his brother's girl? Is that what this is all about now? He always said that I was his first. Did he mean it?

None of it can be painted that black and white. What happened can't be summed up into a single paragraph. How dare he judge me? He was in on it too. Does he blame himself as much as he seems to be blaming me? Or are his insecurities fuelling a ridiculous notion that wouldn't even cross his mind otherwise? Not that that makes it any better if that's the case.

I just wish he'd snap out of it or at least try to rein it in. I can't play the victim entirely. I have spoken about Kerim too fondly lately and I know that it's not helping, but it is purely innocent. There's nothing between us at all. He's just… my idol or something along those lines. I have so much respect for him. Why does Nathan have to tarnish that? Why does he have to turn it into something dirty and wrong?

CHAPTER SEVENTEEN

<u>Nathan</u>: Please come home. Please. I promise I won't argue anymore. I just want you here.

I read that message at a traffic light and in the distance is a roundabout. I could turn back and continue this, or I could do what he did and stay away for the entire night. I'm not sure what would be better in the long run.

I need ice-cream.

I'm wasting a kid free night with all this moping. Sighing heavily I make a U-turn on the roundabout and drive all the way home.

Nathan, seeming to be watching for me, comes racing out of the house and pulls me into his arms. "I'm sorry."

"Stop." His confusion over my word makes me smile. "You're coming with me for the night."

"Where are we going?"

"For ice cream."

"That sounds excellent," he grins, kissing my moist lips. "Maybe we can take some home with us."

"You're so dirty minded," I giggle, leading him to my car. "I'm driving."

"You're really not," he tells me, pulling me to his. "You're going to sit in the passenger seat and relax."

"Fine, but if you detour I'm not sucking ice-cream off your cock later."

Choking a little, he pulls open my car door and adjusts himself. "Don't tease."

"Hurry up or we won't get my favourite," I call as he rounds the front of the car and folds himself into the driver's seat. I'm relieved that the car is still cool from our previous trip as the outside is so muggy and warm. That's the problem with English weather - when it's hot, it's heavy and damp.

"Thank you for coming back."

"There's a purpose behind my mood swing," I assure him, setting my determined gaze on the road ahead. "Take a left…"

Five minutes later we sit in the staff carpark of my work place. I can tell Nathan isn't pleased by my bringing him here but I couldn't care less.

"You said ice-cream," he murmurs, his brow furrowed with annoyance.

"I wasn't lying about the ice-cream."

"Why are we here?"

"I want you to see my job and meet my co-workers."

"Seriously?"

"We did it for you," I snap, irritated by his attitude. "It's your turn."

"You're right, sorry," he mutters. "Just... don't say anything to Kerim."

"Duh." I take his hand. "Let's go."

"Won't they be too busy?"

"Always," I reply, grinning as we near the building. The beautiful smells waft out of the slightly cracked door. I notice a tin of chillies holding it open and roll my eyes. He shouldn't leave the door open, especially not with food produce. I should purchase a door stop but then I'd be permitting the door to be open.

"Are you sure we're allowed?"

"Stop being a baby." I pull the door open and lead Nathan inside. The glow of the kitchen comes through the light of the glass on the second door. We close the exit behind us and push through.

I smile at the sight of everyone working hard, flipping things at their stations, tossing herbs into pots on the stove, slicing meat ready for cooking. Kerim's orders carry above everyone else's voices.

They haven't noticed us enter, too enthralled by their own world, so I pull Nathan to the private area of the kitchen where customers can't see into and take his jacket.

It's Harold who notices us first and salutes us with two fingers from his chef hat. This draws the eyes of the others and everyone greets me.

"What are you doing in my kitchen on your day off?" Kerim calls over the noise, smiling a little.

"I'm stealing some of your ice-cream."

"It'll cost you."

I roll my eyes and take Nathan's hand. "Come on, to the freezer."

When I slide the large, heavy metal door open, Nathan blinks with astonishment. "This is huge. It puts our little freezer to shame."

"Right?" I laugh and wrap my arms around myself. "See, we don't serve ice-cream normally unless requested and even then it's just the standard vanilla over there." I point to the large tubs stacked in the corner. "We make those in bulk once a month."

"It's freezing in here. How can you stand it?"

"You get used to it," I grin and push a large metal shelving unit on wheels to one side, revealing a narrower shelving unit as tall as me, hiding several tubs of homemade ice-cream. "This is Kerim's secret stash. He makes the *best* ice-cream in the world."

I notice a flicker of jealousy in Nathan's eyes and nudge his arm with my own.

He really has a problem with Kerim.

"Choose your poison." I pick up a tub of white chocolate and grab a bag of fudge pieces for melting. Nathan chooses the same and we quickly exit the freezer.

"My favourite." Kerim snatches the tub away the second I exit the freezer and grins childishly. "Guys, it's ice-cream time. Gwen's paying."

When they cheer collectively, the entire restaurant looks over to see what has made us all so happy.

"Paying?" Nathan whispers, but Kerim heard him.

"Not to worry, my friend. She only has to make the next batch of ice-cream and clean up the mess afterwards."

"First person to touch Kerim's ice-cream loses." I add, giggling.

"Yes and she's lost for the past... three months now?" Kerim grins and reaches out a hand to Nathan. "How are you? I am sorry for not being in contact; you know how time quickly flies."

"I understand; I'm guilty of the same. Gwen has been keeping me up to date." Nathan tucks me under his arm possessively. Kerim, thankfully seeming unaffected by the possessive display, opens the ice-cream, grabs a few small bowls and begins scooping the amazing frozen treat into each one. I pull away from the man I love and pop the bag of fudge into the microwave.

"Too me," Kerim states, smiling easily.

"Me too," I correct him after snorting at his jumbled response. When he realises, he hits my hand with the lid of the ice-cream.

"Your wife is a bully. Forever teasing me."

Shrugging, I cross my arms over my chest and respond, "It's vengeance for all of the yelling."

"Yelling?" Nathan's voice has darkened. I wince.

"It's a kitchen, we yell. We have to; the pressure is crazy," Patience puts in and I'm grateful for the help. "We all yell. Even Gwen."

"Gwen yells?" Nathan doesn't look as though he believes it. "I think I've only ever heard her yell twice in the entire time I've known her."

"Ah," Kerim chuckles. "She has more tolerance for you than me. That is all. This is good. But it makes sense; her passion is in this kitchen." Why did he have to word it like that? "Passion sparks fire in a person, agree?"

Nathan nods but looks as though he wants to kill him. I sense his look isn't missed by Kerim either, even though he doesn't show any signs of noticing.

The microwave pings so I grab the fudge with a gloved hand and begin squirting it onto the ice cream in each bowl.

I love how quickly the top layer of ice cream begins to melt; it makes it taste so much more delicious. The contrast of the warm fudge on the cold, melting treat is divine.

"Oh my gosh," I hum happily as the first bite melts in my mouth. "Literally there is no greater taste in the world than this ice-cream."

Nathan seems reluctant to agree but I can see that it has even affected him in a similar way.

"I'll throw in unlimited ice-cream and fudge if you consider my offer," Kerim tells me quietly, stepping into our bubble. His sudden change in demeanour hasn't gone unnoticed and I feel curious eyes on us.

"We'll need to go over a few things but…" I glance at Nathan out of the corner of my eye and pray he doesn't get upset over this. "I'm definitely interested. It's an honour to work with you."

Kerim beams from ear to ear. "In that case, I will pay the price for the ice-cream and consider this a victory celebration." When he winks at me, I remain passive. Nathan looks about ready to kill and if Kerim has noticed, he isn't letting on. "I must work. Enjoy your ice-cream. Take the tub if you like."

"Chef," Harold calls, waving him over.

"Duty calls." Kerim grips my shoulders and squeezes before taking Nathan's hand once more and promising, "I'll be in touch."

"See you later, guys," I call, taking the tub of ice-cream under one arm with the fudge resting on top.

They call a jumbled, "Bye, see you later, don't get pregnant."

I'm not sure who yelled the last part but I flip the room off anyway.

"See?" I say to Nathan as I walk backwards ahead of him. "Kerim is just Kerim. There's no need to be paranoid."

"We shall see," he mumbles, grabbing me and pulling me to him. "You have chocolate on your bottom lip." When he sucks my lip into his mouth, I tremble and melt faster than the fudge in the microwave. "Tasty."

"Stop teasing me."

"Says you." Grinning, he kisses me again, deeper this time, and grabs my arse with one hand as the other keeps my head pinned in place. I clench and tingle in my womb, especially when I'm backed up to the wall and his lips travel down my neck. There's little I can do to reciprocate or ward him off because of the tub of ice-cream in my hands.

"Nathan," I whisper when his hand that was at my neck now grasps my breast over my shirt. "Seriously, you're killing me."

Smiling, he pulls back, kisses my nose and takes me to the car. I need a fan. I can't recall ever feeling so hot. What came over him and how can I make it come over him again?

And then, lying together in bed, after coming down from one of the best orgasms we've shared, Nathan whispers, "We're passionate, right?"

"If you don't think what we just did is passionate, there's something wrong with you."

Nuzzling my neck and crushing my body under his, we sleep. There's something so soothing about drifting off with him still partly inside of me, connecting us in the most intimate way.

Chapter Eighteen

Awoken softly would be an understatement; soft kisses and a gentle massage of my limbs stirs me from slumber. I sigh with contentment. What did I do to get so lucky?

"Morning," I hum when he moves to my feet and rubs them with his whole hands. "That tickles."

"Shh," he whispers and pushes his fingers back up to the backs of my knees. "I made you breakfast."

"You did?"

"It's keeping warm. Come on, shower," he softly demands and moves away.

I open my eyes and stretch into the mattress, face down and feeling amazing. "What time is it?"

"A little after nine."

"No lie in then?"

"I have something planned."

This piques my attention. "Oh?"

Smiling his handsome smile, he helps me from the bed, laughs at my messy hair and directs me to the bathroom. "Go shower before I ravage you and make us late."

The tingling between my legs definitely doesn't mind that happening.

"Seriously," I grumble after climbing into the car. "What kind of parents don't sleep all day the one time they don't have their kids?"

"The kind that are passionate, fun and love each other so much they want to do things together."

"Yes, like... I don't know, sleeping perhaps?"

He laughs and tugs on my over the shoulder braid. "You're cute."

"Don't call me cute when I'm grumpy."

"You're not grumpy; I've seen you grumpy." He flashes his tongue at me. "This isn't grumpy Gwen; this is hungry and needs a coffee Gwen."

"Is there a difference?"

"Majorly. When you're grumpy, food and coffee don't fix it."

He has a point. I sigh and reach across to stroke the back of his hair with my fingertips. "Your hair is so soft. Let it grow like it used to be when I was pregnant with Dillan."

His brow quirks. "It was dishevelled."

"It was wild. I loved when you could tuck it behind your ears." Pulling gently, I try to do just that but it doesn't quite reach past the curve. "It suited you." Then I scratch my nails over the stubble on his jaw. "Keep this too; you have no idea how sexy you look."

His smile broadens, showing his teeth, and his eyes crinkle at the edges. I love this look on him too.

"I see girls looking at you whenever we go anywhere together."

He hums, concentrating on the road but still listening.

"I hate it and love it all at once."

"Sometimes I wish you were ugly so I wouldn't have to constantly compete for your affections."

"You have all of my affections," I giggle, smacking his arm playfully. "You're my world."

"Then marry me already."

My eyes roll of their own accord but my smile doesn't fade. "Then let's plan it."

Large fingers encompass my wrist and pull my hand to his thigh. "I'm ready when you are."

"Good. So, wherever we're going today we'll finally decide on our top two venues and then next week we will go and view said venues; how's that?"

"Sounds perfect." His mood becomes even lighter than before. "You're going to love what I have planned for us today."

"It does involve coffee, right?" When he doesn't respond I choke out a panicked, "*Right?*"

"Duh."

"You scared me then."

"I know."

I poke my tongue out at him and open the window. I love the feel of the breeze through my hair.

"It's such a gorgeous day. We've had a great summer this year." Nathan comments as he tweaks the dial of the radio.

"That we have. It's a shame we've not had time to spend it together."

"That's changing from now." Nathan insists. "We'll make more time for each other."

"Promise?" He doesn't get the chance to answer because my head is hanging half out of the car window as I cry, "LEE VALLEY?" I turn to him, lit with excitement. "Ice skating?"

"I owe you a session."

"Oh my god! Horse riding and ice skating? Who are you?"

"Sit down." He pulls me back by my shoulder and quickly parks in one of the spots at the far end of the carpark. It's something he always does. He says it's all good exercise. I disagree. There's no such thing as good exercise unless it's ice skating of course.

"I am so freaking excited." I think he can tell by how badly I'm grinning. My entire face hurts.

"I can tell."

"We should make this a monthly thing!"

"Woah now," he laughs nervously. "Let's not jump in head first. We don't know how bad we are yet."

"I bet you'll be a natural!"

"I highly doubt it."

The first mistake Nathan made was stepping onto the ice without holding onto the side. He fell straight onto his arse and I howled with laughter, though I shouldn't have because karma was quick to serve me an ice cold dish of pain. My laughter knocked me off balance and I slid to the ground beside him, no doubt bruising my rear.

Nathan laughed as hard as I did and we somehow manoeuvred our way back up to standing.

Skaters fly by at lightning speed, their bodies seeming to fly. Even little kids have this better than us. I don't care though; every time my ankles wobble I just feel more joy. I will conquer this ice.

Nathan clings desperately to the side as I finally find my footing and dare to enter the oval with the others. It takes me a while to pick up my speed but when I do, I'm gone. Shakily, yet confidently, I whiz past people, feeling the cold prickle my face, feeling proud and free. I totally forget about Nathan still clinging hopelessly to the side.

When I make a full circle back to him, I find him chatting to an unknown man who seems to be giving him tips on how to not fall on his arse. This only makes me laugh even more. Nathan sees me, shakes his head with amusement and yells, "I'm the natural, huh?"

"You can't have it all, Baby. Gotta leave something for me to be good at," I giggle, winking at him and slamming to a stop against the wall in front of him.

"Don't do that again; you'll break your bloody arms," Nathan snaps, concerned but not concerned enough to let go of the rail.

"Hi," I pant, holding my hand out to the man in a red jumper, white scarf around his neck and proper figure skating boots on his feet.

He shakes my hand and smiles. "Hi, I'm Dean; just helping your guy to find his footing."

"I know your accent!" I comment excitedly. "You're from Hull! I'd know that twang anywhere."

"You'd be right," he laughs and does a half twist on his skates to face Nathan. "You need to bend your legs at the knees."

"Go," Nathan waves his hand at me, "while Dean helps me try to find my dignity."

"Nath," I whisper, worried I've upset him.

His smile is reassuring and so soft and sweet. "Go. You look peaceful out there. I'll catch up."

"You sure?"

"I'm sure."

"Go," Dean laughs, giving me a gentle push with a hand on my shoulder. "I'll have him skating in no time."

I don't need telling again. If Nathan wants this time to learn, I'll let him have it. I know he doesn't like to look like a failure in front of me and I just know this is exactly what he'll be thinking if I stay.

CHAPTER EIGHTEEN

Besides I really am loving this. I'm not graceful at all but I feel it. I almost slip a few times but I stay close enough to the rails to stop myself. Every time I circle past Nathan, he's slowly made his way to a new section of rail. This makes me so happy. Poor Dean is still with him too. I notice them laugh at something and feel an immense amount of pride and joy. Nathan is doing something out of character; he's actually being nice to somebody other than me.

Before I know it, I feel a hand in mine and I'm skating by my future husband, laughing and giggling over every near fall, over every near collision. Also, I'm inwardly celebrating that he and Dean promised to seek each other out. Dean is new and has very few local friends and Nathan is Nathan and has no social life beyond me or work.

This really has been the best weekend of my life.

Unfortunately, what goes up, must come down. That's the saying, I think.

Chapter Nineteen

I RECEIVE A PHONE call on the way to work and my curious mind, despite the fact it says spam, doesn't hesitate to answer. I transfer the call to Bluetooth and switch up the volume. My eyes remain firmly on all of my mirrors and the street ahead.

"Gwen speaking," I sing song, my tone high and cheery.

"Hello, Guinevere."

I recognise the voice but I can't be sure who it is. "Sorry, the signal is choppy; who is it please?"

"My apologies, it's Jackson. Are you available to talk?"

"Oh! Of course, sorry, I'm free."

"Great." He clears his throat. "I know you decided not to go through with my services but seeing as you already paid, I just couldn't leave a job half done."

"That's fine," I smile, confident that he found nothing.

"Normally I'd send my clients a file with details of when and where the person they're looking in on have been, but I don't feel I need to in this case."

Even though I knew this would be the answer, my heart swells with relief and tears sting my eyes. "He's a good man, isn't he?"

"Yes, beyond his crazy work schedule, you, his kids, and visits with his mother, he doesn't have a social life. No texts, calls, anything that can't be linked to you, work or close family."

That swelling in my heart freezes and my head feels fuzzy. "Just a second, I need to pull over."

"Certainly, should I call back?"

"No!" I practically yell. "I need to... just one second."

He goes silent as I pull over with trembling hands on the wheel, almost cutting off a man on a bike in the process. Fuck.

"Sorry, I'm good now." Swallowing the lump in my throat I nervously ask, "His mother?"

"Yes."

"Not my mother?" Please, please be my mother.

"No, a Mrs Patricia Weston."

"You're sure?"

"It's my job to be," he says a little haughtily.

"Sorry, I'm just a bit... how often do they meet?"

He goes quiet. "I'm sensing something here."

"You'd be right," I confirm, feeling my anger build, not with Jackson though. Definitely not with Jackson. "How often have they been meeting?"

"Every few days."

"Oh my god." That *liar*. "Every few days?"

"Give or take. Would you like the list? I took pictures too."

"Please, if you would. I'd appreciate it." My eyes sting with threatening tears. "Are they friendly?"

"Definitely," he states, leaving no room to question. "Though he remained distant, your children seemed familiar with her..."

"WHAT?" I screech. "This can't be happening."

"I shouldn't pry, but..."

"She's an awful, horrid woman."

The phone crackles on his end as he seems to move, probably to get comfortable. This is all just another day in the office to him. "Do you need my assistance further? I could squeeze you in if necessary."

"No, no, I'm okay. I can take it from here. Thank you."

"If you're sure."

"I'll call you if not. Please send over the photos if you can, as soon as possible. I need to see this for myself."

"No problem, I'll send it all over immediately. Are you certain you don't need further assistance?"

Another thought jumps to mind. "Do you by any chance know when they'll be meeting next?"

"I do actually; from his messages I'd say Wednesday."

Wow... this private detective stuff really is invasive. "Wednesday?"

"Noon." When he says this I have to choke back a sob. That's the day Nathan is supposed to be going to a parent and child event with the kids while I work. He's done nothing but lie to me. "I'm already placing it into the email with the rest of the information I have. I'm sorry this didn't have the ending I expected."

"Me too," I murmur, embarrassed by my reaction, so I hang up as swiftly as possible. "Okay, deep breaths. It's all just one huge misunderstanding."

Then the email comes through and I'm unsure whether or not I want to open it or remain blissfully ignorant.

Too late now. When the email comes I don't hesitate to subject myself to an entire world of pain and rage. There he is, just as Jackson said, in the park with *my* children and that vile bitch. What the hell is going on? Is this why he brought her up? Did he really want to tell me this? What is wrong with him?

I scream and bash the steering wheel with my fists. Have my children been around the abuser too? Or just the bitch? I need to know everything!

My phone rings, startling me from my steering wheel slapping and inside the car screaming alone match.

"Shit," I curse, slamming my hand again against the steering wheel again. Pressing the button on the phone, I quickly blurt, "I'm sorry, I'm on my way."

"You better be!" Is all Kerim responds and then hangs up.

I'm late. I've never been late.

Fuck you, Nathan.

I type a text to Nathan reading, 'How's Patricia?' but with a shaky thumb I press delete and let my head fall back heavily against the headrest. A tear falls in the same spot my thumb just vacated on my phone so I wipe the screen on my thigh and drop my phone onto the passenger seat. I need to calm myself enough to drive to work, though I really want to call in sick. It wouldn't be a lie; I'm one wave of nausea away from throwing up.

What am I going to do? I can't allow this. What is going through his head?

It takes me a short while to gather the strength to unfold my weakening body out of the car. The cool breeze helps the pain in my head but not the pain stabbing through my heart.

I keep trying to convince myself that there's some reasonable explanation to this but I won't allow myself to permit him to lie to me so badly. He's had my children around that monster. What is wrong with him?

There's no excusing this, even if there is a reasonable explanation, which I doubt there is. There is no rationalising his lying to me. How will we get past this? It feels impossible. I'm not sure I'll be able to look him in the eye.

"Don't be late again!" Kerim shouts the second I step through the door. "I should send you home but Patience is ill."

"Sorry, Chef," I say quietly as I pass him, my head down.

I get changed in record time and put myself into the kitchen, relieved to see I don't have to oversee anything today. I'm not sure I have the willpower or strength.

Preparing food for meals I should have finished already, I dive into my work, distracting myself from the realities of life.

Kerim blanks me. I can tell he's upset with me and rightfully so. My home life shouldn't be interfering with my work. I've never seen anybody else in this kitchen come in late because of a marriage spat or similar. There's still so much growing up I must do. Maybe Nathan wouldn't lie to me if I wasn't so naïve.

The day goes by and I'm proud of myself for not checking my phone a single time.

When the restaurant begins to empty and cleaning in the kitchen begins, I feel trapped. I want to go home to my kids but I know that the second I step through the front door, everything is going to change. I'm terrified.

My colleagues start filtering out of the exit, saying tired goodbyes. I hang back and wait for Kerim to exit his office. I owe him an apology.

"You're still here?" He blinks, his eyes red rimmed and tired.

I nod unnecessarily. "I feel bad for being late, especially seeing how busy we were."

"It happens." He waves me off and leans back against the wall. "Is all okay?"

Smiling, a lie on my face, I respond, "Of course, I was just a bit ill."

"I think something is going around."

"Yeah." My hands tuck my hair behind my ears. "I'll see you tomorrow."
"Good, on time?"
"On time."
"Have a good night, Gwen."
"Goodnight, Kerim."

He walks me to the door and watches me to my car. Just before I climb in he yells, "Don't be late!"

"I won't." Although I'm not sure what is going to happen now with regard to childcare.

Why can't my life just be as easy as it was while I was pregnant with Emily? I was so happy then. Things were calm, stable, settled. Nathan was a dream. We were in heaven.

How do I approach this?

The man I love and trusted with my life is a liar and has been taking my children around a monster without speaking to me. What is wrong with him? Why would he hurt us like this?

I make it home and the house is dark. This is good. I don't think I can fake it tonight. What I need is sleep and a clearer mind. Maybe I should write a list to tackle as I talk to him. Will it do any good?

I'm so terrified of everything that is going on with us. I have this horrible churning in my gut that whatever happens next is going to break us so badly there will be no return.

All I can see in my future is myself alone, two kids to two different fathers, a failed career and grey hairs before my time. So bleak and scary.

Have I given up on him already? What else can I do? The trust between us is shattered. I don't see how this can be excused or rationalised.

Every part of me wants to avoid Nathan right now. I've never felt this way before. I don't want to climb into bed beside him, though I know I have to. Until I figure how to go about this, I need to act normal. He can't know that I know. I need to see this for myself and catch him with her. He'll be too flustered to lie anymore and I'll be too angry and focused for him to convince me that this is my fault.

After I reach our bedroom, I stare at his sleeping form and visualise myself shaking the answers out of him. Words would fall from his skin, answering all my questions with perfect truth. If only questions could be answered this way.

Nathan grumbles quietly in his sleep, sprawled on his front, his face directed towards the window. I slip out of my clothes and into my pyjamas as silently as possible.

Every grunt that Nathan seems to make in his sleep has me wanting the couch. The thought of his arms around me at this point makes me want to cry.

Carefully I pull back the blanket and tuck myself into a ball right on the edge, as far away from him as possible. My mind, though a torrent of thoughts, soon settles in its exhaustion and darkness claims me.

"Daaaaaaaa!" Dillan squeals and I feel Nathan shift beside me. "DAAAAAAADDDDYYY!"

"I'll go," Nathan whispers and kisses the shell of my ear. "Don't open your eyes; you had a late night."

I do as I'm told, mostly because my eyes are filling with tears. How can such a perfect man be so imperfect? Does he know how badly his lies are going to break my heart? Does he honestly think I'm never going to find out?

Staying in bed because I just don't have the strength to exit it yet, I listen as he chases Dillan around downstairs. Emily must still be sleeping, the lazy git that she is. Part of me wants to go back to before the phone call yesterday. Why did I have to answer it?

When I do finally get up it's as Nathan is coming to collect Emily. He kisses my cheek, pinches the skin of my hip and opens the bathroom door for me.

I can do this. Chanting this to my reflection in the mirror, I grip the basin with both hands and then mentally pep talk myself. He's been living a lie for months now; I can handle just three more days.

Chapter Twenty

The days don't exactly fly by but it's easy enough to pretend that things are normal. That is until Wednesday comes around. Watching him leave with my children, knowing where he's going with them, makes me want to claw at something. He seemed so normal, so at ease with his lies.

But then again, so did I. When I told him I was definitely working tonight, it fell from my lips so easily and tasted bitter on my tongue. I've never been a liar and when I've tried I've never been good at it. Because of this, he could sense something was wrong. I could tell because he kept giving me glances when he thought I wasn't looking. Fortunately, he didn't bring up his outing today beyond reminding me of the time and I didn't ask because I was worried I wouldn't be able to keep my cool. It sliced through me like a knife through butter when he acted as though today was just another normal day.

Even though I'm inwardly raging, I manage to calm myself down enough to follow him to his destination. I already know where he's going, but I don't want to risk missing any changes in his plans so I stick as close behind him as possible without him noticing.

My heart is such a frantic melody, I feel like I'm the one doing something wrong and maybe I'm going about this completely the wrong way, but I can't help it. I'm doing this alone. Maybe I should have spoken to somebody first, Sasha or Tommy or even my mum. I just don't feel as though they'd understand without knowing Nathan's background and I'd never out him like that to them.

"Fuck," I cry as we finally pull into a playground in Edmonton, London, quite far from where we live and never an area I must cut through to get to work so there's no risk of me catching him.

He put a lot of thought into this web of lies.

Parking isn't too difficult and I wait for him to get himself and my babies out before I pull into my chosen spot, only a few cars down from his. I love seeing how much he loves the kids; he's holding Dillan's hand as he skips along beside him, kicking up the grass as he goes. Emily is balanced on his hip; she's lazy and so happy to be carried everywhere at the moment. Her dad is too happy to oblige.

Climbing from my car, I rest against it, watching as he cuts across the grass to the playground. Kids run riot, their parents close by. He's never brought me to this park before, though it's not that different from the one near our house.

The hairs on the back of my neck stand up on end and I know that I'm in the presence of a demon. I feel her before I see her and when I do see her I have to press my back against the side of my car to remind myself why it's a bad idea to launch myself at her and rip her hair out.

The kids don't rush to her, both too eager to play in the park. This makes me feel a little bit smug. At least she hasn't fooled them, not yet anyway.

Nathan doesn't go to embrace her either. They share a few words. She smiles at him warmly and places a hand on his arm. He shifts away, clearly uncomfortable with the contact.

This is insane. Why is she back in his life? What does she want from him?

I feel like a crazy stalker as I watch them interact, trying to build the courage to let them know that I'm there. Should I? Or should I just let them have their hour and then approach Nathan later?

Tears fall from my eyes as I try to figure out my reasoning behind all my choices and all of his.

"What am I doing?" I ask myself and slam the palm of my hand onto the roof of my car. As I pull the door open and climb back in, I hold tightly to the steering wheel until whiteness bleeds into my knuckles. Putting the car in gear after turning the key, I give one last glance to the man I thought I knew. Unfortunately, as if my scent carried on the wind, Nathan whips around and his startled eyes hit mine. I see them fill with regret and panic but I don't linger.

"Gwen!" I see him mouth and take a step in my direction.

CHAPTER TWENTY

I should drive away but I can't find the courage to, so instead I wait for him to reach my car. He pulls on the handle as I keep my eyes ahead on the children. That vile bitch is watching us, her face twisted with faux concern.

"Open the door," Nathan orders softly.

I wind the window down instead, still refusing to look at him.

"I can explain but I need to get back to the kids." When I don't look at him, he reaches through the window to guide my face in his direction. I pull away; his fingers against my skin feel poisonous. "Baby," his plea is a mournful whisper. "I'm sorry."

"I know," I murmur and put the car into gear. "So am I."

"Why are you sorry?" He leans forward so as to see me better and I lean sideways so as to avoid him better.

"Because I don't think I'll ever be able to forgive you for this." Tears fall and a sob tears its way up my throat, clogging it with a lump I just can't swallow.

"I…" He presses his forehead to his hands that rest on the empty window frame. "I'll get the kids and meet you at home."

"No," I snap, shaking my head, my eyes on my beautiful babies racing around the park with such joy. His mum stands off to the side looking awkward and too formal for a park. She looks suited for a wedding party, not a muddy play area. "I'll get the kids."

"The car seats are in my car; it makes no sense to swap it all over when I'm going straight home to you," he implores, his voice low and soft.

I nod my agreement, still avoiding eye contact. As much as I want to snatch my children away from this situation, it wouldn't be good for them.

He backs up, still staring at my profile before turning and calling for the kids. When he stops to speak to his mother and points at the car, I see her place a hand on her chest. Whatever she says has Nathan shaking his head and pulling away as she reaches for him. She looks over at me and the glare she throws my way is pure poison, so I raise my middle finger and smile sardonically at the stuck-up bitch.

I also don't leave until Nathan has my kids back in the car and is taking the lead home. I never should have let it get this far. It's unfair that the kids are now suffering because of us. They'll forgive me when I pull out the craft box. I hope.

My home seems such a soul sucking place as I walk through the door with Emily in my arms. Nathan and I haven't spoken and we don't speak as we cross the threshold and place the children in the living room. As silently promised, I pull out the baby safe craft box and smile when they cheer with glee.

Nathan waits for me in the hallway, his face a grim mask.

"You need to leave," I demand softly, not meeting his eyes.

"What?" He breathes, his body stiffening immediately. "We just need to talk..."

"I don't want to listen." My whispered words fall from my mouth faster than tears fall from my eyes.

"Gwen..." His hands cup my face. I don't push him away; I let him search my eyes. I want him to see the pain he has inflicted. "I'm sorry I lied."

"I guess that's okay then." My voice is a dull note as my hands wrap around his wrists to either side of my face. "It's all fixed."

"You don't understand."

I push his hands outwards away from me and wipe the wetness from under my eyes.

"Leave."

There's a loud knock at the door. It recurs for at least seven seconds before either of us make a move to answer it. Instead we stand, staring at one another, my stare full of heartbreak, Nathan's full of regret.

When he opens the door I see him close his eyes and his lips thin to a white line before I look from his profile to the person knocking.

"What is she doing here?" I angrily growl, my eyes on Nathan and not on the hideous creature standing on my doorstep.

"I don't know." He blows out a breath and barks, "Did you follow us?"

"I wanted to help." His mother responds and I scoff incredulously.

"You're not helping," Nathan whispers and goes to close the door, but her hand reaches out and presses against the wood.

"We have a huge bridge to build." She says this to me, her eyes gentle and seeming sincere.

"Well then you can both build one together, behind my back. You seem to have been doing a brilliant job so far!"

"We really need to talk about this," Nathan implores, turning to me with his hand still on the door handle. "Let me explain."

CHAPTER TWENTY

My jaw hits the floor. "Explain what, exactly? I know what's been going on and I'm beyond caring why."

"Please."

"You don't get it," I snap. "The fact you didn't trust me to be understanding is..." I glare at his mother. "I'm not doing this in front of *her*."

"You're being very childish," she remarks.

How dare she? I'm being childish?

"Are you kidding me?" I snarl and Nathan's hand grips my trembling bicep. "Get off."

"This is spiralling; you're getting mad." His hand tries to pull me back into the house. "Mother, you need to leave."

"You both need to leave." I pull my arm free and peer into the room where the kids are drawing all over a black mat with their multi-coloured blocks of chalk.

"I didn't deceive you because I wanted to." Nathan completely ignores my wishes. I can feel a stress headache begin to throb in my temples. "We didn't." He points between himself and his mother. "I didn't mean to cause you pain."

"Well you did."

"And what of the pain you inflicted on Nathan?" Patricia puts in, her face twisted with a scowl.

"Sorry?" Confusion is the most prominent thing I feel at present, followed shortly by anger. "Have you been discussing our relationship with her?"

"No." Nathan's eyes widen. "What are you talking about? What pain?"

"He doesn't need to tell me; every time I see him it's been obvious. He's always so tired, especially considering you won't accept help from outside sources. Poor Nathan is running himself ragged," she sneers, sounding every bit as pompous as she looks.

"Excuse me?" I hiss, my fists clenched by my side.

"Mother," Nathan snaps. "That's not true. It was I who refused help."

"A real woman would have noticed and called for help anyway. There's no excuse."

How dare she question my parenting? How *dare* she? "I'm going to punch her in the fucking face," I snarl, taking an aggressive step towards her.

"Gwen." Nathan grabs my arm to stop me from unleashing my wrath. "That's hardly helping."

"Sorry?" I turn to him, my mouth hanging open in horror. "You're defending her?"

"No, of course not, I just…"

"You just what?"

"She's changed."

"Because she wants something from you," I yell after relinquishing a harsh laugh. Why can't he see reason? "She allowed you to be abused for years."

"Abused?" Patricia questions, acting the picture of innocence.

"She was under a lot of stress with Caleb's health."

"THAT'S NO FUCKING EXCUSE!"

"Gwen…"

"No!" I raise my hand to silence him and turn to the evil woman in my presence. I hate myself for losing control but I can't help it. "If you even step within a million feet of my children again, I will kill you." She blanches, probably seeing how serious I am and I am deadly serious. No pun intended. "You stay away from them."

Nathan frowns. "It's my decision too."

"No, I'm taking that away from you until you come to your senses."

"Excuse me?" His tone is dark and dangerous.

"You heard me, Nathan. I take away your rights, all of them, until you grow the fuck up."

"You wouldn't dare," he spits bitterly, stepping into my space. "They're my kids too."

"And you're willing to endanger them."

"You can't keep them from me."

"Oh I can. If you insist this vile being must see them, then you can take me to court and trust me when I say I will air EVERYTHING." His face visibly pales and I hate myself for hurting him this way. "To protect my kids, there's little I wouldn't do."

"If you take those kids away from me, Guinevere, I will *never* forgive you."

"And if you choose her over us, I'll never forgive you either." I respond honestly, hurt by his words so badly that tears spill down my cheeks as I speak mine. "But then again, after your deceptions I'm not sure I could forgive you anyway."

"You're being unfair," he says, gripping my arms to stop me from turning away. "You're being entirely unreasonable."

"If that's true then the courts will see that too, won't they?"

"I can't believe this is happening."

"Me neither," Patricia snaps, her hands on her hips.

"Just go!" Nathan yells at her and then closes the door in her surprised face. "Gwen, let's calm down. This has all been entirely blown out of proportion."

"So you keep saying." I move away from him, checking on the kids again. Dillan spots me and smiles before throwing a plastic tube that rattles at me. Smiling, I wrinkle my nose up at him and then return my attention to Nathan. "I need you to leave."

"I'm not leaving you."

"You don't have a choice." Hands come to touch me but I step backwards. "Leave."

"Why? I'm sorry, but you have to understand it from my point of view. I know how much you hate her."

"With good reason!" I cry. "My God… I don't even know who you are anymore."

"I could say the same."

"You don't trust me with something so important that you lie to my face to conceal it." I prod his chest. He snatches my hand the second I do and holds it tightly to him. "Let go."

"Listen…"

"No. I'm done listening."

"You haven't started yet."

"You're right." Yanking free from him, I walk to the door and fumble with the key to unlock it for ten seconds before I realise it's already unlocked. "The time for listening was months ago, before you started sneaking around."

"To see my mother, not to have an affair."

"And after all she has done, I'm not entirely sure what's worse."

I yank the door open but his hand comes over my shoulder and presses it shut again. "We've hardly seen each other; I didn't know how you'd receive it all."

"If you want to have a relationship with that bitch then by all means, go ahead, but how dare you bring my kids into it."

"Stop calling them your kids; they're our kids and I'd never do anything to hurt them."

I shake my head. "Once upon a time I'd have believed that."

He spins me around and presses me back against the door, violently enough to shock me but not hurt me. "You question my parenting?"

"I question your sanity and I also question your love and respect."

"My love and respect?" His eyes twinkle with anger. "I break my back to make you happy!"

"Wow," I breathe, hardly able to believe my own ears. "You break your back to make me happy? You say that as though I've asked for it or as though it's a bad thing you're forced to do?"

"Now you're just picking a fight."

"I just want you to leave."

"Do you really?"

"Yes."

"Prove it."

"Is this suddenly a game to you?" I snap. "What part of 'I don't trust you anymore' is so hard to grasp?"

"I'll regain your trust."

"I don't want you to!" I yell, this time shoving his chest so he steps backwards out of my space.

His handsome face falls blank and his chin raises defiantly. "You don't want me?"

"I don't know you."

"You don't *want* me?" He repeats harshly. "You don't trust me?"

"No."

His hand snags the collar of his jacket and yanks it down, revealing the scar that he received two blissful years ago. "You don't trust this?"

"I can't believe you're holding this against me."

Ignoring my words he spits, "If you truly don't trust me, return the ring."

My heart falters painfully and for a moment I worry it has stopped. The finality of what he's asking hurts but my hand immediately reaches for my ring finger and begins to twist and tug the smooth piece of jewellery over my knuckles.

His breathing stops and watery eyes come to mine. "That was too easy." He yanks the ring from my hand and throws it onto the ground behind him. "Too easy. You didn't want this, did you?"

I move to the right but he grips my forearms and pushes them up to my chest, pinning me against the wall.

"You didn't want any of this. That's why you put off marrying me. You were going to leave me; I remember. I've always had my doubts. We never came to a conclusion on any of it before the fire. You got pregnant."

I try to tug free as his hands hold tighter to my wrists, causing a burning discomfort to stretch my skin. "Let go of me."

He doesn't; he continues his ridiculous heart wrenching ramblings. "We almost died. That's the only reason you stayed with me, isn't it? That and because of Emily? Did I force your hand? Did you feel guilty that we almost died?"

I've never seen this side to him before. I don't know what to do. I feel panicked as he holds me tighter still, crushing my wrists in his hands to my chest.

"I could never be him."

"Nathan, you're hurting me," I say calmly, trying to diffuse the situation. There has never been a time like this in our relationship that I've felt scared of him, not since I found out about his life of abuse and he punched the wall beside my head. Was that a warning of things to come?

"And now, now you just throw me away so easily." He releases my wrists, not wincing when I rub one and then the other to help relieve the ache. "Now you've found an untainted man who can cook, somebody you share *passion* with. Yet another perfect fucking heart throb for Gwen, just like Caleb was."

"Stop," I order, trying to escape the cage of his arms.

"You didn't even hesitate!" He shouts and I hear the pain in his voice. "It's clear now though. I'll become the weekend dad, looking after *your* kids while you go and fuck my friend. Something tells me that was your plan all along."

My hand whips around and with a loud crack it connects with his cheek. My palm tingles and aches with the force of it and Nathan staggers back a step with the force of his head turning.

We both hear a peculiar crunching sound with his step and both of us look down as he lifts his booted foot, revealing a bent and broken ring.

"Figures," he laughs and bends to pick up the broken sign of our commitment. "If that's not a sign then I don't know what is. Maybe I can make it into a charm and you can put it on your necklace besides Caleb's ring."

"You've lost your mind," I sob, rubbing my chest with the very hand I struck him with. He's never been so cruel in all of the time that we've been together.

"Probably." He pockets the damaged ring and stares at me in the eyes. I can't tell what he's thinking or feeling. The carefully guarded mask that he once used constantly is in place. I'm too angry to try and tear it off. "As promised, I'll leave."

"I think that's best."

"Daddy!" Dillan comes diving into the hallway and immediately latches onto his father's leg. Emily toddles in shortly afterwards, covered in chalk. I manage to laugh a little at the state of her. I'm unsure how; I've never felt worse. "Emy pull ma hair."

"Emily," I chastise when Nathan doesn't say anything. Upon looking up, I notice his swollen, sad yet still achingly beautiful eyes on me. "Just go, Nathan."

"As you wish," he hisses and when his breath hitches, my chest stabs with the most powerful ache. "I love you with every fibre of my being, Guinevere. Why can't you just feel the same?"

He exits the house, leaving me winded and cold and none of it is because of the breeze.

"Daddy gone now?"

"He's gone to work," I lie and lift my boy into my arms.

"Yes," he says cutely as his little hands stroke the back of my hair. "Daddy work with sparkly."

"That's right, baby." My teeth find my trembling lower lip and pin it between them.

"Sparkly, shiny, wings and waces."

"Shall we tidy the room?" I whisper and nuzzle my nose against his.

What am I going to do about work? How will I explain this to anybody?

The night passes slowly and I'm relieved when the children go to bed, though not so relieved when I notice Nathan hasn't been in touch at all. I'm not sure why I'm expecting him to. I guess I just feel wronged and feel as though he should be grovelling a little. It's messed up, I know that. The last thing I want to do is inflict pain on him but I need to follow my heart and head and both of those aren't in this relationship right now. I can't be with a liar. It hurts too much. Caleb damaged me for life.

Nathan's words swim around my mind, echoing over and over again. Does he truly feel so little for me?

Does he really think I only wanted him out of obligation to the fact he nearly died and I was pregnant with his child?

Why has he never spoken to me about these worries? It's unfair that he's suddenly blaming me for all of this now without giving me any chance to defend myself. I love him, with all of my heart I love him. How can he not see that? He makes me happier than anyone. Even Caleb. Every moment with Nathan is full of such fiery passionate sparks. It's just a shame he can't get past his insecurities for long enough to realise that.

<u>Gwen</u>: Can you by any chance have the kids while I work tomorrow?

<u>Jeanine</u>: Of course, is everything okay?

<u>Gwen</u>: It could be better. Shall I bring them to you and pick them up the next morning or would you like to come here? I really appreciate it. I owe you so much.

<u>Jeanine</u>: Not at all. Bring them to me. I'll take those little beauties out for the day. Don't you worry about a thing.

<u>Gwen</u>: Thank you so much; you're the best.

<u>Jeanine</u>: I know ;)

A weight has lifted now that I'm sorted for work tomorrow. Thankfully. It's a question of what else I'm going to do until this is resolved that has me worried.

I don't want to keep the kids from their father but until his head is sorted, it's probably best that he remains absent for a while. When he's in a better frame of mind I know he'll understand.

I am just so sorry that it has come to this.

Chapter Twenty-One

"It's so good to see you." Jeanine hugs me tight, her arms around me and Emily who tries to push her away in protest.

"You too," I grin, though it falls flat. I didn't sleep well last night and it hasn't gone unnoticed. Jeanine looks at me with concern, her warm eyes help to alleviate the tension I feel.

"What's wrong?" She asks and I shake my head to alleviate the throbbing in my throat. Sensing my need to take a moment, she removes Emily from my arms and ushers Dillan into the room.

"You have a full house," I grin, waving to her daughter Jennifer and her son Tyler. "How are you, Jen?"

"I'm great, thank you, yourself?"

"Brilliant."

She smiles a smile so similar to her mother's and takes the toy train Dillan hands to her. "Do you want to play?"

"Would you mind keeping an eye on the kids while I help Gwen with her things?" Jeanine asks quietly, her soft hand on my arm.

"I can help and you stay?" Jen suggests but Jeanine waves her off and replies, "Not at all. We have much to discuss, two birds one stone."

"Go ahead then. These little cuties will be fine with Tyler and I, won't you?"

My kids ignore her, far too enthralled by the many toys available. Jen and I share a smile before I exit the room after her mother.

"Okay, let's get their stuff from the car." Jeanine follows me to the boot and helps me lift their individual backpacks and double buggy out. "Now, let's dump this in the hallway and you can follow me into the kitchen for what looks like a well needed cup of coffee."

"Thank you."

"So, what's happened?"

"What didn't happen would be a shorter list."

"Oh dear." We place the bags and cot at the bottom of the stairs. "Come on, let's boil that kettle."

"Sounds great." I find a seat at the round wooden table in her kitchen and turn a chair to face her. "Nathan has left."

The spoon in her hand clatters onto the worktop and she spins to face me. Nothing but the sound of the kettle hissing as it heats can be heard in the stillness of the kitchen.

"I made him leave," I clarify so she doesn't think it was all his fault. "And I don't think he's going to be coming back for anything other than to be a father and at the moment, even that hangs in the balance."

"Oh good lord! What on earth has happened?"

My eyes burn, familiar tears threatening to spill over my cheeks. "It's complicated."

"When isn't a break up complicated?" She turns to the cupboards and pulls out two cups from the one by her head. When she turns back to me I see the sadness in her eyes. "You both love each other so much."

"I know. He's changed," I whisper, wishing I never had to say the words out loud. "His insecurities are too hard to penetrate and he won't even let me try. All he does is lie to me."

"Well that just won't do."

"No it really won't."

"Is he going through something? Depression perhaps?"

I shrug. "Maybe, I'm not sure. He won't talk to me and he won't seek help. Well not from anybody but his mother anyway."

"His mother?" She squawks, looking as shocked as I did when I first found out about their secret outings.

Nodding, I watch as she stirs the drinks and adds milk. "Like I said, it's complicated."

"It sounds it. Do you want to tell me more?"

"I do, oh how I want to just let everything off my chest..." A ragged sigh leaves me and even though my chest deflates it feels as though a weight is pressing on it. "I can't. He'd never forgive me if I were to bare his secrets, even to you."

"That is something I understand." She hands me my drink and places a gentle touch to my shoulder. "It'll all work out, you'll see."

"I sure hope you're right."

"It will; you've been through worse."

I don't think we have but I don't say this. It all seems so hopeless and I miss him so much. If it weren't for the children I don't think I would have gotten out of bed this morning.

Should I text him? Should I extend the first branch?

No. I need to let this sit for a while, as crazy as it will drive me. We need space to organise our thoughts. This is all going to come to a head eventually and I'm not sure poking the bear at this point will help us resolve anything.

Or maybe it's my need to shy away from conflict that is making me weak?

Am I weak? How does one spot weakness in themselves when weakness is overcome with strength?

"What are you going to do?"

"I don't have an answer for that." Sipping my drink I rest back and close my eyes. Jeanine moves behind me and plays with the ends of my hair. It's one of the nicest feelings in the world.

"It'll all work out. You and Nathan are such a lovely couple and he loves you more than the earth."

"I know he does; I just wish he knew that I felt the same."

"Have you told him that?"

"I thought I had," I murmur. "There's only so much a person with deep set insecurities can absorb, I guess?"

"He'll get past it."

"Probably. Will I, though? There's only so much a deceived person can take before they lose the ability to trust."

"You'll heal. He just has to step up and show you he can be different."

Too right. "I don't think he's going to."

"Silly man. I'm so sorry, Gwen." She releases my hair and pinches my cheek. "You get off and go have a nap before you have to start work. You look wiped."

"I am," I honestly reply. "Though I doubt I'll be finding solace in sleep anytime soon."

"You'll work it out. I have faith."

I'm glad somebody does. "Thank you again for having the babes. I pray they're well behaved."

"Nonsense, they're just babies. They don't know how to be naughty on purpose."

I wish that were true. Laughing a little, I hug my friend and allow her to lead me from the house. Such a long drive home lies ahead of me. It feels daunting knowing that I'm escaping to an empty house, one that brings me nought but pain at present, although the house can't really be to blame in this scenario.

"Screw it," I whisper to myself as I put the car into drive with only one destination in mind. Sleep won't help me now; keeping busy will. I just know that if I go home to a house that smells of Nathan, I won't be able to resist calling him and begging for him to come home. Life seems bleak without him but it also seems bleak with him when I think about how he's made me feel lately.

"You are three hours early," Kerim comments when I walk out of the staff area. I managed to avoid his view upon entry. The kitchen is empty save for Kerim and Patience working on updating the menu. They were both absorbed by what they were doing.

"Is that a problem, Chef?" I inwardly plead that it isn't but keep my face blank so he doesn't feel pressured into allowing me into his kitchen.

"Not at all, I could use your insight." I nod and tighten my jacket as he assesses me in my uniform. "You've lost weight."

My clothes have been feeling looser. "I've been working hard."

"It hasn't gone unnoticed." He winks and steps to the side so I can see what he and Patience are working on. They have notes scattered around numerous saucepans on the counter. I've never been a part of the menu creation. This is exciting. "Try them all. Sniff them, taste them, try the texture on a spoon and let us know which one you favour."

I do so, tasting the different flavoured soups. There are so many that are tasty, it's hard to know which one to choose. That is until I taste a certain type of vegetable soup that is divine. I've never tried a soup like it.

"That one," I tell them both without hesitation. "I want to eat the whole pan."

CHAPTER TWENTY-ONE

Kerim claps and yanks the spoon from my hand to try it himself. "I told you, Patience."

"I still think the lentil soup would be better," she grumbles, but he ignores her.

I help to clean as he finds the recipe in the notes and sets about making another batch for when the others come in. That'll be a while yet.

"Why are you here so early?" Patience hisses and I know she's going to be annoyed with me purely because I've interrupted her private time with Kerim. When is she going to make her move? How can she live like this? I'd be losing my mind pining for somebody for so long.

"That's not your business why she is here early," Kerim snaps, clearly having overheard her. We both jump at the sound of his voice, me even more so when he moves behind me and places an arm across my shoulders. "She is welcome in this kitchen anytime."

I don't respond. I can't be bothered with more drama, so instead I ask, "Does this mean we can finally be rid of that awful fish and cabbage dish?"

"Hell yes," Kerim agrees. "What was I thinking?"

"We can't all be perfect all of the time."

His smile turns into a shit eating grin. "You think I'm perfect?"

"I think you're going to get slapped if you don't stop bothering me." I remark haughtily but it only seems to garner laughter from him. He has a pleasant laugh, a contagious one. I smile with him, though it's weak in comparison to his, which lingers long after his laughter has ceased. "Okay, so, let's find a nice fish replacement for that mess."

"Yes, Chef." Kerim salutes and practically skips to the pantry. "How about seabass?"

"That does seem to be popular at the moment."

"I vote Salmon!" Patience adds excitedly and together we work on a new menu, unbiased and happy.

In the end we decided on Salmon. This new menu is going to be the best one yet.

When I awake the next morning I call Jeanine and speak to the kids. Luckily for me she can have them again, but only until the morning. This is great as it means I'm set for the evening, but what am I going to do long term? Nathan and I really need to find a common ground here.

Gwen: We need to talk.

His response is immediate and floods me with relief.

Nathan: When?

Gwen: 1pm?

Nathan: I'll be there.

Well that's something. Now I just need to list my grievances so we can at least try to stay on track. I really hope he doesn't start being bitter and insulting again. I hate that; it enrages me and hurts me all the same. I find myself wanting to spit back vile things that I'd never normally say in a bid to hurt him. My self-control is better than that.

I'm better than that. I won't stoop so low. I won't hurt him like everybody else has done in his life. I just wish he'd honour me the same.

As I tidy the house, deciding to use what little portion of freedom I have to get my many chores done, there's a knock at the door.

I drop my rubber gloves onto the worktop and smooth my shirt down. I notice orange marks across the white fabric, all caused by splashes of bleach. Am I the only one with cleaning clothes? Surely I can't be.

"Just a second," I call as I rinse my arms and hands.

The person, whomever it may be, doesn't knock again and I hope they haven't left. I'm far too curious. Maybe Nathan is early? That wouldn't surprise me. It's only half an hour and I don't mind. I know what I want to say and the sooner we get past this the better.

As I walk to the door, I pull my messy hair bun a bit tighter to my head. The tendrils at the back tickle my neck as one errant lock at the front falls across my nose. I blow it out of the way just as I pull the door open, keeping my face stoic in preparation for Nathan to enter. Is it so wrong that I don't want him to see how upset I am?

The breeze hits me almost as fast as the shock at seeing Kerim standing on my doorstep, a box in his hands.

"I come with cake!" He raises the box a little higher and gives me a handsome smile that I'm unused to seeing.

Except for when we went for dinner, I've never seen him out of his uniform. Light blue jeans and a grey polo suit him. He looks younger and more at ease than usual. His hair is messier too but in a nice way, not a lazy way.

"Come in," I blurt after an awkward pause. My wits finally gather and I motion for him to enter. "Please ignore the state of me, I've been cleaning the kitchen."

"Not to worry," he grins, looking around my cosy little home. "Where are your babies? With their father?"

"With a friend," I respond and lead him into the kitchen. "Can I get you a drink?"

"I would love chai."

"Black tea it is," I grin, knowing what chai is. "Though I only have PG; is that okay?"

"Perfect." He places the box onto the breakfast bar. "May I use your kitchen as my own?"

"Of course." If somebody had told me two years ago that my favourite chef would be making himself at home in my kitchen, I'd have tapped them on the head to check for a brain. This is unreal. Even though I work for the man, I'm a little bit star struck. "Anything you need in particular?"

"Plates and forks." He finds my favourite oval shaped presentation plate as I'm boiling the kettle. "Make yourself a chai or coffee too. This cake has to be eaten with a hot drink."

He reveals the caramel coloured cake. It looks like a simple sponge covered with almonds but I know that it'll be far from simple. My stomach growls hungrily.

"I'm sure you're not just here to ply me with tea and cake," I comment as he slices the rectangular shaped sponge into squares. He places them onto the plate, piling them neatly before setting them directly into the centre of the surface.

"Here." He suddenly appears beside me and takes the almost boiled kettle. Watching as he pours a small amount of water into our cups, swirls the teabags around the bottom and then dumps the water into the sink before clicking the boil on the kettle again. "Always wash the teabags first or they get such a metallic taste to them."

"I've never noticed but I usually drink coffee."

Flashing his teeth at me, he helps me finish the drinks and then pulls out a bar stool for me to sit on. One would think this was his house, not my own. I feel like such a blundering idiot in comparison to his ease and grace in my own kitchen. "As for my visit, I'm here simply as a friend. Out of concern and because I enjoy your company."

"Oh. Concern?"

"Yes, I've noticed recently that you've not seemed yourself. Your early visit yesterday has been testament to that."

"So it was a problem?"

"Not at all." His hand covers my wrist as my hand grips the handle of my cup. "Eat the cake; it's one of my best."

I do as I'm told, hungry for the first time in over a day and sip my tea as I swallow. "It's lovely."

"Thank you." He looks around my kitchen. "As is your home. It feels so warm and full of love in comparison to my third floor, one bedroom apartment."

"Home is what we make of it."

"Something my mother tells me." He gets such a look of love to his eyes that a lesser woman would have swooned.

"Do your parents live in London? I've not seen them in the restaurant."

"They do, but they're visiting my sister in Turkey for a few months."

"I bet you miss them."

"Surprisingly, I miss my mother's cooking."

This definitely makes me smile. "Is she better at it than you?"

"I learned a lot from her but not enough. When she comes back I'll take you to her house for dinner."

Blinking, I stammer, "I wouldn't want to intrude."

"Not at all, you can't intrude in a Turkish household. We love guests." He sips his own tea and takes a large bite out of a cake square. "So, how are you and why have you not been yourself lately?"

I wasn't prepared for his question any more than I was prepared for his visit. Shifting uncomfortably in my seat, I try to lie. "I'm fine. I'm not sure what you mean."

"Of course." He places his hand on my wrist again and dips his head to draw my eyes to his. "But if you need an ear, I'll give you mine. I'm only an away call."

CHAPTER TWENTY-ONE 219

His language muddling makes me giggle. Unfortunately it makes me giggle right as Nathan steps into the kitchen, takes one look at us sitting at the breakfast bar sipping tea and eating cake and reacts in a way I never would have thought him capable of.

A scream rips from my chest and my hand flies to my mouth when Nathan grabs Kerim by his collar and shoves him up against our American style fridge. Magnets fall to the ground, clattering around their feet.

"Nathan!" I yell in horror. "What are you doing?"

"Me?" He releases Kerim who calmly smooths himself down. I step to his side, wanting to apologise profusely. "What are *you* doing?"

"I feel my presence may be causing offence," Kerim sighs, shaking his head and frowning at Nathan. "But I don't feel comfortable leaving you alone with a man in clearly such a state of distress."

"This is insane," I hiss, grabbing Nathan's arm and ripping him backwards. I put myself between the two of them and glare at my fiancé. "Are you crazy?"

"Are you?" He asks, his eyes swimming with hurt. "Did you plan this?"

"You think that little of me?"

"I showed up unannounced," Kerim states, raising his chin indignantly.

"Do you make a habit of showing up at the houses of your staff unannounced?" Nathan tries to step towards the man at my back but my hand on his chest stops him. I honestly can't believe this is happening.

"Yes," Kerim steps forward too and my arm presses against his chest. "When I feel as though they're going through something, that's exactly what I do. I never imagined it could be this."

"How chivalrous." His sarcasm isn't lost on either of us. Nathan growls in response so I push harder against his chest.

"I am so sorry, Kerim." I turn to him and bite my lip. "Nathan's not himself right now."

"You're kidding?" Nathan breathes. "You're apologising for me?"

"You need to calm down or I won't talk with you," I yell, willing myself to calm down. I take a breath and look at the man on my left. "Kerim, I really appreciate your visit but I have things to... solve."

"Of course," Kerim whispers and pinches my chin between his finger and thumb. "I apologise for the intrusion. Are you sure you'll be okay?"

"She'll be fine," Nathan snarls and I feel him tense with anger. "Just leave us."

Kerim ignores him as I lead him to the door and thank him for the cake and apologise once more. He asks me if I'll be okay and I assure him that I will be, before shutting the door after him. I take a few heavy breaths to calm myself. I want to throw things at Nathan. I want to scream at him. I don't. Part of me knows that it won't do any good and I know I'll feel worse afterwards.

"Before you open your mouth," I tell him, my voice deceptively calm as my fiery gaze catches his, "and say something that'll never earn you my forgiveness on top of your physical assault on my boss." At my words his eyes soften and a muscle in his jaw tics. "Let's take a moment to calm down before beginning this conversation. Okay?"

"Why can't you see that he wants you?" He asks, his tone one of exasperation.

"Oh my God," I laugh, my tone more exasperated than his. "Are we ever going to get past this?"

"I want to," Nathan whispers and rushes to me. "I want to stop feeling like this. When I'm not with you I make myself all of these promises that I'll be different, that I'll be able to trust with all of my heart, but... I just..." His hand threads into the back of my hair as the other one goes to my hip. "I can't get the images of you and him together... you and any man."

"That's not fair on me."

"I know." He kisses my forehead and inhales deeply. "It's my issue that I need to deal with. That's just so much easier said than done."

"It really isn't. The sooner you take that leap of faith, the easier it becomes."

"Gwen," he whispers and slides his hand from my hair to cup my jaw. "I love you, with all of my heart, and before your aversion to us getting married, I did trust you, but," he pauses and looks away. "Ever since you started postponing the planning of our marriage, I've been waiting for you to leave."

"I've just not been ready to marry you yet. I don't understand why you've felt as though we need to rush into it."

"Because I love you."

"Marrying me won't stop me from cheating on you!" I snatch his hand away from my jaw and place it against my chest. "Only I can stop that and you need to trust in my love for you as I trust in your love for me."

CHAPTER TWENTY-ONE

"I know that, okay?" Pulling away, he turns and looks at himself in the mirror. "I feel like with every passing day I become more desperate to keep you, despite the fact I know it's wrong."

"It'll ruin us."

"Hasn't it already?"

"No," I murmur and see the hope in his eyes come but then leave swiftly when I add, "The lying has. I could have worked past the fact you don't trust me; I could have helped you with that. I can't forgive the lying."

"Gwen..."

"It's all another form of distrust." I shrug, feeling my eyes sting. "You don't trust me enough with your inner thoughts."

"So what happens now?" He asks softly, so softly a tear falls from my eye.

"You need to find somewhere else to live," I respond and when his face crumples with pain it takes everything I have to not mirror it.

"You're kicking me out? For real?" He asks, his voice cracking.

"Yes."

"But..." His hands push through the front of his hair. "I can change."

"Prove it."

"How can I prove it if you're forcing me to leave?"

"I don't know, Nathan. I just know that I can't live with a man who spits venomous words to hurt me while his mind deteriorates from a fictitious belief that I'm going to leave him for my boss."

He rolls his eyes. "It's hardly fictitious when that man wants you."

"You're just not getting it. This is hopeless."

"It's not hopeless; how can you say such a thing?"

"Maybe you were right," I whisper and move into the kitchen. My throat is dry so I down the rest of my tea.

"About what?"

"About us never concluding what happened. We just threw ourselves into a relationship with so much lingering between us."

"I was angry. I said many things I should never have said."

"That doesn't mean you were wrong." I rub my eyes and then tug on my bleach stained shirt. "I love you but I feel like it's never enough because you constantly question it."

"Do you have any idea how frustrating it is knowing that you work in close quarters every single day with a man that wants you? A man that I know gets whatever he wants when he sets his sights on it."

"You're being…"

He interrupts, pressing his chest to mine and holding my biceps with his hands. "A man who is far better suited to you than I ever will be." My lower back presses against the sideboard as he keeps his body tighter to mine. "Do you know how that feels?"

"Why don't you talk to Kerim? Clear the air? I can only promise you that I'd never cheat on you. I can't put your mind at ease with how he's feeling because I can't control that."

He seems to stop breathing for the longest moment before he nods. "Fine. I'll call him."

"Just don't bring me into it anymore."

"I won't," he promises, but his lack of trust has rubbed off on me. I don't believe him at all. "Give me another chance, Gwen. Let me come home."

"No," I reply adamantly. "For now I think it's best for both of us and the kids to separate."

"I refuse to lose you."

"Then show me you can change."

"I will," he assures me and kisses the tip of my nose. "I promise I will." His lips touch mine softly. "Starting this second."

I really hope he means it. "Until then, we need to schedule our work rotas to make it so the kids have constant care."

"So I still can't come home?"

"No."

"But…" He stops his argument and sighs heavily. "Fine. I understand. Where are the kids now?"

"With Jeanine."

"Good, they love her."

I smile softly and move from between him and the counter. "Is it so wrong that I want a drama free relationship?"

"No, I want that too."

"Then we're on the same page." I smile and clear the mess from the counter. "I just hope it's a reachable goal."

"It is."

"I have every hope." Then I add. "We also have the matter of your mother to discuss."

"Let's tackle that another day." He winces and helps to clear up. "For now let's celebrate this small victory with a coffee and a movie?"

"I'll not allow her to visit with my children until we've discussed it."

"That's fine, she knows." He's spoken to her since then I'm guessing. This annoys me but I don't let it show. "Maybe we can all sit down together and work something out?"

"Maybe." I give a little. "That doesn't dismiss anything you did, though."

"I know." He steps into my space and slides his warm, large hands down my sides. My body shivers without permission and my throat dries as other places moisten. When his lips touch my neck and kiss a gentle path down to my shoulder, that shiver turns into a shudder and my knees become weak. "I'm sorry."

His hand that rested on my hip slips under the waistband of my trousers and begins to tease as his other hand moves to grasp my breast.

"Nathan," I whimper, my strength waning, not that I have tried to push him away at all. No matter how mad I am with him, he knows exactly how to torment my body to the point of no return.

"Shh," he hisses in my ear and then takes the lobe in between his teeth.

Groaning, my head falls back onto his shoulder. He grinds against me powerfully. I feel his erection and pray that he relieves me of my trousers and slips into me so slowly as his leather clad fingers tease me to the brink of orgasm.

"That's it," he whispers, kissing my neck. "Let me make you feel good."

"God," I moan, wrapping my fingers around his wrist. "I want you."

"No telling me twice," he pants as the belt of his trousers clicks free. I hear it thread through the metal loop before his fingers part my folds and seek out my entrance. "Are you sure?"

"What?" I breathe as he taps against me.

"I know you don't like doing it when we're mad."

"Are you fucking kidding me?" I cry. "Just do it already!"

He doesn't hesitate another moment before he's filling me and I'm sighing with relief. The orgasm I receive simply by the fullness makes me spasm so badly he has to hold me up.

"This way," he whispers and walks me to the breakfast bar.

I squeal when he bends me over it, pressing my chest to the hard surface.

"I thought I'd never feel this again," he admits, moving to a soft rhythm.

With more speed and power he keeps going, driving me over the edge more times than I can count. It seems to go on forever yet it doesn't last long enough. Before I know it, he's collapsing onto my back, crying out with his own release and I'm squirming beneath him, needing to breathe.

"Please don't make me leave," he whispers in my ear, keeping me pinned.

"Nathan."

"Please. I can't bear to be apart from you."

He allows me to stand and turn into his open arms. They envelop me with so much love and warmth.

"I don't trust you. You've hurt me too much."

"I know," he murmurs as he buries his face into my neck. "I'm so, so sorry."

"I know."

"I'll give you the space you need for the time being." He promises and kisses me gently. "Text me your work hours so I know when to come and look after the kids. I miss them."

This breaks my heart. "They miss you too."

"Also..." He bites hard on his lip, his eyes showing an internal struggle that I wish I could help him through. "Everything I said to you...I was angry and hurt."

"I know."

"I love you."

"I love you too."

He sighs heavily as he tucks himself into his trousers. "Things are such a mess right now."

"You can say that again."

"It'll get better."

I nod my agreement. "It definitely will. I have faith."

"Don't ever lose faith in me." He kisses me once more so sweetly and tenderly it leaves me aching for more. "Promise?"

I don't promise because I never break a promise if I can help it. Instead I usher him out of our home and quickly text him my work dates.

Work...there's a thing I'd like to avoid. I'm humiliated by the way Nathan reacted. I should have called Kerim the second he left. I shouldn't have allowed Nathan to get away with such behaviour so easily.

I'm nothing but a massive screw up.

Nothing about the way I've handled this makes any sense, even to me. My love for him blinds me to the reality of all that is going on.

CHAPTER TWENTY-ONE

Sneaking into work with my head hanging low, I busy myself with tasks as far away from Kerim as possible. I've never been so mortified. He must think me such a burden.

Patience - Miss Hot and Cold as I call her - is being especially nice today and is keeping me occupied, as well as the rest of my co-workers. Kerim hasn't acknowledged me which I'm grateful for and also not so much because I don't know what he's thinking.

Will he terminate our arrangement if he thinks my baggage might interfere with my work?

I'll just have to show him that I love my job.

So I stay late, exhausting myself as we work together in amicable silence. Then I stay late the next night and the next. Nathan doesn't question it and Kerim remains the same as always.

Maybe things will change for once.

I sure hope so.

Chapter Twenty-Two

"I'm coming this weekend," my mum states. "I'll be there on Friday."

"Yay!" I'm so relieved but also I'm nervous about having to explain why Nathan isn't staying here. I have yet to tell a single soul but it's nobody's business so I don't plan on it. Now I guess that I'll have to.

"I miss you all."

"Me too. I'm sorry we haven't been in touch; it has been so hectic."

"Same here." She yawns to confirm this. "How are things?"

Deep breaths. "Unfortunately, not great."

"Oh dear, still rocky?"

"One could say rocky. I prefer the term... separated."

"Separated?" Her voice squeaks and I'd laugh if I weren't so tense. "What does that mean?"

"I wish I could tell you. He's gone from the house but not from our lives."

She's silent for the longest moment before finally asking, "Was he cheating?"

"No, I wish." I snort, shaking my head. "I can't really talk about it. Just know that I feel as though it's right."

"I'm here; you know that?"

"I do. As am I."

"Thank you." She sighs heavily. "I'm so sorry, babe. I know you love him."

My eyes burn. "I just wish he loved me the same."

"I'm sure he does."

I don't respond because she wouldn't understand without knowing the full story. My words are true though; if he loved me the way I love him, he wouldn't hide things from me.

There's a gentle knock at the door. "Mum, I'll call you back."

"Okay, no rush."

As I'm walking to the front door, I hang up the phone and peer through the peep hole.

"What is she doing here?" I hiss as my hands begin to tremble. The adrenaline is rushing through my body already and I've not even come face to face with her yet.

She knocks again, just as gently as before, knowing I'm home no doubt because my car is across the way.

"Get some balls," I tell myself and then yank the door open. "I'm not interested."

"Gwen," his mother says softly. Her familiar brown eyes make my heart ache for a man that no longer lives on this earth.

Caleb, how I miss you. Regardless of what you did, I'll always love you.

"I made a lot of mistakes in my life. My bitterness caused me to miss out on a lot but I'd like to be there now." Her hand rests against the door to stop me from slamming it in her face. "I'll do anything. Anything you ask. Parenting classes, group sessions, a lie detector." My eyes meet hers and my heart warms a little at her words, though not enough for me to stop hating her. "*Anything*."

"I'm not interested. I don't trust you."

"I don't blame you. I neglected him. I was an awful mother to both of my boys. I want to rectify that. Let me be there for my son and his babies." Tears fill her eyes. "I won't visit without you present. I'll do all you ask. Just please..."

My mouth drops open. "Why do you think you deserve this? Why should I let you into the life of my kids?"

"Because I finally know how to love again and I don't want the feeling to die. I love my grandbabies. I love them to the bottom of my heart. Please." Fuck. Is she talking me around? How bad could things be if visits are supervised? If I'm present, then maybe she does deserve a chance? "Please, Gwen."

"I need time to think."

"No," she blurts, pushing on the door with a wrinkled, delicate hand. "If I let you think about it alone you'll never change your mind. I can be relentless." Her mouth twitches with a weak smile. "I don't want to hound you but I can't lose this. I can't lose him and those kids again." Her eyes bore into my own, full of desperation and hope. "Please, Gwen."

"Fine," I relent. "Supervised visits only."

Her smile is blinding and it reminds me so much of Caleb, my heart aches. "Thank you. *Thank you!*"

"Don't thank me yet. You only get one chance. Just one."

"Understood."

"I'm not kidding. Don't think that I'm giving you permission to suddenly start giving me tips on how to parent."

Her smile is blinding. "I think it's I who needs the tips." Isn't that the truth? "When can I come to see them? With your planning and permission of course."

"I'll let you know. But let me set one thing straight before we proceed." She nods.

"Under no circumstances will you be seeing these kids without me present and without my knowledge. If I find out you have been conspiring with Nathan again, not only will you lose all rights to my children, but so will he." My gaze levels and I hope I'm nailing her with a look that could kill. "I will do everything in my power to protect them, as is my right."

"I understand." She releases her hold of the door and steps back. "I'm very sorry for all of the pain I've caused you and for the things I said."

"Let's just not discuss any of that because it'll only piss me off." I check my watch. "I have to go."

"Shall I call you or..."

"No. I'll text you later with a date and time."

She nods, smiling, and fluffs up the back of her short white blonde hair with both hands. "You have my number?" That's a good point. When she sees me hesitate, she pulls her phone from the leather bag dangling from the crook of her elbow and unlocks it then places it back into her bag after texting the number I tell her with a simple, 'Hi'. "I'll not take any more of your time. I look forward to getting to know you all properly this time."

I disagree internally and finally get my chance to close the door.

"God!" I whisper shout and punch the air. I loathe that woman. *Loathe*. Why did I agree to any of this?

This year has been my most stressful yet, which is saying something considering I almost died in a fire.

Nathan comes to look after the kids while I work. We don't talk much or even look at each other much. He touches my back as I walk past him, but other than that there's a stillness between us that wrecks my heart and no doubt wrecks his.

The longing look he pins me with as I leave forces me to hold back tears. He's giving me the space I asked for but he's letting me know that it's hurting him and I loathe that he's hurting, possibly even more than I loathe his mother.

I just can't get past this until he understands what he's done or at least gives me a good enough reason for why he's done it.

If his reasons for this deception speak to my soul and enable me to forgive him and trust him again, he can come home. For some reason, I don't think that's ever going to happen and that depresses me more than anything else. Our entire relationship is resting on whether Nathan can finally open to me in a way he never has.

After checking the rota at work, I send Patricia a text letting her know that she's welcome to join us in the morning after breakfast. She immediately responds to let me know that she'll be there and my skin crawls with the thought of her stepping foot into my house. I just feel like I need to give her this chance for the kids and for Nathan. I don't want to look as though I've been unfair at all.

"You're with me," Kerim tells me the second I stepped out of the staff area and into the kitchen.

"I am?"

"Yep." He throws a ladle at me which I somehow catch between my hands and chest. "Gel."

Gel in Turkish means for me to come there. I've picked up quite a few new words since starting here. More swearwords than anything else, as is usual when people want to learn a new language.

"What are we doing?"

"We are going to make more of that soup," he says as we move to the smaller gas stove top. A large pot rests on the top. "We are going to give a free sample out to all customers today in return for an honest review."

"Good plan," I smile and help him chop and dice the vegetables. We follow his recipe that is on a sheet of paper behind the metal work top, only tweaking it with salt because Kerim never weighs salt. He says it's a waste of time.

"If they love it, I'd like it if you could stay late and help me to make it in bulk."

I nod. "That's fine." I don't tell him I'm relieved for the excuse to not go home. If I have to see Nathan again before nightfall I'm not sure I can handle it.

"Excellent. We'll start at around ten and finish for midnight-ish."

"Do you need us too, Chef?" Harold asks, not too far away, overseeing the fish as it's filleted into perfect portion sizes.

"No, we can manage. You already know what to do; Gwen has yet to learn."

Harold nods, winks at me and moves around my co-workers. I turn to Kerim. "Do you ever go home?"

"I can't remember," he chuckles and tosses a batch of shredded cabbage into the pot. The water bubbles gently so he turns down the heat and I stir the cabbage around it.

"You love your job. I think if I didn't have the kids, I'd always be here too. Especially to experiment with all of your fabulous utensils and extremely high quality goods."

"You can, you know? Any time you like. This is your kitchen too."

"Thank you. I might do just that. I miss working in a bakery; my oven at home just doesn't make cake the way theirs did and don't get me started on the bread!"

Kerim flexes his fingers and pushes the carrot that he was dicing to the side. "Then it's settled. When you get a free day, you will impress us with your baking skills."

"I would be honoured."

"I shall look forward to it." He brushes past me, placing his hand on my arm to hold me steady. "You continue; I'll re-join you soon."

"Sure." I'm used to following his recipes so this doesn't worry me. It's just that the batch is quite large and requires a lot of cutting. I might not get it done in time for it to cook ready for the customers to try. Soup is no easy thing to prepare.

Patience, as expected, sours towards me for the rest of the day but I just can't be dealing with her crap. She needs to calm the hell down before she pushes me over the edge I'm already teetering on.

Patricia arrives at ten in the morning as promised. She doesn't make herself at home at first, not until she sees how tired I am and keeps the children busy in the living room while I prepare for dinner later. I always prepare the food early because if I don't, Nathan will and it's not that he's a bad cook, it's just that the kids are used to eating my food. They won't even eat fast food so we can't just stick a kid's meal in front of them. Little food snobs. They make me so proud.

"You look dead on your feet," she says to me. She's right. I have huge bags under my eyes and I didn't get nearly enough sleep after Nathan left last night. He didn't even say anything, just kissed my cheek and left. It's wrong that I want him to chase me, to fight for what we have. How is it that after all we've been through, we aren't made for each other?

"Would you like a tea or a coffee?" I call from the kitchen, hoping she hears me so I don't have to go and speak to her. The kids are running riot in the living room and they sound as though they're having a great time. I loathe her for that too.

"I would love a tea. Thank you." She calls back and I make quick work of preparing two mugs. "No sugar and only a splash of milk." Her raspy aged voice adds.

I already put a sugar in so I dump it and start again, yawning powerfully as the kettle boils.

When I take both cups into the room and hand hers to her, she thanks me and takes a sip as I curl my legs under me in the corner of the couch.

My body is tense, unable to relax in her presence. This all seems so surreal.

"He looks so much like Caleb," she murmurs quietly as Dillan runs a toy train over her thighs while making noises.

"Yeah," I agree sadly. "He'd have loved him so much."

"He would." She smiles in a way that seems so genuine it makes every other smile I've seen look fake. "I'm sorry I didn't tell you about him."

"Sorry?"

"About his illness. There's nothing I regret more than how I treated you all."

CHAPTER TWENTY-TWO

What do I say to that?

She sips her drink and we enter a silence that's not quite awkward but certainly lacks comfort.

After an hour she leaves and I release all of the air in my chest before rubbing my eyes so hard they hurt. Then I wrestle the kids into their napping spots and pray they sleep so I can too. Dillan doesn't acquiesce and instead spends the fifteen minutes Emily remains sleeping lying on my back and stroking my hair. He loves stroking hair.

Being a mum is hard but I love it so much.

Chapter Twenty-Three

"I don't get it," Nathan snaps suddenly. He was all happy a moment ago, playing with the kids in the room, ignoring me like he has the past few weeks.

"Huh?"

His gorgeous brown eyes twinkle dangerously. "My mother…"

"Oh." My lips linger in the shape of an O. "I figured she'd tell you."

"She'd tell me?" He looks insulted and I can understand why. "Suddenly we're separated and on different planets? I've been here almost every day."

"I don't know how to approach you at the moment."

"You don't know how to approach me?" Now he looks hurt so I snort and spew, "Yeah, how does *that* feel?" His mouth instantly clamps shut.

I continue. "I just haven't been able to approach the subject. She's visited a few times. We've come to a mutual understanding."

"Yet I'm still not allowed home?"

For crying out loud. I huff with annoyance. "This is why you're not allowed home, because you just don't get it!"

"Don't get mad." He holds his hands up. "Let's talk about this."

"I have said this so many times, Nathan. I'm tired of spelling it out for you. If you don't know what you've done and you don't agree that it's wrong, then you're just going to do it again." I calm myself and lower my voice. "It's not about you seeing your mum. It's that you didn't tell me. You openly lied to me numerous times and made me feel as though I was losing my mind!"

"I couldn't…"

"Talk to me." I stare at him, absorbing every single inch of him. Burning him to memory. "I know. You've said and that's what hurts the worst."

"I feel so lost." He turns away from me and realigns the kettle with the sugar, tea and coffee pots. "I thought I was just giving you space. I didn't realise you needed me to grovel."

My mouth falls open. "Grovel? You broke my trust!"

"With good reason."

"Tell me the reason so I can judge!"

"DADDY!" Emily screams from the hallway. It's a happy scream, not a sad or scared scream, so neither of us panic and I allow Nathan to step out of the room to deal with her. When he comes back in with Emily in his arms, he diverts his eyes and the conversation.

"You've been staying later at work a lot lately."

Shrugging, I remove Emily from his arms and place her in the highchair. Dillan comes racing in as soon as he hears the fridge open. I give them both a yoghurt each and smile when they fall instantly silent.

"Anything you want to tell me about that?" Nathan presses, seeming nervous.

"I've been working."

"Why so late?"

"We're building a new menu so I've been staying to help prep."

He nods and licks his lower lip. It glistens and I miss kissing it so badly. When he realises I'm staring, his pupils dilate and I know he feels the same.

"With everyone?"

"Why are you questioning me?" I sigh, knowing exactly where this conversation is going.

His brow quirks as he snaps, "You've been alone with Kerim."

"And so it begins," I laugh humourlessly. "This is one of the reasons I haven't spoken to you at all these past couple of weeks."

"I have a right to know."

"No you don't," I whisper shout. "Not anymore. You lost that right!"

The tension between us thickens and I can see Nathan battling with the urge to retaliate. He doesn't. He turns and leaves the room to calm down and I'm glad for it. When he comes back in, he helps me to clean the kids up but doesn't talk again at all before I leave for work.

This isn't getting any easier. At all.

CHAPTER TWENTY-THREE

As the work day draws on, I lose interest in it and find myself thinking back to my own mum's visit a couple of weeks ago. She's glowing and so in love. I wish I'd seen her like this as I was growing up. She was also so helpful around the house that when it came time for her to leave, I hid her suitcase. To say she was impressed would be a complete lie. It was funny though.

"Staying late again tonight?" Kerim asks quietly as he passes my station. I nod. "If that's okay. I need to make a cake for my friend Tommy."

"What's the occasion?"

"They're coming to visit and he loves cake."

Kerim smiles. "I shall help. It will be a cake fit for a king."

"You don't have to; I know you're busy."

"It'll be my pleasure."

Tommy will never want to leave.

Thinking of Tommy and Sasha makes me realise that Sasha hasn't brought up a possible proposal in a while. Has she moved on from it now? I should really tell her about Nathan and I too. She'll be hurt if she finds out and I didn't warn her.

Telling people just seems so final and I'm just not ready for final. Am I holding onto something that no longer exists?

As the rest of the staff leave, eager to get home after a difficult night, I start to take the ingredients I need from the pantry.

"What are we making?" Kerim asks from the doorway. I hand him what's in my arms and respond, "Triple layer triple chocolate fudge cake."

He grimaces and I laugh lightly.

"It's not my first choice either. Tommy has a major sweet tooth."

"Tommy is..." He prompts waiting for more from me.

"My best friend, who is almost engaged to my other best friend Sasha."

"Oh, I've heard you mention her."

I nod and grab the final few ingredients. We exit the pantry and dump them onto the middle worktop. It's closest to the ovens.

"What shape?"

"Circle."

He grabs the round cake tins and places them onto the worktop beside the ingredients. "I've never made cake without a recipe, not including the ones I know by heart. I feel as though I'll be learning something new today."

"I hardly even weigh anything. I'm so lazy with it." I admit, grinning as I crack eggs into a glass bowl and Kerim adds the water he just collected. "Thanks again for letting me stay almost every time I've worked."

"It's been a big help." He bites on his bottom lip. "Though..." He clears his throat and pulls himself up onto the counter before beginning to mix the bowl of water and egg on his lap. "I can't help but feel as though you're staying for a reason and not just to help? Forgive me for prying."

"It's fine." I slowly sieve the flour into the bowl, giggling when it goes over the side and onto his apron. "Sorry."

"I'll be a walking cake by the end of this myself."

"Probably. You should have seen me when I worked in the bakery. I wore hair nets and I still managed to get jam in my hair."

"Not hard to picture."

Cocking my head, I give him a cheeky grin and add the sugar, being careful not to spill it onto him this time.

"So... all is okay? Is Nathan okay?"

This time I bite on my lip, worried about what to say next. "It's a process sometimes but... I don't know. Things will get better, right?"

"You tell me." He sneezes into the arm of his jacket and curses before going to clean himself up. There wasn't a mess but Kerim is a stickler for hygiene.

We place the cake into the oven and joke around as we clear up the area covered in flour and other ingredients. We then prepare the different types of icing.

"We're still going to be here for a couple of hours. You don't have to stay," I tell him when the clock strikes midnight.

"I'm fine. I'm not working tomorrow so I don't need the sleep." He assures me, twisting the end of an icing pipe. "Besides, I'm excited to try this delicious yet sickly looking cake."

"Me too." I grin, the smile mirroring my excitement. "Oh my gosh, it's hardly started cooking yet and already it smells delicious."

We both sit on the side, our legs swinging. This is going to be a long hour of waiting for it to cook and then waiting for it to cool.

"Let's watch a movie."

"Where?"

He takes my hand and pulls me from the side before leading me into his office.

CHAPTER TWENTY-THREE

"Sit." He points to the sofa to the side, its brown leather shining in the dim light glowing through the window.

"You really do live here," I snigger when he turns on a projector above my head and a square image lights up the white wall.

"Yes. I truly do."

I wait for him to connect the laptop on his desk to the projector. When he joins me with a remote in hand, we choose a comedy and sit on opposite sides of the couch, silent and tired though enjoying the scent of the baking cake.

My phone vibrates in my pocket. I pull it out and blink as the light from the screen blinds me. "Hello?" I whisper.

"Hey," Nathan whispers back. I'm unsure why he's whispering. "Why are you whispering?"

"Because it's quiet." What kind of explanation is that? "Is everything okay? Are the kids okay?"

"They're fine, sleeping." He falls silent for a long moment. I catch Kerim's eye and mime an apology for disturbing the peacefulness. "Can I stay tonight?" My lips part. "Just on the couch. I'm tired; I just woke up and I don't think I should be driving."

Who am I to deny him such a request? It is his house too. "Of course you can."

"Thank you." He mumbles and I hear him drop, no doubt onto the couch. "I love you, Gwen. I know I don't show it as well as I should, but I do."

"Me too." I whisper even more quietly than before. "Goodnight."

"Don't work too hard."

If only he knew what I was really doing. Am I being as bad as he was, withholding information from him? No, this isn't the same thing. I'll tell him in the morning. I can't help it if Kerim wants to stay. I certainly didn't ask him to.

"Are you enjoying the movie?"

I nod in reply and snuggle deeper into the side of the couch. "Don't let me fall asleep."

"I'm going to say the same to you."

Laughing through my teeth, I try to prop myself into a more uncomfortable position, purely so I don't doze. That cake can't be in for a second longer than necessary or it'll dry faster than the desert sands.

The movie drones on and even though it keeps us occupied it doesn't stop my head from drooping with exhaustion. I have never been more relieved when the chiming bell of the timer on the oven goes off, signifying the end of cooking. Jumping up, I almost collide with Kerim who does the same. We laugh and he pulls me back to race me to the cake.

"Ladies first then," I call after him and he quickly stops and allows me through, too proud to be called a lady. That's a win for me.

He still beats me to the oven and removes the cake carefully. It looks wonderful. I'm so excited for it to cool so I can cut it horizontally and add the frosting.

"The icing is ready; shall we finish the movie?" I suggest. It seems better than standing around doing nothing.

He nods.

When I woke up this morning I had this feeling of impending doom, as though something really bad was going to happen, so when I made it to midnight and all was well, I felt relieved and I unfortunately let my guard down. As I lifted the cut, frosted and decorated cake to place it into the box, it slipped off its stand.

"Oh my God, Gwen!" Kerim yells angrily as I try to catch the cake between my arms and chest. I drop the stand in my attempt to save the cake but it's unfortunately not to be. I miss and it topples in the wrong direction when I try to correct its descent.

It smashes on the tiled ground, sending chunks all large and small in different directions.

"What the fuck happened?" He yells, looking as angry as I feel. His anger isn't helpful; I feel awful as it is. "Hours of wasted effort. Hours!"

"I don't know," I scream back at him. "I guess I must be fucking stupid!"

He throws the box across the room and it folds in on itself, becoming little more than a piece of shiny white card.

Then I feel him, his hand on the back of my head, his other at the base of my spine, and then firm lips on mine. My gasp only proceeds to allow him entrance and he swiftly pushes his tongue into my mouth.

A deep groan rattles through his throat as he holds my tight, unsure body closer to him. My dazed, confused, tense form does nothing as he prompts me to kiss him, giving me no escape, and for a stupid fraction of a small moment I lose myself in the passion that just built up between us. But then reality hits and I shove him away from me.

"Oh my god," I breathe, choking for air, my lips swollen and tingling. I touch them with the tips of my fingers. "Oh my…"

"Gwen," he whispers, stepping into my bubble, so I take a step back. "I apologise. I see that I've upset you. That wasn't my intention."

"You just kissed me." I shake my head and place my hand against his quickened heart to stop him from coming closer. "I love my fiancé."

"I know… he's a dear friend. I had a moment of weakness."

"A moment of weakness?"

He inhales slowly to level his breathing and swallows. "You torture me, daily. Every single inch of you."

This isn't happening. "I should go."

"No," he insists, looking around the kitchen and then at the mess on the floor beside us. When he reaches for me again and tries to draw me closer, I duck under his arm to escape, twisting my arm so quickly my skin stretches. My foot sinks into the spongey mess of cake on the ground and I almost slip as I try to hop away from it.

"Fuck," I hiss under my breath.

"Gwen," he panics, moving to block my path. "You lost yourself too. I felt it. You kissed me back."

"For less than a second."

"More like three," he corrects, looking away as if ashamed. "I apologise. It wasn't the right time."

"The right time?" My voice hits a high pitch. "There will never be a right time! That can't ever happen again."

"It won't. You mustn't tell Nathan. Do you understand? It will ruin you both."

My jaw hits the floor. How dare he? "I have more faith in my partner than that." Not that we're together, but we aren't exactly not together. I know it will upset him. I know he's been struggling with my relationship with Kerim. I should throttle myself for not believing him when it came to Kerim's intentions.

"Feel free to tell him, though take it from a man who knows, he'll never trust what you have here."

Deep down I know that he's right and that frightens me. I don't want to lie to Nathan but I don't want to fuel this treacherous fire. "Why are you so worried what I do or don't say?"

"I'm just trying to clear your mind before you leave."

"Clear my mind?" I laugh once though there's nothing funny. "You're insane. You're my boss... my chef."

"We'd be perfect for each other."

"I'm perfect already!"

Pushing around him, I aim directly for the staff room to gather my belongings. I need to put as much distance between myself and Kerim as possible.

"I know you feel the same way. It's why you hide here with me instead of with your fiancé."

"You are deluded," I murmur as I pass him once more. I'm relieved when he lets me go.

It isn't until I'm outside that he yells after me, "You kissed me back. It might have been just for a second but it happened. Think about that before you make any more decisions about me."

My feet pick up the pace, eager to reach my car and drive home.

I don't want or need this drama. I just want a quiet and happy life without all of these hidden little extras waiting to test my strength and patience. If there is a god, he certainly put me on the sour side of his plan.

Chapter Twenty-Four

"You have no idea how happy I am to see you!" I go to hug my friend but stop in my tracks when I see how different she looks. Her hair is jet black and flowing in thick waves past her shoulders. "You look gorgeous! You've changed your hair."

She bites her lip, stifling a stretched, uncontrollable grin. Then her left hand rises higher and higher until the sparkling rock on a thin gold band catches the sun and blinds me entirely with happiness.

We both begin to scream together like school girls and finally hug, still bouncing up and down on the spot.

"You told her then," Tommy chuckles, stepping to her side and wrapping his arm around her shoulders after we separate. "She hasn't stopped looking at it since I gave it to her yesterday."

"What took you so long?" I beam, pulling him in for a hug.

They follow me into the house as he replies, "Well I knew she was excited, so I wanted to make her wait."

"You're a nob," she states but her smile remains. He kisses her cheek and looks around my kitchen.

"No cake," I wince apologetically and his face contorts with a mixture of horror and disappointment. "I dropped it."

"I would've still eaten it."

"I'm sorry." I go to hug him but he shuns me playfully. Sasha hugs me instead and then asks the dreaded, "Where's Nathan and my babes?"

"He took them to the park so I could get you settled and deliver the disappointing news about the cake to Tommy."

She quickly becomes distracted by the picture of Caleb on the microwave. "Oh my gosh! It has been too long since I looked upon this face. It's making me emotional."

"He was a good-looking guy." Tommy shakes his head slowly. "What a waste of life."

"I miss him," I admit aloud and Sasha returns the photo to its resting place.

"We all do." Then she grins and adds, "He'd want us to celebrate my engagement."

"The kids," I pout.

"We don't need to go out to celebrate."

Waking up in the morning is the worst thing to happen to me. My head hurts, I feel sick and my back is sweaty from where Nathan is crushing me, breathing vodka fumes into my face. He's using my cheek to cushion his cheek and my back to cushion his body.

"Get off," I grumble, elbowing him in the ribs. "I'm going to puke."

He immediately hops up and follows close behind as I rush into the bathroom. Counting to three, I inhale deep and expel the remains of last night from my stomach. It aches. I need water.

Nathan, sensing this, rushes away after tying my hair back and returns with a fresh bottle of water.

"Little sips," he whispers, helping me into a sitting position.

"Why did I drink so much?" I flush the toilet and lean back against the wall. Nathan crouches in front of me, looking a bit unsteady himself. "It's all such a blur."

"You had fun." He responds, smiling warmly.

"Maybe too much."

"No such thing."

I recall trying to get him to tie me to the bed. I also recall him tripping on the blanket I kicked onto the floor and falling into a heap. My lips tip up with a smile. "You were also drunk."

"I think I still am." He flashes his eyes at me and holds out a hand for me to take. "Come on: teeth, shower and let's face the day."

"The kids."

"No need." He kisses my neck and places my toothbrush into my hand. "Sasha took them to breakfast with Tommy. Apparently she likes to eat away her hangover."

"What time is it?"

"Almost eleven."

"I am the worst hostess ever."

He kisses my neck again. "And the sexiest." Then he orders, "Teeth."

"Yes, boss."

Did we make friends last night? I can't recall much beyond the first three drinks and trying to have sex with him. He didn't though, forever the gentleman even when plastered on vodka. I'm such a harlot. If I keep giving Nathan mixed signals he's never going to recover or pay attention to the actual issues at hand. I also can't just throw him out now; that would be entirely unfair.

"We will talk when we're feeling better," Nathan whispers, seeing my internal struggles through my eyes reflected in the mirror. Before guiding me into the shower, he kisses my cheek and breathes in my ear, "I love you. Forever. Whatever decision you make with regard to me and our future, I'll always love and cherish you and I always only ever want your happiness."

Holy crap. I'm a puddle. He always says the right things, usually at the wrong time, but he says them and I have no doubts that he means them.

Instead of responding, I climb into the shower. When I finish I check my phone ready to text Sasha but she beats me to it by walking through the door with my babies in tow.

"Wing A WOSES!" Dillan screeches so loudly I hear glass crack.

"POSES A PO!" Emily joins in.

"A TISSUE A TISSUE!" Tommy chants with them, just as loud and irritating. Sasha looks on cloud nine and I can already see her planning the birth of their first child. I just hope she waits a while longer before the squawking of a new-born can be heard in her home.

"We all fall down," I finish.

Nathan steps into the hall and scoops both kids up, one on each arm. How he has the strength for that I have no idea; I'm barely hanging on.

"I hope you don't mind but we're going to go and do a bit of sightseeing," Sasha politely tells me.

"Of course! You don't have to spend all of your time here."

"We'll be back in a few hours."

"It's fine," I reassure her because it really is. There's nothing worse than being tied down and made to feel guilty over wanting to do your own thing. I know that feeling all too well. "Go and explore."

"Are you sure?"

"Go," I laugh, shoving her to the door. "I'll have a small, non-fancy cake ready for when you return to replace the one I dropped."

"You dropped one?" Nathan enquires. I nod and give him a look that says I'll tell him about it later.

What exactly I'll tell him I don't know.

Sasha leaves soon after, taking Tommy and Emily with her because Emily will sleep through the entire outing in her pram anyway, whereas Dillan will run them ragged. Still, it's nice to get some alone time with my boys. They're wrestling already and the draft from behind Sasha has yet to leave.

"ROAAARRRR!" Nathan roars and an excited Dillan giggles loudly.

"Oh no, a scary monster," I feign fear and hide with Dillan behind the chair. "Whatever will we do?"

Dillan hides his pudgy face in the crook of my neck, still giggling so violently his body is shaking. Nathan snatches him from me and, still growling, begins to chomp on every chubby area of our little boy. I sit back, smiling at the sight of their happiness. Why must relationships be so complex?

"Who's hungry?" Nathan asks as Dillan dangles from his back, arms tight around his neck.

"I need to make cake."

"Why don't I go and pick us up some lunch?"

Smiling I admit, "That does sound good."

He leans in and kisses my cheek. "I'll take the brat; he'll only cry if I leave him with you anyway."

"True."

"Daddy's boy."

He returns before long with a bag full of food and a sleeping Dillan resting on his shoulder.

"Bless him," I whisper and take the bag. "Go and settle him."

"And then we'll talk?"

I nod and smooth a hand over my baby boy's hair. "And then we'll talk."

Before he leaves the kitchen he turns and says, "That smells wonderful, by the way."

"Right?" I grin, looking to the oven where my cake is rising happily.

When Nathan steps back into the room I bite hard on my lip and speak. "Before we get into the heavy stuff, I... I need to tell you something."

"Go on." He eyes me warily, cautiously, and remains poised only a foot from me.

"Two nights ago when I stayed late to make Tommy's cake."

"The one you dropped?"

Nodding, I continue, "Kerim..." Fuck, this is hard to say. I avert my eyes. "You were right about Kerim wanting more than I thought he did."

"What?" He hisses dangerously and his hands fist by his sides.

"Please don't make an issue of it."

"An issue of the fact another man, a *friend*, has shown his true intentions to my wife?"

Oh dear.

"What exactly happened?"

"He kissed me." I think back to the forcefulness of his mouth on mine and then I shudder at the memory with guilt. "And for less than half a second I may have reciprocated." He freezes, his face paling, so I quickly add, "It was the surprise of it and I'm not kidding - it was only for a split second."

"Half a second or a second?" He barks, shaking with anger.

"Does it matter?"

"I suppose not." His tone is biting, furious. "And then you pushed him away?"

"Of course!" I duck my head to catch his eyes that are looking down as he tries to collect himself. "I'm not interested in Kerim. I would never hurt you like that either."

His lips thin to a white line and then my heart soars when he pulls me into his chest and mutters, "I believe you."

"Thank you." Is he finally learning to trust me? "I don't know what to do."

"You won't have to do anything," he says softly and rests his chin atop my head.

This makes me question, "What are *you* going to do?"

"I don't know." He pulls away and lets out a sad breath. "You're not really mine anymore, are you?"

"That's a difficult question to answer."

He nods once, looking as if he knew exactly what I'd say. "I do trust you. I know you think I don't, but I do."

"I know you think you do but you don't."

"Can't we have some things separate from each other? Do we have to be forthcoming with every small detail?"

"Not at all." I place my hand on my heart. "I'm not that unreasonable." He tries to speak but I raise my hand to silence him. "But suddenly getting into contact with your mother and involving our children isn't a small detail."

"Fair point." He rubs his face with both hands and sighs. "I don't know what I'm doing. I don't want to keep hurting you."

"Then don't."

"It's not that easy when what you need from me isn't something I can give."

"Why though?" I grab the sleeve of his shirt, desperate for him to give me more than that. "Why can't you?" When he doesn't answer I give his shirt a tug. "I've been indebted to you since the fire."

His look is questioning.

"I've let you walk all over me, Nathan." I whisper, looking away. "The things you've hidden, the way I've responded... I've essentially been enabling your behaviour because you literally almost died for me."

"You don't owe me anything."

"I know, but I felt as though I did so I've been letting you lie. I've been letting you treat me badly because I thought I didn't deserve better." I explain softly. "It's not going to be like that anymore. You can't treat me how you have been anymore. The jealousy, the mistrust, the lying..."

He nods solemnly. "I know I've been a bit intense lately. I'm really trying."

"I hope so, because it's not fair. I'm not completely blaming you for everything. I should have listened to you about Kerim. I didn't trust your judgement and for that I'm sorry."

"Your cake," he states, hiding any emotions from my view.

"Shit," I hiss and dart for the oven. I pull the cake from it just in time. It looks perfect but only time will tell if it is or not.

CHAPTER TWENTY-FOUR

"Stop cursing; it doesn't suit you."

"Sorry." My heatproof gloved hands place the cake tin on the wire rack. Fingers crossed this one doesn't end in disaster like the last one. "And I'm sorry that I kind of kissed him back. It wasn't because it was him… I don't know how to explain it any more than I know why I did it."

"It's okay; you're confused and under a lot of stress right now. We both are." I feel his heat against my back as I stare at the cooling cake.

"Why are you being so nice to me?" If the shoe was on the other foot I'd be going insane, despite how irrational it may be.

"Because I don't want to lose you. I promise I'll do better. You're right… about everything. I feel terrible."

Wow.

I can hardly breathe. His words have made me weak.

He kisses the curve of my neck and moves away. "May I stay a while longer?"

"Of course." I finally turn and tilt my head at my kind of fiancé. "Stay as long as you need."

"I need forever."

"One step at a time, okay?"

He grins, though it's a mixture of sadness and amusement. "Understood."

"Well at least you understand something I say." I jest and he answers by pinching my hip and pushing his lips onto mine. Is this a normal thing to do when separated? Who knows?

Chapter Twenty-Five

Nathan's mum shows up at ten on the dot, holding a bag full of gifts for the children and even a new, beautiful hat and scarf set for me ready for the winter. I thank her and leave her to have some privacy with the kids. She has visited so many times now it's getting easier and I'm starting to enjoy her company. The woman before me doesn't resonate with the woman I once thought I knew. She's so much more carefree, happy and seems to be almost at peace, though there's a tortured look to her that I can tell she tries to Botox away. She'd deny it if I asked.

Nathan has moved back in and sleeps in Dillan's room. I can't trust myself with him in bed. Who can blame me? He's a male God. His body is perfection, his love for me and his personality even more so.

As for work, I haven't been in much over the past couple of weeks and when I have been in Kerim hasn't been there or he's been busy. Thankfully he hasn't approached me about what happened and I'm hoping we can move past it without issue.

Nathan doesn't want me to say anything to him but Sasha thinks I should get things squared out about it all and our possible partnership and my promotion. What worries me is that the partnership was a promise based on us sleeping together and now that's off the table I'm out, which would mean I'm not as good as Kerim said I am.

This reality will devastate me. *Devastate me.*

The alarm on my phone rings, reminding me of my appointment at the doctors today. I'm booked in to get the coil, birth control, and I completely forgot. I should have set an earlier reminder.

"Damn it!" I hiss and twist my hair around one hand as I try to think about what to do. I could rebook but it'll take at least two months and I can't handle another day on this pill. It's making me so ill. Why am I such a bone head?

"What's wrong?" Patricia asks softly, placing her cup of tea on the side out of reach of the kids.

"I forgot about an appointment I have," I wince, checking the time on my phone again. "Would you mind me calling an end to this visit a bit earlier than expected?"

She looks disappointed and I don't blame her; she only just got here. "May I watch them for you? It would really be no bother."

My heart hammers in my chest at the thought of it. I'm not sure I can, despite our numerous meetings.

"It's fine." She holds up her hand and gives me a reassuring smile. "I understand your reluctance. Maybe another time?"

"Would you... just hold on for one second. I'll call Nathan."

She smiles again and watches me exit the room. This feels all kinds of wrong and of course I'm scared but I also want to give her a chance. She didn't ever physically abuse Nathan and she really does love the kids, I can tell. I wouldn't make that mistake.

This is such a hard decision. What if I make the wrong one?

"Hey," Nathan greets me, sounding breathless through the receiver of my phone. "What's wrong?"

"I'm getting the coil today."

"You are?"

"I completely forgot." I lean back so I can see Patricia sitting on the ground with the kids, playing with their toy trains. "I could take them with me but..."

"But?"

"Your mum said she wants to look after them."

He stops breathing as do I and then he whistles long and high. "That's... I'm not sure I'm comfortable with that. What do you think?"

"That's why I'm calling you."

"How long will you be?"

"An hour, maybe an hour and a half."

He makes a ticking sound with his tongue before replying, "She deserves a shot. Right?"

"I agree. She's been here more times than I can count."

"I just... Go. She'll be fine."

"You sure?" I ask cautiously. "You sure you're sure?"

He chuckles quietly. "I'm sure. I'll video call her. It'll be fine. Good luck."

When I re-enter the room I pick up Emily and kiss her cheek. Then I gather the courage to finally ask Patricia, "Are you sure you don't mind?"

Her face lights up so bright it warms my heart. "I could never mind." When her eyes begin to glisten with tears, I shuffle uncomfortably on the spot and nuzzle Emily to divert my attention. "This means a lot. Too much."

Too much? "I hopefully won't be too long. Nathan said he's going to video call you at some point."

"That's fine, go. All will be perfect. You will see."

And leave I do, my heart beating rapidly and my legs carrying me faster than they ever have.

When I return, my stomach cramping and aching in an awful way, I stagger into the toilet and vomit almost immediately.

"Oh my goodness, Gwen, are you alright?" Patricia raps on the bathroom door.

"That was the worst experience of my life," I whimper, recalling the aching pain as the coil was inserted. The cramps are making it so hard to see straight. I hurt.

"I'll make you some peppermint tea."

"Are they okay?" I yell, as she descends the stairs.

"They are fine. Emily is napping on the couch," she calls back, only just loud enough for me to hear.

I'm relieved they're all okay but deep down I knew they would be or I would never have walked out of that door. I kind of wish I hadn't walked through that door. My stomach hurts so badly. The procedure itself wasn't terrible - it hurt but not like I imagined - it's the after cramps. I feel so achy and drained. The doctor said it'll go away after a good sleep. I sure hope she's right.

"What happened? You look ghastly."

Ghastly? That's a word you don't hear every day. She's right though, I look as white as a sheet and probably shiny too after splashing my face with cool water and not having the energy to dry it properly afterwards.

"Should I call Nathan?"

"No." I shakily lower myself onto the couch behind Emily and tuck her into my side. "My stomach hurts so badly."

"I'm not surprised. What did you get? That awful T shaped thing they insert into your lady parts?"

Lady parts? Snort. "Yeah, it'll be worth it. No more horrible chemicals and even worse hormonal spats to contend with."

The kettle boils and Patricia leaves the room once more, returning a few minutes later with a pleasant smelling peppermint tea, the bag still in the water.

"I added a sugar."

"Thank you." I wait for her to place it on the smaller table by the couch before reaching for a handle, reaching my body far over Emily's and taking a small sip. "That's perfect."

"I know my time is almost at an end but I'd feel terrible leaving you in your condition."

"I'm sure I'll be fine," I wave her off and shut my eyes, praying that Dillan doesn't start climbing all over me.

"I doubt it and I shan't risk it. If it's alright, I'll stay and keep an eye on the kids while you rest."

Who is this wonderful woman and where did she come from? "Thank you, Patricia."

"It's no bother. Close your eyes and sleep. I'll fetch you a blanket."

A soft, warm hand touches my forehead followed by even softer lips.

"You smell good," I whisper, reaching for Nathan as he lifts me from the sofa and into his arms. "I'm heavy."

"This brings back memories." I hear the smile in his voice. "That night you stayed in the house, back when you were pregnant with Dillan. I found you asleep on the sofa."

"I remember vaguely," I murmur. My eyes won't open. "My stomach still hurts. What time is it?"

"Bed time. You missed work."

"What?" I jolt as he carries me up the stairs.

"It's okay, I spoke to Harold. He understands it can't be helped."

My eyes peel open though the light hurts so I shut them immediately. "I think I'm getting ill."

"I think you're just exhausted." He lowers me onto the mattress and begins to help me out of my clothes. "I called the doctor and she said this is normal for some people. You just need rest and to check the strings in the morning, whatever that means."

"Right." I raise the top half of my body so he can help me out of my top and bra. "Where are the babies?"

"Sleeping. Like I said, it's late. My mother was putting them to bed just as I got home."

"Oh my god, now I feel bad."

"It's fine." He lowers me down and tucks the blanket up to my chin. "She said you were dead to the world."

"I can tell." Rolling onto my side, I tuck the blanket between my legs. "Tell her I owe her one."

"She seemed to be enjoying herself just fine. She was singing to Emily. I've never heard her sing." He sounds happy and wistful. "Is it possible that I might actually…"

"What?" I try to turn to look at him but he pins me and curls into my back.

"Nothing, it's a silly thought."

"There's no such thing."

"I just feel content," he sighs softly and kisses my shoulder. "As though all things are going to work out better than I could have imagined."

"I really, really hope you're right."

"Well!" I grin, stretching tall. "The doctor was right. I just needed sleep."

"Twenty hours' worth," Nathan laughs, handing me a tray with toast, cereal, a mug of coffee and a cup of tea. "I wasn't sure what you'd prefer."

"This is perfect. I'm so hungry." My stomach confirms that with a growl. "You're the best."

"Then maybe you'll reconsider the bedroom ban?"

I smirk after filling my mouth with rice pops. "We shall see."

"What if I promise to never lie to you again?"

"Is that a promise or are you asking me if you should?"

He hesitates, confused by my question.

"I don't want you to make me promises that I don't want nor expect you to keep." I rub my eyes and place the spoon in my bowl. When I offer him the toast he politely declines with a slight shake of his head. "Like you said, we should have our own things. They just shouldn't compromise our happiness."

"Right." He seems just as confused as before. "This relationship thing is hard for me to grasp. There are so many rules that didn't apply during my life of solitude." When he sees my frown he adds, "I'm not complaining, I'm enjoying the experience... mostly. I just wish I could figure this out."

Damn, now I feel awful. He really is trying and I've majorly spat my dummy out in a way that isn't helpful to either of us. "You're right." I place my hand on his. "I think we both need to be a bit more understanding and less demanding of each other."

"So... does that mean the bedroom ban is off?"

I laugh and place the tray to the side. "Okay. The bedroom ban is off." Then he dives on me.

<u>Gwen</u>: Thank you so much for all of your help yesterday. We all really appreciate it.

<u>Patricia</u>: It's no problem. That's what family does. Correct?

<u>Gwen</u>: If you need anything at all, we're also here. We look forward to seeing you again.

I think back to yesterday when she got tears in her eyes after receiving my permission to be on her own with my children and my heart twangs in the same way it did then. For once, just this once, make it so Nathan gets what I know his heart must desire – a mother who loves him to his very core. She won't be able to get that time back and neither will he, but she's found a good place to start in his children. Our children.

Kerim is at work today and I make a note to approach him at some point before nightfall. I want to clear the air between us; there's no use being a coward anymore. We have things to discuss, not just about our relationship but about the promotion he offered me. I need to know where I stand.

The second he's free, I follow him out into the smoking area and wait for him to light his cigarette before I sidle up to him, hands tucked into my pockets.

"The dreaded conversation," he grins and inhales a long drag before blowing it out into the air away from me. "I've been waiting for when you were ready."

"Oh." I chew on my lip and kick at the ground with my shoe. "Now I don't know what to say."

"Look," he takes another drag, this time blowing the cloud of smoke towards the ground, "I know I've been too forward with you, but what I said about your talent is all true. I wasn't just offering you a promotion to seduce you. I wouldn't be idiotic enough to try." He smiles warmly and reaches out to take my hand in his. "I like you, as a friend. I'd like to be more, as I've said, but I respect that your heart belongs elsewhere and instead offer you my kitchen."

Thank God.

"I can see your relief," he smiles, his eyes twinkling with amusement. "Do you think so little of me?"

"No, of course not." I slide my hand from his. "I'm just grateful. I'd like to still accept, as long as things aren't weird between us."

"Not at all. That was all my mistake and I'd hate for it to ruin the ease we had."

"Me too." I waft my hand through the smoke, pushing the silvery floating threads around the air. "You should quit."

"So you keep saying."

"I'm going to head back inside." I nod to the door. "Thank you for not making this weird."

"You too," he laughs, flicking the cigarette stub into a plant pot full of them. "Now get back to work before the others begin to suspect that we're having an affair."

"Not funny," I call over my shoulder.

"Yet very true!"

<u>Gwen</u>: All is well with Kerim. I feel like everything is finally getting back on track.

<u>Nathan</u>: Good. I'm glad. We miss you.

<u>Gwen</u>: I miss you all too. I'll bring ice-cream. Has Dillan been on his potty today? We've been slacking a bit.

Nathan: Once but he mostly peed on the floor. We'll get him there. Don't worry. It's been a hectic time.

He can say that again.

"Back to work, Gwen," Harold calls, though his tone is kind and not aggressive like Kerim's would be.

"Just a sec," I call back as I type one final text to Patricia.

Gwen: Are you coming tomorrow, usual time? If I don't respond it's because I'm at work.

She doesn't respond at all. Nor does she the next day.

"Dillan probably exhausted her," Nathan says in jest but the worry in his eyes shows me that he's not entirely positive that's the case either.

"She's not answering you?"

He shakes his head. I sit back and help Emily take a bite of her sandwich before sipping my latte.

"You don't think your dad did something to her, do you?" I whisper so as the babies and the rest of the café can't hear. Not that the babies will understand, but I'd still like to shelter them from as much drama as possible.

"I..." His tongue swipes across his lower lip. "I'll make a few calls."

"Good." I take his hand over the table. "I'm sure she's fine; she's probably just exhausted."

"Yeah," he responds, though he looks unconvinced. "Come on, the kids are excited to play."

I remove Dillan's shoes while Nathan plucks Emily from the wooden highchair and together we make our way over to the children's play area, well-fed and ready for a few hours of family fun.

When we return home, Nathan disappears into the bedroom to make the calls. He's gone a while and my panic grows. Busying myself with the kids, I try not to clock watch as desperately as I want to. I also place my phone on the microwave by Caleb's picture to avoid calling Patricia again.

Who would have thought that a woman I once hated would now be the cause of my sympathies and concern?

"Give me strength," I beg of my deceased lover. "And take my headache away while you're at it."

A shiver rushes through me, creeping me out.

"If that was you, Caleb, that's not funny."

"Wee!" Dillan yells, distracting me.

"Good boy!" I cheer and lead him to his potty. "I'm so, so very happy!"

Nathan enters the room just as I'm pulling Dillan's trousers up. "I called around a few acquaintances and she's fine."

I blink, confused. "What does that mean?"

"She's probably just needing some space."

"That makes no sense."

"My mother is... you know she's complex."

"Yeah." I loop my hands around the back of his neck and tip my head back so I can look into his eyes and kiss his jaw. "Overload of emotion keeping her away you reckon?"

"Maybe. Who knows?" He sways us on the spot, gently rocking us from side to side. "We'll figure it out." Lips press against my own and I deepen it swiftly. He tastes so good. "Speaking of figuring things out." His right hand takes my left and when he steps back, he brings my hand to his lips and shows me a sparkling new ring sitting on my ring finger. It's similar to the last but not an exact replica. It's beautiful. "Don't take it off this time."

"I won't. So long as you don't treat me like that again."

"I won't."

We share another kiss and turn back to our kids. Before we move on from the conversation entirely, I rest my temple against his shoulder and say, "Thank you for my ring and don't worry about your mum; she'll be in touch."

Chapter Twenty-Six

The days go by and even when I receive the contract from Kerim to stabilise my place as a leading chef in his kitchen, my thoughts don't drift from Nathan. He seems so sad, so lost and alone. He's throwing himself into work to distract himself from thinking of his mother. I fear that he'll spiral to a place I can't pull him back from. As sad as that sounds, if his mother vanishes I worry he'll never put his trust into anyone again. I sent her a text earlier begging her to contact us before this weekend. The kids miss her so much. It's unfair of her to be doing this to them. I'm starting to get past the point of caring and I'm beginning to get angry.

"I really need to find a solicitor to look this over," I say to Nathan, who is looking over images of his finished products for the Essex store. It won't be long now until it's complete, though Nathan's excitement seems to be diminishing. His love for me and the kids still soars; it's more his soul that seems to be fading to a dull aura.

"I have one in mind who deals with those types of contracts." He kisses my hair and flips another laminated page in the red binder. "What do you think to the new line of charms?"

"I still think you should do a mermaid one and a unicorn one!" I push my leg beneath the folder and over his lap.

"I was thinking of adding a fairy-tale line. It would be great for kids."

I slap his chest. "I love fairy-tales and I'm not a kid."

"That could be easily protested."

"Hey," I whine but it's swallowed by his kiss. He throws the contract and folder away and leans into me, devastating my nerves and senses with a deep, all-consuming kiss. "Christ." I whimper as his lips move down my neck and to my breast, where he nuzzles and snuggles with a happy, contented sigh.

"Any charms you want, any at all, you just tell me and they're yours."

"I want a penis one."

He sighs again, this time from exasperation. "That's not happening."

"Boobies?"

"And you got upset when I called you a child?"

I grin happily and adjust my body beneath his. "You still haven't taken me to the gym yet."

"True. I miss having one ready in my basement."

"In a few years we can afford a bigger house again," I assure him and tickle the back of his hair with gentle touches.

"As soon as we get married, we'll start exploring our options."

"I want land, like we had before."

"Me too," he agrees, smiling. "And a room for a gym."

"And an office for you and a greenhouse!"

"And a conservatory that leads onto a deck where we can hose the kids down and host barbecues."

Grinning, I grab his hair and lift his head so I can look at his stunning eyes, a shade lighter than melted chocolate. "I want a huge kitchen, a dining area and a living room."

"You can have it all. Anything you want, it's yours."

I release his head and he kisses the top of my breast. "Promise?"

"That's a promise I can definitely make."

"Go get me some doughnuts then from that doughnut place."

"Fine, but only because I have a craving for the raspberry one and not because of my undying love for you."

"Right," I giggle, which turns into a squeal when he starts nibbling at my neck. "Go. I'm hungry."

"You just ate."

"I need calories to keep up the size of my rear."

"And what a lovely rear it is." He grabs it and rolls over me. "I'll be back soon."

"Thank you, baby, you're the best."

"That I am. Now choose a venue and get wedding planning."

"Aye aye." I salute him and whistle at him as he leaves.

CHAPTER TWENTY-SIX

Gwen: I need help planning a wedding.

Sasha: Me too!

Gwen: We can do this.

Sasha: That we can, my lady bitch.

Gwen: Let's not turn this into a Bride Wars thing and accidentally book our weddings on the same day.

Sasha: And no talk about a joint wedding. My day is MINE and your day is YOURS.

Gwen: Agreed. I think I want to get married at the HAC.

Sasha: You would think that the amount of time I've spent wanting to marry Tommy, I'd have a clue where and when.

Gwen: You baffle me.

Sasha: I already have my dress picked out.

Gwen: Well, that's a start.

Opening my laptop, I flick through images of dresses that I find on a search engine. There are so many gorgeous styles, though none call to me in the sense that a particular style cries out, "I'M THE ONE."
But then it happens. I find the perfect one. The one that I'll need to replicate to a T or I'll never be happy with another.

Gwen: I just found my dress too and the maker is local!

Sasha: Well duh, everything is in London... Shall I come next weekend?

Gwen: YES! Though with or without you I'm going to find it alone. You can just see it next weekend.

Sasha: Whatever, but I get dibs on seeing it before anyone else.

Gwen: Deal.

"Why are you so happy?" Nathan asks, standing in the doorway with a box of doughnuts in his hands.
"I didn't hear you come in." I can't contain my smile as I snatch the doughnuts away and open the box, only to discover a doughnut missing. "Greedy git. Who said you could have the first one?"
"Me." We both drop onto the couch side by side, and he chooses a movie as I choose my first doughnut.
"Okay," I announce. "This will be my very last piece of junk food until our wedding in July. I know it's a way away, but I want a summer wedding because I don't want to be freezing my nipples off when we take photos outside of the venue, which, I believe should be the HAC, not only because you get it at a discounted rate but also because it's beautiful…"
"And breathe," he chuckles, smiling from ear to ear. "I'm loving the enthusiasm."
"I'm excited."
"Me too. That makes me happier than you can imagine."
"This doughnut makes me happier than anyone could ever imagine." I hum loudly with joy as I sink my teeth into the gooey centre. "Promise me you won't enable my bad eating habit."
"I promise." He twists a lock of my hair around his finger. "You too. No more fattening dinners for me."
"Agreed."
"What do you want to watch?"
I shrug. "Whatever, just don't make it a long one. I have a busy day tomorrow."
"Doing…?"
"Dress shopping." I bounce a little. "I think I found the perfect one."
"I wish I could come with you."
"You could go suit shopping."
"Not until you give me the colour scheme."

"I'll let you know." He kisses the chocolate from my lips and tastes it with his tongue. I love this man.

Jeanine joins me on the hunt for the wedding dress expedition, mostly to help me look after the babies. I'm relieved to have her here, not just for her help but also for the company.

"I've missed you," I admit. "It feels like whenever I see you it's always fleeting."

"You've been busy; I understand. We get to catch up today instead."

"Exactly."

Heading into the wedding store I found online, I browse the rows upon rows of dresses until an attendant comes to help me. I show her the one that I saw online, annoyed when she tells me it was an exclusive for that particular model and would be, *'above what I can afford.'* No kidding, she said that so I left.

We hit all of the mainstream wedding boutiques, looking at table centrepieces and colour fabric blends. Nothing appeals to me and by the end of the morning I'm feeling disheartened and bored of it all. The kids are beginning to get restless too. The only person who looks to be having a good time is Jeanine.

"Let's stop for lunch," she suggests, pulling us into the next restaurant we see. Her phone comes out the second we stop at a table. "We need to stop going to all of these commercial places. They're overwhelming you with their business cards. How many photographers do you now have in your pocket? How many caterers?"

My cheeks puff out as I blow out a breath. "Too many."

"Give them to me." She drops them into the middle of the table. "Forget about all of that. Planning a wedding should be a happy time and you look rotten."

"I feel it."

"Which is a shame because this morning you looked so happy." She checks her curled hair in the mirror on the wall and flags down the waitress. "You'd think they'd put menus on the table."

Smiling at said table, I wait for the waitress to bring some over and tell her my drink order before she leaves.

"So, I propose we spark that fire in your eyes that was there this morning and have another look at the beautiful dress you fell in love with."

At her command, I open the image on my phone and we stare at it, smiling with joy and love for it.

"Right, let's see if we can't find us an independent dress maker."

"Won't that cost a fortune?"

"Not if you find the right one." She winks and turns her phone to me. "Well, would you look at that? It's fate. There's one just around the corner."

"If you consider five miles away just around the corner then sure."

"It's nothing when you're driving." She waves her napkin at me and turns to the kids. "Are you babes hungry?"

"Nom nom," Emily says quietly as Dillan bangs his hands against the plastic surface of his highchair.

"I'll take that as a yes," I whisper and we both laugh together.

Feeling rested, full and fresh, we head out to the car and find the independent dress maker. It isn't easy as it sits below a townhouse down a side street. I leave the kids with Jeanine at first to check that it's open and also because if this is a failure like the rest I'll feel awful for getting them in and out of their car seats for the hundredth time today.

At first I assume I have the wrong place because of the numerous dream catchers on the inside of the window and the strange dark purple, sparkly net that hangs just behind them. It seems to be a display for one of those palm reading stores. The sign above the door reads,

'Altered Illusions.'

The name seems... well strange, but who am I to judge?

I knock on the glass of the door before opening it and it rattles and jingles in such a cute, old timey store way.

The store itself is very dimly lit and smells wonderful, spicy and sweet all at once. I can't decide what it smells like, I just know that I like it.

The reason I immediately know I'm in the right place is because along every wall are rolls and rolls of fabric. It seems very disorganised but I bet the creator of the beautiful dresses on mannequins in the centre of the room knows exactly what she's doing.

"COMING!" Comes a yell from the doorway, draped in purple beads, behind a small, rectangular shaped wooden desk. "Ouch." The lady stumbles on something I think because she begins cursing under her breath after knocking a few things over.

When she finally comes into view, she is not what I expected. Though after walking into this store, I'm not entirely sure what I expected. What I didn't expect was a petite, stunningly pretty young woman with light blue hair. It's almost grey but not quite. Her fringe is a perfect block against her forehead. It really suits her.

I see a white peace sign tattoo on the side of her neck. White. I didn't know they could tattoo in white. It looks amazing.

She pops a pink bubble from between her thick, dark brown lipstick painted lips. "I'm Adriana, the owner of this lovely little crap hole. And you are?"

"Oh, I'm umm..." I look at her outfit. Her top is a white lace crop top over a bralette. Her dark jeans are slashed all the way down to her ankles. White converse with sparkly silver gems on the toes cover tiny feet. "I'm..."

"You got a problem with how I look?" Her hands go to her hips and she chews the bubblegum angrily before popping it again.

"No, God no," I raise my hands, my eyes wide. "I love it. I wish I had the guts and style to dress so... wicked?"

She grins, seeming appeased, and holds out her hand which also has a tattoo, this one a black lace design, going from her wrist to her middle finger.

"I can stylishly flip people off," she giggles, noticing me staring. "Okay, I'm done being the walking object. How can I help you...?"

"Gwen," I respond when she waits for me to tell her my name. I release her hand and pull out my phone. "I want a wedding dress made like this."

She snatches the phone from my hand and places glasses over her eyes. They were hanging on a chain around her neck but I didn't notice them as I was too busy checking out how perky her breasts are in that tiny bralette. I think I might fancy this woman a little. "This is gorgeous, but it's not my design."

"I know."

"Which means I can't make it, but I can take inspiration from it and design you my own."

My lips part. "Really? What if I don't like it?"

"Oh you will love it. I've yet to disappoint," she grins, still chewing away. "You want this colour too?"

"Yes! I absolutely love that colour."

"It needs more sparkles to make it pop."

"Sure," I agree for the sake of agreeing. "How much do you think it'll be?"

"I'll have to measure out the materials and whatnot before I can give you a definite price. It won't be cheap, but it'll be cheaper than what you've been quoted for that dress. I only charge for time and materials."

That's what I figured. "Okay. Do you have a portfolio or something I can flip through?"

"Yep." She finally gives me my phone back and I follow her to her desk. She hands me a black folder. "I'm the best. People don't know it yet, but it's true." As I flick through the images, I completely believe her. "You really made all of these?"

"I did. And they're all cheaper and better quality that anything similar instore."

"You're so talented."

"Thank you." She pops her gum again and cocks her head at me. "I take a fifty quid deposit just so I know you're serious and if you don't like the dress I sell it on and try again, but trust me... you will *love* the dress."

Can I really put my faith in somebody for something this huge? "I'm in. Could you possibly make a few matching ties too?"

"Whatever you need, you email it to me," she hands me a business card, "and I'll add it to your bill."

"This is great!" I beam, stuffing my phone back into my pocket. "Shall I email you the image too?"

"Nah, it's cool. I got it up here." She taps a finger to her temple, flashing me the Deathly Hallows symbol tattooed on the side.

"Thank you."

"No problem, sweets. Now let's get your details then." She opens up her diary on the desk. It's a large leather journal with cotton paper. "When do you need it for?"

"Not until July, but..."

"Good, that'll give me enough time. You need to lose weight and get fit, I bet?"

"That's the plan."

"Stop eating bread, hype up the protein and you'll be golden." She tweaks the hoop piercing in her nostril and then flexes her impressive, defined biceps. "I know what I'm talking about."

"Right." I quickly give her my details. "Do you need the deposit now?"

"No, not until I start. I'll call you when I'm ready and when I have the invoice. You're a ten, right? It'll take a few days. My turnaround is usually quicker but I am fully booked for a while."

"That's great, I'm happy for you," I smile and she just gives me a disbelieving look. "So I'll go and you call?"

"Yep, I'll call you and you'll need to come in closer to the time for measurements too, but for now I'll calculate the cost based on an average size ten." She leads me to the door and all but shoves me out. "Happy engagement!"

I skip back to the car and climb into the driver's seat with a broad grin on my face.

"Sorted?" Jeanine asks and I nod frantically. "Excellent. That's such good news."

"I think we got lucky. You should have seen the few dresses she had on display. They were ostentatious but they were amazing. This one dress had three layers and the top layer was this see through black lace. It was so gothic but so beautiful and well made."

I turn back to look at the kids, both in car seats on either side of the rear bench. Dillan is drawing pictures on the window with his finger and Emily is napping as per usual.

"I can't wait to see what she does with your dress." Jeanine buckles up her seatbelt, as do I, and we set off once more, this time for home. "Though I can't say it took long?"

She's concerned I'm going to end up with something I hate. Me too.

"She's going to get me a price for the style I want and then we're going to finalise everything… probably." My hand clicks the signal and we turn right, almost hitting a man on a bike as he flies across the road, uncaring of oncoming traffic. Well, this is London. I don't expect any differently. I'm used to it now, forever prepared for any eventuality. "This is fate; it'll be fine."

"I'm so happy you and Nathan are okay again."

"Me too," I agree, because I really am. I got scared for a while there. "Oooh, it's that book store!"

"The one you're always harping on about?"

I nod. "They do some lovely leather journals. I get one or two for Nathan every year. I haven't had chance this year though."

"He still writes in his journals?"

"Yes, he lets me read them when they're full too. They really have helped me to understand the way his mind works."

"Poor boy," she mutters solemnly. "I wish I'd done more to help him growing up."

"You had enough kids of your own to deal with. He doesn't hold it against you at all."

"He's a good man when he wants to be." She pats my hand on the gear stick and offers, "Go in, I'll wait in the car with the kids again."

"Are you sure?"

"Of course. No use getting the kids out again, especially not while Emily is sleeping."

"Thank you." I park as close as I can and race across the street, weaving through people as quickly as the crowds will allow. It doesn't take long for me to find the perfect journal either. Nathan doesn't like the ones with clasps and such; he prefers just a plain brown leather with a rope to seal it shut. That's exactly what I buy him and before I know it I'm back in the car and I'm driving Jeanine home.

After an emotional goodbye, despite the fact I see her far more than my regular friends, I head home with the babies where a happy looking Nathan waits for me and helps me remove the kids from the car.

Once they're settled in front of the TV, I take the journal from my bag and race it upstairs before he can see. I have a little box where I hide things worth hiding. It sits at the back of my closet on the ground, hidden beneath a pile of shoes. Well it used to. I notice how the shoes that are usually stacked neatly in that area are in a bit of a mess. It's been a while since I took a set of heels from the pile; I must have forgotten to tidy it.

Unfortunately, I discover the reason for the mess and my heart stops. It stops so suddenly I begin to choke for air and then nausea takes over. As I attempt to calm myself, my hands throw the shoes out of the closet.

I yell repeatedly, "No, no, no, no... this can't be happening!" Shoes fly backwards as well as Nathan's journal and the box itself until there's nothing on my closet floor. "FUCK!"

"Gwen?" Nathan calls up the stairs. "Is everything okay?"

"No," I honestly reply and then bury my head in my knees.

"Babe, you need to come here. I can't leave the kids."

"Did you take it?" My voice is muffled by the foetal position in which I'm holding my body.

CHAPTER TWENTY-SIX

"I can't hear you; come here."

"Did you move the DVD?" I lift my head, tears streaming down my face.

His silence finally draws me from my protective position. I stand upright and make my way to the stairs. He stands at the bottom, frozen in place and staring up at me with blank, almost lifeless eyes and pale skin.

"Did you?"

"I wouldn't. He waits for me to go down before racing up after me. The sound of drawers sliding open and slamming shut brings the kids to where I stand. Dillan grips the bars of the stairgate and Emily clings to my leg. "Did you put it somewhere else maybe?"

"No. It's always been there."

He continues looking around before coming back down, looking dishevelled and panicked. "We haven't had a break in." His shoulder accidentally bumps mine as he goes into the room and checks the cabinet full of DVDs and books. "We'd have noticed."

I let out a sob. "That's why..."

"What?" He looks at me for a brief second, pulling DVDs off the shelf. I see his face get paler.

"I'm so sorry," I whimper and press my hand to my aching heart. "Nathan, I am so sorry. I never should have left her alone."

"That's all she wanted, wasn't it?" His voice is monotone as he sits back onto his knees and surveys the mess of cases on the ground around him. "She used us, tricked us and the kids, to keep him out of prison."

"How did they know we had it?" I ask, stepping into the room, feeling lost and out of breath. "How do they know we haven't made a copy? How did she know where it was?"

He doesn't answer; he continues to stare blankly at the cases. I kick them out of the way and crouch down in front of him.

"Nathan..."

"It doesn't matter," he whispers and stands abruptly. "There's no use dwelling on it. Come on, the kids need dinner."

I watch him leave, his tense body taking long, eager strides to remove him from the room.

"Nathan," I say quietly, softly, as I follow him close behind. "It's..."

"I *don't* want to talk about it."

"We have to."

"We don't!" He snaps, his voice loud and his tone final. "I don't ever want to discuss this again. It's done."

That spiteful, vile bitch. "I know you're hurting."

"Then you don't know me well."

Ouch. "I'll give you space."

"I don't need space." He turns to me, his eyes blazing. "I need you to help me make dinner and to just go back to normal."

"Please..."

"Wipe that pity from your eyes, Gwen. I can't stand it. I don't want it and I don't need it."

"Don't shut yourself away from me."

"I'm not. Why are you forcing me to confront something that isn't even bothering me? It's over."

"The hell it is," I mutter, seething with anger, not at him but at this situation. "I'll kill her."

"What's the point?" He turns away and begins rooting through the cupboards before grabbing a bag of pasta and dropping it onto the side. "They've won; it's over. Let's just safeguard our children and learn from this. Okay?"

"I can't believe this is happening," I whisper to myself, though I know he hears it because he laughs. "Oh I can." His hands frantically rip at the bag and he dumps too much pasta into a sauce pan. He has yet to boil the kettle but I don't think he's realised. He's too consumed by the hurt I know is eating at him. "Of course she didn't come back because she could ever love me or my kids. I'm a fool."

"You are not a fool."

"Aren't I? I lied to you because deep down," he turns and looks at me with a weary gaze, "I knew this would happen and I didn't want to face the pity you'd give me, the pity in your eyes right now."

"That's not..."

"Because why, after years of torment, years of begging her and *him* to let me stay with my brother, would she suddenly be there for me? Why?" He yells and steps towards me. "Because clearly I haven't been punished enough, have I?" His hands grab my biceps and hold tight. Fingers bite into my arms but the pain is nothing compared to the throbbing in my chest. My heart is truly breaking, for him, not for me. "My entire childhood was stolen from me. I have no good memories. I'm a mess, Gwen, a mess. And

CHAPTER TWENTY-SIX

the one time, the one time I let myself believe that things might actually be going perfectly, it gets ripped away."

"You don't need her; you have us."

"Is it so wrong?" He asks sadly and his voice breaks. His brown eyes shimmer and a tear slowly leaves a shiny trail as it falls from his lashes and onto his cheek. "Is it so wrong that I just wanted her to love me?"

"No." I cup his face with my hands, my own tears falling freely at the sight of his. "That's not wrong. They are wrong. They are losing, not you."

"Why doesn't she love me, Gwen?" His voice is barely audible and I choke back a sob. He buries his face in my neck and with trembling arms he holds me to him so tightly I find it hard to breathe. "Why would she let them do that to me?"

I don't know what to say so I don't say anything. I just hold him as he cries, something I know that he has likely never done.

"I'm so sorry," I sob, holding him just as tight as he holds me.

Frantic lips find mine and I let him kiss me. It's painful, it's rough but we both need it. He lifts me onto the counter and knocks the saucepan full of pasta onto the ground. My arms wrap around his neck as our mouths tangle as well as our tears. A strong hand grips the back of my head, disallowing me to move away, making it hard to breathe, but I don't care. I let him. I absorb him. All of him. All of his pain. If I could take it into myself I would, but for now this will do.

"Uh-oh," Dillan cries from the doorway and we both separate and look at where he's pointing a chubby little finger. "Mess."

"Naughty Daddy." I playfully smack Nathan's shoulder and wipe my cheeks on my sleeve. "Shall we get the brush?"

"Yeah." Dillan goes straight for the cupboard under the stairs where we store the dustpan and brush.

Nathan grabs my wrist before I leave the room and yanks me sharply back to him. "Thank you for loving me, Gwen."

With the back of my fingers, I stroke his still moist cheek and whisper, "I don't know how anybody can do anything but love you, Nathan. You don't know what you're worth."

He kisses me again, sweetly this time, and quickly turns away, his eyes glistening once more. I chase after Dillan, giving my fiancé the escape and privacy he needs.

"Let's clean up this mess," I tell Dillan, who is sweeping the hallway already despite it being sparkling clean. "In the kitchen, baby." Emily toddles along after us with a feather duster.

Nathan stands at the back door with a glass in hand. It's clear and I can't tell if it's vodka or water. When he downs the glass and his profile grimaces, I decide it must be vodka. As the kids are pushing the mess around the floor, I sneak up behind him and wrap my arms around his middle. He places a hand over my locked ones and sighs gravely.

"You go have a bath," I tell him, my cheek pressed between his shoulder blades. "Relax."

He nods, turns, kisses me and then stalks upstairs.

"Right," I tell my beautiful babies. "Let's clean this up and go."

"Daddy gone," Emily says, looking at the doorway.

"He's gone to have a bath," I assure her, though this doesn't appease her. She can tell something's wrong. Our daughter is a lot like her dad, brooding yet observant. "Come on." I lift her into my arms and she rests her head against my shoulder. "What shall we eat?"

"Hey," I say to Mum quietly through the phone as I step into the hall and close Dillan's bedroom door quietly.

"Everything okay?" She asks. "You sound sad."

"I only said 'hey'. How can you tell I sound sad?"

"I'm your mum."

"Good point." I blow out a breath and silently creep to my bedroom. Peeking through the crack in the door, I spy Nathan sitting on the side of the bed, his shoulders slumped. Leaving him, I pad downstairs and fight back tears as I say, "I need you to have the kids for two nights."

Her tone changes to one of serious concern. "What's wrong?"

"I..." My voice cracks. "It's Nathan."

"Christ, what's happened? Is he okay?"

"Physically he's fine, but mentally... I'm worried. I need to... I just need to get him away for a little while."

"Why? What's going on?"

I exit the house and stand in the garden. The breeze blows my hair across my face so I turn to face it.

"I wouldn't even know where to start."

"At the beginning."

"Mum... Nathan was... I shouldn't even... I..." Fuck. "I found DVDs of him being abused by his grandfather as a child and that's why his dad burned the house down, because one of the DVDs showed that his dad knew and didn't care because he needed money to keep his business afloat and Nathan's grandfather paid for that. But you know his mum has come back into our lives? Well it was to double check that we didn't have any more copies of these DVDs. Well we did. We had one and she took it and Nathan... Nathan is broken. Not because of the DVD but because she's a lying sack of mouldy shit and I hate her. I *HATE* her for what she's done."

My breath is lost after that tirade and my stress is high.

"I don't even know what to say to any of that." She goes silent again. "Do you want to bring them here or shall I come there?"

"I'll bring them to you, first thing. Is that okay?"

"That's fine, I'm free." Pause. "That poor boy."

"I know," I whisper. "I wish I could kill them all."

"Karma. Don't ruin your good fortune for them. They aren't worth it." I hear a door open and close and then the wind hit the speaker of her phone. "Was Caleb molested too?"

"No, that was one of my first questions too. I think it was because he was terminally ill."

"This is crazy, Gwen."

She's right. I still can't wrap my head around any of it. "I know. I'll be there at about ten tomorrow. Thank you for doing this."

"Of course. I love you. This is what families do."

That's basically what Patricia said too.

"I'll let you go," she says. "Try to sleep."

Immediately I race back inside and up the stairs to quietly pack the kids' bags. Nathan probably won't be happy to be away from them on his days off but right now, with everything that has happened, he needs some healing and so do I.

The kids don't need to be around us for this. They'll have much more fun with their nan.

When I return home from dropping off the kids with my mum, Nathan is still sleeping. It's almost one in the afternoon. I'm worried about him. He didn't sleep last night; he just laid beside me, holding me in his arms, staring into space.

I kiss his temple though he doesn't stir. He's wiped, not just physically but mentally and emotionally and no doubt spiritually.

He needs me to take care of him today and that's exactly what I'll do. Right after I send that vicious bitch a very angry text.

<u>Gwen</u>: I don't believe in the existence of a higher being. I don't believe in a lot of things that I can't see. Except love. We gave you that. Nathan, after all you did, gave you that. I gave you that. My kids gave you that. You didn't deserve it any more than he deserved a lifetime of what he had before me and our kids. I know that you probably won't even read this. I just know that I can't let this go unsaid. You have ruined him. Not because of what you took from our house, but because of what you took from his soul. He was happy. For once he was fucking happy. You were back, his mummy, the person who was supposed to protect him. He genuinely believed that you didn't know about the abuse. I let him believe it, despite my doubts.

How can you sleep at night knowing what he's been through? How can you sleep at night knowing you're protecting a man who ruined your son's childhood?

How can you just walk away from him again and our kids?

I'd ask what did he do in a past life to deserve this, but I don't believe in reincarnation. This, to me, is the only life we get. This is the only life you'll get with us. How can a man that abused you and your son for so long make you happy? Are you willing to lose everything that's worth a damn in your pathetic existence in order to protect a man who made your existence pathetic in the first place? You won't get another chance at this. Do the right thing. It won't repair what has happened and it won't bring you back into our hearts, but at least when you're old and on your death bed, you won't be begging for Nathan's forgiveness just like your father in law did. Nathan didn't forgive him, by the way, just like he won't forgive you.

Bring the DVD back. Let Nathan have his justice. Fucking redeem yourself. Don't be weak. Any ounce of motherly instinct you have left needs to be channelled right now.

Chapter Twenty-Seven

"Hey." Nathan blinks a few times, sounding and looking tired.

"I made your favourite soup and your favourite cake," I whisper, placing the tray onto the bedside table and then sitting beside him on the bed.

"What time is it?"

I glance at the digital clock on my side of the bed and respond, "just gone five."

"In the afternoon?" His face is flat. He doesn't seem upset at his late awakening. I nod and gently caress his jaw. "I should get up."

"You'll feel better after a shower and some food."

He doesn't answer, nor does he look convinced.

I place the tray onto his lap, relieved when he starts to eat.

"This is good," he murmurs, smiling a little. "Where are the kids?"

"I took them to my mum's."

"You drove all the way to Skeg and back?"

"It was nice to clear my head."

He doesn't object, only frowns, and I know he isn't happy but I also know he's too tired to argue.

"Finish your soup and eat your slice of cake; you need the sugar."

"Yes, boss." His attempt at jesting falls as flat as the expression on his handsome face.

"I'll go and start the shower. I need one myself." I tuck his hair behind his ear, relieved to see it's grown long enough to do so. Only just.

The hot water is a relief. It spills over my curves perfectly, taking my aches with it. If only it could dissolve the hate in my heart.

Nathan joins me after a few minutes and presses me against the wall with his solid chest. I run my hands over his back. It feels so silky under the water, which his body is sheltering me from. I begin to catch the chill in the air which causes my nipples to pebble as my breasts tighten. He ducks his head, the water hitting the top of my head and running into my mouth when he takes my nipple into his mouth. I cry out with surprise and hold his head gently. Fingers part the folds between my thighs and dip into me slowly and softly. I can hardly handle it. My body is burning so badly. It jerks and tenses with each pulse of pleasure.

Finally his mouth releases me. I whimper at the loss of it and then whimper again when he begins to kiss his way down to my navel. The fingers tormenting and probing inside of me remain as such. His head gets lower and lower until he's on his knees. I don't have time to protest because I don't fully understand what he's doing until I feel his tongue there. Right there. He seeks my clitoris and then he finds it and it's as if he has done this a thousand times. He hooks my leg over his shoulder and kisses me below as intensely as he kisses me above.

"Oh," I pant and press my back against the wall. I need to grab something and twist it in my hands. I daren't grab his head for fear that he'll stop.

He pushes deeper, vanishing entirely into the space between my thighs, and I know I'm close. I can feel it ready to release.

"Nathan," I grit. My eyes squeeze shut and I stop breathing. It's too late and if he knows it, he doesn't care because he won't stop teasing and tasting me. My climax explodes through me in a way it never has and he doesn't relent. I jerk and pull away from him but he holds me tight, still tormenting me. It's painful but the pain goes as quickly as it started and as soon as my second orgasm begins, he stands, lifts me, pins me against the cold, tiled wall and sinks into me. His dilated pupils find mine right before his mouth hits mine and I get to taste the tanginess of myself on him before the water washes it away.

"You're amazing," I sigh, pulsing around his solid, thickening length. He smiles at me, looking proud of himself. "That was amazing." Now he looks even prouder and then he tenses, losing himself faster than he ever has, just as my orgasm begins to dwindle.

CHAPTER TWENTY-SEVEN

"I figured I owed you one." He says each word accompanied with a powerful thrust and then he groans and stops still. Resting his forehead against mine, we both wait for the sensations to diminish into a dull tingle before separating and taking due care of each other's bodies.

Best shower sex ever.

Best sex ever.

Nathan is literally the best ever.

Unfortunately, all good feelings and all good things must come to an end.

When we're dried, dressed and in the middle of watching a movie in peace, the Police arrive on our doorstep with news, a note and a black and gold urn.

A note from his mother and an urn full of Caleb's ashes.

Nathan paces back and forth in the sterile hallway as I nurse a plastic cup of terrible hot chocolate between my hands.

I blow on it, even though it has already cooled. It's to distract me from counting the seconds on the clock. Time goes too slowly when I do that and I need it to go quickly.

"She's been in there for almost four hours." Nathan hisses just as a nurse comes out of the room on the right, smiling sadly.

"Mr and Mrs Weston?"

"Yes?" Nathan holds out his hand to me and I rush to his side.

"She's okay. Her jaw is broken, as are two of her ribs and her right kneecap." She explains and I feel like vomiting. "But fortunately, the breaks aren't terrible and should heal nicely after a couple of months."

Nathan blows out a breath. "What about her jaw? How will she eat?"

"At the moment it's bandaged up, but the doctor will need to wire it in a few days when the swelling goes down." She gives us a firm look. "It's imperative that she doesn't talk at all."

"Understood." I nod and squeeze Nathan's bicep. "Thank you so much."

"Don't thank me, I'm just the messenger. The doctor will be back shortly. He would have been here to explain the procedure, but he has another emergency to attend to."

We don't waste another second to enter the room where his mother lies on a hospital bed, railings up either side, leg bandaged and propped on a pillow, face bandaged so much all we can see is her eyes, nose and top lip, all of which look swollen.

When she sees us her tired eyes light up and she immediately begins to hum, eager to speak. Nathan rushes to her side and whispers, "Don't you dare talk. Don't say anything."

A sob wracks her body and tears spill from her eyes. I stand by the door, too scared to move to her for fear of hurting her.

Nathan takes her hand. "You don't need to say anything. It's done. He's done. Okay?"

She nods slightly and closes her eyes, still sobbing. My own eyes fill with tears so I turn away to give them a moment of privacy as their bond of mother and son finally takes form, a bond lost for such a long time.

'Dear Nathan and Gwen,

I am uncertain where to start. I am afraid you won't read this because I know I do not deserve forgiveness from either of you, especially you, my son. My son whom I should have protected. My son whom I failed, whom I lost because of my selfishness and fear.

I just want you to know that I didn't know and I didn't plan on all that happened. When you left me with my beautiful grandchildren, my husband arrived on the doorstep with three men I didn't recognise. They pushed their way into your house and the men set about looking for something. I didn't know what was going on. All I knew was fear. Fear for my grandchildren playing in the living room.

My husband wouldn't speak, so I took the babies into the garden and waited. Whatever he came for, it wasn't for me or the children. I hadn't seen my husband since before the trial, but he had been watching me and waiting for an opportunity to enter your home.

I protected him by not calling the Police. I protected him by not telling you and my shame forced me back to him. Not because I wanted to be with him, but because I had to know what it was he was looking for.

The men left with a DVD and threatening glances and I saw the DVD in one of their hands. I acted as though nothing had happened. I will never forgive myself for that.

Well, I found the DVD just now. I am uploading it to the Police right now. I am writing this letter as the percentage gets higher and higher. The Police are waiting for it. I won't waste time driving it down there, though I will if I have to.

I just want you both to know that I didn't know. I was blind to that because I refused to believe it. That does not mean I wasn't at fault because I was. I didn't protect any of you when I should have.

When you accepted me into your family, that first night we ate dinner together and you allowed me to help bathe and put the kids to bed, I have not felt happiness like that since before Caleb fell ill. I didn't want to lose that. I do not ever want to lose that but I know I may have to and that's okay. I understand.

So I gift to you something I should have given to you so long ago - Caleb's ashes. They belong to his fiancée, his son and his brother and his niece.

I apologise for everything. Every single thing that has befallen you because of my life choices.

I wish you both all the happiness and joy in your lives away from the poison spread through me and my husband and our family. You're lovely people and, son, I am so proud of you for becoming the wonderful man and father you are today, despite your upbringing and lack of role models. I am SO proud.

Call me anytime you like, both of you. I love and miss you all. Genuinely, I love and miss you all so much. You were correct in saying love is the only believable thing, Guinevere. I wish I'd learned that sooner.

Yours truly and honestly,
Patricia Victoria Weston (Soon to be Kipling again after my divorce is finalised. I'm filing as soon as my solicitor allows it.)

That letter changed everything, especially when coupled with the fact that when Nathan's father arrived home, he caught Patricia just as the file finished uploading and he whaled on her. He beat her so badly the Police thought she was dead on arrival. She had still been on the phone speaking to her contacts in the Police force to let them know what a sick and twisted bastard her husband was when he arrived, so they heard the entire thing. He'll be going away for a very long time. The charges against him are too many.

Patricia had been a victim for so long. We know it doesn't excuse her, but now she has her courage back and mind back, we're both willing to work with her in making her whole again. Though trust is one thing she'll need to spend a long time working for. For now we'll let her rest and take comfort in the fact that the choice to prosecute Nathan's father was taken from us.

It's going to be a long and bumpy road ahead but we'll get through it together.

We can get through anything together.

Epilogue

THREE DAYS AFTER NATHAN and I got married, I in the most beautiful rose gold, ballgown style wedding dress, totally fit for a queen, Nathan's father was sentenced to forty years in prison for the offences of child endangerment, neglect, trafficking, assault and battery, stalking, abuse, and the list goes on. He had three different trials for three different crimes and the years just kept adding up. He'll likely be dead before he ever sees daylight again and Patricia and Nathan get his assets and other belongings. Patricia got it all in the divorce, but all of the stores and businesses she handed straight to Nathan almost immediately. He now owns the leading jewellery supplier in the whole of the UK.

We were in Italy when his final sentencing was called, on the holiday we never got the chance to go on due to helping to care for Nathan's mother as she recovered. We didn't complain and we had a better time without the kids, I'm ashamed to admit. We wouldn't have gotten that freedom last time.

Upon returning we revisited the charred remains of the first home we lived in together and instead of leaving the land tainted or selling it on, we had it all cleared and together we designed the most perfect home to raise our children.

Mum and her new husband moved closer to us too, finding solace by the seaside in Essex. Mum is now manager of Nathan's Essex stores. He has two and she loves every second. She's good at it too.

Though we have spent years celebrating and building a beautiful home life for our babies, today is an unfortunate day of mourning.

Dillan, so tall, strong and handsome, stands side by side with his father on the sands of Skegness beach. It's not the most glamorous place but it's where I grew up, it's where Caleb and I met and it's the town where Dillan was conceived.

Emily, now nineteen, is at home looking after her thirteen-year-old sister Ashlyn, my mini-me. They both could have come but they both, being the angels they are, wanted to give us space to say a final goodbye.

A final goodbye to Caleb, Dillan's biological father, my first love and Nathan's brother.

Dillan has known about his father since the day he was old enough to understand. He turned to his spirit in times of need as he grew up. I often heard him speaking to himself in bed as though praying and even though it was sad and sometimes a little disturbing, it made me proud and joyful to know that even in death Caleb still gets to know his son and his son still gets to know him.

Now, though, it's time to set him free. Dillan, now at the age Caleb was when we first met, feels as though it's time to let go and let Caleb be free. I'm so proud of him and the man he is becoming. He's so head strong, loving and kind. He's a replica of his father, not just in looks but in his spirits too. Caleb's ashes which we've kept in hiding for years are out and ready to be scattered into the sea and sand.

Dillan takes the first handful and releases it, whispering something under his breath that I can't quite make out. I watch the shimmering grey vanish into the water.

Next goes Nathan, silently taking the next handful, his arm around the shoulders of his son. He releases it too and I smile warmly at my favourite men. One has greying hair, yet is no less handsome than he was when we first met. I kiss his cheek. The other is a replica of Caleb; they are almost identical when compared in photographs. I kiss his cheek too. Then I snatch the urn and dump it upside down. The ashes hit the sand with a poof that fans around my ankles. Creepy.

"Mum!" Dillan gasps and Nathan looks up at the heavens as if hoping for help. "What the fuck?"

"Don't curse," Nathan snaps at his son, now frowning in his direction.

"You had your moment, I deserved mine." I respond haughtily. "Caleb will understand." I kick his ashes towards the slow crawling waves.

"Stop!" Dillan cries, though I hear the laughter in his voice. "What is wrong with you?"

"Caleb knows."

"May I know?"

"No, but he deserved it." I grin, ensuring the ashes are entirely gone so some poor unsuspecting kid doesn't end up building a sandcastle with them. "What shall we do with the urn?"

"I don't know. What do people normally do with urns?" Nathan asks and Dillan immediately pulls out his phone to ask Google.

"We could donate it to charity?" He suggests, shrugging as he walks backwards ahead of us.

"What if they don't know it's an urn and use it as like a fancy gravy dish or something?" I grimace with horror at the thought.

"Eww," Dillan sniggers, still walking backwards. "Gross, Mum."

"We'll use it as a plant pot," Nathan tells us, taking the urn from me so I don't break it.

"I like that idea."

"Me too," Dillan agrees. "Shouldn't I be sad or crying or something? I feel..."

"At peace?" I ask, smiling warmly.

"Yeah, I feel like I got to meet him properly for the first time ever. Thanks for letting me do this."

"It was a good idea," Nathan puts in, taking my hand in his. It seems such a long time since he was afraid of sand. He's walking on it so easily now, as though it never bothered him. There's a lot of things he can do now that would have once bothered him. His leather gloves remain, though. I don't think they'll ever go and I don't think I ever want them to.

Then Dillan scrunches up his nose and states, "I'm hungry. Shall we get fish and chips?"

"You just scattered ashes; how can you be hungry?" I balk.

"I want spice on my chips," he adds, ignorant to what I just said.

"Oh good lord," I sigh, looking up to the heavens for help much like Nathan just did. "Wash your hands first, you weirdo."

"I want gravy," Nathan grins, releasing my hand to chase after his son.

"You guys are sick, you know that?" I yell after them, grinning broadly.

"Says the woman who just kicked her dead husband into the sea!" Dillan shouts and the couple walking past me stare at me in horror.

"He was my fiancé and he deserved it," I giggle and race after my men. "Wait for me!"

THE END

Acknowledgments

Normally I'd know exactly what to put in this, who to thank and how to thank them but it's impossible. Throughout this entire writing journey I have met and fallen in platonic love with more people than I can name. Each and every single one of you have left a mark on me in some way that will never fade.
Adriana Rizak-Healing, Samantha Louise Heaney, Elisia Goodman, Elizabeth Butts, Melissa Teo, Zean Maskell, Charlena Barclay, Rivka Spicer, Addi Whillock, Siobhan Long, Gina Paul, Alyssia, Aydin
The list goes on and on and on. Thank you. Simply, thank you for everything, to the people I know personally and to my readers. I'm supposed to be good with words but instead, your constant support and love that I'm not even sure I deserve, has rendered me emotionally speechless.

About The Author

A. E. Murphy is the queen of sarcasm and satire, she likes long walks in the park, as much as ice cubes like to chill in a roasting oven. She's efortlessly independent and so good at adulting it's unfair on the rest of the world. She only napped twice today and has only avoided the dishes for three days before making the child slaves do them this morning. Winning! (Kidding, she has a dishwasher now.)

Her favourite hobby is writing, her worst hobby is reading through that writing. Also, she has four cats that carry toys to the top of the stairs and drop them down so they can chase them. They do this repeatedly in the middle of the night. Who cares if she has work the next morning? Not the cats, that's for sure. And if it's not the cats doing the waking, it's the ridiculous amount of children and bonus children she has constantly asking for a snack, or the fiancé being a needy bear. This is likely why she is so happy all the freaking time, but not without coffee and chocolate.

P.S. Please leave feedback, if not on the book then on this ridiculous bio she wrote herself. It's the least you can do seeing as she'll forever talk in the third person now.

Alex loves her readers. Alex says thank you. Alex smiles.

CONTACT

Facebook
www.facebook.com/a.e.murphy.author
Email
a.e.murphy@hotmail.com
Instagram
aemurphyauthor
TikTok
@authorxelaknight
@authoraemurphy

ALSO BY THE AUTHOR

Standalone Novels
VICIOUS
Becoming His Mistress
NAKED OR DEAD
DANCE OR DIE
Masked Definitions
HIS FATHER
STEPDORK

Seas of Seduction
Seizing Rain
Freeing Calder

The Little Bits Series
A Little Bit of Crazy
A Little Bit of Us
A Little Bit of Trouble
A Little Bit of Truth
A Little Bit of Guilt

The Distraction Trilogy
Distraction, Destruction, Distinction
The Broken Trilogy
Broken, Connected, Forever

A Broken Trilogy Spin-off
Disconnected (Dillan)
Sweet Demands Trilogy
Lockhart, Lockdown, Unlocked

Colouring Books
NAKED OR DEAD colouring book edition
Laurie's Life Lessons a colouring book novella (Becoming His Mistress Spin-of)
VICIOUS colouring book edition
Audiobooks
NAKED OR DEAD
HIS FATHER
BECOMING HIS MISTRESS

XELA KNIGHT
(Paranormal Books)
Syphon 1A, Syphon 2A, Syphon 3A

Printed in Great Britain
by Amazon